HERE
TO
STAY

ALSO BY MARK EDWARDS

WITH LOUISE VOSS

HERE
TO
STAY

MARK
EDWARDS

THOMAS & MERCER

Published by Thomas & Mercer, Seattle

www.apub.com

Amazon, the Amazon logo, and Thomas & Mercer are trademarks of Amazon.com, Inc., or its affiliates.

ISBN-13: 9781542006613 (hardcover)
ISBN-10: 1542006619 (hardcover)
ISBN-13: 9781542044905 (paperback)
ISBN-10: 1542044901 (paperback)

Cover design by Tom Sanderson

Printed and bound by CPI Group (UK) Ltd, Croydon, CR0 4YY

HERE
TO
STAY

Before

They had been driving for an hour before he finally snapped.

'Can't you make her shut up?'

Lizzy stared straight ahead, knuckles white as she gripped her knees. They had the windows wound down but the air that blew in was warm and thick and did nothing to blast the tension away. The landscape of south-western France rolled by, vineyards stretching in every direction. They passed a chateau, shadowy in the distance, then drove through a hamlet of crumbling stone buildings. Jeff kept expecting to see blue lights in the rear-view mirror. But nothing. Only the occasional truck, leaping out of the dark like a monster in a movie, setting his nerves jangling again.

'She's been through a lot—' Lizzy began, but he cut her off.

'She's been through a lot?'

Lizzy reached across, squeezing his knee. 'Calm down. If you hadn't lost your temper back there . . .'

He shot her a look that made her change tack.

'She loved him, Jeff.'

A gasp, a catching of breath, came from the back seat, and the keening noise that had accompanied them the whole journey – that terrible sound that made it impossible for him to concentrate, to hear his own thoughts – grew so loud he would almost have welcomed a siren, blue lights, the silence of a cell.

'Shut up!' he yelled, thumping the wheel.

The keening dimmed, then stopped. She sniffled and he was about to shout again, but she fell quiet.

Now it was silent, he was able to think clearly, to push away the image of the dead boy. So far, since they'd left that burning wreck behind, he'd been acting on pure instinct. And instinct had told him to drive further south, steering clear of large towns, towards the blank patches on the map. For the first hour, escape had been all that mattered, getting distance between themselves and the incident. But it had left him with a feeling he hated.

Lack of control.

The absence of a plan.

Now, though, as the sweat dried on his back and all he could hear was the rush of wind, the smooth drone of their tyres on the road, he began to formulate one.

'We're the Robinsons,' he said, not realising he'd spoken aloud until Lizzy looked over at him. He reached out and took hold of her hand, squeezing. There was love in her eyes. Love for him, for their family.

A family of survivors. It was what they did, whatever the world threw at them. They had been doing this for years.

And they would survive again.

PART ONE

PART ONE

Chapter 1

Shadows were beginning to creep across the lawn, the sun that had blazed all afternoon preparing to turn in for the day, and I was about to go indoors and pour myself something cold when a woman poked her head around the gate.

She wore an inquisitive smile. 'Are you still open?'

I'll admit it: if she hadn't been so attractive, I might have said no. She had slightly scruffy dark-brown hair and was wearing large sunglasses that hid much of her face, but she reminded me of someone, an American actress I'd had a crush on when I was a kid. She was wearing blue jeans and a white T-shirt emblazoned with a cartoon dinosaur, with pink Converse on her feet. As she stepped into the garden she seemed a little awkward but determined, like she really wanted to look around. So instead of telling her she was too late, I said what I'd been saying all day: 'Come on in.'

She rewarded me with a huge smile, removing her shades for a moment so I could see that smile reach her green eyes. 'Thank you,' she said, and she held my gaze for a moment before turning away.

I remained seated at the trestle table on the patio. I had learned that most people didn't want to be shown around. They preferred to explore the garden at their leisure, without the owner breathing down their neck. Of course, a good number of the visitors had approached me to share tales of their own gardens, to offer praise and, on several occasions, advice. Some of it had actually been pretty useful. I'd spent ten minutes chatting with an elderly hippy about whether it was possible to deal with slugs humanely.

Lots of people had brought children with them, and I'd told them if they were quiet there was a good chance they'd see one or two of the frogs that had made a home in the pond near the back wall.

It had been a good day, even better than expected. When I had told Amira, my business partner, that I planned to let people look around as part of the local Open Gardens day, she'd pulled a face. 'What, let strangers traipse all over your property?'

I'd laughed. 'Yes. It's a nice thing to do for the community. Plus it'll be fun.'

'Hmm. Rather you than me, Elliot.'

But it had been fun. And nearly everyone who'd come through the gate had left a donation, which would go towards improving local public green spaces, specifically a nearby playground that had fallen into disrepair. A number of my neighbours on Cuckoo Lane were taking part, and we'd taken turns to visit one another's gardens, exchanging gifts. Edith next door had a bottle of her own rhubarb wine for everyone, and the Singhs down the road produced an enormous batch of samosas. People will tell you that in cities like London there is no such thing as community anymore, that we all live inside little bubbles, but that certainly wasn't true today.

I'd recognised quite a few of the people who had visited my garden – some of them were the parents of kids I'd taught or worked with – but the young woman who was looking around now wasn't familiar.

I tried not to watch her, but there was something about her that magnetised my attention. She did a slow circuit of the garden, taking in the wisteria, the lavender bush which hummed with visiting bumblebees, the little pond, the crocuses and tulips. She paused by the vegetable patch – my first, semi-successful attempt to grow my own food – and she must have felt my eyes on her because she turned and headed over.

Her sunglasses slipped on her nose where she was perspiring a little in the lingering afternoon heat. She pushed her hair back from her face and faltered for a moment; a moment in which, for some irrational reason, I feared she might turn and flee, out through the gate, back out of my life. And even though I didn't know her, had barely spoken to her, I knew I didn't want that to happen.

But she didn't leave. She stopped at the edge of the patio. 'It's beautiful,' she said. Her tone was wistful. 'I've never had a garden. Not a proper one, anyway.'

'Really?' I got up from my seat and went closer to her. Standing before her, I discovered she was a good few inches shorter than me, her head coming to my shoulder. When she spoke she revealed a little gap between her front teeth. I tried not to stare at it.

'Since I left home I've always lived in flats,' she said. 'And my parents . . . Well, we did have a garden, but it was paved over. The nearest we had to flowers were a few thistles and dandelions growing out of the cracks.'

She shifted on the spot again. She seemed a little uncomfortable, worried about something.

'Are you all right?' I asked.

'Actually . . . I know this is a terrible imposition, but could I use your loo?'

'Of course. It's not an imposition at all.' I gestured for her to cross the patio.

'Thank you.'

The back door opened straight into the kitchen, which was divided into two spaces, with a dining table on the left-hand side as you went in. I hardly used the table; I had got into the habit of eating dinner in the living room in front of whatever Netflix series I was into at that moment, a plate on my lap. The dining table, meanwhile, had become one of the favoured sleeping spots of my ginger cat, Charlie, who was curled up there now, enjoying the sun that streamed through the window and warmed his fur.

'The toilet's just along here,' I said, showing her into the hallway that ran from the kitchen to the front door. 'First door on the right.'

I waited in the kitchen, tickling behind Charlie's ear and trying to remember the last time I'd had a woman in my house. Amira, of course, had been round several times; I'd invited her and her boyfriend, Colin, to dinner recently. A few months ago, there'd been that woman I met on Tinder, which was my one experience of using the hook-up app. The sex had been okay but left me feeling weirdly unsatisfied. One-night stands really weren't my thing. I'd explained this to Amira the next day, when she'd asked for 'all the deets'.

'So, basically, you need a girlfriend, Elliot.'

'I don't have time for a girlfriend.'

'Oh, come off it. How old are you? Thirty-eight? You should be settled down by now, with a wife and two-point-four children. That house is far too big for you to rattle around in with a cat.'

The toilet flushed and I busied myself with filling the kettle while I waited for her to come into the kitchen, trying to think of something interesting to say.

'Better?' I heard myself asking as she entered the room holding her phone.

I winced – *Better?* What was wrong with me? – but she laughed.

'Much better,' she said. 'Thank you. I should leave you in peace now. You've probably had a long day.'

'I have. But I was about to make tea . . . if you'd like one?'

'Um.' She glanced at her phone. I guessed she had somewhere to be. And she wanted to get away from the weirdo who'd asked her if she felt better after she'd been to the loo. 'Actually, tea would be lovely. Though I feel like I'm massively imposing.'

'Don't be silly. It's nice to have company.'

She met my eye. 'So, do you live here on your own?'

'Yeah. Just me and Charlie.'

She stroked his back. 'I'm a veterinary nurse so I see lots of cats, but few are as handsome as Charlie here.' She looked around. 'This place is pretty immaculate for a bachelor pad.'

'Everyone says that. I guess I don't like mess. Mister Anal.'

She laughed and I groaned. I'd done it again.

'Actually,' I said hurriedly, 'call me Elliot. That's my name. Elliot Foster.'

She grinned. 'I'm Gemma. Gemma Robinson.'

'Lovely to meet you, Gemma.'

The kettle clicked off and I found a couple of mugs, putting a tea-bag in each and hoping she wasn't the type who insisted on tea being brewed in a pot. She didn't seem bothered, though. She was too busy looking around the room.

When I turned back, she was staring at me. She flushed, pink creeping across her collarbone.

'I'm sorry,' she said, taking a mug of tea from me. 'I'm just sure I recognise you from somewhere. Have we met before?'

'I don't think so.'

We definitely hadn't. I'd have remembered. But this was quite a common occurrence. I was a very minor celebrity, known by tabloids as a 'boffin' and by listeners to Radio 4 as a 'philanthropic scientist'. I occasionally appeared on TV as an expert when there was a science-based story in the news, something I did not because I enjoyed attention – I hated seeing myself on screen – but because it helped the not-for-profit I ran with Amira.

'Maybe you've just seen me around.' I was reluctant to tell her how she might know me, because it was difficult to say it without sounding like I thought I was special. 'Do you live locally?'

'Kind of. Bromley.'

That was further out – a fifteen-minute train ride away – and much livelier than this part of south London. 'So, what brings you to West Dulwich?'

'I was visiting my brother Stuart. He lives in Herne Hill.' That was the neighbouring area, a mile or two up the road. 'But I saw the ads for this Open Garden event and couldn't resist. I looked round a couple of others before I came here, but yours is the best.'

'I bet you say that to all the—' I stopped myself. 'Sorry. For some reason my mouth keeps working without a filter today. But I'm very happy you like my garden so much.'

'I like your house too. It's beautiful.' She made a self-deprecating noise. 'Sorry, I'm one of those people who's addicted to property shows, especially the ones where someone buys an old wreck and does it up. That's my dream. To buy a big Victorian place like this and do it up.'

I put down my cup of tea. I was enjoying this woman's company and didn't want her to leave yet. Here was a way to get her to stay for a little longer. 'Do you want me to show you round the rest of the house?'

'Really? That would be amazing.'

'Great. Let me show you number twenty-six Cuckoo Lane.'

Chapter 2

I gave her the tour. As Gemma had said, the house was Victorian – semi-detached, with three bedrooms and two reception rooms arranged over three floors. It had steep staircases and all the original features: sash windows, ceiling roses, fireplaces in many of the rooms. There was stained glass over the front door and polished floorboards throughout. Most of the doors were bare wood too; I had stripped off the paint and removed the nasty modern handles that had been put on at some point, replacing them with replicas of the originals, which I'd gone to great lengths to track down.

'I pretty much restored the whole place,' I said, crossing to the window in the living room at the front of the house. 'It was a total mess when I moved in. An elderly couple had lived here for years, allowing it to crumble into total disrepair. And it had been modernised during the sixties. People did some terrible things back then. A kind of mass vandalism.'

'You did it all yourself?'

'Pretty much. I hired someone to do the plumbing and electrics, but I did most of the rest.'

'That's amazing.'

As I showed her upstairs – the spare bedrooms and the main bathroom, with its claw-footed tub – I couldn't help but study Gemma. I loved seeing her reactions, the way she really seemed to appreciate my home, the light that came into her eyes as she took it all in.

There was an awkward moment on the middle floor. We were standing in the doorway of the only room I hadn't shown her yet and I said, 'And, er, this is the master bedroom.'

She poked her head into the room and said, 'Nice', but didn't go inside. The atmosphere between us shifted and went a little flat.

'I really feel like I'm imposing,' she said. Her cheeks were flushed. 'But thank you so much for showing me around. It's perfect. But I think I should probably make a move now.'

We went back downstairs and into the kitchen, where she'd left her bag. I had a horrible deflated feeling, which I knew would linger all evening. Gemma, too, looked sad, like she had something on her mind.

'What is it?' I asked.

'Nothing. Just . . . I was thinking that I'll never be able to afford somewhere like this. I'll never live anywhere so beautiful.' She forced a smile. 'God, I sound so self-pitying, don't I?'

'No, not at all. You know, I was only able to afford this place because I had some luck. When I left university I set up a website – just a hobby, really.'

'What kind of website?'

'An educational site. About science. Like a resource for teachers and students.'

Gemma nodded. She was standing by the door, and behind her the light was shifting, still bright and warm but more muted as late afternoon turned to evening.

'The lucky part was that it got really popular and a bigger web company approached me and offered to buy it. That's how I was able to afford this place and do it up.'

'That's so cool,' she said. 'I used to have a blog, but only about three people ever visited it.'

'And one of them was your mum?'

The last traces of her smile vanished. 'No. Not my mum.'

That was intriguing but I didn't want to pry. We went back out into the garden. Despite what she'd said about needing to go, she seemed reluctant to leave. And that was fine by me. We stood on the patio and I had a sudden yearning for a glass of wine. Should I offer her one?

'So . . . science,' she said, interrupting my thoughts. 'Is that what you do? You're a scientist?'

'Yes. A science teacher, really, although it's slightly more complicated than that. The other thing I did with my website money was set up a little business. A not-for-profit. We go around teaching kids about the wonders of science, especially in underfunded areas. We run workshops and take children on field trips. My mission is basically to get working-class children excited about chemistry and physics.'

She stared at me. 'That's really cool. And now I know where I recognise you from. I'm sure I've seen you on TV. You were arguing with this stupid politician about their education policy. I thought you were brilliant.'

I might have blushed. 'Oh, thank you. That's—' I cried out in pain. 'What is it?'

As we'd been talking I had put my hand down on the patio table – and a lightning bolt of pain had shot into my palm. I snatched up my hand and saw a bee, half-dead, wriggling on the wooden surface. There was a red welt on my palm, a tiny stinger protruding from it.

Gemma saw the bee too, and the way I was holding my wrist. 'Did it sting you?'

I nodded, hardly able to speak. The pain was intense; it was as if there were a direct line between the point of the sting on my palm and my heart – a burning, pulsating line.

Gemma spoke, her voice sounding like it was coming from a long way away. 'You're not allergic, are you?'

'I don't know.' I had never been stung before. But the garden appeared to be spinning around my head and my torso had begun to itch. I pulled up my T-shirt. Half a dozen scarlet hives had appeared on my chest and belly.

She said something else but I couldn't make out the words. Because suddenly the whole world was shifting, collapsing in on itself, and I collapsed too.

Chapter 3

I must have come to only a few seconds later. I was lying on the concrete with Gemma crouching beside me, her hands on my shoulders.

'Elliot. Elliot! I think it's anaphylactic shock. Do you have an epi pen?'

I shook my head and tried to speak but nothing came out. I tried not to panic, grabbing hold of Gemma's arm and attempting to pull myself up.

'Call 999,' I whispered.

'That'll take too long.' She seemed very calm, which helped to keep me from freaking out. 'Do you have a car?'

I nodded. My throat was closing up and the hives on my torso itched and burned. Beneath the panic, I knew exactly what was going on. The bee sting had released a flood of chemicals in my blood, including histamine. My blood pressure must have plummeted, causing me to faint. My throat and tongue, which felt like a fat lump of meat in my mouth, were swelling. I was having a generalised allergic reaction. I needed an injection of epinephrine.

'Where are the keys?' Gemma urged.

'Kitchen,' I managed to say. 'Next. Kettle.'

She sprang up and sprinted into the kitchen, coming back seconds later with the car key in her hand.

'Can you stand?' she asked.

With her help I got to my feet, and Gemma pulled my arm around her shoulders and put hers around my waist. 'We're going to walk to your car, okay? Is it close?'

I nodded.

The journey across the garden seemed to take hours. My legs were as wobbly as a newborn lamb's and I was only just able to breathe, forcing air down my restricted throat and into my lungs. We reached the gate and Gemma pressed the button on the car key.

The lights flashed on my Audi, which was parked a few cars along, and Gemma raised an eyebrow. 'The Audi? Nice.'

She opened the rear door and I crawled on to the back seat. I'm six foot two so it was a tight squeeze, but that was the least of my concerns. She slammed the door and ran around the car, jumping behind the wheel. She started the engine, then paused.

'I have no idea how to get to the hospital. What's the nearest one? King's College?'

I croaked, 'Yes.'

It was a few miles away, in Denmark Hill. The issue was going to be traffic. It was Saturday afternoon and I knew the traffic through Herne Hill could be horrific.

I was going to die, here on the back seat of my car.

'You're not going to die,' Gemma said, as if she'd read my mind. I couldn't really see what she was doing but later she told me she had punched the hospital's name into the map app on her phone.

'Hold tight,' she said, pulling out. 'I'm going to drive fast.'

She looked back at me for a second.

'Keep breathing, Elliot. It would be just my luck if I lost you.'

A little while later, I was sitting in a hospital bed, a curtain drawn around me, eager to go home. It was still light outside, although I had no idea what time it was. I felt hugely disorientated. But at the same time, I was filled with a kind of quasi-religious mania. I was alive! I had survived! And, like so many other people who have had a brush with death, I was suddenly aware of all the things I hadn't achieved. The things I wanted to do, places I wanted to see. Experiences I had yet to taste. I could see my life with a new clarity, like I was looking at myself beneath a microscope and noticing all the flaws, everything that was missing.

Yes, I had achieved some things in my thirty-eight years. I'd made some money. I had my company. A couple of good friends. A cat. And, of course, I had my house. My beautiful house.

But there was so much missing – and chief among those, of course, was someone to share it all with. I slept and ate alone. I had no one to talk to at the end of the day.

Sitting there in that hospital bed, with nothing else to do but think, I made a vow to myself.

No more wasting time. No more wasting life. From now on, I was going to be impetuous and brave. Willing to take risks.

While I was having this epiphany, a doctor came up to my bed. 'How are you feeling?'

'I feel great,' I said. 'I'm alive.'

She checked me over. 'I'm going to discharge you,' she said, looking at my notes. 'From now on you should keep an epi pen with you. Just in case this happens again.'

The doctor went to walk away, then paused.

'By the way, there's someone here to see you.'

She pulled aside the curtain to reveal Gemma, standing by the entrance to the ward. She came over.

'How are you feeling?' she asked.

'Alive. Thanks to you.'

17

She shrugged. 'Well, I could hardly leave you there to die, could I? I mean, I thought about robbing your house while you lay there but you'd been so nice to me, letting me use your loo and everything.'

I laughed. 'I need to do something to repay you,' I said.

'Hmm, yes, I've been thinking about this. Your car's nice.'

'It's yours.'

It was her turn to laugh. 'I was only kidding.'

'I know, but if you want it, it's yours.'

She pushed her hair out of her eyes. She had faint freckles across the bridge of her nose which I hadn't noticed before. 'I really don't want your car, Elliot.'

'Then what would you like? How about I take you out for dinner?'

There, I'd said it, and now my heart was beating fast again, waiting for the answer. Waiting for this woman, who was out of my league, to say no.

She tipped her head from side to side, making a big show of thinking about it. 'Okay. But it's got to be somewhere good. Not McDonald's.'

She found a piece of paper and wrote her name and number on it, placing it on the table beside my bed.

'I really should get home now,' she said.

She hesitated, then leaned over and kissed my cheek.

I picked up the scrap of paper. Beneath her name and number, Gemma had added a large *X*.

Chapter 4

We met in August 2018, and I could write an entire book about the next two months, that period of intense happiness, the whirlwind that swept Gemma and me into the air and carried us away. Anyone who has ever fallen hard will understand. The magic of those early days, when you are consumed by each other, when your whole body thrums in the presence of this new significant other and aches when you're apart. Two months passed at lightning pace, like one of those speeded-up films of flowers blooming.

It was an October morning, cold and overcast, and Gemma was still asleep, lying on her front, her dark hair fanned out across the pillow. She had one hand balled into a fist, pressed against her face like she was a small child clutching a comfort blanket. The sheets had been pulled down to expose her naked back.

As I watched, she shifted, turning on to her side. Her arms were crossed over her breasts but her belly was exposed.

Her stomach was criss-crossed with scars. Most of them were short, just a couple of inches long, and they were all shallow. But the cumulative effect – as if someone had used a stick to draw dozens of lines on a sandy beach, at every angle on the protractor – was shocking. Of course I had seen them before, but we usually made love in low light, so they had never been so noticeable.

I had made a decision the first time I saw the scars. I would not ask her about them. I would wait and see if she would tell me.

Gently, I kissed her bare shoulder and she stirred in her sleep. She muttered something.

I wasn't one hundred per cent sure, but it sounded like, 'I'm sorry.'

'Gemma,' I said when she opened her eyes. 'You might think this is mad, but I've got a suggestion. Well, a question, actually.'

She sat up, blinking sleepily, and I asked her.

ᗯ

'Wait. You're getting married?'

Amira had stopped walking. We were in Streatham, on our way into what was – according to Ofsted – a failing primary school, where we had been invited to talk at an assembly.

I met Amira at university, where I was reading physics and she was doing microbiology. She was clever, probably the smartest woman in our year. Actually, scrap that. She was the smartest person. But unlike some of the brainiacs at our college who had the social skills of a laptop, Amira was warm and funny and wise. Her family were Syrian, and had migrated to the UK in the 1960s.

It was raining lightly and I wanted to get inside, but Amira didn't seem to care.

'How long have you known her?' she asked.

'Two months.'

'That's what I thought. Wow, Elliot. Just . . . wow.'

'Listen, I know you're going to say it's too quick. That's what everyone is going to say. But I'm not going to change my mind. You know when I was stung by that bee? I made a vow to myself then that I wasn't going to waste time anymore. I wasn't going to allow fear or doubt to rule me. She makes me happy, Amira. So happy.'

'You've certainly been in a much better mood recently.'

'Exactly.'

We began walking again, towards the squat, grey school buildings.

'As long as you're thinking with your head and not just your penis.'

I laughed. 'What about my heart?'

She rolled her eyes. 'Oh, please.'

We entered the school. It had the air of so many of the schools we visited. Rundown. Poor. But full of energy and hope, with walls that showed off the work of the pupils, kids from impoverished homes who were statistically destined to fail.

Our mission, the reason we had set up Inquiring Minds, was to turn kids on to science. To show them that it wasn't boring or hard or out of reach. That they could learn skills that would give them a bright future. If we could change the prospects of just one child at each school or youth centre or juvenile prison we visited, we considered that a success.

'So have you met her family yet?' Amira asked as we headed down the corridor towards the head teacher's office.

'Her parents and sister live in France.'

'Doesn't she have a brother in Herne Hill? Have you met him?'

'No, not yet. But we're going round for dinner this Saturday.'

'Ah. That's good.' She stopped walking again. 'I'm pleased for you, Elliot. I really am. You deserve to be happy.'

'But?'

'But you're crazy. Completely bloody mad.'

I laughed. 'You know what? I'm going to take that as a compliment. I've spent my whole life, since my parents died anyway, being this buttoned-up, reserved Englishman. Mister Science.'

'And now you're the nutty professor?'

'Exactly. And it feels great.'

ω

Gemma's brother Stuart lived in a small terraced house on Milkwood Road, which ran parallel to the railway track that linked Herne Hill and Loughborough Junction.

Gemma and I turned up at the allotted time, six thirty on Saturday, and Stuart opened the door and let us in.

'Stuart, this is Elliot. Elliot, Stuart.'

We shook hands. Gemma and Stuart didn't embrace or kiss but, being an only child, I wasn't sure if that was unusual.

He was thirty-four, two years older than Gemma. I hope it doesn't sound vain to say he looked a decade older than me, even though he was four years my junior. He had lost most of his hair and had dark bags beneath his eyes. He was jittery too, like someone who'd had too much caffeine.

'Welcome to our humble abode,' he said, grinning broadly. The smile lit him up and suddenly I could see his resemblance to Gemma.

He took the bottle of wine I'd brought and inspected the label. It was a very good wine from my 'cellar' – not a real wine cellar, more a collection of decent bottles that I saved for special occasions. I had no idea if Stuart knew anything about wine but he nodded approvingly.

Stuart led us to the kitchen, where we found his wife, Jane, making dinner. She was skinny and mousy and, like Stuart, she had a jittery air. For a moment I wondered if they were drug addicts. They had that look, and I found myself glancing at their teeth for the telltale signs of heroin use. But no, their teeth were fine. Perhaps they were just nervous people, I thought.

'What are we having?' Gemma asked.

'Pasta,' Jane replied. 'Stuart, why don't you take Elliot and Gemma into the front room? Dinner will be about fifteen minutes.'

We went into the living room. There was a threadbare sofa and a massive TV, and a pair of mismatched armchairs. There were, as far as I could see, no books in the house, and the walls were decorated with reproductions of well-known paintings. Van Gogh's *Sunflowers*. Degas's ballerina. There was no sign of their six-year-old daughter apart from a box of grubby-looking toys in the corner.

Stuart sat in one of the armchairs and Gemma and I took the sofa. I had been hoping he might open the wine I'd brought but we weren't offered any kind of drink. He sat and stared at us, occasionally licking his lips, which were cracked and dry.

I clutched Gemma's hand.

'Where's Katie?' Gemma asked.

'In bed, fast asleep.'

'I thought you might let her stay up to see me,' Gemma said.

He shrugged. 'Routine is very important.'

'Gemma tells me you're a taxi driver,' I said, filling the silence.

'That's right. I should be out there now. Earning a crust.'

'Oh.'

'You're a scientist, are you?' he asked.

'Yes.' I began to describe my job but he cut me off.

'You live in West Dulwich? Very nice. *Very* nice.' He gave Gemma a meaningful look, a 'you've landed on your feet' look.

'We've got some news, actually,' Gemma said, shifting closer to me and squeezing my hand. 'We're getting married.'

Stuart's mouth gaped open. 'Well,' he said. 'Well, well.' Then, for good measure, 'Bloody hell.'

'We're very excited about it,' Gemma said.

'I bet you are.' He pushed himself to his feet with great effort, like a man thirty years older, hands braced against his thighs. I was expecting him to start telling us we were mad, but his beam of delight seemed genuine and brought him to life. Maybe my initial assessment had been wrong. Perhaps he and Jane were just getting over the flu or something.

'That's brilliant, sis,' he said. 'This calls for a drink to celebrate.'

He went off to the kitchen, calling out, 'Jane? You'll never guess . . .'

Gemma whispered, 'I'm sorry. I told you he was awkward.'

'It's fine,' I said. 'He's just . . . very different to you.'

'This isn't going to put you off me, is it?' she said, still whispering.

'Of course not.' I kissed her. 'I love you.'

Stuart came back into the room holding a bottle of white wine and some glasses. It wasn't the bottle I'd brought. It was coated with dust and was, when I tasted it, sweet. I forced myself to swallow the first mouthful.

Stuart held his glass aloft. 'Congratulations, little sis.'

'Thanks, big brother.'

He winked at me and said, 'Welcome to the family, mate.'

And then he laughed, like he'd cracked a joke I didn't understand.

Chapter 5

Two weeks later, Gemma and I stood in a chapel in Las Vegas, grinning as we read our vows to one another. It felt surreal, like the most insane thing to be doing. But she looked so beautiful and happy – and as the white-haired official told me I could kiss the bride, Gemma's shoulders shook with emotion and I realised she was crying.

'Happy tears,' she said as I studied her with concern, and then she wrapped her arms around me and pulled me close.

That night, we hit the Strip, going from casino to casino, watching the fountains dance outside the Bellagio, riding the rollercoaster on top of the New York-New York. We drank cocktails and fed coins into slot machines, and I was expecting a miracle, that it would be apt if we hit the jackpot, could imagine a crowd gathering around and whooping as money poured forth, making us rich.

But that didn't happen. We didn't win a cent, not that it mattered. We were married. We were ecstatic. Caught in the whirlwind.

ᚹ

We had only been back from Las Vegas a few days when I came down from my morning shower to find Gemma in the kitchen looking worried, her phone lying on the table before her. There was black toast in the toaster, smoke curling upwards, and a cold mug of tea beside the kettle. Charlie snaked around Gemma's ankles but she was oblivious to all of it.

'What's the matter?' I asked, sitting opposite her.

She didn't answer immediately.

'Gemma?'

She picked her phone up. 'I've had an email from my mum and dad.'

I assumed they'd given her terrible news. A death in the family. A cancer diagnosis. Financial ruin. I reached out and took her hand, but she pulled it away like she couldn't bear to be touched. She took a deep breath.

'They're coming back to the UK,' she said.

'To visit?'

She shook her head. 'No, for good, apparently. Chloe too.'

That was her younger sister. 'Oh? That's . . . great, isn't it?'

'I guess.'

'You don't sound very sure.'

'It's just . . . I haven't seen them for a while.'

'But it will be good to see them, won't it?' As someone who had lost his parents as a teenager, I found it hard to understand why she wasn't jumping for joy. I would have given anything to see my mum and dad again.

'Yeah, of course.'

It was almost eight, and Gemma needed to leave to get her train. 'I'd better get to work. Can we talk about this later?'

'Of course,' I said, kissing her goodbye. Though I wasn't really sure what we needed to talk about.

ᙡ

She told me over dinner that night, when I brought the subject up.

'So, your parents, are they heading back to Winchelsea Beach?' That was, as I recalled, the name of the seaside village where the Robinson family hailed from.

Gemma shook her head. 'No, we don't have a house there anymore. We were only ever renting.'

'Oh, right.'

She had a forkful of food halfway to her mouth. 'I'm not sure where they're going to stay, actually. They can't stay with Stuart because he doesn't have enough room.'

'Okay.'

'I suppose they'll have to rent somewhere.'

I put my fork down. 'Hang on, have they not sorted this out? Don't they have anywhere to go?'

Gemma pushed her plate away, as if her appetite had deserted her.

'Gemma, you clearly have issues with your parents—'

'Why do you say that?'

'Because you told me you had a strange relationship with them.' This was something she'd said when she'd first mentioned her mum and dad.

'Hmm.' There was a flicker of anger, something I'd hardly seen her display before. I'd seen the odd flash of temper – impatience with other drivers, for example, when we were in the car. Anger at stories on the news, especially ones involving cruelty to animals. But in our almost three months together, we hadn't had a single argument. I knew that wasn't particularly healthy and I was almost looking forward to seeing how we would deal with our first row. I just didn't want it to be about her parents.

'I didn't mean to give the impression that I have issues with them,' she said. 'No more than average, anyway.'

'Okay. I understand.' I didn't understand really. 'All I was going to say was, if you don't want to see them, if their return is causing you stress, you should tell me. You're my wife now—'

'What, and you think that means you own me?'

She stood up, making the cutlery rattle on the table.

I was shocked. 'Of course I don't. Where did that come from? Gemma, please, sit down. Let's talk about this.'

But she didn't sit. She crossed the kitchen, taking a bottle of wine out of the fridge, filling her glass and downing half of it in one go. She exhaled, eyes closed.

'Talk to me,' I said.

'Okay. I'm sorry, Elliot. I'm nervous, that's all.'

'About seeing your mum and dad?'

She took another big swallow of wine. 'Yes. It's been a long time. And I'm worried about what you'll think of them.'

'I'm actually really looking forward to meeting them,' I said. I wasn't lying. I was intrigued. 'If they brought you up, there can't be too much wrong with them.'

She stared into her wine. 'They're not like you.'

'What do you mean?'

This conversation was clearly causing her pain. 'Well, you're clever. You have a great job. A big house. And my parents aren't—'

'Wait, are you going to say they're not middle-class like me? You think I'm a snob?'

'No! Not a snob, but . . .'

'Gemma, I told you, we didn't have any money when I was growing up. My parents didn't leave me a penny. You know I was only able to buy this house because I was lucky with that website I set up. I'm actually working-class myself.'

She laughed. 'No, you're not. Maybe you used to be, but I heard you talking to that mechanic when you took your car in to be fixed.

You did that whole thing of calling him "mate" and pretending to be into football.'

'I do like football.'

She'd sat back down by now, and she reached across and touched my face. 'Elliot, you're lovely, but you own a beautiful house in Dulwich. You run a not-for-profit. You know about wine and have opinions on which are the best international airports. You're not working-class. Not anymore, anyway.'

'Okay, you got me. But I'm not a snob.'

She kissed me. 'I know. I'm sorry.' She put on an Eliza Doolittle accent, pre-elocution lessons. 'And I'm proper chuffed you took in a poor girl like me, sir.'

We went through to the living room, taking our wine glasses with us. It was unusual for Gemma to drink on a work night, but she grabbed another bottle and brought that too.

'Let's talk about this,' I said. 'When are they coming back?'

'Tomorrow.'

I blinked at her.

'Tomorrow?'

I'd expected her to say 'next month' or 'after Christmas'.

'Yeah. They land at Luton Airport at four thirty.'

'And they haven't arranged anywhere to stay? What about a hotel?'

She laughed humourlessly. 'They don't like hotels.'

'Where are they going to stay, then?'

Gemma put her wine glass down and took my hand. She stroked my palm where the bee had stung me. The diamonds in her wedding ring glinted beneath the artificial lights.

'Is it okay if they stay here? Just for a couple of weeks, until they sort themselves out.'

Suddenly, her weird mood made sense. She'd been scared of asking me.

'Of course!' I said. 'There's plenty of room. I'm sorry I didn't think to offer. To insist! Your parents can have our room and Chloe can sleep on the sofa bed in the little bedroom.'

'But you use that as your home office.'

I shrugged. 'It's fine. I hardly use it anyway, and if it's only for a couple of weeks . . . We can go up to the spare room. We were thinking about moving our bedroom up there anyway, weren't we?' The top bedroom was a little smaller than the master bedroom, but it had an en-suite bathroom and would give us more privacy while her parents were here.

Gemma flung her arms around me and kissed my face. 'Oh, thank you, Elliot. You're so lovely.'

'I know.'

She kissed my lips lightly and pretty soon we were kissing properly, and then we were taking off our clothes.

Afterwards, I sat panting beside her as she pulled her clothes back on, still not speaking.

'Sex on the sofa,' I said with a smile. 'We won't be able to do that while your parents are here.'

I expected her to return the smile. But she didn't.

Chapter 6

Amira gave me a lift home the next day. Gemma had borrowed my car – which I insisted she see as 'our' car now, anyway – to pick her parents and sister up from the airport. I wanted to be there when they got back.

'Sure you don't want me to stay, to provide backup?' Amira asked, leaning out of the car window.

'In case they have tentacles and horns, you mean?'

'That's quite an unusual combination, but yes.'

I looked up at the house. Not long ago, it had been just me. Now, for a couple of weeks anyway, it was going to be full of people and life. I was looking forward to it.

'I'm good, thanks.'

Amira drove away, leaving me standing outside my front door. I took a moment to look up and down the street. The first time I'd walked along this road, on the way to the house viewing, I'd known I wanted to live here. All the lovely, sturdy Victorian houses, the wrought-iron railings, the well-kept front gardens. Even when it was dark, like now, there was a gentle, welcoming atmosphere here. Of course, some of the neighbours were a little snooty, and a few were nosy, and there could be disputes over noise and car parking spaces and trees overhanging gardens, but people generally got along. And we knew how lucky we were to live on such a pretty street.

I was looking forward to showing it off to Gemma's family.

ɯ

I heard the car pull up outside at just after six thirty. Moments later, the sounds of doors opening and shutting, and voices, a woman and a man. I thought I heard him say 'Impressive', but couldn't make out the woman's response.

I opened the front door.

Gemma's parents were on the pavement, with two large suitcases in front of them, and Gemma was getting more bags out of the boot. A young blonde woman, presumably Chloe, remained in the back seat, staring straight ahead.

I hurried out and went straight up to Gemma's parents, sticking out my hand. I knew their names, of course. Jeff and Lizzy. The Robinsons.

'Hi, I'm Elliot.'

I shook Jeff's hand and we smiled at each other. His grip was firm, almost painful. He was strong, like someone who spent a lot of time lifting weights. He held on to my hand for another couple of seconds, squeezing harder, and I wondered if he was doing it deliberately or if he didn't know his own strength. Finally, he let go.

Gemma had told me that her parents had had her when they were in their mid-twenties, meaning they were both in their late fifties now. Jeff had grey hair which was slicked back using, I assumed, Brylcreem, and he wore a leather jacket over a dark T-shirt. His eyes were dark and small, and when he grinned he showed off two rows of small, yellowish teeth.

'Very kind of you to invite us to stay,' he said.

'The least I could do. You're Gemma's family.'

'We are indeed,' he said, running a hand over his hair.

'We're *your* family now too,' said the woman standing behind me, and I turned to face Lizzy. 'We couldn't believe it when Gemma told us she was married,' she said. She stood on tiptoe and kissed my cheek, pulling me into a hug. She was about the same height as Gemma, five foot six; maybe an inch shorter. Like Gemma, she had dark-brown hair and green eyes but she was very thin, with a prominent clavicle over which hung a gold chain bearing a locket. She was tanned, her skin a rich brown colour, like she had spent a lot of time sunbathing.

'Aren't you handsome?' she said. I was taken aback. No one had ever described me as handsome before; not even Gemma. 'He looks a bit like that actor, doesn't he, Jeff?'

'Which one?'

'You know. From *Notting Hill*.'

'Hugh Grant?' I said with a laugh. 'That's flattering.' I looked nothing like him, apart from being a similar height and colouring. 'Or do you mean the Welsh one who was always walking round in his underpants?'

They both laughed like this was hilarious.

'I assume you won't be walking round in your boxers while we're here,' Lizzy said. She looked me up and down. 'Not that I'd mind. You look like you work out, Elliot. Do you?'

Before I had a chance to tell her I never went to the gym, she turned to Gemma and said, 'You've done very well here, Gem.'

'I know,' Gemma said, coming over with the remaining suitcases. She put her arm around me while Lizzy continued to stare at me like I was a side of beef.

Jeff stepped in. 'Leave the poor lad alone, Lizzy. I apologise, Elliot.'

'It's fine.'

'Besides,' he said to Lizzy, 'he definitely doesn't look like he works out to me.' He clapped me on the shoulder. 'Brains not brawn, am I right?'

Gemma said, 'Elliot has an MSc.'

33

'Ooh! Hear that, Lizzy? A Master of Science. Impressive.'

I couldn't tell if he was being mocking or sarcastic, and decided to give him the benefit of the doubt. Keen to change the subject, I said, 'Is Chloe all right?' She was still in the car.

'She hasn't been very well,' Jeff said. 'The poor lamb picked up some kind of virus in France, just before we left.'

'Oh no,' I said.

'Probably best if we leave her in the car while we get these bags indoors, if that's okay with you.'

'Yes, of course. Let me give you a hand.' I picked up the largest suitcase. It felt like it was full of bricks.

'I can carry it if it's a bit heavy for you,' Jeff said as I struggled with it.

'No, it's fine.'

I lugged the suitcase into the hall and dropped it with a thud. It had made me sweat, but I didn't want Jeff to think I was a wimp who couldn't carry a heavy case. Both Jeff and Lizzy were looking around, clearly impressed by the house. Jeff whistled.

'This is gorgeous,' he said.

'Perfect,' added Lizzy.

'Thank you.' I beamed like a proud parent. 'I'll show you round in a minute. But why don't you go through to the kitchen? Make yourselves at home.'

'We will,' Lizzy said. 'Thanks, Elliot.'

I went back outside with Gemma to fetch the other bags, while her parents went into the kitchen.

'Everything okay?' I asked in a low voice.

'Yes, fine.'

'They seem . . . nice,' I said.

'Do you think?'

'Yeah, why wouldn't I? And you look like your mum.'

She winced.

'You're much more beautiful. I mean, not that I'm saying there's anything wrong with your mum . . .'

Gemma looked up at the house. 'I hope she didn't embarrass you with that comment about you in your underwear.'

'I thought it was funny.'

'And all that stuff about you working out. I'm sorry.'

'It's fine.'

We carried the remaining cases into the house.

'What do you want me to do about Chloe?' Gemma asked her parents, who were seated at the dining table. They exchanged a look, like they were communicating telepathically.

'Have you made up a bed for her already?' Lizzy asked.

I answered. 'Yes, on the middle floor.'

'Thanks, sweetheart. Because I think she's going to have to go straight there. Come on, Jeff, we'd better fetch her.'

They went back outside, and Gemma and I followed. Jeff and Lizzy had already reached the car.

My next-door neighbour, George Whiteley, was standing by his door. He was in his seventies and had lived on Cuckoo Lane for over forty years. He and his wife, Edith, had brought their family up here, and for a long time they'd been hinting heavily about what great family homes these were, how nice it would be to hear the sound of children's voices through the walls. They had been ecstatic when I'd told them I was getting married, and had come round when we got back from Vegas with a wedding gift: a set of Le Creuset pans that must have cost a packet.

'Got company?' George said, lighting his pipe. He always came outside to indulge in what he called his 'final vice'.

'Gemma's mum, dad and sister have come to stay with us for a couple of weeks,' I explained. 'Except Gemma's sister isn't very well. A virus, apparently.'

George was a retired doctor, a GP who had worked at the heart of this community for decades. His ears pricked up. 'Oh dear. What are her symptoms?'

'I'm not sure yet. Nothing deadly, I hope.' I laughed and looked over at Gemma, who was standing by the front door. The drive to the airport and back, perhaps combined with the emotional impact of seeing her family after so long, appeared to have taken its toll. 'Jeff and Lizzy are going to put her straight to bed.'

'Very sensible. Let me know if I can help in any way.'

George went back inside as Jeff and Lizzy helped Chloe out of the car.

She had long, blonde hair but a closer look revealed dark roots. In fact, it looked like she hadn't bleached her hair in a while. She was taller than Gemma, almost six foot, and quite shockingly thin. Her skin was as pale as her mum's was tanned.

'Come on,' Jeff said. 'Let's get you to bed. Do you think you can make it up the stairs?'

An almost imperceptible nod, but she staggered as Jeff guided her towards the house. I hurried over to help, but Jeff waved me away. Before I could say anything, he lifted Chloe up and carried her into the house like a groom taking his bride over the threshold. Lizzy turned to follow.

'Has she seen a doctor?' I asked her. 'She looks really poorly.'

'Oh, she'll be all right. It's a little virus, that's all. She'll be as right as rain in a day or two.' Despite her words, there was a definite hint of concern in her voice.

I followed her back into the house. Jeff had already gone up to the middle floor and was waiting on the landing, still holding Chloe. Lizzy started to climb the stairs but Jeff said, 'Don't worry, darling. I've got this. You rest.'

'If you're sure,' Lizzy said, and she and Gemma headed for the kitchen while I went up the stairs.

'Which room is it?' Jeff asked when I reached him.

'This one.'

I opened the door to my office. I had already unfolded the sofa bed and prepared it for her. Jeff set her down on it as if she was still a child rather than a twenty-eight-year-old woman, and she closed her eyes immediately. Jeff sat on the edge and eased Chloe's shoes off.

'I'm surprised they let her on the plane,' I said.

'Oh, we gave her some paracetamol and Lizzy slapped some make-up on her cheeks.'

'Have you taken her temperature?'

'What? No, it's not worth it.'

I didn't agree. I headed to the bathroom and fetched the thermometer from the cabinet. When I returned, Jeff was standing, staring down at his youngest daughter, who appeared to be asleep.

'Chloe's always been a drama queen,' he said. 'Ever since she was born. Flipping 'eck, she used to scream the house down if she got the slightest graze.'

Jeff obviously knew his daughter better than I did, but this seemed like genuine sickness to me.

I held up the thermometer. 'I really think you should check her temperature.'

'Nah, it's fine.' He waved a hand dismissively.

We were at an impasse. It wasn't my place to check Chloe's temperature but Jeff showed no sign of taking the instrument from me.

I tried again. 'I really think you should—' I moved towards the bed and Jeff stepped into my path, like a bouncer barring entry to a nightclub. He folded his arms, which accentuated the veins that snaked around them, the rocky swell of his biceps. He was still smiling but there was something in his eyes, a warning, that made me instinctively retreat a few inches.

'Jeff, I—'

A crash came from downstairs, followed by a shriek.

Chapter 7

I rushed downstairs, followed at a much slower pace by Jeff.

Lizzy was standing on the far side of the kitchen, by the back door. Charlie was sitting on the counter, in the warm spot near the kettle where he liked to sleep. And Gemma was crouching on the floor, sweeping shards of glass into a dustpan.

'Your cat,' Lizzy said. 'It knocked the jug off the worktop.'

'Really?' Charlie had never done anything like that before. Like most cats, he possessed the enviable skill of being able to weave around household objects without touching them. I gave Gemma a quizzical look.

'I was in the loo,' she said, emptying the dustpan into the bin.

'I hope it wasn't valuable,' Lizzy said, eyes fixed on Charlie, who sat blinking at her.

'No. Not really.' I was lying. The jug had belonged to my parents, and whenever I used it I would picture my mother pouring lemonade into tall glasses on summer days. But I didn't want to make a big deal of it.

'You didn't tell me there was a cat here,' Lizzy said, moving to sit down opposite Gemma and rubbing at her nose.

'Mum's allergic,' Gemma said, with the slightest roll of her eyes.

'Oh.'

'Don't worry, though,' Lizzy said. 'As long as it doesn't come too near me or try to sleep on our bed.'

I was taken aback, but picked Charlie up and carried him over to his cat flap, coaxing him through it. As I watched him through the window he paused for a moment, flicking his tail, before padding off into the darkness of the garden. I felt a little guilty, like I'd betrayed him.

'He usually stays down here. Though he does have that cat-like habit of jumping on people who don't like him.'

'It had better—'

'Lizzy, stop fussing.'

Jeff had finally come into the kitchen, and his voice made his wife change tack instantly.

She turned to me. 'I'm so sorry, Elliot. It's your cat and this is its home.'

Jeff came over and clapped me on the back before sitting next to his wife at the table. 'And a beautiful home it is too. How long have you lived here, Elliot?'

'Yes,' Lizzy said, joining in, 'I want to hear all about you as well. Our new son-in-law. It's *very* exciting.' She winked at Gemma.

So I told them my story. How I had bought the house four years ago and restored it to its original condition. I told them about the work I did, teaching science to disadvantaged kids. They seemed fascinated by all of it, asking lots of questions about the house and the work I'd done. Jeff seemed particularly interested to hear how I'd raised the funds to buy this place.

'So are you one of those dot-com millionaires?' he asked.

I laughed. 'Far from it. It all went into this house.'

'Well, you did a great job,' Jeff said. 'Bricks and mortar, that's what it's all about. You're an Englishman and you need your castle. Am I right?'

'I guess.'

'Of course I'm right.'

39

Gemma hadn't spoken much during this exchange. But now her dad turned his attention to her.

'So how did you two meet, then?'

'She saved my life,' I said before she could respond. Jeff and Lizzy raised their eyebrows in unison, and I gestured for Gemma to fill them in with the rest.

'Well done, Gem,' Lizzy said when she'd finished. 'So, you have allergies too, Elliot? Me with cats and you with bees. That's two things we have in common. Allergies and thinking Gemma's lovely.'

'I taught her to drive, you know,' Jeff said, focusing on the part of the story where Gemma drove me to the hospital. 'Didn't I, sweetheart?'

'Yes, Dad.'

'Bloody terrible, she was, at first.' He reached across the table and patted her hand and I was surprised to see her flinch, until I remembered Gemma telling me she wasn't very tactile, something I hadn't witnessed before myself. 'I thought she was going to kill us both. But she got there in the end.'

'Everyone's terrible at first,' I said.

'Yeah, but Gemma . . .' He stopped, held his hands up. 'But now you're a lifesaver. Good for you, girl.'

I got up from the table. 'Would anyone like a drink? I'm going to open a bottle of wine.'

'We don't drink,' Lizzy said.

'Teetotal,' added Jeff.

'Oh.' I hadn't expected that. They didn't seem religious. Perhaps it was a health thing. Or maybe they were both alcoholics. I paused. 'You don't mind if I drink, though, I hope?'

'Knock yourself out,' said Jeff. 'We're not in the programme, in case you're wondering. I just don't like that feeling of being out of control.'

'And I've always preferred a cup of tea,' said Lizzy.

I poured a glass for myself and one for Gemma, passing it over to her, before filling two glasses with water for my in-laws.

'Been drinking a lot, have you?' Lizzy asked Gemma, eyeing her wine.

'Not really.'

'Hmm. I thought it might account for your weight gain.'

I almost spat my own wine back into the glass. Gemma was looking down at herself, a hand on her belly. She was far from overweight. She wasn't skinny like her mother and sister, but she was average-sized. Healthy. I was stunned by her mother's words, and Gemma was clearly stung, though she didn't seem greatly surprised.

'I haven't put on much,' she said.

Lizzy grunted. 'I suppose there's nothing wrong with a bit of winter padding. Have you thought about—'

For the second time, Jeff interrupted her. 'I think she looks great. Cuddly.'

I could see the muscles in Gemma's jaw flexing as she bit back a retort. I put my arm around her shoulders. 'I'd go with perfect.'

'He's a keeper, isn't he?' said Lizzy. 'Jeff's the same with me. That's how we ended up with three kids. We were supposed to stop with Gemma but Jeff could talk the knickers off a nun.'

'Mum, please. Elliot doesn't want to hear about that.'

Lizzy's eyes shone. 'What about you two? Are you planning on starting a family?'

This conversation was like being thrown one live grenade after another.

'We haven't talked about it yet,' Gemma said.

'Well, don't waste too much time,' Lizzy said. 'It would be lovely to have grandchildren.'

'You have Katie already,' Gemma said.

'Oh, I know. But . . . well, it would be lovely to have a couple more. Extend the bloodline. Anyway, maybe an accident will happen. I remember what it was like being a newlywed. We were at it non-stop, weren't we, Jeff?'

'Mum!' Gemma protested.

'Oh, come on, Elliot's a scientist. A man of the world. I'm sure I haven't shocked him.'

I laughed. 'You've come very close.'

She laughed too, and gave me another of her winks. 'I'm sorry, darling. You'll soon get used to my ways, I'm sure.'

Jeff took a sip of water. 'Do your mum and dad live around here, Elliot?'

'No. They died when I was eighteen. Just before I went to university.'

'Oh, that's bad luck. What happened?'

His directness was refreshing. Most people would express sympathy and leave a gap, hoping I would fill it without them having to ask.

'They died in a hot-air balloon crash.'

'What? You're having me on.'

I shook my head. 'No. It was a freak accident. Apparently when it was landing a gust of wind blew it into an electric cable and it caught fire.'

It had been all over the news at the time. Hot-air balloon accidents were rare, especially fatal ones. The pilot had died too, and three other passengers were seriously burned.

'Bloody hell,' Jeff said.

'You'd never get me in one of those things,' Lizzy added.

'Elliot was meant to go up too,' Gemma said, squeezing my hand. 'But he wasn't feeling well that day.'

Jeff whistled. 'So you've had two lucky escapes, Elliot. Seems like somebody up there likes you.'

'I suppose you could put it like that.'

'I'm a firm believer in fate,' he said. 'I mean, obviously it's a massive shame about your mum and dad but it seems to me like you're a lucky bloke. And luckiest of all, you met our Gemma.'

'I'll drink to that,' I said. I raised my wine glass and, after a beat of hesitation, Gemma did the same. Jeff raised his water but Lizzy's remained on the table.

'I reckon Gemma's the lucky one,' she said. 'So, Elliot, tell me. Did you sue the hot-air balloon company? Did you get loads of compensation? I'd have screwed them for every penny they had.'

'I couldn't,' I replied. 'My parents had to sign an agreement before the flight, which absolved the company of any responsibility.'

Jeff shook his head. 'Bastards.'

'Well,' said Lizzy. '*You* landed on your feet, anyway.'

Chapter 8

'Your mum is . . .'

'What?' Gemma said. We were lying in bed together, in our new bedroom on the top floor of the house. My three in-laws were sleeping one floor below and I spoke quietly, unsure of how well sound carried here and thinking I should have tested it out before the Robinson clan arrived. I didn't want to spend the next two weeks whispering.

'A character,' I said, completing my sentence.

Gemma covered her face with her hands. 'I'm sorry. She's so embarrassing. She's always been like that.' She removed her hands. 'I'm not embarrassing like her, am I?'

'Not at all.'

'Thank God.'

'I'm sure her heart's in the right place,' I said, rolling over and propping myself up on one elbow. 'But I couldn't believe what she said about you gaining weight.'

'Oh, that's nothing. When I was a teenager she was always going on at me about the importance of having a "good figure", how no one would want me if I was fat.'

'That's awful.'

'It's because she's obsessed with her own weight, not that she ever does any exercise, or never used to when I lived with them. She lived on cigarettes and white grapes.' She laughed. 'I don't let it get to me. Not anymore. Thank you for sticking up for me, anyway.'

I didn't think I had. Not really. Next time, I decided, I would challenge Lizzy if she insulted Gemma. This was Gemma's house now, as well as mine, and her parents had no right to come here and upset her.

'Is it nice to have them here, though, despite that?' I asked.

'Yeah, of course. I mean, it's weird. It's been so long since I've seen them, let alone lived with them . . .' She sighed. 'But I'll get used to it.'

'And it's only for two weeks.'

Gemma made a noise of affirmation. 'Let's change the subject, please. Tell me about something that happened at work today. Something that has nothing to do with my family.'

'Okay.' I told her a story involving the amusing antics of a couple of kids I'd been teaching earlier that day. She laughed and moved closer to me.

She was wearing her habitual T-shirt and pyjama bottoms. Even now, almost three months in, she was reluctant to let me see her naked before and after sex, so she would usually get into bed wearing clothes, then pull them back on before getting up. I was still waiting for her to tell me about the scars on her torso. It had reached the point where it seemed like I'd left it too long to ask, but it was also beyond the point where she might tell me without being prompted. I wanted to know the story behind them, because I loved her and wanted to know everything about her. I wanted her to trust me and feel close enough to me that she could tell me anything. I also wondered if she was waiting for me to ask.

I had a good idea what had caused the scars anyway. But I wanted to hear it from her.

I reached out a hand, touching her hip. 'So, are we going to let them cramp our style?'

She sighed. 'I'm really not in the mood tonight.'

'Oh.' I withdrew my hand. 'Okay.'

'I know I shouldn't worry about it, but knowing they're down there . . . I don't think I'll be able to relax.' She leaned over and kissed my lips. 'It'll do us good to have a night off and recharge our batteries.'

We turned out the lights, and before long I heard Gemma's breathing shift as she fell into sleep. I tried to follow her but was struggling to switch my brain off. The house felt strange with other people in it, and I thought I could hear voices too, so quiet they might have been in my head.

The problem was I'd lived on my own for too long, and I reminded myself that even having Gemma here had felt odd at first. I'd soon get used to having other people around.

ᴡ

I must have been awoken by a noise, or perhaps it was a shift in pressure somewhere else in the house, an instinctive reaction that pulled me out of my dream. I sat up, images of a burglar creeping about downstairs setting my pulse racing. But then I remembered. We had houseguests. And now I was awake, I needed to pee, so I got out of bed and put my dressing gown on.

As I came out of the en-suite, I heard it. A definite noise coming from downstairs. I strained to hear. Was it just Jeff or Lizzy moving around in the master bedroom? I listened more closely. No, it was fainter, like it was coming from the ground floor.

It was almost certainly one of Gemma's family, getting a glass of water or something completely unremarkable. But what if it was a burglar? I couldn't remember if, with the change of routine, I had locked the back door – and the more I thought about it, the more convinced I became that I'd left it open. I headed down and walked past the living room towards the kitchen.

A shuffling noise came from inside the living room.

I froze, heart banging against my ribs. There was someone in there. Should I continue to the kitchen, grab a knife or heavy object? I stood motionless, unable to hear anything except my own breathing. I was paralysed, unable to decide what to do.

Then someone inside the room coughed and the spell was broken. I peered into the room and saw Lizzy, standing there fully dressed in the dark, with just the glow of the moon from outside illuminating the room.

She had something in her hand: a small square object.

'Lizzy?' I said.

She spun around, clutching her chest. 'Oh my Lord, you frightened the life out of me.'

'Is everything all right?' I asked, entering the room. She had her other hand behind her back, so I couldn't see what she was holding.

'I couldn't sleep, that's all, so I was looking for something to read.' She gestured to the bookcase.

'Want me to recommend something?'

'You are sweet. But, actually, I've suddenly come over all tired. I think I'll go back to bed.'

'Okay. Goodnight, then.'

'Goodnight.'

I went into the kitchen and heard her go up the stairs behind me, the familiar creak of the fourth step. I checked the back door – it was locked and secure – then looked around for Charlie. There was no sign of him, which wasn't unusual. He often stayed out all night.

I drank a glass of water, then headed back up. It was only when I slipped into bed beside Gemma that it came to me: the square object in Lizzy's hand had looked like a tape measure, one of the ones where you press a button and the stiff plastic tape comes whizzing back in.

But what on earth was my mother-in-law doing with a tape measure in my living room in the middle of the night?

My brain was too tired to process it. I went back to sleep.

Chapter 9

'So how was it?' Amira asked. 'The first night with the in-laws?'

'It was . . . interesting.' I gave her a rundown, leaving out the more sensitive parts like Lizzy's comments about Gemma's weight. I knew Amira would be outraged and angry on Gemma's behalf, but also thought Gemma might not like me talking about it. I didn't mention seeing Lizzy with a tape measure either, because by morning I had convinced myself I must have been mistaken. Remembering what Gemma had said about her mum existing on a diet of cigarettes and grapes, I deduced it was more likely that the object was rectangular, not square, and was in fact a pack of cigarettes. My guess was that she had actually been planning to sneak out for a smoke.

It was four o'clock now, and Amira and I were waiting outside the Inquiring Minds lab-cum-classroom in Tulse Hill. Our classroom was in a council-owned building that was carved up into business and retail units. It wasn't glamorous, and got far too hot in summer, but it was cheap. This afternoon's workshop was for children aged eight to eleven from a couple of local primary schools that couldn't afford the equipment that Amira and I had. Their teachers did the best they could, but with classes of thirty children, and an uninspiring curriculum to stick to, they were unlikely to find the next Marie Curie or Stephen Hawking.

That was where we came in. The sessions were, of course, free. All the children needed to show was enthusiasm, although I suspected that many of the kids who came were those with parents looking for free childcare at the end of the school day. No matter. It was one of the most enjoyable sessions we ran, mainly because of one particular kid.

'Rather you than me,' Amira said when I'd finished telling her about my first evening with my in-laws.

'It's only for two weeks,' I said.

'So, what, are they looking for somewhere to rent?'

'I don't know. We didn't discuss it last night.'

'I see.'

'What do you mean, "I see"?' I asked.

She patted my arm. 'You're a nice guy, Elliot. Too nice sometimes. My advice is, don't make them feel too welcome.'

'Why? It's not like they're planning to stay forever.'

The minibus that brought the children to us pulled up by the kerb. Kenneth Chase, a teacher from Tulse Hill Primary who had volunteered to bring the children from both his and the neighbouring school to our door, was behind the wheel. Kenneth opened the bus doors and a dozen children spilled out and filed past us, chatting excitedly and jostling each other. They were the usual multicultural mix found in London, which was one of the reasons why I loved this city so much. Amira and I had attended a couple of school concerts at Tulse Hill Primary in which children whose parents came from all over the world performed side by side, as if racial and national differences were a stupid concept invented by adults.

Spend enough time around kids like these, I had discovered, and you might begin to feel optimistic about the future of humanity.

And one of our favourite little humans filed past us now, Pikachu backpack slung over her shoulder, showing us her customary grin. Effia Mensah, Effy for short.

'Hi, Mr Foster. Miss Nasri.'

'Hi, Effy.'

I know one shouldn't have favourites but it was hard not to where Effy was concerned. She was eight years old, a skinny little kid who lived in a block of flats on an estate between here and Brixton. Her parents were Ghanaian immigrants, she was obsessed with Super Mario and Pokémon and she was the brightest child I had ever taught, with infectious enthusiasm that reminded me, even on the toughest days – when the other kids were difficult or we were locked in a battle with some bureaucratic body or other – why we did this.

'Okay,' I said, once we'd joined the kids in the classroom and Amira began setting up the equipment. 'Today we're going to do some chemistry experiments. We're going to make things fizz and go pop and maybe even bang. How does that sound?'

A low murmur of enthusiasm. One of the boys was playing with a mobile phone. I went over and plucked it from his hand, eliciting a squeal of protest.

'My dad'll kill you if you damage my phone,' the boy said.

I ignored his threat and returned to the front of the classroom. 'I said, how does that sound?'

'Amazing!' a couple of them yelled, including Effy.

'That's more like it. Okay, who can tell me what happens when we put oil and water together.'

Effy, as expected, put her hand up.

'Come on then, Effy, enlighten us,' Amira said, and the little girl was happy to oblige.

Later, when the lesson was over and the kids had returned to the minibus, Amira and I hung back to talk to Kenneth before he drove them all home.

'They're doing great,' I said. 'Especially Effy. How's she getting on in the rest of her lessons?'

'Fine, I think. Although she most comes to life when she's with you guys. I was actually talking to her dad last night. He said Effy's talking about wanting to be a nuclear physicist or possibly study quantum mechanics. You know she asked the school librarian if they could get in a copy of *A Brief History of Time*?'

'That's brilliant.'

It was almost six by the time we got back to the office, and Amira said, 'Why don't you knock off? Go home and talk to your in-laws?'

'I don't know. I need to file that application with—'

She cut me off. 'I'll handle it. You go home. Honestly, I really think you need to find out how long they're planning to stay. Have I told you about my friend Syed? His mother-in-law moved in for a week. That was in 2011 and she's still there.'

'Bloody hell. Okay. I hear you.'

'Good man. I'll see you tomorrow, okay?'

'Okay.'

'And Elliot? Don't take any crap. Pin them down.'

ϖ

When I got back to Cuckoo Lane the house seemed empty. Gemma had her yoga class on Tuesday nights but I had expected Jeff and Lizzy to be here. I went through to the kitchen and called, 'Hello?'

No response.

There were half a dozen dirty plates and mugs stacked up in the sink. That was a little irritating, but maybe they'd been planning to do it later or weren't sure how to use the dishwasher. It wasn't a big deal.

As I was putting the last plate in I heard a drumming noise coming from the back door. It was Charlie, pawing at his cat flap.

This happened occasionally. The cat flap got stuck, usually when Charlie went through it too fast and knocked the lock. But when I crouched to open it I saw the lock was all the way across. I slid it open and Charlie clattered through, rubbing against me and heading straight to his empty dish. I opened a pouch of cat food and stroked his back while he ate, looking over at the cat flap.

Had someone deliberately locked him out?

I stood up and went into the main body of the house. The living room was empty and undisturbed. I went up to the first floor and lightly rapped on the door of the master bedroom. There was no reply so I pushed it open.

The room was a mess. The quilt was bunched up in the centre of the bed, there were more dirty cups on both bedside tables, and the two large suitcases the Robinsons had brought with them were open, their contents spilling out across the carpet.

Don't get stressed, I said to myself. It was, temporarily, their room. They were adults. I could hardly ask them to keep it tidy. I was being irrational, a result of having lived on my own for so long and keeping everything immaculate. My bedroom was always tidy. I rarely even left the bed unmade. Gemma was the same. But I had guests now and needed to chill out.

I needed the loo so I went into the bathroom – and the smell hit me immediately.

Somebody had used the toilet but hadn't flushed it. I put my sleeve over my mouth and nose and grabbed the chain, flushing away the offending objects. I found the air freshener and sprayed it around, then took in the rest of the room.

There was talcum powder – which wasn't mine as I never buy the stuff – all over the floor, and two wet towels left in sodden heaps on the tiles. Shaking my head, I scooped up the towels and dropped them into the washing basket, then felt the need to wash my hands.

There was no hot water. Somebody must have recently emptied the tank. There was a citrusy smell in the room too, and it took me a moment to recognise it. It was Eau Sauvage. I rarely wore aftershave these days, but Sauvage had been my go-to aftershave when I was younger and there was a dusty bottle of it here in the bathroom cabinet. I guessed Jeff had helped himself.

I left the bathroom. Leaving their bedroom untidy was one thing, but it certainly wasn't on to leave communal spaces in a mess. This wasn't a hotel. Aware that I sounded like my mum telling me off when I was a teenager, I tried to make excuses for them. Perhaps they had been planning to clean up before I got home from work. Maybe something had made them need to go out suddenly. I was torn. I didn't want to be uptight and unwelcoming, but I also didn't want to have to keep cleaning up after my in-laws.

I was about to go back downstairs when I heard a noise come from the room at the end of the hall. The room where Chloe was staying.

I was worried about her. She was unwell, yet her parents had gone out and left her on her own. I went over to the door and listened but couldn't hear anything. After hesitating for a moment, I knocked.

There was no response.

'Hello?' I said. 'Are you okay in there?'

Again, no response.

What if her sickness had got so bad that she couldn't speak? She could be in there, suffering, needing help.

'Chloe,' I said. 'I'm going to come in, all right?' I turned the handle.

The door wouldn't open.

All of the doors inside the house, apart from the bathrooms, had Chubb locks fitted. It had been like that when I moved in, a strange quirk of the house that I'd never encountered before. This, being my home office, was the only room I ever locked because it contained lots of important paperwork. When the Robinsons had come to stay, I had left the key in the lock.

Okay, I thought, trying to come up with an excuse for her, *she wants her privacy*.

I was about to step away when I heard another noise from inside the room. A sniff.

It sounded like someone laughing. Or . . . crying?

'Chloe?' I said.

Nothing.

'Chloe? Are you okay?'

But she had fallen silent. And then came a burst of noise from downstairs as the front door opened. I headed down and found Jeff and Lizzy coming in, struggling with half a dozen shopping bags full of groceries.

'Elliot!' Jeff exclaimed. 'You're home!'

'Yes, I—'

'I hope you didn't see the messy bathroom,' Lizzy said. 'Chloe had a bath and then I had to put the poor lamb back to bed and I got distracted. I was going to clean it up when we got back.' She gestured to the bags. 'We thought we'd get some shopping in for you.'

'That's nice of you.'

'Well, you're putting us up. We don't want to eat you out of house and home.'

'Thank you.'

'Jeff,' Lizzy said, all smiles, 'you unpack, put the kettle on, and I'll go and sort out that bathroom.'

She paused on the stairs and turned back.

'What must you think of us, eh?'

I smiled, feeling guilty for allowing myself to get so wound up by the mess, for thinking the worst of them. It was going to be fine. Of course it was.

Chapter 10

Gemma got home from her class a little later and headed straight for the shower, complaining when she came out that there wasn't much hot water.

'Sorry about that,' Lizzy said. 'We'll have to be careful not to use it all up.'

After dinner, which Lizzy cooked, Gemma told me she had a headache and needed to go to bed.

She pulled me aside while her parents cleared up in the kitchen, demonstrating that they did know how to use a dishwasher. 'Are you going to be all right?'

'Of course. It'll give me a chance to get to know them.' To ask them the questions I'd meant to ask when I came home that afternoon.

Gemma kissed me. 'I'll probably read for a while, so hopefully I'll still be awake when you come up.'

'Okay. Love you.'

I went to the wine rack in the kitchen and was looking through the bottles, intending to open a red, when Jeff came over.

'I don't know anything about wine,' he said, 'but is this where you keep the good stuff?'

I smiled and showed him the bottom two rows of the rack. 'These are all really nice, but this is the best one.' I pulled out the bottle of

Cappellano Barolo Piè Franco, handling it like I would a piece of delicate china. 'I'm saving this for a very special occasion.'

Jeff went to take it from me and, reluctantly, I let him. The wine dated from 1995 and was one of my most treasured possessions.

'Expensive, was it?' he asked, holding the label up to the light.

'I think so.' I explained that it had been a present from one of my old college professors, who gave it to me when I graduated. He'd promised it to me if I achieved a First, and although at that age I was more likely to drink cheap cider than fine wine, the prospect of gaining his approval – this father figure, who had stood in for my own dead dad – had helped drive me on.

'You got the First, then?' Jeff asked, still holding the bottle.

I pulled a modest face.

Jeff whistled. 'You're the whole package, aren't you, Elliot? Nice guy, brains, money.' He winked at me. 'All you're missing is a bit of brawn. Not harbouring any dark secrets, are you? Skeletons in the closet?'

From the other side of the kitchen, Lizzy said, 'Bodies buried in the garden? That's what they always say, don't they, when they arrest some serial killer? "He seemed so normal. So nice . . ."'

'There are no bodies in my garden or skeletons in my closet,' I said. Jeff was now holding the bottle by its neck and I was convinced it was going to slip from his grasp and smash on the floor.

But Jeff looked me up and down. 'Nobody's perfect, though,' he said with another wink. 'For all you know, we could be a pair of serial killers.'

I laughed nervously and Jeff noticed how I was staring at the precious bottle.

He handed it back to me. 'You should drink it. Live today, that's what I say. You never know when something terrible's going to happen. I mean, what if that bee sting had killed you? You'd have died without ever getting to enjoy this vino.'

'I will,' I said, sliding the bottle back into its place on the rack and remembering the vow I'd made in the hospital. Marrying Gemma had been the only really impetuous, out-there thing I'd done. Since then I'd slipped back into my old, cautious habits. 'But not tonight.'

A little later, we were sitting in the living room and I suddenly remembered Chloe.

'Have you checked on her this evening?' I asked.

'Oh, yes,' Lizzy said. 'She's sleeping. It's the best way to fight a virus.'

'Has she eaten?'

'Yeah, I made her some chicken soup earlier, just before her bath.'

I was going to ask if Lizzy knew that Chloe had locked herself in, but I assumed she must do. I had also intended to ask them if they knew anything about the cat flap being locked, but both Jeff and Lizzy had been in such good spirits since getting home with the groceries, and the meal had been so delicious, that I found myself feeling generous. It must have been an accident. Charlie had done it himself. Silly cat.

'Whereabouts in France did you live?' I asked.

'Hmm?' said Jeff, who had been studying the TV remote like it was an ancient artefact that he didn't quite understand. The TV was off and I wondered if he was itching to watch something.

I repeated the question.

'The south.'

I waited to see if he'd be more specific but he continued turning the remote over in his hands.

'Any good . . . vineyards nearby?'

'I told you, I don't know anything about wine.'

I decided to leave it. It wasn't really important. 'What did you do out there? Job-wise, I mean.'

'Oh, this and that.'

'Were you running a business?'

They exchanged a look, one I couldn't read. A conspiratorial look, with a hint of humour but something else too.

'Yes. Yes, we were,' Lizzy said.

'Managing,' added Jeff.

Managing what? They didn't say any more. But although the way they were acting, their secretiveness, made me uneasy, I didn't really need to know. I moved on.

'What made you leave?' I asked.

Jeff put down the remote. 'We were missing home, weren't we, Lizzy?'

'That's right. And opportunities had run out over there. It was time to come back. We were missing our kids too.' She reached out and squeezed Jeff's hand. 'And little Katie.'

Jeff picked up the remote again and I had to resist the urge to snatch it from him, tell him to leave it alone. His knee bounced up and down and he raised his chin, as if a thought had occurred to him.

'We should go and see Stuart tomorrow, Lizzy.'

'Oh yes. We should. It'll be lovely to see him.'

'You can invite him round here if you like,' I said.

'Oh, thank you, Elliot. I can't wait to see that lovely granddaughter of ours. From the photos I've seen, she's the spitting image of Chloe when she was that age. I'm looking forward to giving her a big squeeze.'

The conversation was slipping in the wrong direction. I tried to pull it back.

'So, what are your plans now you're back? Are you going to be . . . running your own business over here?'

'That's right.' Jeff's knee continued to bounce. 'We're exploring a couple of opportunities, aren't we, Lizzy?'

'We certainly are.'

This was like trying to get information out of my cat. I was used to dealing with children, many of whom were shy and closed off, but Jeff and Lizzy took reticence to a new level.

It was time to ask the big question.

'So what about finding somewhere to live?' I asked. 'Are you looking for somewhere near here?'

'We are,' said Jeff.

I waited. 'I guess you want to live close to Gemma and Stuart?'

They both nodded.

'It's expensive round here,' I said, keen to get some idea of their financial situation. They had been so vague about their business that they could have been minted or completely skint. It was impossible to tell.

'Oh, I know,' said Jeff. 'The prices here are crazy. But that's not a problem.'

So they weren't skint. That was a relief. Maybe they had sold their property in France or had made a lot of money from their business, whatever that was.

'Are you going to try to rent a house?' I asked. 'Or a flat?'

'We prefer houses,' Jeff replied. 'Don't we, Lizzy?'

'Oh yes, we like to have room to spread out. And I'd go mad cooped up in a little flat with Jeff.'

'Hey!'

He grabbed at her and I was surprised to see him tickle her ribcage, making her squirm. It was nice, I supposed, to see a middle-aged couple acting like a pair of loved-up teenagers.

'Actually,' Jeff began, 'do you have a computer we could use? To search for properties?'

'You haven't started yet?' I had assumed they'd started looking before they returned to England. That's what I would have done.

'We've made a few inquiries,' Lizzy interjected. 'But nothing perfect has come up yet.'

'Right. Yes, of course you can use the computer.' I reeled off the names of a few property websites, the ones most people used to search for places to buy or rent. 'It's in the snug.' That was what we called the little room at the front of the house.

'Not that we know how to use a computer, do we, Lizzy?'

'We haven't got a bloody clue.'

'Neither of us. We usually get Chloe to do all that stuff.'

They laughed, with that odd pride that people sometimes display when they're telling you they are crap with technology. As if being unable to use a phone or computer is a positive trait.

'That's okay,' I said. 'I can help. I can show you now, if you like?'

'Hmm, I'm exhausted,' Lizzy said. 'I won't be able to concentrate. It'll just bounce off my thick skull.'

'Me too,' said Jeff.

I tried not to let my frustration show. 'Okay, how about I show you in the morning, before I leave for work?'

'Sounds good.' Jeff waved the TV remote at me. 'Now, how do you get this bloody thing to work?'

Chapter 11

The next morning, Wednesday, I showed Jeff and Lizzy how to use the computer and set up a search for them on Prime Location, which aggregated all the listings from local estate agents. There were quite a lot of houses available for rent in the area, most of them eye-wateringly expensive. Still, the Robinsons didn't seem bothered by the cost and told me they were looking for somewhere with at least three bedrooms and a garden.

'Like this place,' Jeff said. 'That's what we're after.'

They both acted as if the computer was an alien form of technology, grappling cack-handedly with the mouse and prodding the keyboard with a single finger. I left them browsing a list of properties and headed off to work.

'How did you get on?' I asked when I got home that evening. Gemma was in the kitchen with her mum, drinking tea.

'Not bad, not bad,' Lizzy said. 'We've made a couple of appointments.'

'That's great, isn't it, Gemma?' I said.

'It's wonderful.' Her tone was flat. I was confused. Didn't she want her parents to find somewhere to rent? Or had she just had a bad day at work? This was one of the most frustrating things about having my in-laws to stay. The lack of privacy and opportunity to talk to my wife.

Gemma had been fast asleep when I went up to bed the previous night and I hadn't had a chance to talk to her that morning.

'Did you speak to Stuart?' I asked Lizzy.

'Yes, he's coming round with her in a bit. I hope that's okay?'

'Yes, of course.' I looked around. 'Where's Charlie?'

'Out somewhere,' Gemma replied.

'I haven't seen it all day,' Lizzy added.

'That's weird,' I said. Charlie was always there to greet me when I got home from work, wanting his dinner. It was part of our routine, which hadn't changed when Gemma moved in.

'You must have been wrong,' Lizzy said. 'You were making out that cats always jump on people who don't like them, but yours has been steering well clear of me. Its fur's still everywhere, though. It gets right up my nose.'

She faked a sneeze, as if to demonstrate.

I went over to the back door and opened it, stepping out into the cold air and calling Charlie. Usually he would come running but there was no sign of him.

I stayed in the garden for a few minutes, waiting to see if Charlie appeared. I felt too irritated to go back inside. Through the window, I could see Lizzy talking to Gemma, who was frowning. What was Lizzy saying? Was she telling her she was overweight again?

I was about to go inside when I sensed something above me. I looked up towards the window on the middle floor. Chloe's room.

She was standing there, staring out at the garden, her face so pale it could have been a reflection of the moon. She was wearing a long white nightdress and had one palm pressed against the glass. She looked like a woman from a fairy tale, a princess locked away in a tower. Or, with the misted glass obscuring her features, like the ghostly heroine of a Victorian gothic.

Perhaps she saw me looking, because she stepped back from the window and vanished from sight.

ᗯ

I was going to say something about Chloe when I went back indoors, to ask Lizzy if her daughter was feeling better and why she was still in her room, but the doorbell rang the moment I entered the kitchen. It was Stuart with his daughter, Katie.

This was the first time I'd met Katie. She was cute, even if she did look a lot like her father. Actually, her presence brought Stuart to life. His eyes shone with love when he looked at her, and he clearly enjoyed being a dad. It made me feel a little envious, and I imagined what it would be like to have my own child. I tried to meet Gemma's eye, to attempt to telepathically transmit what I was thinking, but she was too busy watching Katie.

'Say hello to your gran and grandad,' Stuart said, as we all convened in the living room.

She hid behind him, clinging to his trousers, and it struck me that this was the first time she'd met her grandparents since she was a baby.

Lizzy got down on her knees on the carpet and reached out her arms. 'Come on, sweetheart. We don't bite.' But Katie backed away further. I studied Lizzy's face. She was clearly hurt.

Stuart tried to coax Katie out from behind him, but she wasn't budging.

'She's shy,' he said with a nervous laugh.

'There's no need to be shy of your gran,' Lizzy said, trying to get closer to the little girl, but Katie gripped her dad's trousers even harder and shut her eyes.

'It's not her fault,' said Jeff, who had been watching from the sofa. 'We're strangers to her. Let's leave the poor little mite alone.'

Stuart turned and picked his daughter up, and she held on to him as if he were about to hand her over to the Child Catcher. She whispered something in his ear.

Stuart turned to Gemma. 'Can she watch your iPad for a bit?'

'Of course.'

Gemma left the room to fetch her tablet. Lizzy was still on her knees on the carpet, still smiling at Katie, who really wasn't going to play ball. Lizzy's eyes were wet and she turned to give Jeff a pitiful look. He seemed unmoved but helped Lizzy get up.

Gemma came back with the iPad and we left Katie on the sofa watching YouTube while the rest of us went into the kitchen.

'She really looks like a Robinson, doesn't she?' Lizzy said.

Stuart seemed displeased by this. 'I think she looks like a mix of me and Jane.'

'No, she's definitely more Robinson,' Jeff said. 'She's got our eyes.'

'Shame she doesn't want to know us,' said Lizzy. 'A child, scared of her own grandparents, of her own family.'

Stuart bristled. 'Maybe if you'd brought her a present back from France you could have used that to break the ice.'

Jeff tutted. 'A present! Kids today are totally spoiled.'

'Well, you didn't get her anything for any of her birthdays,' Stuart said.

'I'm sure you and Jane got her plenty of stuff. We wouldn't have known what to send her, anyway.'

Stuart opened his mouth to retort but must have thought better of it because he just stood there, glowering.

Gemma put a hand on his upper arm. 'Want a beer?'

'I can't. I'm doing the night shift later.'

'You're not still driving a cab, are you?' said Jeff. 'I thought you would have moved on from that by now. No wonder you can only afford that tiny house. And renting too. What a waste.'

Again, Stuart bit his tongue. I could almost hear him counting to ten beneath his breath. 'I enjoy my job,' he said eventually. 'And I like renting. It means I'm not tied down. I thought you'd approve of that, seeing as you've never owned your own place.'

Jeff grunted. 'We're looking to settle down for good now.'

'Oh, really? Going to buy somewhere, are you? Planning on rob-bing a bank?'

Lizzy jumped in. 'Come on, what must Elliot think of us, having a family argument when we haven't seen each other for five years? Give your old mum a hug. Katie won't hug me so you'll have to do.' She pulled Stuart into an awkward embrace.

I decided now would be a good time to slip out of the room and leave them to it. I really didn't want to get involved in their family politics, although I had been unsettled by Stuart's comment about Jeff and Lizzy needing to rob a bank in order to get their own place. I went back into the living room, where Katie was staring at the iPad, enrapt. I sat down on the arm of the sofa.

'What are you watching?' I asked.

Shyly, she tilted the screen towards me. It showed a couple of kids breaking open a large papier mâché egg. I knew from my work that videos of children opening surprise eggs to reveal toys were enormously popular.

'Didn't you want to meet your gran and grandad?' I asked.

She shook her head.

'Why not?'

She didn't take her eyes off the iPad. On the screen, the children were leaping around, clutching their new toys.

'Mummy and Daddy had a big quarrel about me coming here,' Katie said.

'Why?'

She finally looked at me. 'They didn't think I heard, but I did. Mummy said Gran and Grandad are . . .' She stopped.

'Are what, Katie?'

Her eyes were wide. She glanced at the door, then looked back at me.

'Evil,' she whispered.

ω

'I'm concerned about your sister,' I said later, when Gemma and I were in bed. She was reaching for the eye mask she'd taken to using when she slept.

I explained how I'd seen Chloe staring out of the window.

'It's very strange,' I said, 'having someone living in my house who I've barely met. And what if she's really sick? I don't understand why your parents haven't taken her to see a doctor.'

'They don't like doctors,' Gemma said. 'They were like that when we were kids. They never took us unless it was really serious.'

'Really? Well, it's freaking me out a little, having this silent stranger hidden away in what's supposed to be my office.'

Gemma didn't say anything for a little while, and I was about to prompt her when she said, 'Chloe needs time, that's all.'

'What do you mean? Time to get better?'

Blue lights strobed across the ceiling: a passing ambulance. I wanted Gemma to say more because I didn't understand her relationship with her sister. It was as if they were strangers. I knew they hadn't seen each other for a long time but they were flesh and blood. Why did Gemma seem so unconcerned?

'I'm tired,' Gemma said, yawning. 'Let's get some sleep.'

'But . . .'

She had already slipped on her eye mask and turned away. I was annoyed. I hadn't told her what Katie had said yet. It was another mystery I wanted to discuss. Why had Katie's mother said Jeff and Lizzy were evil? What had they done?

I was going to shake Gemma's shoulder, but then her breathing changed and I realised she was already asleep. A frown seeped through from whatever she was dreaming about.

I closed my eyes, but I couldn't relax and my heart was beating too fast. Years ago, after my parents died, I had been through a terrible period of insomnia which had forced me to go to the doctor to get sleeping pills. It had taken a long time for me to wean myself off them but since moving into Cuckoo Lane I'd had no trouble sleeping at all. The house had always felt so safe, so nurturing, like a mother rocking a baby, and I had enjoyed eight hours a night, easy.

Not tonight, though. In fact, I hadn't slept well since the Robinsons arrived. I had put it down to a shift in atmosphere, and to being in a different room, but tonight I felt anxious and frustrated. Gemma and I hadn't had a proper conversation for days, and the lack of privacy was starting to get to me.

Come on, I said to myself. *It's only been a few days. It'll all return to normal soon.*

But they haven't found somewhere to go yet, said the other voice in my head. *They could be here for weeks.*

And the reasonable voice said, *Don't be so unwelcoming. They're Gemma's family. Why does it matter if they stay a little longer?*

Because they're evil, said the other voice, and that sounded so crazy it killed the internal dialogue.

I felt myself sinking, but in those final moments before I fell asleep I became convinced there was someone standing outside my bedroom door. I could hear them – no, *sense* them – breathing. And then I was dreaming – dreaming that someone, too shadowy and liquid to make out, was coming into my room, creeping towards the bed, watching me, wanting to smother me and take everything I had.

I jerked awake, cold and sweaty, and as I lay there I heard a voice, then another. *It must be the TV downstairs*, I thought. I tried to get back to sleep but now I'd heard the TV I couldn't tune it out.

I got out of bed. I was going to go downstairs and ask Jeff, because I presumed it was him, to turn it down. But when I got to the middle floor I realised it wasn't the TV, it was Jeff and Lizzy. They were on the ground floor.

I crept towards the staircase and strained to hear what they were saying. But all I could make out was the bass rumble of Jeff's voice and the treble of Lizzy's. Normally I would have left them to it, but I was desperate to hear. They might be talking about their plans for moving out. Or they might be saying something about the situation with Chloe. I trod lightly down the first few steps.

'. . . think we've got away . . .' That was Jeff. I couldn't make out the end of the sentence. *Got away with it?* That seemed the obvious conclusion.

They were in the snug, where the iMac was. Lizzy said something – a question – possibly 'Are you sure?'

Then Jeff said, 'Look. There's nothing.'

Were they using the computer? I didn't think they knew how, although even the most computer-illiterate person was surely capable of using Google or email.

I heard Lizzy yawn before saying something else. This time I heard it more clearly: 'You don't think she'll say anything?'

Jeff replied, 'No. Don't be stupid.'

Lizzy's next words were inaudible, but the ones after that were easy to make out. 'I'm going back to bed. Are you coming?'

Quickly, I ran back up the stairs and slipped beneath the covers, heart beating fast. Replaying the conversation in my head, I was increasingly sure Jeff had said, 'I think we've got away with it.'

But got away with what?

Chapter 12

I pushed the mower over the lawn, thinking this was probably the last time I'd need to do this until spring. Fallen leaves lay in piles beneath the trees, and treading over them I was hit by a wave of melancholy. The changing of the seasons, the move indoors, a nation preparing to hunker down for the long, cold, wet months ahead. I stopped the mower and stood there for a minute, thinking how much my life had changed since last winter. I had been alone then; content but with a hole at my centre, a hole that Gemma had filled.

'Penny for them.'

I was startled back to the present, realising I was standing in the middle of the lawn, the grass half-mown. George was talking to me over the fence that separated our gardens and Edith, his wife, stood behind him wearing a pair of gardening gloves. I left the mower where it was and went over to the fence.

'You looked like you were miles away,' George said.

'I was. Just thinking about . . . Christmas.'

Edith came over. 'Christmas? Oh my goodness, it's only just November. But I expect it'll be exciting for you this year. Your first with your lovely new wife.'

'*Just* me and Gemma, I hope.'

George's eyebrows, which were like two furry grey caterpillars, shot up. 'Uh-oh. In-laws not showing any sign of moving on?'

I waved a hand. 'I'm only kidding. They're looking for somewhere to rent, so they won't be here much longer.'

I glanced back at my house. Jeff and Lizzy were inside now. Gemma had gone out to meet a friend for lunch and Chloe was still in her room. Apart from trips to the bathroom, she hadn't emerged once since coming to stay. And Gemma still didn't seem concerned about it.

'They've only been here five days,' I said. 'I've been encouraging them to look online for somewhere to rent, although they don't seem keen. They're pretty hopeless with computers.'

'Really? We love ours, don't we, George? We were FaceTiming Terry in Australia earlier.' That was their son. 'And I love looking at property sites, having a nose round all those houses. I found a really good new site called Forever Homes. You should get them to take a look.'

'I will. Do you still have your Facebook page?'

George and Edith ran the local Neighbourhood Watch scheme, for which they had set up a Facebook page where residents of Cuckoo Lane and the surrounding streets could share messages and coordinate campaigns – for example, the quest to get speed bumps installed on the road.

'We do,' George replied.

'I might need to post on there about Charlie,' I said with a frown. 'I haven't seen him since Tuesday.'

'Oh no.' Edith put her hand to her lips. 'You must be worried sick.'

'I am.' I had lain awake the night before, straining to hear the clatter of his cat flap, having checked to ensure it was unlocked before going to bed. 'But he's probably gone off to his second home. Most cats have one, don't they? I think he's waiting for my in-laws to clear off so he doesn't have to listen to anyone moaning about his fur setting off their allergies.'

George laughed. 'Like that, is it? Send me a photo of the little chap and I'll put it on the page, get everyone to check their sheds and what have you.'

'Thanks, George.'

I was about to say I needed to get back to my lawn when George lowered his voice and said, 'So apart from the cat-allergy problem, how are you getting on with the in-laws?'

'Not too bad, I guess.'

I hesitated to mention all the little things that were irritating me, like there never being any hot water, Jeff's constant watching of TV with the volume turned up so loud it made my head throb, and the fact that one of the pair – Jeff, I assumed – didn't seem to know how to flush a toilet. I had tried to make a joke of this last one with Gemma, who had promised to have a word, but so far there was no improvement. Every day I found something nasty lurking in the loo.

There was the smell of cigarette smoke too, which wafted out of their bedroom. I had been right about Lizzy being a smoker, and I had asked her directly if she wouldn't mind smoking outside – it was far less embarrassing than asking them to remember to flush the loo – and she had said, 'Yes, of course.' But I knew she was smoking out of the window in the bedroom, like a sneaky teenager.

'What about the sister?' George asked. 'Is she feeling better now?'

'I don't know. Actually, maybe you could—'

'Elliot?'

I jumped. It was Lizzy, standing in the doorway to the kitchen. 'There's someone on the phone for you.'

'Can you take a message?' I said. 'It's probably a junk call.'

'He said it's really important.'

I sighed and addressed my neighbours. 'I'd better go and see who it is. I'll send you that photo of Charlie.'

I went inside the house and through to the living room, where the landline was. Jeff was lounging on the sofa, his feet on the coffee

71

table, watching the football. The volume was, once again, cranked up to eleven.

'Hello?' I said into the receiver. There was no one there, just a dead tone. Sighing, I hung up.

I spoke to Jeff. 'George and Edith were telling me about a new property site. We should take a look.'

'What?' He cupped a hand behind his ear.

'I said . . . Wait.'

I found the remote and turned the TV down. Jeff looked disgusted. I repeated what I'd said.

'Remind me who George and Edith are?'

'They live next door.'

'I see. The nosy neighbour brigade.' He shook his head, as if he'd felt a wasp clinging to his forehead, and softened his tone. 'I can't get my head round those websites. I'm going to phone an estate agent. You know, an actual human—'

There was a yell of excitement on the TV – someone had scored – and Jeff's attention snapped back to the screen.

Realising I wasn't going to get any sense out of him while he was engrossed in the football, I left him to it and went back through to the kitchen. Lizzy was standing in front of the cupboards. She had removed most of the cups, mugs and glasses and had them stacked up on the counter.

'They'd gone,' I said. 'It must have been a sales call. What are you doing?'

'Just giving these cupboards a clean. They were really grimy inside.'

'Really?' That surprised me. 'Just please don't rearrange anything. I'm quite anal about having everything just as I like it.'

She turned and gave me a wink. 'Quite anal, eh? Gemma talk you into that, did she?'

I was too shocked to speak.

Lizzy's eyes shone. 'Has Gemma told you her nickname among the local lads? Not-So-Precious Gem, that was it.' She turned away from me to carry on scrubbing the inside of the cupboard. 'Don't worry. I won't mess up your precious arrangements.'

I had to get out of the kitchen, away from her. I went back into the garden. *It's just her way*, I told myself. *She's crude. She probably thinks it's funny.* Jeff and Lizzy weren't evil. They were just crass and impolite. The thing they'd got away with was probably a business deal. They weren't terrible people, I told myself. We had bad chemistry. That was all.

After sending a photo of Charlie from my phone to George, I went back to mowing the lawn. But my head was full of what Lizzy had said about Gemma, and Jeff's lack of interest in the important topic of finding them somewhere to rent, and the next thing I knew there was a loud bang and the mower cut out.

I had run over the power cord. I cursed. The lawn was half-mown and Lizzy was standing by the back door.

'Careful, Elliot,' she called. 'Don't want to make Gemma a widow, do you? Not this soon.'

Chapter 13

The doorbell rang, waking me up. Gemma was still asleep, her eye mask askew. I squinted at my phone. Who was ringing my doorbell at quarter past nine on a Sunday morning? I had been awake half the night, worrying about Charlie, who still hadn't come home.

The doorbell sounded again and I forced myself to get up, pulling on my dressing gown and running down to the ground floor. There was no sign of Lizzy or Jeff.

I opened the door. It was George, looking dapper in a blue blazer. Charlie was in his arms.

'Oh my God.'

The moment Charlie saw me, he began to wriggle, jumping out of George's arms and shooting into the belly of the house. He looked fine, maybe a tiny bit thinner but unharmed.

'Where did you find him?' I asked.

'It wasn't me. Mr Singh got up early this morning, checked our Facebook page and went out to look in his shed, like we asked.'

'And there he was?'

'There he was.'

'Ah, that's brilliant. I'm so relieved. Cats, eh? They know how to make their owners worry.'

Charlie had re-emerged and was sitting in the hallway, staring up at me, probably wondering why I hadn't fed him yet.

'Do you want to come in for a cup of tea?' I asked George. 'Or coffee?'

'That would be lovely.'

I put the kettle on and George took a seat at the dining table. It was a fine morning, crisp and bright; a perfect day to finish the gardening I'd started the day before, once I'd been out to buy a new lawn mower cord. I made the drinks and took them over, sitting opposite George.

'Amazing what you've done with this place,' George said. 'You should get a medal. The place was in such a state when the previous owners lived here . . . I had this horrible feeling it would fall into disrepair and ruin the street.'

'I'm sure that wouldn't have happened.'

'Perhaps. But you have to be vigilant about these things. Like that Japanese knotweed. Once it gets a grip . . .' He clasped his throat. I tried not to smile, wondering if this was how he'd spoken to his patients when he was a GP. *Sorry, Mrs Smith, but you're doomed.*

'I'll go round and thank Mr Singh later,' I said. Charlie was busy wolfing down a double helping of breakfast.

'He'd appreciate that. The funny thing is, Mr Singh can't understand how the cat got in the shed. It was secured with a padlock and Mr S hasn't been in there for a week, he says.'

'Maybe there's a hole somewhere. Cats can squeeze into some pretty tight places.'

'True. But he swears his shed is in perfect repair.'

'Hmm.'

I was sure that either there was a hole or that Mr Singh or one of his family had been into the shed and forgotten. It was no great mystery.

But George went on. 'The other weird thing is that Mr Singh swears some things in his shed have been "interfered" with.'

'What, by Charlie?'

George laughed. 'Not unless Charlie is capable of picking up a hammer and walking off with it.'

'There's stuff missing?'

'That's what he thinks.' George shrugged. 'A hammer and a bag of nails. And he swears the container of kerosene he keeps has been half depleted. A couple of other things too. Gardening gloves, some twine. Maybe our Charlie here is some sort of – wait for it – cat burglar.'

I groaned, then we both laughed.

'What's the big joke?'

It was Lizzy, coming into the kitchen. George got to his feet, ever the old-fashioned gentleman, and I introduced them.

'Lovely to meet you,' George said.

'Likewise. Oh look, the cat's back. Where was it?'

I explained.

'Little bugger,' she said, before conjuring up a sneeze which sounded fake to me. 'Sorry, Elliot, but he makes my eyes itch and I find it hard to breathe when he's around.' She made a terrible wheezing sound.

I stared at her. Could she or Jeff have put him in Mr Singh's shed? There was a padlock, but it was possible that Mr Singh had left the key hanging around somewhere. I glanced at George and he was giving Lizzy a curious look too, as if he might be thinking the same thing.

'You can put up with him for another week or so, can't you?' I asked.

'Why, where's he going?' Lizzy replied. Seeing my reaction, she quickly added, 'Oh, until we move out, you mean. I suppose so. I mean, yes, yes, it's your cat. This is your home.'

She adopted what I assumed was meant to be her most charming smile. 'I have no right to complain, do I? You're very graciously letting us stay here. I'll just have to put up with it.'

She narrowed her eyes at Charlie then left the room, sneezing as she went.

Chapter 14

'This is so lovely,' I said, putting down my knife and fork. 'I feel like I've barely spoken to you during the last week.'

Gemma and I were in an Italian restaurant in Soho. It was Monday night, and the Robinsons had been staying with us for seven days. In all that time, apart from some brief chats at bedtime and snatched phone conversations during the day, my new wife and I had been like strangers living under the same roof. So, today, I had booked a table and asked Gemma to meet me at the train station after work. We needed some quality time. A date night.

'I'm sorry,' she said. 'It's my fault.'

She had changed into her civvies, jeans and a Breton top, and had her hair pinned up, exposing her pale, slender neck. Seeing her in a different environment, surrounded by other people, reminded me how beautiful she was. We had walked here from the station hand in hand and had stopped on the corner of the street to kiss, drawing whistles from a group of passing teenagers. I felt how I imagine parents must feel on a rare night out without their kids.

'Don't be silly, it's not your fault,' I said now.

'No, it is. I'd forgotten how hard I find it to relax when my parents are around. Even when they're on their best behaviour.'

'Wait. They're on their best behaviour?'

I expected her to laugh, but tension rippled across her features. 'I should have warned you what they're like, but I felt . . . responsibility. And I thought you might not let them stay if I told you how . . . difficult they are. How rude they can be.'

'Has your mum been making comments about your weight again?' I asked in a soft voice.

I hadn't told Gemma what Lizzy had said about her supposed teenage nickname: Not-So-Precious Gem.

'Yeah. Constant little barbs. About how I eat too much, drink too much, how I'm wasting my time being a veterinary nurse, how I'd better get a move on if I want to have children.' She stopped. The woman at the next table was clearly listening in.

'Shall we get the bill?' I asked. We had both finished eating. 'Go somewhere more private?'

'Good idea.'

We ended up in the bar of a hotel at the far end of Tottenham Court Road. I bought a bottle of Sancerre and we found a quiet table in the corner, our conversation masked by the plink-plonk of the pianist who was providing the background music. As we sat down, Gemma leaned forward and kissed me again, her lips cool and warm at the same time, and my breath caught in my chest. Her kiss, the sight of her collarbone and the little glimpse of flesh around her throat made all the desire that had been bottled up since her parents arrived come rushing out.

'Shall we get a room?' I think I was panting slightly. A dog in need of water.

She didn't reply immediately. 'Let's just go home to our own bed.'

'Okay.'

I waited for her to continue what we'd been talking about in the restaurant. Finally, it felt like she was opening up to me, preparing to show me her dark corners.

'What are you thinking?' I asked when she remained silent.

There was another long pause. 'I've been waiting for you to ask me about my scars. The ones on my stomach.'

'I thought you'd tell me when you were ready.'

The pianist was between songs and Gemma didn't speak until he started up again. 'They're from when I was a teenager. When I was at my most unhappy.'

I waited.

'I . . . I used to cut myself. I'd use a little knife . . . a fruit knife, the one my dad used for cutting up apples. He went mad when it disappeared, blamed my mum, but I had it in my bedroom. In my hiding place under the carpet.'

Her gaze was fixed on a point directly ahead. Talking about this was clearly very difficult for her.

'Gemma, you don't need to tell me.'

'No, I want to. I haven't talked to anyone about it for a long time.' She laughed drily. 'I used to hope my mum and dad would see the cuts and that they'd demand to know why I did it. Chloe was still a little kid back then and Stuart spent most of the time in his bedroom, playing video games, so they never noticed. We lived in this remote place and I didn't have many friends, not real ones. I felt invisible, and part of me was happy about that. But another part of me wanted the world to notice how much pain I was in.' She shook her head. 'I'm not explaining this very well, am I?'

'You don't have to explain it at all.'

'I do, Elliot. Let me.'

'Okay. I'm sorry.'

The piano music had grown more sombre and the bar was half-empty. People were heading home or to their rooms.

'When I cut myself, I felt better. It was like this enormous release. Like I'd walk around for days feeling all this stress and tension build up in me. I could actually feel it filling me, like I was a balloon and my skin was going to burst. Using the knife gave me relief, temporarily anyway. And afterwards, I'd feel good. Kind of high.'

'That would be the endorphins,' I said.

She nodded. 'Yeah. I read that. Those lovely, addictive little endorphins. I blame them for half the stupid things I've done in my life.' We laughed, but the sadness returned to her eyes. 'Most of the time, the cuts were shallow, more like scratches. They'd bleed a little but I'd clean them up and they'd heal quickly. But sometimes, when things were particularly bad at home, I'd cut a little deeper. Those are the ones that left scars.'

I didn't want to point out that there were a lot of scars.

'So your mum and dad never found out you were doing it?' I asked.

'No. And I managed to make myself stop when . . .' She didn't complete the sentence and I didn't want to push her.

'I haven't done it at all, not even thought about it, since I left home and moved into the squat.'

'Wait. You lived in a squat?'

'Yep. It was fine, actually. Kind of. It was fun for a while, especially the first summer. But then it got darker . . . Everyone was drinking too much and some of the guys were sleazy, nasty, and summer ended and I was always hungry and cold. I even thought about going home.'

I wondered if this was the period Lizzy had been alluding to when she told me Gemma had been promiscuous.

'And then,' Gemma said, 'I met someone. A guy. Henry. He saved me.'

'You haven't mentioned him before,' I said.

'No.' The pianist was playing something I recognised. A Lana Del Rey song. 'Henry was older than me, in his late twenties then. He had his own house, quite near the park in Hastings. A lovely place. His parents had died when he was young and left it to him.'

'Sounds like you've got a thing for orphans.'

'Ha. Yeah, maybe. Anyway, I moved in, cleaned up, lived with him for a while.'

It seemed to be getting harder for her to speak.

'What happened?' I asked.

'Things went bad.'

I waited for her to elaborate, but there were tears in her eyes and I sensed she didn't want to say any more right now. She didn't need to. I could imagine what had happened. The death of the relationship. The ending to most love stories. There was something I needed to ask her, though.

'What about your mum and dad? I can't quite get my head round your relationship.'

'Me neither.'

'Yeah, but seriously. How do you feel about them?'

'I don't know, Elliot. It's been . . . difficult. When they went to live in France I thought I might never see them again. And you know what? I wouldn't have been that bothered. When they told me they were coming home, though, suddenly I did want to see them. Firstly, because no matter what they're like, they're my mum and dad. I love them. I can't help it. But secondly, I wanted to see if they'd changed.'

'And have they?'

She tapped the edge of her now-empty glass. 'I don't know yet. But living under the same roof as them – that isn't any easier.'

'Do you want me to kick them out?'

She looked up at me through her lashes. Her eyes were dry again. 'Would you do that?'

'I'll do anything you want, Gemma. I mean that.'

A little smile. 'No, don't kick them out. It would be hideously awkward and they might never speak to me again. They'll be gone soon, anyway.' She reached across and took my hand. 'Then things can go back to how they were.'

She kissed me.

'I love you,' she said.

'I love you too. And I just want to say one more thing. You're nothing like your parents.'

'Thank God for that. If you told me I was like my mum I'd have to kill you.'

Chapter 15

When we got home the house was quiet and all the lights were off. It was midnight and I guessed Jeff and Lizzy were in bed. Gemma and I were still tipsy and we bumped into each other as we both tried to get inside at the same time.

The door to the snug was open and, conversely, the living room door was shut. I only noticed because this was the opposite of how things usually were, and it jarred.

'Are you tired?' I whispered.

'Why are you whispering?'

'I don't know. But you are too.'

We both laughed, and I was still grinning as I entered the kitchen and flicked on the light.

'Oh my God.'

I looked around, unable to believe what I was seeing. The room was immaculate. Every surface had been cleaned. The counter was shiny, all the cups and plates put away, and even the cables that snaked from the chargers had been neatly wound around the plugs. The sink was gleaming and all the papers that had been scattered across the dining table had been stacked up.

'Have the elves been in?' I asked. Charlie was curled up in his favourite spot beside the kettle and I scratched behind his ear, eliciting a purr.

Gemma didn't seem as surprised as I was. Instead, she headed to the fridge and took out a bottle of wine.

'Are you sure you want another?' I said. 'We've got to work in the morning.'

She shrugged. 'I'm just going to have one. Are you going to join me?'

I hesitated. 'Oh, go on, then. Sod it.'

She filled two glasses. She handed me mine and I set it aside after one sip, pulling her into an embrace. Her kiss was warm and she wrapped her arms around me, pulling me hard against her, one hand going up the back of my shirt, the other to my groin, then she broke away from the kiss and whispered in my ear, 'I need you inside me.'

Lust overtook us. I unbuttoned and shrugged off my shirt and watched her pull off her top, revealing a white lacy bra, and I pulled her against me again, skin on skin. I was about to unbutton my jeans when I heard a thump.

I broke off the kiss. 'Did you hear that?'

'Huh?'

'I'm sure I heard something outside.'

I went over to the back window. The blinds were closed and I pulled them aside, trying to peer into the back garden, but all I could see was my own reflection in the glass.

'I didn't hear anything,' Gemma said.

But I was certain I'd heard a noise, like something being knocked over, or possibly the shed door banging shut. Gemma was still standing there in just her bra and jeans and all I really wanted to do was forget the noises and take her upstairs. But after the possible robbery at Mr and Mrs Singh's, I knew I wouldn't be able to relax.

'Let me take a quick look,' I said.

I opened the back door and looked out. It was dark, the sky overcast so there wasn't even any moonlight, and I couldn't see anyone. All was quiet. But I put my shirt back on, went outside and headed straight over to the shed.

The padlock that secured the shed door was gone.

Was there somebody in there now? The same person who had stolen the hammer and other items from the Singhs?

I walked quickly back into the house, as quietly as I could, and grabbed a knife. 'I think there's someone in the shed,' I said to Gemma, who was now fully dressed again.

'Wait, Elliot, it might not be safe . . .'

But I needed to see. I went straight back into the garden and strode across the lawn, wanting to do this before my courage deserted me.

I pulled open the door, holding the knife out in front of me with my other hand.

The shed was empty.

Exhaling, and suddenly aware of how fast my heart was beating, I leaned against the workbench that I hadn't used for ages. There, among the half-empty tins of paint and scattered tools, was the padlock. Looking up, I had a perfect view through the window of next door's house. A light was still burning on the top floor and, as I watched, either George or Edith appeared behind the frosted glass of the bathroom.

I tried to remember when I'd last been in the shed. It must have been when I'd mowed the lawn. But I was sure I'd replaced the padlock then. I always did it, as a matter of habit. The key was in the kitchen, hanging on the key rack . . . And I suddenly thought of a possible answer. Lizzy, coming out here to smoke, a place to shelter from the rain. It had been raining all afternoon. Perhaps she'd come out here and forgotten to replace the padlock. The noise I'd heard had simply been the wind banging the shed door.

But when I sniffed the air, I couldn't smell cigarette smoke. Instead, I smelled another familiar scent. Eau Sauvage. My old aftershave, which I had last smelled in the bathroom next to Jeff and Lizzy's room.

Had Jeff been out here? And why would he come into my shed? I looked around but couldn't see any signs of activity.

I left the shed, fastening the padlock, and went back into the kitchen.

'Well?' said Gemma.

'Nothing. But—'

The door opened and Jeff appeared. He was in his pyjamas.

'All right, you two?' he said. 'Good night?' Then his eyes widened. 'Blimey, Elliot, you're not planning to stab my daughter, are you?'

I looked down and realised I was still holding the knife. I quickly slid it back into its block.

'What's the matter?' Jeff asked. 'You seem on edge.'

I stepped close to him, trying to see if he smelled of the aftershave. Too close, obviously, as he stepped back. 'What on earth are you doing?'

Gemma was looking at me as if I'd gone crazy.

'Did you go into the shed earlier?' I asked Jeff.

He didn't answer immediately. It was as if he was trying to weigh up his options. 'Oh, yeah.'

'You forgot to put the padlock back on,' I said.

'Elliot thought we had a burglar,' Gemma said.

'Oh, right. Sorry. It's an age thing. I'd forget my head if—'

'What were you doing in there?' I asked.

He grinned sheepishly. 'Just trying to get five minutes' peace and quiet. Don't tell your mother, Gemma.'

Gemma laughed. 'I won't.'

So there it was. No great mystery.

Jeff turned to me. 'I spoke to an estate agent tonight. He's taking us to look at some properties tomorrow.'

'Oh, that's brilliant,' I said, the shed instantly forgotten.

'That keen to get rid of us, are you?' Seeing me groping for words, he said, 'Only teasing. We're keen to find a place of our own ourselves. You've been very kind letting us stay here. I know we're not the easiest family in the world.'

'Oh, no, you're fine.'

He laughed. 'Anyway, sleep tight, you two. Don't let the bed bugs bite.'

He left the kitchen and I listened to his heavy tread as he went up the stairs. One, two, three, *creak*, five, six.

When the bedroom door clicked shut I went into the living room to turn out the light that Jeff and Lizzy had left on. An object on the table caught my eye.

A square tape measure.

I held it in my hand. So it *was* a tape measure I'd seen Lizzy holding that night. What had they been doing? Measuring the dimensions of my living room? Why would they do that?

Gemma appeared behind me. 'Come on. Let's go to bed.'

Exhausted, with a headache coming on from all the alcohol I'd drunk, I left the tape measure and followed her upstairs. On the way, I nipped into the bathroom on the middle floor and grabbed the bottle of Eau Sauvage, taking it upstairs to the en-suite. I hadn't been bothered before about Jeff borrowing it but now I felt proprietorial. He could buy his own aftershave.

Chapter 16

'Could I have a quick word, Elliot?'

Kenneth, the head of science at Tulse Hill Primary, approached me while the children, including Effy, took their seats on the minibus. I was teaching on my own today because Amira had a meeting with a potential corporate sponsor.

'How was today's session?' Kenneth asked. He was in his late twenties, keen and friendly, with his shirtsleeves always rolled up to his elbows. It was him who had pushed the head teacher at his school to get Inquiring Minds involved.

'Really good. We made elephant's toothpaste.'

He beamed. 'I love that one.'

The experiment involved taking hydrogen peroxide, washing-up liquid, food colouring and yeast. As long as you used the correct concentration of hydrogen peroxide, when you mixed them together in a plastic bottle it created a thick foam which came gushing out. The kids got really excited about it and it allowed me to talk about using different concentrations of chemicals to achieve different results, as well as explaining exothermic energy. It was an easy, safe experiment.

'Effy grasped it straight away,' I said. 'Actually, it was a little simple for her. She was helping the other kids and was telling me about all these experiments she's watched on YouTube. She gave me a long list of stuff she wants to try out.'

'That's brilliant. Actually, it was Effy I wanted to talk to you about.'

I braced myself. Was she going to move away? Go back to Ghana? Seeing my expression, Kenneth said, 'It's nothing bad. But her dad came in to talk to me yesterday. He wanted to know if it's possible for Effy to have extra, private tuition.'

'With you?' I asked.

'No. With you. Mr Mensah sees me as a mere servant of the government, while you're a guru.'

I laughed. 'I like the sound of Mr Mensah. But we don't usually do that. We don't think it's fair, to give individual children extra attention.'

'I understand. But Effy is very special, isn't she. It wouldn't surprise me if she was ready to take, and ace, her science GCSEs before she leaves primary school. And nothing like that has ever happened at Tulse Hill Primary before.' He met my eye. 'And I'm sure that would be excellent publicity for you, which wouldn't harm your funding efforts, and even the bean counters at the LEA would be impressed.'

He was right. We needed to keep the local education authority sweet to do what we did, as well as seeking sponsorship from private companies. And it got increasingly harder as the novelty of what we were doing wore off and budgets were stretched. It could be an enormous help to be able to demonstrate a case study where we had helped a young girl get her qualifications six or seven years earlier than her peers. Effy was in the perfect socio-economic bracket, and I could imagine the press. And more than all that, despite our policy not to favour individuals, it would be a wonderful feeling to help Effy achieve her potential. One hour a week in the classroom wasn't enough.

'Let me think about it,' I said.

Kenneth clapped me on the shoulder. 'Good man.'

Chapter 17

George was putting his bins out when I got home, ready for the next morning. Watching him drag them across the pavement made me hope I'd be that fit and healthy when I was his age. He waited for me as I got out of my car.

'Good day?' he asked.

'Yeah. Not bad.' I lowered my voice. 'Fingers crossed it's going to get even better.'

'Oh?'

'Jeff and Lizzy were going to look at some houses today, so I'm hoping I'll get my house back soon.'

'Really? I didn't see them go out. Not that I would have, necessarily,' he added hurriedly. 'I mean, it's not like I sit and watch your house all day.'

My eye fell on the Neighbourhood Watch sticker in George and Edith's front window. 'Any news about Mr Singh's shed mystery?'

'No. He tried calling the police but they weren't interested. He's talking about setting up security lights and cameras, as if someone's going to come back and nick the rest of his weedkiller and his spare flower pots.' He tapped the side of his head. 'Between you, me and the gatepost, it wouldn't surprise me if he's misplaced that hammer and the other stuff. It happens when you get to his age.'

I was sure Mr Singh was only a couple of years older than George but didn't point this out.

'Speaking of weedkiller, how are the Knotweeds?' he said, with a twinkle.

'Huh?'

He chuckled. 'It's what Edith and I have started to call your in-laws.'

'That's good. Maybe I should start using it.' I thought about telling him about the tape measure but really didn't want to get drawn into a long conversation about Jeff and Lizzy.

'By the way,' George said, 'I was going to ask if you can recommend a good restaurant. It's my and Edith's wedding anniversary next week and I want to take her somewhere special. Somewhere expensive.'

'Oh, lovely.' I reeled off the names of a few places I thought he might like. 'How many years?'

'Forty-nine.' He grinned. 'I know, I don't look old enough, do I? I was only twenty-one when we got married, and Edith was twenty. Different times. You know, she's the only woman I've ever been with.'

I was slightly taken aback by his frankness. 'Wow.'

'And you know what? I haven't missed out. She's the most wonderful woman. My best friend as well as all those other things.' He nodded to himself. 'It's the big gold one next year. We're going to have an enormous party and then go off and visit all the places we've always wanted to see. A world cruise. Then we're going to stay with Terry and his kids in Australia for a while.'

'Sounds amazing.'

He had a faraway look, perhaps already imagining barbecues in his son's garden in Melbourne. He came back to the present. 'You hang on to that Gemma. She seems like a good 'un to me, even if her parents are a little iffy.'

'Don't worry. I intend to.'

ѡ

I went inside. I was in a good mood as I went through the door, touched by what George had said and wondering if I should get them a gift for their anniversary. Forty-nine years . . . It was hard to comprehend that length of time with someone else. Gemma and I had only known each other a few months and there was still so much about her I had to learn. But it appealed to me, that idea of knowing someone inside out, of your lives and selves being as intertwined as George and Edith's. I wondered if my parents would still be together now if they hadn't died young.

I found Jeff and Gemma at the kitchen table, peering out through the back window into the garden. I could see his face reflected in the glass, and was startled by the transformation that took place when he heard me come in. He had been scowling – close to anger, I thought – but by the time he turned he was smiling. There was no sign of Lizzy.

'How was work?' I asked Gemma, taking a bottle of beer out of the fridge. Gemma already had a half-empty glass of white wine in front of her.

She sighed. 'Awful. Somebody brought in a Dalmatian that had been hit by a car. Such a beautiful dog.' Tears filled her eyes.

'They couldn't save it?'

Her reply came in a whisper. 'No.'

'You ought to be used to all that by now,' Jeff said. 'You were always too soft where animals were concerned. Remember that hamster, Chips?'

Gemma got up. 'I don't want to talk about that, Dad.' The look she gave him shocked me. It was laced with contempt. She left the room without another word.

I was about to go after her but Jeff said, 'Leave her. She'll be all right. The kettle's just boiled if you fancy a cuppa.'

I didn't want a 'cuppa'. I held up my beer bottle. 'I'll stick with this.'

'Suit your ugly.' He made himself one. Watching him, sipping his tea in the artificial light of the kitchen, I was hit by a wave of revulsion. He smelled strongly of Brylcreem, and after each sip of tea his tongue darted from between his lips like a lizard's. He was wearing a T-shirt with tight sleeves and his biceps looked pumped, as if he'd spent the day working out. Beside him, I felt unfit and out of shape, despite my relative youth. Perhaps it was my own insecurities making me feel such revulsion. Or perhaps it was a hangover from the weird sensation that had hit me as I entered the house. This man and his wife, and to a lesser extent their reclusive daughter, were making me feel like a stranger in my own home.

'How did it go today?' I asked.

'Hmm?'

'The houses you were going to see. What were they like? Did you find one you want to rent?'

He smirked. 'You really do sound like you want rid of us, Elliot.'

'Well, you don't want to be here forever, do you?'

He put his mug down with a thump. 'Of course we don't. But we had to cancel the appointments.'

I didn't bother trying to hide my dismay. 'What? Why?'

'Because Lizzy's not well.'

'Not well?'

'Yeah. She's been in bed all day, the poor thing. Says she feels rotten. You know, achy and weak with a dodgy stomach. She's got a sore throat and ear too. And a headache.'

That seemed very convenient.

'I think she must have caught what Chloe's got.' He rolled his eyes. 'Women, eh? The weaker sex. I expect Gem'll go down with it next. In fact, it wouldn't surprise me if she's got it already, the way she's acting.'

I stared at him. 'But you feel all right, do you?'

'Oh yeah. Fit as a flea, I am.' He narrowed his eyes. 'Come to think of it, you look a bit peaky yourself, Elliot. Although I suppose you always look like that so it's hard to tell. You should be careful if you do start feeling ill. You don't want to pass it on to all those kids you teach, do you?'

Charlie came clattering through the cat flap and jumped up on to the table beside me. I stroked him absent-mindedly.

'Couldn't you have gone to look at the houses on your own?' I asked.

'What? Me, choose a place for us to live without Lizzy? You clearly don't know much about women, do you?' He chuckled. 'Besides, I needed to stay here to look after her. Cater to her every bloody whim.'

The cat leapt across the room and landed beside Jeff. To my horror, Charlie rubbed his cheek against Jeff's arm and Jeff rubbed his ear. Charlie began to purr.

Jeff winked at me. 'You know what? I actually quite like it when Lizzy's sick, when she's all weak and vulnerable. It's sexy, isn't it? There's something highly erotic about screwing a woman when she's too weak to resist.'

Charlie continued to rub himself against Jeff's arm. I wanted to snatch my cat up and forbid him from going anywhere near this man.

Jeff glanced at the clock on the wall. It was half seven. 'The football's about to kick off, so if you don't mind . . .' He strolled towards the door and, to my horror, Charlie jumped down and followed him.

'But what about . . . ?'

He was gone.

Chapter 18

I needed to talk to Gemma. I went up the stairs, skipping the creaking step, and by the time I reached the middle floor I could hear her moving about upstairs in our bedroom, singing along to an old pop song. She must be feeling brighter, or perhaps she was trying to cheer herself up. It was something I did often when I was down: put music on and belted it out, enthusiastically but tunelessly. Maybe I should go up there and join in. Sing it out together.

But as I passed the door to the master bedroom, I made a snap decision. I knocked lightly.

'Who is it?'

'Elliot. I just wanted to see how you are.'

I went in. Lizzy was sitting up in bed, reading a paperback. It was a book she must have found on my shelves downstairs, a horror novel called *Sweetmeat*. As soon as I entered the room she set it aside and hoisted the duvet up around her shoulders. She was wearing what appeared to be men's pyjamas. She sniffed and coughed pathetically.

'How are you feeling?' I asked.

'Like crap. This book isn't helping. It's giving me the willies, and not in a good way.' She shoved it so it fell to the floor. 'That's better.'

I took a step closer to the bed, but didn't go too close. If she was genuinely sick I didn't want to catch it.

'Do you think you've got the same thing as Chloe?' I asked.

She frowned. 'Probably. But I'm sure I'll be okay in a week or so.'

A week?

'I'm sure you'll be better before that. But maybe you should go and see a doctor?'

'With a virus? There's no point. Besides, I'm not registered anywhere.'

She lay down, looking up at me over the edge of the duvet. The room had the sweet, unpleasant smell of a sick room, and looking at her, all weak and bleary-eyed, I experienced a pang of guilt for suspecting her illness might be fake.

I picked the fallen paperback up. The spine was cracked and she'd folded over the corners of some of the pages. 'Speaking of Chloe, how is she? I've barely seen her since you arrived.'

'She's not too bad. Still a little under the weather.'

'Perhaps she should go outside, get some fresh air?' I suggested. 'It might make her feel better.'

'No.'

She had her head half-buried beneath the duvet and I wasn't sure if I'd heard correctly. 'No?'

'She doesn't need fresh air. She needs to rest, that's all. Like me.'

I backed out of the room and closed the door behind me. Upstairs, Gemma was singing along to a different track now, something by The Cure. 'I'm living in a madhouse,' I said to myself, my eyes falling on the office door. I approached it and put my ear to it. From within, silence.

Lizzy was wrong. Being cooped up in this room wouldn't be doing Chloe any good. And I was getting tired of having someone in my house who I'd hardly exchanged a word with. In fact, I couldn't remember if we'd done even that. I rapped lightly on the wood.

There was no response. I stood there for a moment, trying to decide what to do. I didn't want to invade Chloe's privacy but, as I reminded myself, this was my house. It was beyond weird that she had barely come out of the room since she'd been here. What if she was seriously ill? Could she have brought back something deadly from France, something that was spreading through the house, infecting us one by one? I needed to see for myself how she was.

I tried the handle but the door was still locked.

Slowly, I dropped to my knees and peered through the keyhole. I thought if she'd locked the door the key would be blocking my view, but I could see straight through.

The room was dimly lit – I assumed the main light was off but the desk lamp was on – making it harder to see. I blinked until the shapes in the room came into focus.

The bed was empty, the duvet pulled back and heaped up in the centre of the mattress. I could see one curtain too, drawn to the left, and as I squinted into the gloom the curtain swayed, touched by a breeze, indicating the window was open.

I stood up and knocked on the door again. 'Chloe? Are you there?'

Silence.

Where the hell was she? I was gripped by a sudden conviction that she had gone, that she had climbed out of the window. Jumped. I had a crazy vision of her flying away, like Wendy heading to Never Never Land. Crazy, yes, but I was convinced something was very wrong. I needed to see inside the room.

When I had moved in, there was a clay pot in the kitchen containing keys to all the rooms in the house, labelled by the previous owners. That was where I'd found the key to the office. Although I never used the others, I knew there were two copies of most of the keys, so there was a good chance there was a spare key to the room in the pot.

I tiptoed past the room where Lizzy lay, not wanting her to come out and get involved. This was something I needed to see for myself. Downstairs, Jeff was yelling at the TV, telling the ref he was a wanker, and he didn't notice as I passed the living room.

The pot of keys was in the drawer where I kept all the junk that might come in handy one day. I tipped the keys on to the counter and sorted through them. I was in luck. I found the key to the office – labelled *spare room 2* – and clutched it in my fist, hurrying back upstairs and inserting the key in the lock and turning it.

The door opened with a creak.

'Chloe?' I said in a soft voice as I went in, leaving the key in place. The desk was to my right and, as I'd surmised, the lamp was on, filling the room with pale, watery light. As I breathed in, I was hit by the rank smell of body odour and sweat. Something else too, the stink of meat gone bad, and I quickly located the source: a ham sandwich on a plate on the desk that looked like it had been there for days, dry and curled at the edges. Both these odours were, thank God, lessened somewhat by the breeze coming through the open window.

The clothes Chloe had arrived in were scrunched up at the foot of the bed but, apart from that and the rotten sandwich, the room hardly appeared to have been touched. The filing cabinet stood beside the desk, drawers firmly shut.

I looked left and right then crossed to the window, peering out at the dark garden. Beneath the window, the patio was illuminated by light from the kitchen, and I braced myself, expecting to see a crumpled body. But there was nothing. She must have gone out.

I was about to go out and talk to Jeff or Lizzy, to ask them if they knew Chloe wasn't at home, when I heard an intake of breath.

I stopped, looking around me and switching on the overhead light to chase the shadows away.

'Chloe?' I said again.

This time, the noise sounded like a sob.

There was a cupboard on the left-hand side of the room, about three feet high and built into the wall. I used it to store old papers and sentimental items, including some of my parents' former possessions that I couldn't bear to part with. The noise had come from in there.

I pulled the cupboard door open.

Chloe was sitting with her back pressed against the wall, curled in a ball as if she was trying to make herself invisible. Her face hidden between her knees, fingers interlaced on top of her head. She was wearing a white nightdress and had bare feet. Her toes wiggled up and down, the only part of her that was moving.

Once again I said her name, and crouched before her. She didn't move or look up. Now that I was close I could feel waves of heat coming off her. I could smell her too: stale sweat and the sweet stink of bad breath.

'Chloe,' I said. 'It's me, Elliot.' I was aware that, even though she was living in my house, she didn't know me. We'd only met briefly. 'Why don't you come out of there?'

Slowly, glacially, she lifted her face and turned it towards me. Even in the darkness of the cupboard I could see her eyes were bloodshot and she was as pale as snow.

I shuffled closer. 'Come on, Chloe. Why don't you get into bed? I'll get you a drink, something to eat. Or medicine. Have you taken anything?'

She opened her mouth but nothing came out. I noticed how dry and chapped her lips were. She licked them and spoke a single word.

'Out.'

'You want to come out?' I reached out a hand. 'Come on, let me help you.'

But she didn't move. I tried again, but still she remained huddled and motionless. I didn't want to touch her in case it made her freak out. What could I do? I decided to go and fetch Gemma. I was certain she would be horrified if she saw the state her sister was in.

I pushed myself to my feet and behind me a voice said, 'What's going on?'

Chapter 19

Jeff came into the room. He looked pissed off, like I'd done something wrong.

'What's going on?' I said. 'That's what *I* want to know. I found your daughter like this, hiding in a cupboard, acting like she's having a breakdown.'

Jeff rolled his eyes like I was making a big fuss about nothing and tried to get past me. I stepped to the left and blocked him. Glancing over my shoulder, I saw that Chloe had buried her face between her knees again.

'She needs a doctor,' I said. 'She's clearly in a bad way.'

Jeff grunted. I couldn't believe how unconcerned he seemed.

'What's wrong with you? How can you not want to help her? It doesn't make any sense.' I gestured to the uneaten sandwich. 'I assumed you and Lizzy were looking after her, but it's as if you've shut her away in here and forgotten about her.'

'You don't know what you're talking about, Elliot.' His voice was low, menacing. He stared at me for a moment, jaw muscles working furiously. A vein throbbed on his forehead. Then he seemed to stop himself, visibly took a breath and, when he spoke again, his voice was quieter. 'It's not my or Lizzy's fault if she hasn't eaten all the food we've brought her. But we have been looking after her. One of us has been sitting in here with her every day while you're at work.'

'Really?'

'Of course. We're not monsters. It's just . . .'

'What?'

'It's a family matter.' He said it like that was it, subject closed. And, having not been part of a family for a long time, I didn't know what to say.

He motioned for me to move aside and, reluctantly, I did so. He stepped past me, bending down to talk to Chloe. 'Isn't that right, sweetheart? Mum and Dad have been looking after you, haven't we?'

She lifted her face and nodded. Her skin was almost grey, her hair greasy and stringy. Beads of sweat clung to her upper lip. She looked scared, like an untamed animal.

'Now, why don't you come out of there?' he said, using a gentle voice. 'It doesn't look very comfortable.'

He held out his hand and this time she responded, allowing him to take hers. She crawled out of the cupboard and let him lead her over to the bed, her bare feet dragging on the floorboards. She lay down with her head on the pillow.

'Let's tuck you in,' Jeff said, pulling the duvet over her. 'There, that's much better.'

She didn't speak.

He put a hand on her forehead. 'You're still burning up. I'll get you some nice ice water and some paracetamol. That's why she's acting like this. It's the fever.'

'But if she's had a fever for ten days, she seriously needs to see a doctor. She should be in hospital.'

'We don't like doctors.'

I turned. It was Lizzy, standing in the doorway in her pyjamas. Gemma was behind her, wearing a sheepish expression. I had been wondering when they'd appear.

'I don't care if you don't like doctors,' I said. 'She needs to see one. It's not normal to have a fever for this long. Or to hide away in cupboards.'

'Actually, it's not that unusual,' Lizzy said. 'If you have the flu, the fever can easily last up to ten days.'

Was that all this was? Flu? I stared at Chloe. The idea that she might be having a breakdown came back to me. Or maybe she was always like this. I had no way of knowing. Gemma had never said anything about her sister having problems. All I could do was go by what the Robinsons were telling me, so I took a step back. But I still didn't feel comfortable. Something was wrong here. I just couldn't figure out what. Though whatever it was, I was certain Chloe needed medical attention of some kind.

Gemma went off to the bathroom and came back with the thermometer, which she handed to her dad. Chloe lay still, eyes fixed on the ceiling. Jeff inserted the thermometer in Chloe's ear and waited a few seconds. 'Thirty-seven point four,' he said. 'It's coming down. I reckon she'll be back to normal tomorrow.'

He stuck the thermometer in his pocket before I could see the reading.

'Come on.' Jeff ushered me out of the room. 'We should let her rest.'

He pulled the door closed. Lizzy went back to bed and Jeff muttered something about missing the football before going back downstairs. I stood on the landing with Gemma, unable to tear myself fully away from the office door.

'What do you think?' I asked Gemma. What Jeff had said sounded so reasonable, but I was still uneasy.

'About what?' Gemma replied. She sounded exhausted.

'The way your parents are behaving with Chloe. I don't understand why they won't take her to see a doctor. How can your mum say she doesn't believe in doctors? It's like saying you don't believe in science!'

'They've always been like that. They're the same with any authority figures.' She laid a hand on her belly and changed the subject. 'I haven't eaten yet and I'm starving. Let's order a takeaway.'

She went to move away and I caught her arm. 'Wait. Are you really not worried about Chloe? You don't think we should take her to see a doctor?'

She sighed impatiently. 'I don't think it's a doctor she needs.'

'What do you mean by that?'

'She needs a break from our parents, that's all. She needs fresh air, friends, a normal life.'

'She needs her siblings too. You and Stuart. And you don't seem like you want to help her.'

Gemma narrowed her eyes at me. 'Unlike you. You seem awfully keen to help her.'

'What do you mean by that?'

'Forget it.' She looked like she was about to say something else, then changed her mind. 'Look, I do care about her, Elliot. Of course I do. But I've never been able to get close to her because my parents are always there, getting in the way. I find it hard to communicate with her.'

'Maybe now's the perfect time to change that.'

'I know. And I will make an effort. It's just very hard to do when my mum and dad are around. Now, please – can we eat? I'm starting to get hangry.'

We went down to the kitchen and I watched in a daze as Gemma searched through the drawer for menus, asking me if I'd prefer Indian, Thai or Chinese. I told her she could choose. I had lost my appetite.

Chapter 20

'That is seriously weird,' Amira said.

It was the next day and we were in our office. Amira had started the morning by telling me all about the 'date night' she'd had with her boyfriend, Colin, who was a police officer. They'd been bowling, and listening to her laughter as she recounted how many strikes she'd got and how the guy in the next lane had applauded her made me feel even more glum. If only my evening had been so carefree.

'It definitely sounds like she needs to see someone,' she continued.

'Except Jeff and Lizzy don't like doctors. Gemma says they've always been like that. She said her parents never took any of them to the doctor when they were kids, unless they absolutely had to.'

Amira tapped at her keyboard, then said, 'Perhaps you should sneak her out of the house.'

'Who, Gemma?'

'No, silly. The sister. Chloe. Take her to the hospital.'

'I'd never get her past Jeff and Lizzy.'

'Hmm. Then perhaps you should bring a doctor to her.'

Now there was an idea.

Amira swivelled away from her computer. 'Now, tell me about yesterday. What exactly did Kenneth say to you about Effy?'

I pulled my chair up to her desk and told her. I had been thinking about the offer all night, when I wasn't worrying about goings-on in my house.

'So, what do you think?' Amira asked. 'Shall we do it?'

I had made my mind up. It would be good for business and great for Effy. It would also, I had decided, be a distraction from all the stuff that was going on at home.

'Yes. Let's do it,' I said.

'Excellent.'

But although I was happy about it, my voice didn't contain the enthusiasm I expected to hear. I was too distracted, thinking about what Amira had said. *You should bring a doctor to her.*

ϖ

I knocked on George and Edith's door when I got home from work, before going into my own house. It was a crisp evening and my breath clouded before me as I waited.

George opened the door.

'Hi,' I said. 'Can I ask a favour?'

He gestured for me to follow him into the kitchen.

Edith was in the living room, watching the evening news, and she waved at me as I passed. The layout of George and Edith's house was identical to mine but in reverse, so it felt like I'd stepped through a mirror, except here there were smiling photos of grandchildren on the walls and knick-knacks on every surface. A cabinet on the wall housed George's prized toy car collection. He had been collecting old Dinky cars his whole life but had stepped up his hobby in retirement. Some of the cars here, including a red Maserati racing car that was worth £1,000, were pretty valuable, but George assured me he loved them as objects of beauty and nostalgia and didn't care about their price tags. I believed him. He had even appeared in the local paper recently, showing them off.

There was something baking in the oven, its rich smell filling the kitchen, and as I entered the room I was hurtled back in time to my childhood, getting home from school to find a cake cooling on the side, a tea towel draped over it, my mum warning me with a little smile not to touch it. The memory was so powerful that it almost knocked me off my feet; I was unsteady and tears pricked the backs of my eyes.

'Banana loaf. Smells good, doesn't it?' George said. 'I got the recipe out of this book Edith bought me last Christmas.'

My dad had always loved cooking. Sometimes I allowed myself to entertain a fantasy in which George and Edith were my family, that they had adopted me after my parents died. I had been too old to be taken into care but that hadn't stopped me, then and many times in the years that followed, yearning to be taken in by some nice older couple. The therapist I'd seen briefly when I was in my twenties told me it was because my childhood had ended so abruptly. I hadn't been given the chance to leave the nest in a normal, natural way.

Part of you is still stuck there, the therapist had said. *Unable to grow up.*

Thinking about this now, it struck me why I was so disappointed by Jeff and Lizzy. I had unconsciously hoped that they might be the parent figures I had longed for. I had been so happy about inviting them to stay partly because I thought they might help me be part of a family, complete with the siblings I had yearned for too.

George chuckled, shaking me from my self-examination. 'I'll bring you and Gemma a slice later so you can sample it and tell me what you think. Beer?'

He handed me a bottle of lager and we sat at the table.

'What's this favour, then?' he asked.

'It's Gemma's sister, Chloe. Did I tell you she wasn't well? That Jeff and Lizzy told me she'd come back from France with a virus?'

'You mentioned it.'

'Well, last night I went in to see her . . .'

I told him everything that had happened the previous evening. He listened, his eyebrows climbing higher with each turn of the tale.

'They're refusing to take her to a doctor,' I said. 'But I'm worried. Especially as Lizzy appears to have it too. Although . . .'

'What?' He leaned forward.

'I probably shouldn't say this, but I suspect she's pretending to be sick.'

'Why would she do that?'

'So she and Jeff have a reason not to look at any houses. I'm worried they're getting a little too comfortable. I don't know about their finances either. Like, can they actually afford to rent somewhere? That's just one of many things I don't know about them.'

George gave me a knowing look. 'Knotweed.'

I sighed.

'What does Gemma say?'

I didn't want to disclose how frustrated I felt with my new wife. It seemed disloyal. 'She keeps reassuring me, telling me they won't be here much longer and that Chloe is going to be fine. But it's . . . difficult. They're her parents. I think she's . . . afraid of them.'

'Afraid?'

I backtracked. 'Maybe just scared of upsetting them. I don't know. You know I don't have much experience of big families, but from what I've seen there are two types. The type where everything is out in the open, where they argue and shout and slam doors, and where disagreements are dealt with loudly and quickly. And the other type, where no one really says what they mean, where everyone tiptoes around and emotions are kept buried.'

'The Knotweeds are the second type? Sorry, the Robinsons.'

I had started speaking without really thinking it through. 'Actually, they're a mixture. Jeff and Lizzy aren't shy to speak their minds, but the kids keep everything zipped up.'

'That sounds like a very different dynamic to me,' George said. 'One I saw a lot before I retired. Dominant parents, and offspring who haven't learned to stand up to them.'

I nodded. 'Yeah, that's exactly it. I wish Gemma would stand up to them because they're always having little digs at her . . .' I trailed off. 'But I'm sure you don't want to hear about all that.'

He looked like he wouldn't mind at all, but I felt uncomfortable talking about it.

'Could you come round?' I asked. 'Take a look at Chloe and see what you think?'

'How about now?'

'Hmm. That won't work. Jeff and Lizzy will stop you the moment you get through the front door. I know this is crazy, but could you come round first thing tomorrow? They both sleep in till after I leave for work. Will you be up at eight?'

'Of course. I get up when the cock crows.'

'Thanks, George.'

'No need to thank me. I love a bit of intrigue.' His eyes sparkled. 'And if anyone asks, I'll tell them I'm popping round with a couple of slices of banana loaf.'

ಬ

Gemma was in the bath in the en-suite when I got in. I knocked on the door and said, 'Hey, it's me.'

'Come in,' she called in a sing-song voice. 'It's not locked.'

I sat on the edge of the bath, trailing a hand in the warm water. It was full of bubbles that concealed most of Gemma's body but she leaned forward and gave me a kiss, making my face damp.

'Why don't you get in?' she asked. There was a glass of wine beside her, and a bottle on the floor, streaked with condensation, but I was surprised to hear her voice was slurred. It wasn't even seven yet.

'Are you drunk?'

She picked up the glass. 'Maybe a little. Come on, get those clothes off and join me.'

But I couldn't get over the fact that she was drunk so early on a midweek evening. 'Did you stop off for a drink after work?' I asked.

'No. I just fancied . . .' She appeared to lose her train of thought. 'I decided it would be deliciously decadent to have a glass of wine in the tub.'

I picked up the bottle. It was empty.

'More than a glass.'

She grinned. 'Oops. Guess it went down too easily.'

'Gemma . . .'

'Oh God, you're not going to start lecturing me, are you? Come on, get your kit off. I'll be your mermaid.' She tried to wink sexily at me but she was so half-cut it looked more like she had a bit of grit in her eye.

'I'm really not in the mood.'

'What? All right, suit yourself. If you don't fancy me anymore . . .'

'Don't be silly. Of course I—'

'Just go. I'll see you downstairs for dinner.'

I left the bathroom, wondering why I'd turned her down, why I couldn't be chilled out about her having a drink. Actually, I knew the answer. Ever since her parents had arrived, she'd been drinking every night. I had put it down to the stress of having them around after so many years, but now I wondered: did she have a drink problem? I would need to talk to her about it, but not until she was sober.

I went downstairs to the kitchen, aware of the tension in my chest, the skittering beat of my heart.

Jeff was seated at the dining table.

'Have you reorganised those appointments yet?' I asked, taking a glass from the rack and filling it with water.

He smiled, but I could tell the question irritated him. 'What appointments?'

'To look at houses.'

Now he rolled his eyes. 'I can't do that till Lizzy's better.'

He had an Ikea catalogue in front of him. I wasn't sure where it had come from – the nearest Ikea was in Croydon, about five miles away – but I assumed it must have been delivered to the house. Jeff had spent a lot of time leafing through it over the past few days. Earlier, when he wasn't looking, I had picked it up and found that he had circled a number of items: sofas, storage units, footrests, and a recliner similar to a La-Z-Boy. The sight of those scrawled rings around items Jeff clearly coveted gave me some hope. He was planning what they were going to put in their new home.

'Jeff!'

We both looked up and Lizzy called again. She was in the bedroom but it sounded as if she were right there in the kitchen.

Jeff grunted. 'Better go and see what she wants this time.'

He trudged up the stairs, yelling, 'Hold your bloody horses', and a minute later I heard them giggling together. I tried not to think about what Jeff had said about finding sick women sexy.

I sat and stroked Charlie, who had jumped up on to the counter.

'Don't worry,' I whispered to him. 'It'll soon be just us again. The three of us.'

He blinked at me and I wondered what he was thinking. Possibly that everything had been better when it was just me and him. Before Gemma came along, trailing her family in her wake.

Had I made a big mistake, rushing into marriage? There were good reasons why most people waited years before tying the knot. At the time, determined to seize life after my brush with death, I had thought it was exciting and romantic. Gemma and I could find out everything about each other after getting married, couldn't we? But perhaps, I was beginning to think, that had been foolish. A fool rushing in.

And why hadn't she come downstairs yet?

I went up to see what she was doing and found her passed out on the bed, the empty wine glass on the pillow. She was wrapped in a towel and there were wet footprints between the en-suite and the bed. She made a snuffling noise and her eyes flickered, so I thought she was waking up, but she was only dreaming.

I didn't really know her. I didn't know her family. I had invited a bunch of strangers into my home. I was gripped by a sensation of dread – of cold, vertiginous regret. What had I done? What the hell—

I shook my head sharply. I couldn't allow myself to think like this. I loved Gemma. It wasn't a mistake. Everything had been fine before her parents and sister turned up. And everything would get back on track when they were gone.

I had to believe that. Because if I didn't, I would have to admit that I'd made a terrible, stupid mistake.

Chapter 21

Gemma was about to leave for work when I caught her and said, 'Can we talk later?'

She squinted at me. She looked queasy and I worried that it might not be a hangover, that she might have contracted the virus that had struck down Chloe and Lizzy. 'What about?'

'Us. And your parents. The situation here.' *Your drinking*, I wanted to add, but decided to leave that for later.

'Sure.' She went to walk away then stopped and turned back. She put her arms around me. 'I'm sorry, Elliot. I know what a nightmare they are. And I'm sorry about last night. I don't even remember going to bed. I must have been so tired.'

'Hmm.'

She seemed a little put out by my response but kissed me and said, 'Let's talk after work.'

She left and I waited on the doorstep. As I'd predicted, Jeff and Lizzy were still in bed. And at precisely eight o'clock, George came out of his front door. He was carrying a leather bag and he looked left and right as he emerged, then winked at me.

'This is rather exciting,' he said in a hushed voice as he came into the house. He reached into his bag and pulled out something wrapped in tinfoil. 'Here. Banana loaf, as promised. Now, where's the patient?'

I led him up the stairs, warning him not to tread on the creaky fourth step. Not for the first time, I thought how ridiculous this was, creeping around like a burglar in my own home. I also wasn't sure how ethical this was, but Chloe was a grown woman. Ultimately, it would be up to her to grant George permission to examine her.

I knocked lightly on the door and heard shuffling within. But Chloe didn't appear.

I turned the handle. It was locked. Again.

'Damn.' Where had I left the key last time I came in? I thought back. I'd left it in the keyhole, but it wasn't there now and there wasn't another spare. Chloe must have taken it inside the room.

I tapped on the door again, stealing a glance over my shoulder. Jeff and Lizzy's door was shut. The faint rasp of a snore came from within.

'Chloe,' I said, my mouth against the door. 'It's Elliot. I need you to open up.'

More shuffling came from inside.

'She's locked herself in,' I explained to George. I cursed. 'I should have kept hold of the spare—'

'Good morning!'

I whirled round. Lizzy was standing outside her bedroom door in a pair of pink satin pyjamas. The door was shut; she must have sneaked through and shut it behind her silently, but it was as if she'd drifted through it like a ghost.

'Lizzy,' I said, appalled by how defeated I sounded.

'What's happening?' she asked. She was all smiles, her demeanour bright and friendly, focusing on George.

'You've met George from next door,' I said. 'Did I tell you he's a doctor?'

'A retired doctor,' George said. He was looking Lizzy up and down, returning her smile. It struck me, with a kind of horror, that he might find her attractive. She certainly looked better than she had the last few days, when she'd been in her sick bed. Her hair appeared freshly washed and she had colour in her cheeks again. It was an image I had resisted previously but now I saw it: she was an older version of Gemma. The loose-fitting pyjamas suited her and she had a flirtatious twinkle in her eye, aimed directly at George.

'I could tell you were a man of standing, the first time I met you,' Lizzy said. 'Not long retired, I assume?'

'Five years.'

'You must have taken early retirement, surely.'

Her words made him puff up, like a pigeon spotting a potential mate. 'You're flattering me.'

She was close enough now to lay what looked like a freshly manicured hand on his arm. 'I've always liked doctors.'

I couldn't help but laugh. 'Lizzy, can you knock on Chloe's door and get her to open it?'

I expected her to protest but she said, 'Of course.'

She rapped loudly on the door. 'Chloe, it's Mum.'

While we waited for a response, George said, 'Elliot tells me you've been feeling under the weather.'

'Oh, I'm feeling a lot better now. I've got a very good immune system. But you can examine me if you like.' She touched his arm again and I could have sworn he blushed. 'Is that bag full of tools, George? Did you bring a white coat with you?'

This was not going how I'd expected. I was about to ask Lizzy to knock again when we heard a key turn in the lock and the door was pulled inwards.

Chloe stood before us. I couldn't believe my eyes.

For a second, I thought it was a different person. She was dressed, for a start, in jeans and a soft purple sweater. Like Lizzy, her hair appeared newly washed and she was wearing make-up, just enough to be noticeable. She hadn't undergone a miraculous weight gain but she no longer looked like she was about to starve to death. She looked healthy. And she was smiling curiously, her gaze moving from me to George and back before eventually settling on her mother.

'Hello, sweetheart,' Lizzy said. 'This nice man wants to take a look at you. To show Elliot you're not at death's door.'

'I'm a doctor,' George said.

'A doctor?' Chloe said, looking with wide eyes at her mother.

'That's right,' said Lizzy. 'He just wants to take a quick look. Elliot was worried about you.'

'Okay, Mum.'

She sat on the bed, knees together, and George sat beside her. He rifled in his bag and pulled out a thermometer, an otoscope and a tongue depressor. He instructed her to put the thermometer in her mouth, then waited a short while before retrieving it.

'Thirty-five point eight. Perfectly normal. A little low, perhaps.'

'I do feel cold,' she said, touching her stomach.

'You need to make sure you wrap up warm.' He smiled at her. 'Do you mind if I take a look inside your ear, dear?' I was glad he'd glimpsed her the night the Robinsons arrived or he might have thought me mad or a liar, making the whole thing about Chloe's illness up.

He shone the light from the otoscope into her ear and nodded. 'No sign of any infection. Now, if I could just check your throat?'

While he did that, I turned to Lizzy.

'So you're feeling one hundred per cent now?' I asked.

'Yeah, well, ninety-five.'

'Good enough to start looking at houses?'

The smile she gave me was very different to the one she'd given George. Colder. Reaching no further than her lips. 'I'd say so.'

'That's great. Maybe you should call the estate agent in a minute. You don't want to miss out on the perfect property, do you? Places move quickly around here.'

I was turned sideways to George and Chloe so I could only see them in my peripheral vision. But I saw Chloe lean towards him, to whisper something into his ear. He nodded gravely, then said something in return. Lizzy was talking so I couldn't hear exactly what George said but it sounded like, '. . . get you help.'

He stood up and packed his medical instruments away in his bag before leaving the room.

'Everything all right?' I asked as I followed him out.

'Yes, she's in good health. Like I said, her core temperature is a tiny bit low so she needs to make sure she wraps up properly. But apart from that, whatever virus she had has gone.'

'Wonderful,' Lizzy said. 'I told you she was getting better, Elliot, didn't I?'

But her smile had completely slipped away now, her eyes narrowed, darting between Chloe and George. Had she seen Chloe whispering in George's ear too? It seemed like it.

'There is one thing,' he said. 'She asked me if I could give her some pills because she's having trouble sleeping.'

'Pills?' Lizzy said.

'Yes. Well, I would always prescribe sleeping pills, or any medication, as a last resort. There are plenty of more natural remedies for insomnia. But then she said something more troubling. She said when she finally falls asleep she almost always has a nightmare.'

'Oh dear,' Lizzy said, looking in at Chloe, who was still sitting on the edge of the bed, hugging herself.

'Has she undergone some kind of trauma lately?' George asked.

'What? No!'

George raised an eyebrow.

'Well, she was ill. And we moved here. I expect she's adjusting to being in a new place, that's all. She's a bit unsettled.' She took hold of George's arm. 'Let me see you out.'

'But . . .' He glanced at me. 'From the way Elliot has described her behaviour, I do think she might be struggling with her mental health.'

Lizzy shot me a filthy look.

'I know some excellent therapists who are based locally,' George said. 'I can give you their numbers.'

'Fine.'

From the way she said this, I guessed George could tell she would throw any numbers he gave her in the bin. 'In fact, Chloe is an adult,' he said. 'I'll give her the numbers myself.'

He turned to go back into the room, but Lizzy blocked his path. And then Jeff appeared from their bedroom, wrapped in a dressing gown, his hair sticking up at crazy angles.

'What's all this commotion?' he said.

'Elliot invited George round to take a look at Chloe. He was worried about her.'

'And?'

'She's fine,' Lizzy said.

'Except,' I said, 'George thinks she should talk to someone about her mental health.'

I expected Jeff to roll his eyes, to say something about how in his day people didn't have 'mental health', how they just got on with it. But he surprised me by saying, 'Okay, doc. Leave it with us.'

George looked surprised too, but before he could say anything, Lizzy took hold of his arm and said, 'We've taken up far too much of your time, George. Let me see you out.'

She marched him down the stairs. At the same time, Jeff went into Chloe's room and shut the door behind him.

I hesitated at the top of the stairs. By the front door, Lizzy had switched back into flirtatious mode, her hand on George's shoulder as she opened the door. I wanted to go down, to talk to him before he went, but a stronger impulse kept me upstairs.

I pressed my ear against Chloe's door. I could hear Jeff's voice, and Chloe said something unintelligible in response.

Jeff raised his voice and this time I heard what he said, loud and clear.

'What else did you tell him?'

I couldn't make out her response.

Chapter 22

I was so busy at work – calls, meetings, urgent emails, classes, prep – that I didn't get a moment to think about what had happened that morning or even to tell Amira about it. I contacted Kenneth to let him know that I would be delighted to give Effy extra tuition and we arranged to start the following Tuesday, immediately after class.

'Mr Mensah will be delighted,' Kenneth said.

This gave me the glow of slightly egotistical satisfaction one gets from doing a good deed. That emotion carried me through the afternoon, blocking out the unease that was simmering in my belly. But by the time I got in my car to drive home, an hour later than I'd intended, the burble of anxiety was back in full effect.

I pulled up outside the house intending to knock on George's door, to ask him about Chloe. I wanted to know if Chloe had said anything else to him – something about Jeff and Lizzy – and also wanted to get the names of those therapists because I knew my in-laws wouldn't do anything to help her. But as I got out of the car my front door opened and Gemma appeared. She was wearing a blue dress with her coat unbuttoned despite the cold, her hair straightened and face made up. She smiled and stood on tiptoe to kiss me. She smelled of the Miss Dior I had bought her on the way home from Vegas. Every now and then it struck me how gorgeous she was, and this was one of those times. My breath caught in my throat as the kiss lingered, and I wanted to lift her off her feet and carry her upstairs to the bedroom. I temporarily forgot all about George.

'What's happening?' I asked.

She raised an eyebrow. 'Mum and Dad are taking us out.'

My good mood deflated. 'Oh.'

She gave me a wry smile. 'They say they want to say thank you to us, especially you, for letting them stay. Dad's booked a table at that new place in the village.' She meant Dulwich Village, which was just up the road. I didn't realise a new restaurant had opened there. 'I don't want to go out with them but I didn't have the energy to argue.'

As she spoke, Jeff and Lizzy came out through the front door. Jeff was wearing a suit and Lizzy was dolled up in a tight dress beneath an open leather jacket, her cleavage on display. I almost laughed, imagining how George's eyes would have popped out if he'd seen her. She must have been freezing, but didn't show it.

'No Chloe?' I asked.

Jeff shook his head. 'She's gone to see Stuart. Said she wanted to catch up with her big brother.'

'Really? That's great.' I was relieved to hear she'd made such a full recovery that she was venturing out at last.

Gemma put her arm through mine and we walked to Dulwich Village, which took ten minutes, chatting about our days, with Jeff and Lizzy behind us. I had been planning to talk to her tonight about how much she'd been drinking, but that could wait. She looked gorgeous and I was proud to have her on my arm. My mood lifted to the point where I didn't even mind that Jeff and Lizzy were with us. By the time we got to Dulwich Village I felt happier than I had in days.

The restaurant was called The Buzz, which seemed like a strange name to me, but as soon as we stepped through the door I realised why they'd chosen that moniker. The place was airy and spacious, with stripped wooden floors and a long, curved bar at the front. But beyond that, on the back wall beside the opening that led to the kitchen, there was a large glass panel, beneath which something shifted. No, swarmed.

I froze, the noise of the busy restaurant fading to be replaced by a low droning noise. My good mood evaporated.

'Bees,' I said.

Jeff clapped me on the shoulder. 'Amazing, isn't it? They make their own honey here and use it in loads of their dishes.'

A waitress came over. 'That's right. Would you like to take a closer look?'

'Yeah, definitely,' said Jeff, and he and Lizzy went over to the glass.

I stayed well back. Gemma held on to my arm and said to the waitress, 'He's allergic to bee stings. He almost died earlier this year when one stung him. It's actually how we met.'

'She saved my life,' I said, automatically.

'There's no need to worry,' the waitress said. 'They can't get out into the dining area. And besides, they're Buckfasts. Very gentle and calm.'

I wasn't worried about bees attacking me. I knew how unlikely they were to do that. If I had to rationalise it, I would say that I was afraid that one would get loose and crawl into my path, like the bee on the day of the Open Garden. But I wasn't thinking rationally. Without realising it, since my brush with death I had developed a phobia, one that was perfectly understandable, I thought. My breath was short and I had gone cold. I could see the bees crawling around on what looked like a giant honeycomb, a great, teeming mass of them. I shuddered and took a step back.

'Are you sure they can't get out?' I asked.

'Quite sure.'

'Maybe we should go somewhere else,' Gemma said, as Jeff and Lizzy came back.

'What?' Jeff said. Then his eyes widened. 'Oh, bollocks. You're scared of bees, aren't you, Elliot? I totally forgot.'

'Scared,' Lizzy said with a tut. 'Of a bunch of bees.'

'He's not scared,' Gemma said, even though she must have seen how pale I was. 'He's allergic.'

'I can seat you at the far side of the restaurant,' the waitress said with a smile.

'Hear that?' said Jeff. 'You won't have to look at the nasty little insects. That would be great, darling.'

The waitress gave me a sympathetic look and Gemma rubbed my arm. 'Are you going to be all right?'

Jeff and Lizzy were both smirking at me, and I pulled myself up to my full height and took a deep breath. 'Yeah, of course. I'll be fine.'

But as the waitress led us to a table in the far corner, not far from the toilets – which Lizzy moaned about – I couldn't help but glance back at the hive. I hadn't brought my epi pen with me because it's rare to encounter bees in winter. I would just have to hope the waitress was right.

Chapter 23

'Cheers!'

Jeff raised his glass of sparkling water, echoed by Lizzy. Gemma and I had ordered a bottle of red and I had downed half a glass in one go, needing to calm my nerves. Gemma was drinking even faster.

While we were waiting for our food, Gemma's phone beeped and she held it up. It was a message from Stuart, showing a photo of Chloe with Katie, both of them smiling. *Hanging with Auntie Chloe*, read the accompanying text.

'Oh, they really do look alike,' Lizzy said, with a proud smile but a hint of sadness in her voice, no doubt thinking about how her grand-daughter wouldn't talk to her. I had to agree about the resemblance. In fact, seeing Lizzy's face alongside the photo on the phone, I could see a resemblance between all three of them. 'And look at that smile. Chloe doesn't need to see a therapist. She just needed to get out of the house for a bit.'

Again, I had to concede she had a point. But I was still wondering if Chloe had said something else to George, something about her parents.

The food came and we ate, Jeff shovelling honey-glazed pork down his throat like he was starving. I can't remember what everyone else had. I was distracted, not particularly hungry. I ordered more wine for Gemma and myself and she knocked hers back quickly.

Jeff, who had finished eating, rubbed his forehead and frowned.

'Everything all right, love?' Lizzy asked.

'Just a bit of a headache.'

Oh, for goodness' sake. If he told us he was going down with the mystery virus, I'd chuck my wine glass at him.

'Did you talk to the estate agent today?' I asked.

Jeff laughed. 'You're like a bloody broken record, Elliot.'

Lizzy put her knife and fork down. 'Oh, stop it, Jeff. You can't blame him for wanting to get rid of us.'

'I don't—'

'It's okay, love, you don't need to make excuses. We get it. You're newlyweds. You want the place to yourselves. You want to be able to roam around naked—'

Jeff interrupted her. 'If we'd had Lizzy's parents stay with us after we got married I wouldn't have been able to stand it. I'd probably have killed them.'

Gemma made a gulping sound and turned bright pink, her eyes watering.

'Quick, she's choking! Do something, Jeff.'

He stood up and started to move around the table, arm raised to slap her back, and Gemma did something that would, over the coming weeks, play on my mind: even though she was choking, she cowered. Like an animal that was used to being beaten.

I grabbed a glass of water and handed it to her quickly. She took a swallow and recovered her breath, her dad hovering behind her, arm still raised. That huge, meaty hand of his, primed for violence.

'I'm fine,' she said, gasping. 'A bite went down the wrong way.'

Jeff returned to his seat, checking his watch as he did so. 'What were we talking about?' he asked. I stared at him, unable to shake the image of him striking Gemma.

Was that why she had self-harmed? Was that why she had been so unhappy as a teenager? Because her dad had hit her?

'Earth calling Elliot,' Jeff said, snapping his fingers beneath my nose.

'Huh?'

'I said, what were we talking about?'

'I can't . . .' It came back to me. 'I asked whether you'd spoken to the estate agent.' Beside me, Gemma had pushed her plate away. She was flushed and I reached out to stroke her arm. She pulled away, not wanting to be touched. Behind me, I was aware of the bees, trapped behind glass. The tapping of their tiny legs.

'You know what?' he said. 'This headache's getting worse. I think I might pop to the shop and get some painkillers. I'm sure we passed a convenience store on the way here.'

'Can you not wait?' Lizzy asked. 'We were about to order dessert. They've got cheesecake.' She showed him the menu.

'Lovely. Why don't you order for me? I'll only be five minutes.'

He got up and left before anyone had a chance to protest. It seemed to me like an extreme way of avoiding the subject of estate agents. And I was getting a headache myself. I was sure I could hear the bees behind that wall of glass. Could feel them crawling around in my skull.

'He's a total wimp,' Lizzy said to me, with a roll of her eyes. 'The first sign of an ache or pain and he gobbles down tablets like he's going to die. Typical man. If he'd had to go through childbirth . . . When I had Stuart—'

The waitress came over and saved us again. We ordered dessert and I made small talk for a while. I was itching to ask Lizzy about the estate agent but was sick of hearing myself talk about it. I decided that I would have a word with Gemma when we got home, tell her that she needed to speak to them. They were her parents, after all.

'What's Chloe planning on doing?' I asked instead, thinking that if I kept talking I wouldn't be able to hear the drone of the bees.

'Chloe?'

'I mean, about getting a job. What did she do in France?'

That was another thing I was curious about. The Robinsons hadn't given me any details about their life across the Channel. Every time I brought it up they answered in the vaguest terms, saying they'd done 'this and that'. When I'd first heard that Gemma's parents lived in France I'd pictured some kind of *A Year in Provence* set-up; middle-class people renovating a crumbling farmhouse in a picturesque village. But now I knew Jeff and Lizzy I could hardly picture them in that setting. What had they been doing over there?

'A job – Chloe?' Lizzy almost spat out her water. 'That girl hasn't worked a day in her life.'

I was shocked. Chloe was twenty-eight. How had she avoided having a job? Maybe she was one of those eternal students, doing one degree course after another, although that would be prohibitively expensive.

'Was she studying over there?' I asked. 'Learning French?'

Lizzy let out a filthy laugh. 'Yeah, something like that. French oral a speciality.'

Gemma stared at the tabletop. Her ears had turned pink.

'Where's that pudding?' Lizzy asked, peering around for the waitress and cutting off my attempts to ask her what Chloe had been doing if she wasn't working or studying.

'Jeff's been gone a while,' I said.

'He hasn't been gone that long. Probably chatting to the shopkeeper. He does that. He'll be boring some poor bloke with his life story.'

I gawped at her. Jeff was the cagiest person I'd ever met. I wished he'd regale me with his life story!

Dessert came and Lizzy asked the waitress if she could keep Jeff's back till he returned. We ate in near silence. Where was Jeff? The convenience store was, as he'd said, a few minutes away, and though I hadn't checked the time when he left, I was sure he'd been gone fifteen minutes, maybe more.

Needing to fill the silence, I talked about work, telling them about Effy and the private tuition I planned to give her. That led on to a more general conversation about kids and education, which Lizzy thought was overrated.

'I went to the university of life,' she said.

'And the school of hard knocks?'

'Exactly. Still, it's . . . sweet, what you're doing.' She looked at Gemma and surprised me with what she said next. 'Like Gemma, working with sick animals. I know I'm not a big fan of our four-legged friends, but when I look at you, Gem, I think I must have done something right.'

But before either Gemma or I could respond, Jeff arrived, clutching a box of ibuprofen. He was red in the face, a little sweaty. He sat down without a word and immediately popped out three of the tablets, gulping them down with water.

'Sorry about that,' he said. 'I only went and got bloody lost, didn't I? Went off in the wrong direction. I kept thinking, *I'm sure this isn't familiar.* Anyway, I went round in a big flipping circle and eventually found the shop. Ended up having a good chat with the chap who works there.'

'Told you,' said Lizzy.

'Nice bloke. He was telling me about property prices around here, how much they've gone up. He told me your place must be worth well over a million, Elliot.' He wiped his brow. 'Flipping heck, I'm not as young as I used to be.'

'Did you run back?' Lizzy asked.

'Yeah. I didn't want to miss dessert, did I?'

He grabbed the waitress and asked her to bring over the slice of cheesecake Lizzy had ordered for him. And for the next ten minutes he rambled on about all the things he'd do to my house if it were his.

ω

After dessert, Jeff and Lizzy wanted a coffee, and they weren't in any hurry to leave after that so we didn't get home till just after eleven.

Chloe was waiting on the doorstep, pink-nosed and shivering from the cold.

'I thought you'd be back ages ago,' she said.

'Sorry, love,' said Lizzy, putting an arm around her and rubbing her shoulders.

Chloe shrugged her off. 'Well, you're home now.'

We went inside. Chloe went straight upstairs and Jeff and Lizzy announced they were going to bed. Gemma yawned and said, 'Me too.'

I didn't feel relaxed enough to sleep so went into the kitchen – intending to have a drink and listen to an audiobook to wind down – where I noticed Charlie's food bowl was full. That was odd. He rarely left his dinner, which I assumed Gemma must have put down for him before we went out.

I checked the cat flap. It was locked again.

Last time I had blamed this on an accident, but now I was certain. Lizzy hated cats, and she was locking mine out deliberately.

Angry, and vowing to have a word with her about it, I went into the garden to call Charlie, walking down towards the pond and shouting his name. To my relief, he came leaping over the fence that separated my house from George and Edith's. He bolted past me into the house, heading straight for his dish, and I was about to follow him when I noticed something.

My neighbours' back door was half-open. In the summer, this wouldn't have surprised me, but it was freezing. All the lights in the house were off too, as if they were either in bed or had gone out.

So why was the door open? Had they been burgled?

I had left my phone in the kitchen and I thought about going inside to get it, to call the police, but I didn't want to waste their time if there was a simple explanation. I decided I should take a look first. Just a quick look.

There was a gap in the fence between our two sheds which I had been meaning to fix for ages. I slipped through it, and headed towards George and Edith's house.

Chapter 24

I pushed the back door open, slipping through into the dark kitchen and stopping for a moment to let my eyes adjust. Moonlight washed the room in pale, ghostly light.

'George?' I called. My voice sounded croaky and weak in my ears. I cleared my throat and tried again. 'George? Edith?'

Silence. All I could hear was the ticking of the kitchen clock and a watery, rushing sound from somewhere beyond this room. The house felt empty, so quiet and still that when a soft thud came from somewhere beyond the kitchen, I almost jumped out of my skin.

I headed through the kitchen towards the noise – and almost slipped, just managing to grab the counter to keep myself upright. My heart felt like someone had injected it with adrenaline.

I peered at the floor. A mug lay on its side next to the fridge and a pool of liquid had spread out across the tiles. Tea, or possibly coffee.

I stopped, knowing I should probably go back and call the police. But what if George or Edith was hurt and required medical attention? I would never forgive myself if my hesitation, my inaction, led to one of them not receiving the urgent help they needed.

I left the kitchen. The utility room was to my right. A red light blinked in the darkness. That must have been the source of the rushing sound and the thud: the washing machine, ending its cycle.

I called their names again and, once more, got no reply. I waited for a second because it was darker here, moonlight failing to penetrate the hallway. Because this house mirrored the layout of my own, I knew there was a light switch just ahead, to my left. Groping along the wall, I found it and turned it on, closing my eyes against the sudden illumination.

I opened them and my breath snagged in my throat.

There was blood spattered across the wall. Actually, more of a spray than a spatter. My first, fevered thought was that it looked like someone with a nosebleed had sneezed directly on to the wallpaper.

My eyes tracked left to a photo of George and Edith's daughter at her graduation ceremony, smiling proudly in her mortar board, clutching her scroll. More drops of blood clung to the glass surface of the frame.

And there was blood on the wooden floor too. Thin lines and fat spots. A trail of crimson that led towards, and into, the living room.

I took a long, deep breath. I think I knew that if this was a crime scene I would be messing it up. Contaminating it. But I clung to the hope that this was something innocent. Maybe it *was* a nosebleed. Or a common domestic accident. George or Edith – or both – could be in the living room now, needing help. I couldn't turn back.

I went into the living room and turned the light on.

The sofa was in the centre of the room, facing the TV, which was over by the front window. Beyond the sofa was the fireplace, which was surrounded by green tiles, and above that the mantelpiece with all its knick-knacks and a large mirror in which I could see my own white, stricken face.

There was blood on the mirror, spattered across the wallpaper, clinging to the tiles. I could smell it, sharp and metallic, and I could smell something else, sweeter and more cloying, like a soiled nappy. I put my hand to my nose, suddenly unable to breathe through my mouth. Fleetingly, I detected another smell too, so faint I thought I might be imagining it, but then I looked down, past the sofa, and all thoughts of smells and anything else were obliterated by what I saw.

Edith was lying face down on the rug before the fireplace. The rug was soaked in her blood, as was the back of her sweater. So much blood. One arm stretched out before her, like she was reaching out for help. I turned away, the sight of her burning my retinas, but not before I saw the back of her head. The hole there, as if someone had struck her with a hammer, hard and repeatedly. The smashed skull and the blackness within. I didn't need to check if she was breathing. There was no way anyone could survive that injury.

I staggered from the room, almost collapsing against the door frame, holding my mouth in a desperate attempt not to vomit. My hand was shaking and I felt like I had no bones in my legs. Somehow, I managed to stay upright.

I turned towards the kitchen, intending to leave. I needed to call the police, but my phone was next door and George and Edith's landline was in the living room, on a little table behind where her body lay. I didn't want to have to step over her. And I didn't want to leave the house before I found George. He might need help.

I hesitated. What if the murderer was still here? I could have interrupted him and now he was waiting to see if I would come to investigate, the hammer – or whatever he'd used to kill Edith – raised above his head, ready to smash another skull.

I strained to listen and heard a groan coming from upstairs. It was George. I was certain it was George.

I ran up the stairs, switching the light on as soon as I reached the landing.

There was another groan. It was coming from the master bedroom. I rushed inside.

George was lying on his side on the carpet beneath the window. Like Edith, he was covered in what had to be his own blood. There was more spatter on the walls here, on the carpet, smeared across the foot of the bed. His hair was no longer white but red. His arms were stretched out in front of him, his head on the floor.

He coughed, blood spilling from his lips.

I threw myself to my knees beside him, trying not to look at the hole in the back of his head, the broken skull, the little fragments of bone that clung to his hair. Later, I would revisit this scene many times in nightmares, and he would open his eyes and tell me it was all my fault, that I had brought death into this quiet street. But now, in reality, he didn't move, apart from the faintest rise and fall of his breathing.

'George,' I said. 'I'm going to go and get help. Okay? You're going to be fine.'

But as I began to push myself to my feet, he let out a gurgling breath. His eyes flickered like he was trying to open them.

'Take it easy,' I said. 'Don't try to move or speak.'

He made a hissing noise, like air from a puncture, then said, so quietly I could barely hear him, 'Edith.'

I couldn't tell him. Besides, if George was still breathing, maybe there was a tiny chance she was still alive too. I needed to get out and call an ambulance. But George was trying to say something else. These could be his last words. I couldn't deny him the chance to have someone hear them.

He opened one eye and looked at me. I don't think, before then, he knew who I was, who was here talking to him. But I saw recognition bloom, followed by alarm. His outstretched fingers twitched and, not knowing what else to do, I took his hand in mine.

'Elliot,' he said.

'I need to call an ambulance. You're going to be okay.'

He wasn't listening. He said something, but the blood in his mouth choked his words so that all that came out was a ghastly wet noise.

His grip on my hand tightened and he tried again. 'Not w—' Again the blood drowned his words, but the tightness of his grip made me sure he was trying to warn me about something.

'Not what, George?' It made no sense. I put my ear close to his lips but no more noises came out except ragged, faint breathing. I sat up. 'George, who did this? Who was it?'

He made a rasping sound and closed his eye.

'George? George?'

Tentatively, I laid a hand on his back. The shallow rise and fall of his breathing had ceased.

He was gone.

I sat there for a moment, stunned, paralysed, then forced myself to get up, to leave the room, almost throwing myself down the stairs in my haste to get out. I paused by the living room door. Could Edith be alive? I made myself go in, crouching by her body and checking her pulse. Her skin was cold. She was dead.

I almost threw up then but managed to get up and out of the room, down the hallway and through the kitchen. I emerged into the cold night air and, driven by the need to phone the police, made it back through the gap between the fences, through my garden and into my house. I snatched up my phone and, hands still shaking, dialled 999.

PART TWO

Before

The sun was coming up when they came across the house. It was a mile from the closest neighbour, a small stone dwelling, half-concealed by the woods in which it nestled. A red Citroën C1 was parked outside and, slowing down to take a proper look – at the garden with its bright, sunny pockets of flowers, and the single shiny car – Jeff was seventy per cent sure that a woman lived here. He was hoping she lived here alone.

They looped back around on the empty road and pulled up on the verge outside the house.

'What are we doing?' Lizzy asked.

'I need to send an email.'

She narrowed her eyes. 'Can't we find, I don't know, an internet cafe or something?'

'What, around here? Besides, when was the last time you saw an internet cafe? It's not 1997.'

'All right. There's no need to be an arse about it.'

He sighed. 'Sorry, darling.' He unfastened his seat belt and leaned over to prod at his sleeping daughter in the back. 'Hey. Wake up. I need you to come with me.'

He had to shake her, gently slap her burning face, before she came to. Her eyes had massive circles around them, there was drool on her cheek, and her hair stuck up like she'd been tied to the back of the car and dragged down the road. Jeff handed her a pack of baby wipes. 'Clean yourself up, brush your hair. I need you to look presentable.'

The miserable expression on her face, the pout, made him want to slap her harder.

'Come on. We haven't got all day.'

It wasn't quite seven but the sun had risen with a vengeance. It was going to be another hot, stifling day. Jeff pushed open the car door and got out, hearing his bones crunch and pop as he stretched. He probably stank, and he ran a few of the baby wipes over his own face, the back of his neck, reaching up beneath his shirt and cleaning his armpits. That would have to do.

'All right,' he said. 'Lizzy, you get out, stand by the car but wait here. If anyone comes, sound the horn.'

He turned to his daughter. 'You. Come with me.'

They walked up the path towards the house. The wind had dropped and, apart from the heat, he was able to appreciate how idyllic it was here.

'Just follow my lead,' he said. 'Be friendly.'

He needed her with him for two things. Firstly, to translate. Secondly, because he knew anyone hearing a knock at the door this early – or at any time, really – would be suspicious of a man on his own. But with a young woman by his side, with another woman standing in the background by the car, he looked safe. A family man.

There was no doorbell, just a large, brass knocker. He thumped it down once, twice, and waited. Almost immediately there came the sound of movement within the house.

A woman answered the door. She was around seventy, he would guess. Grey hair, laughter lines, petite. She tilted her head, blinking at these strangers on her doorstep.

'Bonjour, madame,' Jeff said, knowing that she would pick up on his English accent straight away. Pretending to be embarrassed, he said, 'Parlez-vous anglais?'

'Only a little,' she replied.

To Chloe, he said, 'Tell her we're on our way to stay with friends who live nearby but we're lost. We need to call them but can't get any reception.'

The truth was, he'd made Chloe throw her phone away as soon as they'd left the scene of the incident. And he and Lizzy only had an old pay-as-you-go mobile, which was unregistered and untraceable.

'Ask if we can come in and use her phone.'

Chloe gawped at him for a second and, once again, he had to fight the temptation to slap her. The Frenchwoman was going to think she was dealing with a moron. He smiled and nodded at the woman, not unlike a moron himself, and gestured for Chloe to speak.

Finally, like a robot being rebooted after a long sleep, she began to convey what he'd said. Jeff couldn't understand her so he was having to trust Chloe not to tell the truth. He studied the woman's reaction for signs of alarm but she nodded and smiled and gestured for them to come in.

It was mercifully cool inside the house. It was rustic, a bit pokey for Jeff's taste, but he could see the appeal. Jeff glanced around, looking for signs that a man lived here, but there were no men's shoes by the door or men's coats on the rack. The woman was attractive, with green eyes, and Jeff wondered what her story was. Divorced? Widowed? Never married? He didn't really care.

She led them into the kitchen, where the phone was attached to the wall. She made a 'help yourself' gesture.

Continuing to nod and smile, and muttering, 'Merci', Jeff picked up the receiver and punched in a random series of numbers, one short of actually making a call.

'Oh, hi, yeah, it's me. We're having a bit of an issue finding you. Yeah, I know . . .' He went on in this manner until the woman drifted away to the back of the kitchen, towards the doors which opened out on to the garden. There was a swimming pool out there, shimmering blue beneath the early-morning sun. The woman had a cup of coffee on the go and she sipped

it – not offering to make him or Chloe one – and lit a cigarette, the smoke curling towards the ceiling. He continued to pretend to have a conversation then hung up the receiver, shaking his head and tutting.

He approached the woman. The cigarette smelled delicious and he had to fight the urge to snatch it from her hand.

He addressed Chloe. 'Can you tell her I've spoken to . . .' He broke off. This was taking too long. 'Can you ask her if she has a computer we can use to look at a map?'

Chloe did as she was asked.

The Frenchwoman stubbed her cigarette out and left the kitchen. He quickly looked around. There were photographs of small children attached to the fridge along with a child's terrible drawing in crayon. So she was a grandmother. There was a photo of an attractive smiling couple on the wall too. The woman's son or daughter and their spouse. Peering out into the garden, he saw an easel set up beyond the pool, complete with a canvas bearing marks and patterns he couldn't make out from this distance.

The woman was taking ages.

'Did you say something to her?' he whispered.

Chloe shook her head. He had never seen her look so exhausted and he was worried she might faint.

He was about to tell her to pull herself together when the woman came back into the room with a laptop.

'Brilliant,' Jeff said. 'Perfect.'

She opened it and logged in, opening Google Maps for him. He smiled and nodded then gestured for Chloe to take over. He had already told her what to do, but he needed to get the woman out of the way so she didn't see Chloe open Gmail.

'I'm rubbish with computers,' he said in English and laughed, pulling a self-deprecating face. The woman looked at him blankly.

He gestured at the packet of cigarettes on the side and said, 'Cigarette, s'il vous plaît?'

'Of course,' she replied, and she took two out of the pack. He followed her into the garden, stealing a glance back at Chloe. She was staring at the computer, fingers motionless on the keys. *That girl* . . . *The way she was acting was doing nothing for his nerves.*

He lit the cigarette and motioned towards the easel.

'Artiste?' he asked. He could handle some simple French words.

'Yes,' she replied.

'And . . . you are a grand-mère?'

'Oui.' But she pulled a face which told him not everything was rosy between her and her offspring.

They stood in companionable silence for a few minutes, smoking their cigarettes, and he was happy about the language barrier. It meant there was no need to attempt to fill the quiet. The garden was surrounded by high hedgerows so any passer-by wouldn't be able to see in. Not that there was likely to be a passer-by. He didn't hear a single vehicle pass while he smoked his cigarette.

Chloe appeared on the patio, squinting into the sun.

'Excusez-moi,' he said to the woman, and approached Chloe. 'What is it?'

'She replied straight away,' Chloe said. 'She said it's not possible. She lives in a tiny bedsit.'

'A bedsit? Pathetic. Try Stuart.'

Chloe looked at him, as if to say, 'Is that a good idea?'

'Yeah, you're right. Reply to Gemma, tell her we're desperate.'

Chloe nodded. Before she could walk away, Jeff grabbed her arm. 'You didn't tell her what happened, did you?'

'Of course not.'

She went back inside and Jeff turned to find the Frenchwoman giving him a curious, disapproving look which pissed him off. He gave her his most charming smile but she didn't return it. He saw her gaze go past him, into the kitchen, towards the phone. She was suspicious, and he suddenly had

141

an image of her going to the police, telling them about the weird English family who had turned up on her doorstep.

Taking another look at the high hedgerows and the empty space beyond, he made a decision.

He walked up to the woman and grabbed her by the throat.

'Sorry, love,' he said, amused by the shock on her face. 'Change of plan.'

Chapter 25

I sat on the kerb, waiting for the police and ambulances to arrive. The night was quiet, a few lights still burning up and down the street, a late-night dog walker strolling past and regarding me as if I were a vagrant, oblivious to the horrific scene behind the door of the house he was passing. Time warped and folded in on itself and I don't know how long passed before flickering blue lights filled the horizon. These lights, combined with the slamming of car doors and the voices of the police and ambulance crew, woke up the neighbours and drew them out of their houses until suddenly the street was busier than it ever got during the day.

Gemma woke up too and came out, shocked to find me on the pavement, even more shocked when I told her – in a series of fragmented sentences that almost choked me – what had happened. As the police and paramedics went in and out of the house, people kept coming up to me, trying to ask me what I'd seen, and Gemma formed a protective shield, telling them to leave me alone. She put her arm around me and rested her head on my shoulder as I sat there, staring at nothing, unable to push away the bloody images of George and Edith.

The uniformed cops had already identified me and asked me if I would wait up – as if I was going to trot off to bed with a nice cup of cocoa and a book – and around one o'clock a woman who introduced herself as Detective Sergeant Amber Rothermel approached and asked me a few questions.

'I'll need you to come in to the station first thing,' she said. She was in her thirties with light brown hair cut in a bob. A kind face, but sharp eyes that appeared to be studying me as I spoke, in the same way I would scrutinise cells beneath a microscope. 'So we can go through it all.'

'I'll be a suspect,' I said to Gemma as the detective went back into the house next door.

'What? Surely not.'

'That's what happens on TV. The person who finds the body always needs to be eliminated from their inquiries.'

Shortly after that – the night is too blurry for me to be precise – another couple of cops arrived and I realised I recognised one of them. It was Amira's boyfriend, Colin. I'd met him a few times before but didn't know him particularly well. He was in his late twenties, over six feet tall with designer stubble and cheekbones that should have been in a magazine. An alpha male. Apparently he'd almost gone into modelling before he decided to become a police officer like his dad before him. He spotted me and came over.

'Elliot. Bloody hell. It was you who found the victims?' I cringed and he said, 'Sorry. I should say Mr and Mrs Whiteley.'

'He was still alive,' I said. 'George. He died right there in front of me.'

'Oh, mate. Were you close?'

I was too choked up to reply so Gemma said, 'They were, yes.'

'That's harsh. I'm really sorry.'

As we were talking, I'd watched two men putting on paper suits outside George and Edith's house. Crime scene investigators.

'I think they're going to be pissed off with me for messing up their crime scene,' I said.

'Don't worry about it. Listen, I'd better get on.'

He went back to stand with the other cops, one of whom was stringing up tape across the front of the house.

I heard a voice behind me. 'Bloody hell. What's going on?' It was Jeff.

Gemma explained what had happened.

'You're joking. And they seemed like such a nice old couple.' He put his hands on his hips. 'Heads bashed in, you say? What a way to go.'

I stared at him. It was as if he were describing something he'd seen in a movie.

Jeff looked up and down the street and blew out a low whistle. 'You wouldn't think it would happen on a nice, middle-class street like this.' He met my eye. 'Still, I guess nowhere's safe nowadays.'

He went back inside, shutting the door with a loud thump.

ω

I arrived at the police station at just after ten and was shown into a dingy interview room with no windows and a sour odour that clung to every surface. I waited for DS Rothermel, yawning so hard it hurt my jaw. I hadn't slept; hadn't even tried. I had sat on the sofa all night and stared at the window, waiting for the sun to come up. It seemed to take forever. Gemma had stayed beside me, refusing to leave me on my own. She nodded off at around four and twitched in her sleep like she was having bad dreams.

That was one of the reasons why I had stayed awake. I knew nightmares were waiting for me.

DS Amber Rothermel came into the interview room holding two takeaway cups of coffee.

'I thought you might need this,' she said, putting them down along with a couple of sachets of sugar.

'Thank you.'

She started by asking me for my personal details – 'I thought I recognised you,' she said when I told her my occupation – then got me to talk her through what I'd found next door, wanting to know the exact sequence of events. Her tone was soft, sympathetic, and I didn't get the impression I was a suspect.

'Are you able to estimate what time they died?' I asked, when I got to the end of my account and she had gone back to clarify a few points.

'We're still waiting for the pathologist's report,' she replied.

I nodded. 'I went into the house at quarter past eleven and the washing machine was just finishing its cycle. I don't know how long—'

'Two hours,' she said. 'So the attack must have happened at some time between quarter past nine and the time you arrived home.'

'Did anyone see anything? Any witnesses?' I continued to blurt out questions. 'Was there any sign of a break-in? Was anything taken?'

She sat back and folded her arms. '*I'm* interviewing *you* here, Mr Foster.'

'I know, but . . . I live next door. I need to know if I should install extra security. You read about this sort of thing. Burglars targeting neighbourhoods.'

DS Rothermel gave me what was intended to be a reassuring smile. 'I understand that you've been through a horrible trauma. But please try not to be too fearful. I can tell you that items were taken – jewellery and some valuable model cars.'

George's cars. In the panic of the moment, when I had been fixated on Edith's body, I hadn't even looked over at the cabinet that housed his collection.

'You think they were after the cars? That George and Edith were killed over some stupid toys?'

'Stupid, maybe, but quite valuable as I understand it.'

I shook my head. 'But there was another break-in last week. The Singhs, a few doors down. Somebody broke in and took some gardening stuff. Kerosene, maybe.' I could hear my own voice becoming louder, higher-pitched. I rubbed my eyes. I felt jet-lagged, finding it hard to keep a grip on reality. The walls of the interview room shimmered like a mirage. 'They stole a hammer too. What if that was used to kill George and Edith?'

'Mr Foster. Please. Calm down. We've spoken to Mr Singh. He found his misplaced hammer and all the other stuff.'

'What? Really?'

'Yes. It was all in his shed. His wife told us that he's become rather absent-minded recently. Please try not to worry. My suspicion is that someone saw George Whiteley showing off his toy collection in the paper and tracked down where he lived. A burglary gone wrong.'

It was horrific. The idea that my neighbours had been killed for money, because they'd disturbed a burglar.

'Do you have any suspects?' I asked.

'All I can tell you is that we're following several lines of inquiry.'

Which was what the police always said when they didn't have a clue.

ᚈ

Emerging into the morning sunshine, I saw a familiar face. Colin, Amira's boyfriend. He was smoking a cigarette, which he quickly flicked away when he spotted me.

'Don't tell Amira,' he said. 'I'm supposed to have quit.'

I stood there, still feeling a little stunned after my interview, and drunk on tiredness.

'Have they got any idea who did it?' I asked.

'We're following—'

'Please. That's what DS Rothermel said. Be honest with me, Colin.'

'No. Not yet.' He popped a piece of chewing gum into his mouth and offered me one. I declined. 'The forensics team are there now, though, combing the place for evidence.'

'DNA.'

'Yeah. Except, as I'm sure you know, DNA is only useful if the perpetrator is already in the system. We're searching for the murder weapon too.'

'The hammer?'

He gave me a look.

'I mean, I assumed it was a hammer. Or a bat?'

He frowned. 'The pathologist hasn't done his thing yet but, yeah, it looks like it was a hammer.'

I squinted at him, the sun in my eyes and ice in my blood. 'I'm shocked no one saw anything. Whoever did it must have been covered in blood. How did the murderer get away without anyone noticing them? There were footprints in the house too. Well, marks, anyway. Wouldn't they have left a trail behind when they left the house? And what about fingerprints?'

I was bombarding him just as I had DS Rothermel.

'We're going to look into all that. Try not to worry. It's a high-priority case. A nice elderly couple, one of them a retired doctor, battered to death in their million-pound home. We're not going to rest. And Rothermel is good. One of our best. We'll find them, Elliot. Believe me.'

He went back inside, leaving me alone. I was so exhausted I couldn't think straight. But I wished I could share Colin's faith in his colleagues. I was sure there was something they weren't seeing; something I was unable to see myself. Would a burglar really batter an old couple to death in such a brutal manner? Of course, I had read about even worse cases. I was fully aware of the terrible things human beings do to each other. But the attack on George and Edith – it seemed unnecessarily brutal. Personal, even. Driven by anger or hatred. And while it was easy to say George had been talking nonsense because of his brain injuries, DS Rothermel hadn't been there. She hadn't seen the way he'd looked at me. He'd said my name, known who I was.

I was sure the police were wrong. He had been trying to warn me.

And there was a dreadful thought, a suspicion, trying to push its way into my mind. One that was so awful I instinctively tried to push it away.

But it kept coming back. And, as I made my way back to my car, I knew I wouldn't be able to rest until I'd explored it, examined it, just as I would test a theory in the lab.

Chapter 26

'I like you, Elliot,' Jeff said.

It was Saturday afternoon and I was in the snug, catching up on all the work I had missed the day before, the torrent of emails that had poured in, including a number from journalists who wanted to talk to me about 'the tragic events on Cuckoo Lane'. A couple had tried to phone me too, but I had blocked their numbers and ignored them. I'd had a few hours' sleep, surprisingly deep and dreamless, but I still felt restless and on edge. I thought concentrating on work might take my mind off what had happened and I spent a little while replying to an email from Kenneth, detailing the plans I had for Effy's private lessons.

Then Jeff appeared behind me and made me jump. I turned in my swivel chair, unsure if I had heard him correctly. I stared at him.

'You're a nice guy. That's plain to see. Gemma's done well.' He came into the room and, without being invited, sat on the little sofa. 'She went out with some real dickheads in the past. I'm pretty sure she did it just to piss me and her mum off.'

That piqued my interest. Gemma and Lizzy had gone out to the supermarket because the fridge was empty and the cupboards were bare. Since they'd arrived, Jeff and Lizzy had been helping themselves to food and drink and, apart from doing one shopping trip themselves, hadn't offered to contribute. I didn't particularly mind this as I wouldn't have accepted their money anyway. But it did mean we'd had to go shopping twice as often as normal.

'Was this back in Winchelsea Beach?' I asked.

'Yeah. And afterwards. There was this one guy . . .' Frustratingly, he trailed off. 'I'm very happy she found you. A man of science. I mean, that's a solid calling, not like all these artsy-fartsy hippy types she used to go out with, even if you are only using it to teach.'

'*Only?*'

He waved a hand. 'You know what I mean. I bet you could be heading up some, I don't know, biotech corporation. Or finding a cure for cancer. But you've done all right for yourself, haven't you?'

'I guess so.'

'Sure you have. I respect people like you, Elliot. A self-made man. Because your parents weren't rich, were they . . .'

I was taken aback. 'How did you know that?'

'What? Oh, I think Gemma told me.'

He got up, apparently losing interest in the topic. He went over to the front window and peered out. The police kept coming and going, along with various members of the media, and there had been a huge increase in traffic in the street, misery tourists coming to gawp at the 'house of horror', stopping to take photos on their phones which they posted to Instagram. Hashtag murderhouse. I had already been out to yell at a group of teenagers, who seemed shocked by my fury. Shouting and swearing at them had made me feel better for a few minutes, though.

'I wonder what it'll do to property prices round here,' Jeff said.

'I'm sure they'll hold up,' I said drily. 'Speaking of property . . .'

'Yes, yes, we've arranged to see a few places. A bit further out than we'd have liked.' He named a few of the suburbs between Dulwich and Kent. 'Nowhere as lovely as round here.'

That was good news. It would be great to have some distance from my in-laws. Though it could be even better. 'You haven't thought about moving back to Sussex?'

'Huh. No chance.'

'Or what about going back to France?'

'Definitely not a good idea.'

I got up from the desk and stood by the door, blocking his exit. 'You know, you still haven't told me what you were doing over there.'

He shrugged. 'We were living the good life, that's all. It's a beautiful part of the world.'

'So why leave?'

'Because we missed Gemma. It was time to have our whole family back together. Especially now she's married and, dare I say it, there might be the prospect of more grandchildren on the way.'

He was trying to appear nonchalant but there was something there, a tension, and he wouldn't meet my eye. He was lying. I was sure of it. Something had happened in France that had made them come back. I remembered overhearing him and Lizzy in this room, in the middle of the night, talking about getting away with something. I had previously thought it might be a business deal but what if it was something more sinister? Something illegal?

I waited to see if he would feel the need to fill the silence between us but he just stood there like he didn't have a care in the world.

Eventually, I stepped aside and said, 'I need to get back to work.'

I sat down at my desk and immediately returned to the email I was writing. After a minute, I realised Jeff hadn't left the room. He was looking over my shoulder at the screen.

I minimised the email and glared at him.

'Must be time for the football results,' he said, and left the room.

ω

As soon as I heard him put the TV on in the living room, turning it up loud as always, I locked my computer, went into the kitchen to grab a couple of cans of Diet Coke, then went up the stairs. If Jeff wasn't going to tell me why they'd really left France, there was someone who might. And I had another question to ask her too. The question that had been burning a hole in my brain for days.

I knocked on Chloe's door, reminding myself as I did so that this wasn't really Chloe's room, it was my office. It was only temporarily inhabited. But since her recovery from the mysterious virus, or whatever it was, Chloe had been as reclusive as ever, hardly coming out of her room.

I was expecting to have to knock several times but she opened the door straight away.

She looked just as she had the morning George came round: in jeans and a sweater, fresh-faced with hair tied back in a ponytail.

'Hey, Elliot.'

I was struck by how pretty she was when she smiled. Like a completely different person. It was as if she were a butterfly who had arrived here during her cocoon phase. She had the same green eyes as Gemma, but whereas Gemma often struggled with eye contact, or would look at me through her lashes, Chloe's gaze was direct. Searching. It felt a little like she was trying to see into my soul.

Feeling a little exposed, I held up one of the cans of Diet Coke. 'I brought you up a drink.'

'Oh, thank you. That's so kind.'

She took it from me and was about to shut the door when I said, 'I've hardly spoken to you since you got here and I was thinking it would be nice to get to know you a little, seeing as you're my sister-in-law.'

She stared at me, the smile slipping away.

'Can I come in?'

She peered behind me and said in a near-whisper, 'Where are my mum and dad?'

153

'Lizzy's gone shopping with Gemma and Jeff's watching the football results.'

She hesitated for another moment, then said, 'Okay, sure. Come in.'

Chloe shut the door behind me. To my surprise, I found Charlie curled up asleep at the foot of the bed, next to what looked like a journal, lying open and face down, a pen beside it. Chloe snatched up the journal and snapped it shut, tucking it beneath her pillow. She sat beside Charlie. 'I hope you don't mind. He was pawing at the door.'

I took a seat opposite her. 'No, of course not. He used to sit in here with me sometimes when I worked from home.'

'He's a lovely cat.' She stroked him and smiled as his purr filled the room.

It was strange to think that less than a week ago I had found her hiding in the cupboard, acting like someone who was having some kind of breakdown.

'I'm glad you're feeling better,' I said.

'Thank you. Me too.' She laughed. 'It must have been weird for you, suddenly having this sick girl sleeping in your spare room.'

'It was a little.'

She turned her head towards the window. 'It all feels like a dream now. Or a hallucination.'

'We should have got a doctor to see you earlier,' I said, and suddenly the atmosphere in the room shifted.

Chloe cast her eyes down. 'He seemed nice,' she said.

'He was a lot more than nice.'

I was aware that I might not have much time to talk to her before Jeff appeared or Lizzy got home. I didn't think I would get anything out of her if they were around. The furtive way she'd asked where they were before letting me into the room made me wonder if she was scared of them. I was taken back to the restaurant, when I'd seen Gemma cower and I'd wondered if he had hit her when she was a child. I hadn't brought this up with Gemma, partly because I didn't want to accuse her dad of such a terrible crime if he was innocent, but also because I'd been preoccupied, the events at the restaurant overshadowed by what I found when we got home.

Chloe was watching me, waiting to see what I would say next.

'Chloe, George told us you were having nightmares. That he was worried about your . . . about the state of your mind.'

'I know. I *was* having nightmares. But it's all fine now.'

'You're sure? Because if you want to talk to someone, I can take you.'

'Honestly, I'm fine. I've been sleeping like a baby.'

She seemed to be telling the truth. But I remembered Jeff asking her, 'What else did you tell him?' I hadn't heard her response.

'And you didn't say anything else to George?'

'About nightmares?'

'About anything.'

'No, nothing at all.'

She seemed to be telling the truth.

She had gone back to stroking Charlie, and I reminded myself that I didn't have much time.

'So,' I said, trying to sound casual, 'what were you doing in France?'

Chloe must have pressed too hard on Charlie because he jumped up and ran from the room.

'What have my parents told you?'

'Hardly anything.'

A quick lift and fall of her shoulders. 'I guess there isn't much to tell. We moved over there five years ago because . . .'

'Because what?'

She let out a long sigh. 'I met someone. A French guy.'

Finally, something that made sense. 'So you went over there to be with your boyfriend?'

She nodded.

'And your mum and dad went with you?'

'Yeah.'

I waited for her to elaborate. This was so frustrating, like trying to get information out of some of the shyer kids I taught. Again, it seemed strange. I could understand Chloe going to live in France because she'd met a French boy, but why would Jeff and Lizzy go with her? I tried to come up with a rational explanation. Maybe they'd gone on holiday to stay with her for a couple of weeks . . . and hadn't come back. That made sense, knowing what I knew about them. Was this a pattern? Had they gone for a short holiday with Chloe's boyfriend and ended up staying for five years?

Was that what was going to happen here?

I heard the front door open and shut, the sound of Gemma and Lizzy getting home from the shops, Jeff's booming voice greeting them.

'Chloe,' I said hurriedly, 'is there anything you want to tell me? About your mum and dad? I'm just going to come out and say it. You seem afraid of them.'

'Afraid? No, I love them.'

But the way she was looking at me, with wide, fearful eyes, said something different. So did her nervous glance towards the door.

'What is it, Chloe?' I whispered. 'What have they done?'

She stared at me, and for a second I was sure she was going to tell me. But then she laughed and said, 'Absolutely nothing. I don't know what you're talking about and you're actually starting to freak me out.'

'Elliot! We're home!' It was Gemma, calling from downstairs. 'Where are you?'

I got up and was about to leave the room when Chloe said something in a quiet voice. '*I* don't need to be afraid of them.'

'What?'

But she jumped up and pushed past me without responding, running down the stairs and calling, 'Hey, what did you get? Anything nice?'

I stayed in the room for a moment. The notebook Chloe had been writing in was under her pillow. Was it a journal? Were the answers I sought in there? I could look now while they were all downstairs in the kitchen, unpacking the shopping. But I hesitated too long, because Gemma ran up the stairs, calling my name, and it was too late.

Chapter 27

'Has Colin said anything to you about the investigation?'

Amira and I were in the car, heading to a meeting at a school in Crystal Palace. It was a foul day and the wipers were at full throttle, hardly able to keep up with the rain that pummelled the windscreen. Friday afternoon, and George and Edith had been dead for over a week. Police tape still surrounded the house but comings and goings had slowed down considerably, the story had vanished from the media and even the rubberneckers had grown bored. The city had moved on already and the hot topic now, after the stabbings of a couple of teenagers in Tottenham, was knife crime. The funeral hadn't even been held yet – apparently Terry Whiteley, who had temporarily returned from Australia, was waiting for the coroner to release the bodies – and it felt to me like my former neighbours had already been forgotten.

But not by me. And not, I hoped, by the police.

'He doesn't talk about work much,' she said, stamping on the brake as a van skidded to a halt in front of us, spray coming off its wheels.

'He must have said something. Like, whether they've got any suspects at all. I've been trying to get hold of that detective, Rothermel, but she's never available.'

'They're overstretched, Elliot. Too much crime, not enough police. Colin goes on about it all the time.'

'So, what, they're just forgetting about George and Edith?'

We stopped at a red light. 'No, of course not. But he hasn't said anything about there being any new leads.' The lights changed and we moved on. 'Anyway, let's change the subject. What's the latest with your in-laws?'

'Oh God. Don't ask.'

Over the past few days, I had been watching Jeff and Lizzy, listening to them, trying to figure out if my suspicions about them were correct. And that list of suspicions kept changing and growing. First, I was worried about what had happened in France. Had they parked themselves at Chloe's boyfriend's place and refused to shift, and were they planning to do the same here?

Second, what exactly was going on with Chloe? Had she lied when she told me she hadn't said anything to George? And had she told Jeff what she'd said? Something that Jeff was desperate to keep secret?

And then there was her other utterance.

I *don't need to be afraid of them.*

Meaning what? That I should be scared of them? The more the words repeated in my head, the more anxious I felt. Why should I be afraid of them? What were they capable of?

And that question led to the unthinkable, a thought that I didn't want to entertain because it seemed so ludicrous and paranoid, not to mention terrifying.

Had Jeff murdered George and Edith?

It seemed insane. He was my father-in-law. He was living in my house, sleeping in my bed. And although he was boorish and rude and clearly in no hurry to move on, that was a very long way from being a murderer.

Except . . . what about the way Gemma had cowered when he'd raised his hand over her when she was choking? Gemma's reaction told me that she knew he was capable of – or was even prone to – violence.

But then I told myself I was being stupid. Even if Jeff were capable of murder – and I had no evidence that he was – surely he wouldn't have had time. Would he?

I thought it through.

He had been gone for just over twenty minutes, perhaps slightly more. It was a brisk ten-minute walk between my house and the restaurant. I was sure Jeff could have run each way in five minutes, maybe six. He had been out of breath when he got back and a little sweaty, though he claimed that was because he'd run back from the shop.

Another thing in his favour: there hadn't been any blood on him. Would it be possible to kill someone with a hammer without being splattered with their blood? Only, I figured, if you wore some kind of plastic coverall, including glasses – similar to the protective eyewear we wore in the lab. He could have stripped off the coverall before leaving the house and hidden it somewhere before disposing of it later.

It was plausible, just, although when I pictured myself explaining this theory to anyone else, including the police, I felt even less confident. It seemed too far-fetched, especially as all of this – donning protective gear, taking it off and hiding it – would have added minutes to what was already a very tight window of time.

And why would he have done it? What would Jeff's motivation be? The only thing I could think was that Chloe was lying and had whispered something to George about her parents, something incriminating. Something Jeff would kill to keep secret.

I wished I could have made out what George had been trying to tell me with his last words. *Not w—*. Not *what*? Maybe it hadn't meant anything. He had been dying, his brain badly damaged. He could well have been talking nonsense.

I sighed. *Kill to keep secret.* It sounded crazy. Not the kind of thing that happens in real life. The police's theory, that it had been a burglary gone wrong, was far more likely.

And so I pushed my suspicions away. I didn't share them with anyone.

'All right, you obviously don't want to talk about your in-laws,' Amira said. 'How did it go with Effy on Tuesday? I haven't had a chance to ask you.'

I was happy to have something positive to focus on. 'Really, really well. I thought I'd push her, introduce her to gravitational waves. Of course, she'd already watched several YouTube videos about the subject. She got it straight away. Incredible.'

'And did you meet her dad?'

'Mr Mensah. Yeah, briefly. Nice guy. Really ambitious for his daughter, which is great to see. He invited me round to dinner.'

'Are you going to go?'

'I'm not sure. I think it pushes the professional boundaries a bit far. Anyway, like I said, he's a nice guy, and he understands that it needs to be fun. That if we push her too hard it might kill her enthusiasm.'

'I don't think there's much chance of that.'

'No.' I laughed. It felt good, after the week I'd had. Work was getting me through, and the lessons with Effy were a bright spot among the darkness. One thing that was, incontrovertibly, going right.

ω

All of the Robinsons, including Stuart, who had popped round to see his parents, were in my kitchen when I got home. Stuart, on his own this time, was chatting with Lizzy, who was clutching a mug of tea, and Jeff was wearing an apron. The room smelled of baking.

Gemma came over and kissed me hello.

'Dad made a cake,' she said with a raised eyebrow.

'Really?'

I had never seen Jeff show any interest in cooking, or anything domestic, before.

'You seem shocked,' Jeff said. 'I'm a man of many hidden talents.'

Chloe was in the living room, playing with Katie. I could hear laughter from the little girl, and then Chloe said something and Katie laughed even louder. I wondered if Lizzy had attempted to talk to her granddaughter or if she'd given up.

This was the kind of busy domestic scene I'd always wanted to be part of, and as Jeff bent down to open the oven door and peer inside, it suddenly seemed absurd that I could suspect him of murdering my neighbours. They were a flawed, difficult family, that was all. Aren't all families like that? As an only child, I had often fantasised about what it would be like to be part of a large clan. Here, as Gemma slipped her arm around my waist and grinned at her dad, who had burned the tips of his fingers and jumped across the kitchen shaking his hand – and Lizzy and Stuart laughed – it felt like that fantasy was made flesh. Maybe it wasn't so bad having the Robinsons here. Maybe they really could be the second family I had longed for.

'What kind of cake?' I asked.

'Banana loaf,' Jeff said.

My stomach lurched. The slices of banana loaf George had brought round the day he was murdered were still in a tin in the cupboard, untouched.

Jeff winked at me and all my positive thoughts evaporated.

It was deliberate. It had to be deliberate.

But before I could speak, Stuart said, 'Tell Elliot about the houses you looked at today, Mum.'

'You actually looked at some properties?' I said, unable to keep the incredulity out of my voice, my emotions swinging back the other way. I glanced at Gemma, who raised her eyebrows.

'Yeah, we went to see four,' Lizzy said, before launching into an enthusiastic description of the places they'd visited, all of which sounded perfect.

'The main problem is going to be choosing between them,' Jeff said. 'I think my favourite was the one in Sydenham Hill.'

'I really loved that place in Crystal Palace.'

They went on like this, arguing good-naturedly about the merits of the various houses, discussing the cost – they all sounded surprisingly reasonable – and I sat at the table, listening and wondering if I had finally cracked and this was all a hallucination.

It felt like the sun coming out. Maybe I had been wrong about the banana loaf. It wasn't deliberate.

Chloe came into the room with Katie. They were holding hands and Katie looked shy but happy.

'We were wondering if the cake was ready yet,' Chloe said. 'We're starving, aren't we, Katie?'

Katie nodded.

'Not yet, girls,' Jeff said with an affectionate smile. 'I'll give you a shout when it's done.'

'Thanks, Dad,' said Chloe.

'Thanks, Grandad,' added Katie.

He beamed as they left the room.

'When are you going to tell them about the surprise?' Stuart asked his dad.

'What surprise?' I asked.

'I was waiting till I'd served the cake, actually.' Jeff shrugged off his evident annoyance and picked up an envelope from the side, handing it to me.

'What's this?'

'Just open it,' said Lizzy.

It was a printout of an email. 'Stuart helped me with that,' Jeff said as I studied it. 'We thought the two of you could do with some time on your own. I mean, I know it can't be easy having us as guests, and you've obviously been through hell recently, Elliot, finding the old couple next door. We thought it might do you a bit of good to get away.'

They had booked us two nights at the Ashdown Park Hotel in Sussex. A four-star 'hotel and country club'.

Gemma took the sheet of paper from me. She seemed as stunned as I was.

'They've got a spa and do all sorts of massages,' Lizzy said. 'I wish me and Jeff were going.'

'I'm jealous too,' said Stuart.

Gemma narrowed her eyes and started to say, 'How could you—'

Jeff interrupted. 'Don't worry about that, darling. Just accept the gift.'

Two nights away with Gemma. It was just what we needed. 'We will,' I said.

Gemma opened her mouth, then shut it again, shaking her head almost imperceptibly. 'Okay. Thank you.'

But there was a problem. They had booked it for Saturday and Sunday night. Tomorrow and the day after. 'I've got work on Monday,' I said.

'Don't worry about that,' Jeff said. 'I've already spoken to that girl you work with. She said it's no problem. She's going to cover for you.'

'You spoke to Amira? She didn't say anything.'

Jeff looked smug. 'Of course she didn't. I swore her to secrecy.'

I looked at the sheet of paper again. 'Well, thank you,' I said. 'It would definitely be good to get away for a couple of nights.' Away from my in-laws. Away from George and Edith's place, and the memories that smacked me every time I stepped outside.

'And you don't need to worry,' Jeff said with a broad grin. 'Your house will be in safe hands while you're gone.'

Chapter 28

The hotel was in Ashdown Forest, which was famous for being the setting of the Winnie-the-Pooh stories; the real Hundred Acre Wood. We arrived just after midday, driving along quiet country lanes overhung by trees in the last throes of their autumnal glory, a canopy of oranges and reds in every shade. The further we got from London, the more the tension in my stomach had unknotted and melted away. In the passenger seat, Gemma was serene and beautiful, frequently reaching across to squeeze my thigh. Away from her parents, she was transformed. Here was the relaxed, happy person I'd fallen in love with. Rolling up the path to the hotel, I felt as if we'd both been in a pit for the last few weeks, and now, here we were, emerging into the light.

Our room was huge, with a four-poster bed, sofa and armchair. There was a whirlpool bath too, and a bottle of champagne waiting for us. The price hadn't been on the email but it must have cost Jeff and Lizzy a fortune.

I put down our bags and popped open the champagne, pouring us both a glass. After a few sips, I pulled Gemma towards me, kissing her. I slipped my hands up the back of her sweater and she kissed me back.

Afterwards, lying on the bed in the white towelling robes that came with the room, Gemma said, 'This is just what we needed.'

'I know.'

She propped herself up on one elbow. 'I'm sorry about my parents. I know they're a nightmare.'

'I'm actually feeling quite warm towards them at the moment. And they're not going to be staying with us for much longer.'

She hesitated before saying, 'No.'

I should have asked her why she'd paused like that, but told myself she'd been distracted. I didn't want anything to kill the mood.

I had persuaded myself overnight, after a pleasant evening during which Jeff and Lizzy had acted like dream relatives and we had talked about their plans for their new house and garden, that it was crazy to think that Jeff had killed George. A short, post-traumatic period of insanity on my part.

The rest of the day was lovely. We used the spa, walked around the lush grounds, had dinner and went to bed, where we made love again. It was wonderful, just like in the first weeks of our relationship, and lying in Gemma's arms I felt all the tension of the past weeks melt away. I went to sleep feeling sated and exhausted. It had been a good day.

It was the last good day we had.

ω

'Let's go for a walk,' Gemma said, jumping up from the bed.

'I was hoping we could stay here for a while.'

But she was already getting dressed. 'I want to hear the crunch of leaves underfoot. Feel fresh air on my face.' She chucked my clothes at me. 'Come on, husband, or I'll have to go without you.'

The path through the forest was, indeed, carpeted with fallen leaves. We walked hand in hand towards a spot marked on a map at the edge of the trees, not talking much, just enjoying being away from the city. Being on our own. The landmark we were trying to reach was three miles away and it took an hour to get there, but the shouts of children up ahead told us we were almost there.

Poohsticks Bridge. 'It's so ordinary,' I said, because it was: just a simple wooden bridge, with a fence each side, over a narrow stream.

The children we'd heard were on the bridge with their dad. A boy and a girl, around five and seven years old. They did what you were supposed to do here: found a couple of twigs and dropped them in the water, urging them on excitedly as they drifted beneath our feet. The boy's twig emerged first and he acted as if he'd won the World Cup, his older sister congratulating him. Then they did it again, and this time the girl's twig was fastest. Her little brother exploded into tears, stamping his foot on the bridge and wailing. He refused to be consoled and their dad ushered them away.

'Do you want a go?' Gemma asked, bounding off Tigger-like to find some sticks. She handed me the larger of the pair.

'Shouldn't I have found my own?' I said.

She smiled at me. 'Is that a life rule? That one should always find one's own Poohstick?'

I laughed. 'I think it should be.'

We chucked our sticks into the stream and waited. Gemma's came through first. We kept waiting but mine didn't appear.

'It must have got stuck,' I said. 'A stuck stick.'

'Want to try again?'

I put my arms around her. 'I'd rather head back to the warm.'

On the way back to the hotel, Gemma was quiet and I detected a shift in her mood. I put it down to tiredness or a hangover. We'd drunk a lot of champagne and wine the night before, although that wasn't unusual for Gemma at the moment. She'd been coming home with a bottle of wine every night and always polished it off. Once or twice I'd noticed the smell of cigarette smoke on her clothes too, though I didn't want to interrogate her about it. I thought perhaps she'd stood outside with Lizzy while she smoked.

Trying to fill the silence, I said, 'That kid was funny, wasn't he? Having a tantrum when he lost the race.'

'A little horror. His poor dad.'

'Poor? I think he's lucky.' I wasn't just saying it. Watching the father with his children, I had experienced a twinge of envy. It was the kind of thing I'd always imagined myself doing one day: taking my kids for a walk in the woods, playing games, introducing them to nature. Teaching children like Effy over the past couple of years had made me think increasingly about how nice it would be to have kids of my own. I wasn't exactly broody, but I could feel myself heading in that direction.

Gemma wasn't having any of it. 'What, lucky to have a grizzling brat?'

I stopped walking. 'Oh my God. You sounded exactly like your mum then.'

'Don't say that!'

'I'm sorry, Gemma, but you did.'

She glared at me and I realised I'd made a terrible faux pas.

'I told you never to say that!'

In fact, she'd said she'd kill me if I ever compared her to her mum.

A cyclist was coming along the path. We waited for him to pass, nodding hello and smiling, pretending everything was okay.

Gemma and I hadn't discussed children yet, one of the negative side effects of our whirlwind romance and quick marriage. I'd assumed it was a topic that would come up soon.

'Don't you like children?' I said, even though I knew this wasn't the best time and place to bring it up.

'It's not that I don't like them.'

'Then what?'

'I just don't want any.'

I reeled. Even though Gemma and I hadn't discussed it, that didn't mean I hadn't imagined it. Gemma and me and a chubby baby, a manic toddler, a little girl or boy. Of course, I knew having children was hard work, that it wasn't all giggles and contentment – far from it – but I suppose I had assumed it would happen at some point down the line.

It was what most people did. And, as George had said to me shortly after Gemma and I got married, we lived in a house that was perfect for raising a family.

Gemma started walking again, going at full speed. I dashed after her.

'We need to talk about this,' I said.

She stopped. Her throat was mottled pink, fists clenching and unclenching by her side. 'My parents were a disaster. You've seen how they talk to me. If I'm so like my mother, why the hell would you want to have children with me?'

'I never said you were like her.'

'You did! About two minutes ago.'

'No, I said you sounded like her, but just that one sentence.'

'That's bad enough! And you're right. I can feel it sometimes, when I hear myself say or think certain things. I look like her too, more and more every year. I can see myself turning into her.' She pushed her hair out of her face. 'And you know what? It's happening faster now they're around. It's like I could hold it off when they were hundreds of miles away, but now they're here . . . it's like my greatest nightmare coming true.'

'You're not turning into her, Gemma,' I said, trying to take hold of her hand. She shook me off. 'You have been different though, since they arrived. You've been . . .'

'What? Spit it out.'

'Well, you've been drinking a lot.'

'No, I haven't.'

I put my hands up. 'Okay. If you say so.'

She glared at me. 'All right, so maybe I've been drinking a bit more. So what? You're hardly teetotal.'

Her voice was louder than normal. There was a man on the path ahead walking a dog and he looked back at us. Even though it was mid-morning the woods were growing darker, the clouds thickening above us.

169

'We've both been through a lot of stress,' I said, trying to placate her and deciding not to mention that I thought she might have been smoking. I wanted to rewind, to get back to where we'd been thirty minutes ago: happy and relaxed. 'Hey, I thought we were feeling good about your parents this weekend,' I said. 'I mean, they paid for this trip.'

Her laugh was bitter. 'Yeah. *They* paid.'

'What do you mean by that?'

'They used money I lent them.'

I stared at her. 'You're kidding?'

'I wish I was. The other day, they told me they'd run out of cash and asked if they could borrow some. Dad said he was waiting for a payment from some guy in France.'

'What guy?'

'I don't know. He said they'd sold all their stuff to some furniture dealer or something and were expecting payment any day.'

I was shocked. More than that: angry. 'How much money?'

'Let's just say it wiped out my savings account. But apparently I'll get it back soon.' She stared into the trees, not looking at me. 'When they told us about this trip, I assumed they must have received the money, but when I asked my mum about it later she told me it was still on its way, and by then you were all excited about our weekend away.'

'Oh, Gemma, you should have told me.'

'Maybe. But I wanted to come here too. To get away from them for a couple of days.'

A couple of raindrops landed on my face. From the look of the sky, we didn't have long before it would be raining heavily. And with the raindrops came a dreadful realisation.

'Wait. If they don't have any money, how are they going to pay for a deposit on a house?'

She gave me a look, like *now you get it*.

The rain was beginning to come down more steadily now. The woods around us had grown dark. Gemma seemed to weigh up her words before saying, 'You've had a hint of what they're really like. But that's all it is. A hint. You don't know the things they've done. The stuff they did when I was a kid. If you talked to people back home . . .'

'What do you mean? What things?' I had gone cold inside. Gemma didn't respond. 'Come on, Gemma, tell me.'

'No. I can't.'

She set off again, going fast, head down against the rain. I hesitated for a moment, trying to take in what she'd said, then ran to catch up with her. I grabbed her arm but she pulled away.

'Gemma, you have to tell me.'

'No, I can't. I can't talk about it.'

'But—'

'Elliot, please, leave me alone.'

She yelled it, and a pair of women in the near distance, towards the hotel, turned sharply to stare at us as if I had attacked her. One of them made a move towards us but Gemma raised a hand to indicate she was okay.

I said her name but she cut me off. 'Elliot, I think it's best if I'm alone for a little while. I'm going to use the spa, have a swim, try to calm down. Okay?'

'Okay.'

'Why don't you go for a drive or something? Enjoy the peace and quiet.'

She headed towards the hotel and I watched her go, wondering how the hell the day had fallen apart so quickly. But I knew who was to blame. Jeff and Lizzy.

Chapter 29

You've had a hint of what they're really like . . . You don't know the things they've done . . . If you talked to people back home . . .

I headed through the rain to my car. I was going to take Gemma's advice and go for a drive. And I knew exactly where to go.

According to my satnav, Winchelsea Beach, the seaside village where Gemma had grown up, was just over forty miles away. An hour and a half's drive, though I reckoned I could do it quicker if the roads were clear and I put my foot down.

It was Sunday and there was very little traffic. I arrived in Winchelsea Beach, having skirted around Hastings and driven through a pretty village called Fairlight, at half twelve. I parked on a long road that ran parallel to the coastline and got out, pulling up my hood against the rain, then walked across to the beach.

It had been a while since I'd seen the sea. The tide was in and foaming waves clawed at the pebbles, spitting at me and forcing me to step back. There wasn't another soul in sight, unless seagulls have souls. A pair of them were squabbling over what looked like a cuttlefish. To my right were crumbling cliffs which blocked the path, houses teetering on the edge above. Stretching towards the cliffs was a straight row of houses, most of them old and showing all the signs of spending many years being battered by wind and sea spray, with a few newer houses among them. I could imagine Londoners coming down and buying these places up, using them as summer homes. It was so beautiful here, even on a wet and choppy day like today, that I was half tempted to look into doing the same myself.

What exactly was I going to do here today? I didn't even know the Robinsons' old address. But I had driven here thinking there must be someone around here who remembered them. Someone who might be able to tell me something. And where do most people in small communities hang out and trade gossip? The pub.

I checked Google Maps and found there was one pub nearby, a short drive away. I got back in the car.

It was busy, the smell of Sunday roasts filling the air and making my stomach growl, reminding me it was lunchtime. I looked around. I needed to find some people who looked like they'd lived here for a long time, though I knew I couldn't just walk up to them and ask if they knew Jeff and Lizzy. It would be better if I sat down, had some lunch and then tried to start a conversation. There were two men in the corner with an empty table beside theirs. They looked around Jeff and Lizzy's age. I ordered a roast and went over to sit at the table, wishing I'd brought a newspaper with me. Instead, I did what everyone does these days when they're alone or in company: I got out my phone and stared at the screen, trying not to look like a Billy No-Mates.

I was hoping that I might have received a message from Gemma. Something conciliatory. Realising I was being a hypocrite, I texted her: *Hope you're OK. I hate arguing with you. I went for quite a long drive and am just having lunch. Love you xxx*

My food came and I ate, listening in on the chat at the next table. They were talking about a quiz night that had happened here a few days ago, before moving on to talking about fishing. I ascertained they were keen sea anglers. There were a number of empty pint glasses on their table, indicating they were in the middle of a heavy lunchtime session. I kept racking my brains for something to say to them, something engaging that would start a conversation. All I could think of was a research paper I'd read about the increasing amount of chemicals including pesticides and coolants found in fish. But I didn't think that would endear me to them.

In the end I had a stroke of luck. A golden retriever appeared from nowhere and sat at my feet, gazing imploringly at my plate. I gave it the remains of my Yorkshire pudding.

'You shouldn't feed him,' said one of the men, who had a straggly white beard. 'You won't get rid of him now.'

'I don't mind,' I said, ruffling the dog's fur. He sniffed at my jeans. 'I think he can smell my cat.'

The men were about to lose interest in me so I hurriedly said, 'This is a nice place. Great food. A friend of mine recommended it to me.'

The other man, who also sported a beard, this one ginger, nodded at me like he was entertaining an idiot.

I pressed on. 'Yeah, it was a friend who used to live around here, once upon a time. Jeff Robinson, his name is.'

The men exchanged a look. White Beard snorted. 'You don't want to listen to anything Jeff Robinson says.'

Bingo.

Chapter 30

I kept my face neutral. 'You know Jeff?'

'Knew him,' said White Beard. His friend was staring at me through narrowed eyes, one hand pulling at his facial hair. 'I haven't seen him for a long time. Fifteen years or so.'

I nodded. 'Yes, he told me he and Lizzy moved away in the mid-noughties.'

'Lizzy? They're still together, then?'

'Of course they're still together,' said Ginger Beard. He had a gruff voice, as if he'd been gargling seawater. 'I couldn't ever see those two splitting up.'

'Huh, no.' White Beard laughed. 'Nobody else would want them.'

I laughed along, then said, 'I'm Elliot, by the way.'

'Dave,' said the guy with the white beard.

After a long pause, his friend told me his name. 'Dennis.'

Dave and Dennis. They were a proper double act. And they were both, I realised, quite drunk. That was good. It made them more likely to be indiscreet.

'I suppose we should be nice about Jeff, seeing as you're his friend,' said Dave, to which Dennis let out an amused grunt.

'Oh. Well, I wouldn't say we're friends, exactly . . .' As soon as I said it I realised it was a bad move. Dennis had his pint of bitter halfway to his lips but he froze before smacking it back on to the table.

Dave ran his fingers over his snowy beard. 'Then what are you if you're not his friend?'

'Are you police?' Dennis raised an eyebrow.

His words made my heart beat faster, but now I had a dilemma. I either needed to come clean and admit Jeff and Lizzy were my parents-in-law, or go along with their idea that I was with the police. I made a quick decision: I'd let them believe what they wanted to believe.

'What's he done now?' Dave asked.

I cleared my throat. 'I'm afraid I can't divulge that. I'm just looking for information about Jeff's background. Something that might help me.'

The dog, seeing how serious the humans had become and realising it wasn't going to get any more scraps, slunk away. It had reached the other side of the pub before either Dennis or Dave spoke.

Dave opened his mouth to speak but Dennis shot him a warning look. 'You're really going to talk to a cop about Jeff?'

Dennis shrugged. 'I don't owe that bastard any favours.' He looked at me. 'I sold him a car. Paid me half up front and then buggered off without coughing up the rest.'

I really had hit pay dirt here. 'Sounds like him.'

Dave grunted again, then looked over my shoulder, clearly concerned he might be overheard, but the pub was noisy: the hum of conversation and clatter of cutlery, plus a man at the bar telling a joke at high volume.

'I used to know the woman who lived next door to them,' Dave said. 'You know they lived in one of those little places up near the holiday park?'

I pretended I did.

'Janet Stafford. Nice woman. They made her life hell,' Dave said.

'In what way?'

'Constant noise. Complaining about every little thing she did. She had this cat that she doted on but they were always complaining about it crapping in their garden. Then one day it turned up dead – the vet said it had eaten rat poison.' He gave me a meaningful look. 'Of course, they couldn't prove the Robinsons had given it to the cat but Janet knew.'

I pictured Charlie, rubbing himself against Jeff. The way Lizzy kept away from the cat. If either of them was responsible for poisoning Janet Stafford's pet, it had to be Lizzy.

'The worst of it was . . .' Dave trailed off. 'Actually, I think I need to know what they've done before I say any more. Is it one of the kids? Has something happened to them?'

'It does involve their children, yes.'

Dave picked up his pint but didn't drink from it. 'Janet told me she used to hear things in that house. They were always yelling at those kids. Yelling at each other too. Sometimes, she said, she'd hear sobbing in the middle of the night. Screaming too. A child, screaming its head off.'

I could feel the lunch I'd just eaten curdling in my stomach. 'And she never reported it?'

'She didn't think your lot would do anything about it.'

'And she was terrified of them,' Dennis added, his voice a deep growl. He had clearly decided to join in. Perhaps Jeff owed him money too.

'Did she ever see anything? Like Jeff or Lizzy hitting their children?'

'No. But she told me the two older kids . . . What were their names?'

'Gemma and Stuart,' I said.

'Yeah, that was it. She'd seen them playing in the garden in the summer in this little paddling pool they had. According to Janet, they had bruises all over them. Bites too.'

'Bites? You mean . . . human bite marks?'

Dave finally drank some of his pint. 'That's what she said.'

I tried to keep my face blank, like none of this was surprising to me. And the truth was, I wasn't hugely shocked. Appalled, but not shocked. It was all beginning to make sense: why Gemma closed down when she was around her parents, why Stuart was so nervous all the time. I thought about Chloe too, still attached to her parents like a child who hadn't been allowed to grow up.

'I need to speak to Janet Stafford,' I said.

'Know any good clairvoyants?' Dennis asked.

'Oh.'

'Been dead ten years now.'

Beside him, Dave was deep in thought. 'I don't blame their daughter for running off with those hippies.'

'They weren't hippies,' Dennis said, with a roll of his eyes. 'They were born-agains.'

'Seemed liked hippies to me.'

I tried to get them back on track. 'The girl ran off with them, you said?'

Dennis nodded. 'Yeah. They were staying in this caravan in Fairlight, up on the cliffs. A young couple . . . What were their bloody names?' He thought about it. 'I think she was called Delilah. I remember because whenever I saw her I got that Tom Jones song stuck in my head. Also, she was a bit of crumpet.' I had to force myself not to laugh. I hadn't heard anyone use that expression since I was very young. 'Gorgeous, she was. Long red hair, these big blue eyes, like something out of a painting.'

'And Gemma . . . ran off with them?'

'Well, she moved in with them. Into their caravan. Found Jesus, I guess.' Dave leaned forward. 'She wasn't bad herself, young Gemma. I even felt a bit jealous of Mickey, shacked up in that caravan with those two gorgeous birds.'

'When the caravan's rocking, don't come knocking,' said Dennis.

I hoped I didn't look sickened or confused. Gemma had never told me any of this. 'Mickey? That was the guy?'

'Yeah,' Dennis replied. Then he lowered his voice. 'A black guy, he was.'

I looked at my surroundings. Everyone here was white. I grew up in London, so the idea of living somewhere like this, where everyone had the same skin colour, was alien to me. But I could imagine how a young black man who lived in a caravan with two white women must have stood out around here.

'So what happened?' I asked.

'Jeff went mad, that's what happened,' Dennis said. 'According to Janet, he didn't know where Gemma had gone at first, but as soon as he found out he stormed up there, beat the crap out of Mickey and dragged the girl home.'

'Do you know how old she was?'

'I dunno. Sixteen? Maybe seventeen? Mickey and Delilah moved on soon after that. I heard Jeff threatened to chuck them over the cliff if they didn't clear off.'

'I don't suppose you know either of their surnames, do you?'

They both shook their heads. 'But I'm sure you'll find reports about what happened to them in your whatchamacallit. Your database. It was big news around here.'

'You mean Jeff beating Mickey up?'

They exchanged a dark look. 'I don't want to make any false accusations, even against a scumbag like Jeff,' Dennis said.

'Just ask him what happened to the caravan,' Dave said.

I could tell they weren't going to say any more.

'Is there anyone else you can think of who might be willing to talk to me? Like, a former employer? Or old colleagues of Jeff's?'

'Ha!' Dennis found this highly amusing. 'Jeff never had a job, not a proper one anyway. Neither of them did. He did a bit of wheeling and dealing but they lived off the state.'

'I remember talking to him about it once,' said Dave. 'I knew a bloke who was looking for labourers. Good money. I asked Jeff if he was interested but he just laughed.'

'Some people are like that, aren't they?' added Dennis. 'Parasites. They're all take, take, take without putting anything back. Of course, it was easier in those days to scab off the state. "Don't want to work? Don't worry – we'll pay you to sit around and watch telly all day."'

Dave started to rant about scroungers and hard-working taxpayers. I nodded along, distracted by a beep from my phone. It was a text from Gemma: *I hate arguing too. I want to see you. How much longer will you be? Xxx*

'I need to get going,' I said, standing up. 'Thank you so much for all that. It's been really useful.'

Dave seemed surprised, but then glanced meaningfully at the empty pint glasses on the table, their insides streaked with foam.

'Let me buy you both a drink,' I said.

I bought two pints of bitter. As I placed them before the two anglers, Dave lifted his bloodshot eyes to meet mine.

'I'm never going to get that money, am I?'

'It's doubtful.'

He nodded morosely. 'I hope you get them, whatever it is they've done now. And I hope they both go down for a long time.'

ϖ

I left with the feeling that there was more that Dave and Dennis hadn't told me, something even worse – *Just ask him what happened to the caravan* – but I needed to get back.

I was torn. Should I tell Gemma what I'd learned and ask her about her stay with the two born-again Christians? Should I go deeper than that and ask her about her home life with her parents? I had no idea how Gemma would react if I told her I'd been talking to strangers about her.

I drove on autopilot, blindly following the satnav, mind and heart racing. I could understand why Gemma hadn't told me much about her childhood. I guessed she wanted to put it all behind her, to bury the past and not have to deal with it or think about it. Perhaps she had already dealt with it, through therapy or on her own, and didn't want to pick the scab. She'd told me about her self-harming because the scars were visible and she had little choice. But there was no need to reveal the source of mental and emotional scars, was there? Maybe, too, she didn't want people to view her as a victim.

Another question: why had Gemma invited Jeff and Lizzy to stay with us if they had treated her terribly in the past? I had no answer to that, except that families are complicated. Blood is blood, and severing ties with your parents is hard, no matter how much pain it might cause to stay connected. And perhaps Gemma had let them come to stay because of her sister. Maybe she wanted to check Chloe was okay, or she simply wanted to see her, spend time with her. Not that Gemma and Chloe had hung out much since the Robinsons had arrived on our doorstep. In fact, Gemma had shown Chloe very little sympathy at all. There were clearly issues there. Did Gemma think that Chloe had been treated better than herself and Stuart? Was she resentful?

I went back and forth, over and over the same questions, always coming back to the big one: should I talk to Gemma about it? Or should I do some more digging first?

I parked at the hotel and sat in the car for a while, finally making a decision.

I was going to have to come clean. Talk to her. It was the right thing to do.

Gemma had texted me to tell me she was waiting in the hotel bar. I headed there, determined to have it out with her, to ask her to open up to me. But when I got there she was sitting with another couple, two guys she had met in the spa, and they were all half-cut. As soon as I arrived, Gemma ordered another bottle of Prosecco, then another, and we ended up sitting with the other couple for hours, having dinner together, while Gemma got increasingly drunk.

Back in our room, I tried to talk to her but she shushed me. She was barely able to stand up.

She fell on to the bed and managed to push herself upright. I sat beside her and she pulled me into a kiss, moaning as she pushed her tongue into my mouth and grabbed at my hair. She pulled my head away from hers and looked into my eyes, though hers could hardly focus.

'You'd do anything for me, wouldn't you?' she asked, her voice slurred.

She tried to pull her top over her head but couldn't manage it. She slumped back.

'Gemma?'

She had passed out.

Chapter 31

I got up early after a restless night, frustrated by my inability to talk to Gemma, and went for a swim in the hotel pool. When I got back to the room, I woke Gemma and told her we needed to check out. She was so pale she was almost green. I was about to ask her if she wanted anything to eat, if breakfast would help her feel better, when she jumped up and ran to the bathroom. I listened to her vomiting into the toilet. Now was not a good time to talk to her. It would have to wait till we got back to London.

We hit roadworks on the way home, a tailback that stretched for a mile, impatient drivers leaning out of their windows. Every time someone sounded their horn, Gemma flinched.

'Painkillers not kicked in yet?' I asked.

'I'm never drinking again,' she said, for the third time that morning. 'The only thing that's going to help is sleep.'

She closed her eyes and leaned her head against the passenger-side window, leaving me alone with my thoughts as we inched through the traffic. My gut reaction was to feel irritated by her behaviour and the self-inflicted wound of her hangover, but I took a deep breath and told myself she deserved sympathy and understanding, not disapprobation. The more I thought about what Dave and Dennis had told me, the clearer the image of what Gemma's childhood must have been like grew.

More than ever, I wanted Jeff and Lizzy out of my house, for Gemma's sake as much as mine. The sight of her slumped against the car door reminded me of how much she'd been drinking since they arrived, how different she was when they were around.

And how urgent it was to get them to move out.

ᴥ

We parked outside the house. Cuckoo Lane was quiet, wind blowing leaves along the street, the crime-scene tape that still ringed George and Edith's place vibrating in the breeze.

'I'm going straight to bed,' Gemma said.

'Can you not wait? I want to talk to your parents.'

She groaned.

'Come on, Gemma. We need to speak to them about this money they borrowed from you and whether they've received the cash they're owed. If the whole thing isn't a lie, that is.'

She didn't try to defend them.

'I'm going to tell them I want them to move out,' I said. 'It's time we gave them a deadline. One week today. I think that's fair.'

'But . . . what if they can't find anywhere to go?'

'I don't know. Maybe they can move in with Stuart.'

She shook her head. 'No.'

'We need to be united on this, Gemma. Ideally, *you* should tell them as they're your parents.'

'I can't,' she whispered.

Again, I fought back my irritation and reminded myself how difficult this must be for her. She'd had a terrible childhood. Her insides must have been churning with conflicting emotions. 'I understand. I'll do it.'

I went to open the car door but she put her hand on my arm. 'What about Chloe? I can't bear the thought of her being out on the street.'

'They're not going to be on the street.'

'They will be if they can't find anywhere else to live.'

With everything I thought I now knew about Jeff and Lizzy, I wasn't too upset by the idea of them being homeless. But I said, 'Listen, if it comes to it, Chloe can stay with us. For a while, anyway, until she gets a job. Maybe I can find someone who'll give her some work.'

Gemma nodded. She looked sick and miserable. Her skin was grey and damp.

'But we can deal with that separately. Maybe they'll surprise us and tell us the money's come through and they've already found somewhere. Wouldn't that be wonderful?'

'Yeah,' she said. 'So would world peace.'

I left it at that and got out of the car, lifting our bags out of the boot.

'Jeff? Lizzy?' I called as I went inside. 'We're back.'

Silence, and the house felt empty. The post was on the doormat, indicating they'd been out a while, though the postman didn't usually come until mid-morning.

'Maybe they're out looking at a house,' I said to Gemma as she followed me towards the kitchen. 'Or perhaps—' I stopped dead. 'What the hell?'

The kitchen was in total disarray. Dirty dishes and mugs were stacked up in the sink and there were three plates on the table containing what looked like the remnants of a full English breakfast. There was a puddle of milk on the floor by the sink. There was cereal all over the counter and a pile of what looked like cat vomit by the back door.

Worse than this, there was an odd gassy smell and, if I concentrated, I could hear hissing.

I rushed over to the cooker. One of the dials on the hob was turned slightly to the left. I turned it off.

'They left the gas on,' I said, opening the window. 'What are they playing at? And look at the state of this place.'

My beautiful house, that had always been so well ordered and tidy when I lived here on my own. It wasn't just the surface mess; the whole place felt grimy. Tainted. I went into the living room. A pizza box on the coffee table. An unpleasant smell, like stale cigarette smoke. That was when I noticed the burn hole on the sofa and the stain on the rug. I got down on all fours and took a sniff. Red wine.

I got back to my feet. I knew Lizzy smoked, although she always did it in secret, but I thought they were both teetotal. Maybe it was Chloe, helping herself to—

'No. Please,' I whispered.

I ran back to the kitchen, praying I wasn't correct, that the spilled red wine was just a cheap bottle from the supermarket. I rushed over to the wine rack.

'It's gone,' I said to Gemma.

'What?'

'My bottle of Cappellano. The one my professor gave to me when I graduated.'

I thumped the counter beside the wine rack.

'It's just a bottle of wine,' Gemma said in a soothing tone.

'No. It's not. It wasn't just a bottle of wine. It was a gift, a special gift. I was saving it.'

I ran up the stairs, jumping over the creaky step, and banged on Chloe's door. I didn't wait for an answer before pushing it open.

She was lying on the bed, naked, her hair wrapped in a towel. She looked up at me, startled.

I backed away from her room, hot with embarrassment. Gemma came up the stairs, moving towards Chloe's door.

'Don't go in there.'

'Why?'

'She's not decent.' I laughed at my own choice of words and ran a hand over my face.

'Wait. You mean she's naked? Didn't you knock before you went in?'

'Yes, but . . . I don't want to talk about this now.' I pushed past her and ran down the stairs. I was sweating, and as I passed a radiator I touched it. Red-hot. They must have cranked the thermostat up and left it when they went out. More expense. Then I remembered the puddle of cat sick by the back door and went to take a closer look.

What had made him throw up? The gas? With a lurch of horror, I remembered what the two anglers had told me about the Robinsons' old neighbour's cat dying from rat poison.

I called Charlie's name and checked the cat flap, worried it might be stuck again, but it was fine. The chances were he was outside. Safe. But I needed to know. I went through the house, investigating all Charlie's favourite hiding places, but there was no sign of him. A missing – no, stolen – bottle of wine was nothing compared to my cat. If Jeff or Lizzy had done something to him . . .

I found Gemma in our bedroom, unpacking.

'I can't find Charlie,' I said.

Gemma ignored my words. 'I still can't believe what you did.'

'What, walking in on Chloe? It was an accident! This is one of the reasons why we can't have your family here anymore. I should be able to walk around my own house without worrying I'm going to walk in on a naked woman.'

'What, you want to throw her out now, too?'

That made me pause. I had always assumed Chloe would go when Jeff and Lizzy finally left. 'I don't know.'

'What about me?' she said. 'Do you want me gone as well?'

'Don't be ridiculous. I want it to be like it was before. The two of us. Three, actually.' I exited the room – I needed to find Charlie – and went into the master bedroom to see if he was in there.

I stopped. There was something strange about the room. It took me a moment to realise what it was.

The bed. It was different. The headboard, which had been white, was grey. Instead of a divan base, the bed now had black iron legs.

I couldn't believe it. Jeff and Lizzy had replaced the bed, which I'd bought when I moved in here, with a new one. And, staring at it, I realised I recognised this bed from the Ikea catalogue that had been hanging around the house; the catalogue that Jeff and Lizzy had been through, circling items.

I left the room and yelled Gemma's name. But before she could respond, the front door opened and Jeff came in, with Lizzy behind him. I ran down the stairs.

'Ah, Elliot, how was it?' Jeff asked when he spotted me.

'Have a lovely time?' said Lizzy with a wink. I realised Gemma had followed me and was standing behind me.

'Where the hell have you been?' I demanded.

Jeff and Lizzy exchanged an amused look. 'Sorry, *Dad*,' said Jeff. 'We went for a walk. Did we break our curfew?'

Lizzy laughed.

I could feel a tension headache coming on, a pink fog clouding my vision.

'Forget that,' I said. 'What have you done to my house?'

'Our house,' said a voice behind me. Gemma.

I half-turned towards her as Lizzy said, 'Yeah, Elliot. It's not just your house now. Don't forget that.'

I stared at her as she wagged a finger at me. Chloe had come out of her room now too; dressed, thankfully. Jeff and Lizzy looked up at me from below. Gemma and Chloe were above. It felt like all of them, even Gemma, had me surrounded, trapped in my own territory. The headache was getting worse and I had to hold on to the banister to stop myself from falling. But then Gemma came down and put her hands on my shoulders, supporting me, and I took strength from that. I momentarily forgot about my search for Charlie.

It was time I stood up for myself.

'I want to talk to all of you,' I said, keeping my voice firm. 'In the kitchen. Now.'

Chapter 32

We gathered in the kitchen. Gemma and Chloe sat at the dining table. Chloe wouldn't meet my eye. Gemma looked like she wished a magician would appear and make her vanish in a puff of smoke. They kept glancing up at their parents, and in that moment they both appeared awfully young, like they'd been thrown back to their childhood. Except back then, there was nobody to stand up to Jeff and Lizzy. That was my role now. To stand up for Gemma and Chloe and myself.

Jeff and Lizzy stood with their backs to the counter, side by side, arms folded. I was by the back door, facing all of them, the puddle of cat vomit at my feet. I was spinning from the adrenaline that coursed through my system, and I took several deep breaths in an attempt to calm down. Then, out of the corner of my eye, I spied Charlie in the back garden, crouching beneath a shrub. The relief helped me feel a little better and able to dial down my anger. I didn't want this to turn into a shouting match.

'Sorry about the mess,' Jeff said before I had a chance to speak.

'Yeah,' said Lizzy. 'We were going to clean it up but you got back sooner than we thought.'

'The mess is just a minor part of it,' I said. 'First, I want to talk about the bed.'

Lizzy shrugged. 'The old one wasn't very comfortable so we replaced it. The new one's lovely. Great mattress.'

'You've replaced our bed?' Gemma sounded stunned.

'What have you done with the old one?' I demanded, the anger returning.

'The mattress is in the shed,' Jeff said. 'I took the rest of it apart and put it in the loft.'

I could feel my face turning purple. 'I can't . . . I can't even . . . How could you afford a new bed anyway? Gemma told me you haven't got any money. That you had to borrow some off her.' I looked over at my wife. She was examining the surface of the table and I experienced another stab of irritation. It would help if she'd back me up right now, even if it was hard for her. 'I want you to ring the delivery company and get them to take that monstrosity away.'

'Nope. Sorry, we're not going to do that,' Jeff said.

'What the hell is wrong with you?'

'There's nothing wrong with us, Elliot. We just needed a more comfortable bed, that's all.'

'Have you got the money you've been waiting for?' Gemma asked before I could think of some way to respond.

Jeff stopped smirking. 'No.'

'Then when do you expect to get it?' I said.

'Don't know.' His voice was dark, with a hint of belligerence.

I waited to see if he would say anything else. When he didn't, I said, 'Then how are you going to pay for a deposit on a house?'

The room was silent. All I could hear was the drip-drip of the tap, which appeared to have sprung a leak while we were in Sussex. Lizzy seemed to be having a problem controlling her lips; they wobbled like she was trying to suppress a smile.

'Well?' I asked.

'We're going to have to wait,' Jeff said with a shrug. 'It's unfortunate but we can't afford to move out yet. Don't worry, though, mate. I'm sure it won't be too long. This French guy—'

I cut him off. My words came out as a half-whisper, half-shriek. 'This isn't acceptable!'

The smirk became a sneer. 'You're not in the classroom now, Elliot. We're not underprivileged kids that you can lord it over. It's unfortunate, but the fact is we don't currently have the funds to rent anywhere. I don't know what else you want me to say.'

I was aware of a vein pulsing on my forehead.

'Gemma said it would be fine,' Lizzy said. 'We spoke to her before you swanned off for your weekend away.'

I turned to my wife, who looked stricken and more sick than ever. 'I said it might be all right for a little longer . . .'

'I'm pretty sure you said we could stay as long as we like,' said Lizzy.

'I didn't say that.'

'Yes, you did,' said Jeff. 'And now you're backing down in front of Elliot. Two-faced, that's what you are. You always have been.'

'Leave her alone!' I snapped. 'She probably said that because she's scared of you.'

Jeff seemed stunned. He was a great actor, I'd give him that. 'Scared? Of us?' He laughed.

To my surprise, Lizzy interjected, using a soothing tone. 'Maybe he meant "scared of hurting our feelings". Is that right, Elliot?'

I was close to losing it.

'Why did you go and look at all those houses if you knew you couldn't afford to move out?'

Another shrug from Jeff. 'We thought the cash would be here by now. But, like I said, it isn't. And it's going to take a little longer.'

'But how much longer?'

'I told you, I don't know. Jesus, Elliot.' He put his hand to his mouth, showing me his bitten, jagged fingernails. 'Oops. Sorry, Gem. Didn't mean to take the Lord's name in vain.'

I took half a step towards Jeff. 'You should have been honest with me. When you came to stay you said it would only be for a couple of weeks.'

'Yeah, and it's only been three.'

It felt like so much longer. 'But now it sounds like you're saying you want to stay here indefinitely.'

'No, I'm not saying that, Elliot.' The way he kept using my name made me bristle. 'What exactly do you want us to do? Find some cardboard boxes and go and live on the street?'

'You don't need cardboard boxes. You can take your new bed with you.'

Jeff laughed. 'That wasn't bad, for you. Listen, Elliot, I'm sorry we're encroaching on you. I know you're not used to being part of a big, messy family. You're a little orphan boy who's used to having everything just how he likes it.'

I'm pretty sure my mouth fell open at this point.

Jeff was about to go on when Chloe, who I hadn't expected to speak, said, 'Don't be so insensitive, Dad.'

'But it's true. Maybe it'll do Elliot some good, having us here for a longer period.' Jeff made a pained noise. 'Anyway, I'm getting tired of this. Let me call France, see if I can get hold of this guy.' He took a phone out of his pocket. It was the first time I'd seen him with one.

'Hang on, you say you're skint but you bought a new bed and now you've got a phone.'

'Yeah, Stuart gave it to me. It's his old one. And he gave me some pay-as-you-go credit.'

It looked brand new, and expensive, but the story was plausible. Jeff began to wander out of the room, Lizzy following him. Chloe stood up. I wanted to scream. I hadn't got anywhere. I floundered for a second before raising my voice and shouting, 'Wait!'

Jeff and Lizzy stopped. Chloe sat back down.

'I'll lend you the money,' I said. 'Enough for a deposit and the first month's rent. You can pay me back when your money comes through.' I'd had enough. I didn't care if I never got it back. I just wanted them gone.

'Really?' Lizzy asked. 'We need at least three grand.'

I didn't have an enormous amount of savings – almost all my money had gone into this house, and recently I'd spent a fortune on our wedding and honeymoon in Vegas – but three thousand pounds would be a price worth paying for freedom. For getting these toxic people out of my home.

'I can do that,' I replied.

'No.'

Jeff filled the doorway, his arms folded again. His triceps bulged and I had a flash of him wielding a hammer, bringing it down on a skull that cracked like an egg.

But it wasn't George or Edith's skull in this image. It was mine.

'I won't accept your money,' Jeff said.

'It's not a gift,' I said, the pounding in my head coming back with a vengeance. 'You can pay me back.'

I could see him mulling it over. 'It'll have to be cash.'

'What? I didn't mean I'd give it to you directly. I'll pay it straight to the landlord.'

'In that case, forget it. I'd rather stay here for a while longer.'

He left the room. I chased after him, dodging past Lizzy and catching up with him in the hallway. 'Jeff. I need my house back.'

He turned. We were standing so close I could smell his sour breath and see the veins that coiled around his arms. His eyes were cold.

'You're really starting to piss me off,' he said.

'What?'

I took a step back and he looked me up and down, his lip curled. The mask of bonhomie he usually wore slipped away to reveal his real face, and for the first time I saw exactly how much contempt he felt for me.

'You're pathetic,' he said, before putting on a babyish voice and saying, '*I don't want you in my house anymore, you big meanies.* I don't know why Gemma married a worm like you.'

He spoke quietly so no one in the kitchen, with the possible exception of Lizzy, who was standing by the door, could hear.

'People like you make me sick,' he hissed. 'You sit here in your big house, with your fancy wine and your flash car, and you make out it's because you've always worked hard and that you deserve it. Well, let me tell you something. My parents worked themselves into early graves. They broke their backs working in a factory, twelve hours a day, and do you think they could afford somewhere like this? You're a privileged prick, Elliot.'

My dad had always told me to turn the other cheek, to rely on my intellect and wits. *Violence doesn't make you a man, Elliot*, he would say. *Life isn't like the movies.* I was paralysed by years of conditioning, and stunned too; no one had spoken to me like this before. No one had displayed such sneering contempt. All I could do was stand there, trembling with rage and shock and frustration.

Jeff saw all this. And he smiled.

'Why don't you go back to your terribly important job?' he said, his voice slimy with sarcasm. 'Find some little girls to play with?'

With that, he walked calmly up the stairs.

I couldn't move. I wanted to run after him, to yank him down the stairs. I wanted to stamp on him. I pictured myself with a hammer, smashing that smile, permanently removing his smirk.

But of course I didn't do any of that. I just stood there as Lizzy walked around me like someone avoiding dog mess on the pavement, and then Chloe came out of the kitchen.

She stopped beside me for a second.

'I'm sorry,' she said. She put her hand on my arm. Like Jeff a minute before, she was standing very close, but this was a different kind of close. I took a step back but she held on to my arm. She leaned forward and whispered in my ear, just as she had with George. With her big eyes and girlish voice, it struck me again that she was like a child, one who hadn't been allowed to grow up.

'Let me stay,' she said before stepping away.

I staggered backwards. For a few seconds, everything turned grey. When the room came back into focus, Gemma was standing in the kitchen doorway, staring at me.

'Did you hear him?' I said. 'Did you hear what he said to me?'

She nodded. 'I'm so sorry.'

I pointed towards the stairs. 'You need to talk to them. Tell them to go.'

'They won't listen to me.'

'Can't you at least try?'

I had raised my voice and she flinched. Stepping closer to her, I saw that she was trembling. When she spoke, her voice was hushed and thick with tears.

'I'm scared, Elliot. I'm too scared.'

Chapter 33

'You look tired, Mr Foster.'

I looked up to find Effy regarding me with concern. We were working on an experiment that involved the demonstration of Brownian motion in a smoke cell. It was actually a little basic for her but she seemed to be enjoying herself.

'I'm fine, Effy.'

She didn't seem to believe me. 'It's important to get enough sleep, you know. My dad is really strict.' She lowered her voice to a whisper. 'There are some kids in my class who are allowed to take their iPad to bed with them, and Joshua said he usually stays awake till midnight. My dad said no wonder he's bottom of the class.'

'Your dad talks a lot of sense.'

'I know, right?'

Mr Mensah picked her up after the extra tuition session and I drove back to the office. I checked my reflection in the rear-view mirror. Effy was right. I had bags under my eyes that looked like purple bruises and my skin was puffy and sallow. I hadn't slept at all the previous night. I'd lain there, aware of Jeff and Lizzy in the room below, brimming over with anger and shame, trying to figure out what I was going to do.

First thing this morning I had called the solicitor I'd used when I bought my house, Shirley Trent, and asked her what rights I had. She told me she wasn't sure, that she needed to consult one of her colleagues, and promised to call back as soon as she found out.

When I got back to the office, Amira was on the phone.

I sat at my desk and rubbed my face.

'Oh dear,' Amira said after she hung up. 'Trouble in paradise?'

I laughed bitterly. 'There are a couple of serpents in the Garden of Eden.'

'The in-laws? Uh-oh. Have they still not found anywhere to live?'

I told her everything that had happened when we got back from Sussex. I played down the final confrontation with Jeff because it made me feel ashamed. I couldn't imagine Colin just standing there and taking it.

You're weak, whispered a voice in my ear, a voice that sounded very much like Jeff's. *You're not a real man.*

'My God,' Amira said. She had listened to the whole thing with growing incredulity. 'I want to go round there and give them a piece of my mind. What does Gemma say?'

I sighed. 'She was so upset that she went to bed and stayed there for the rest of the day, then got up and went to work early this morning before I had a chance to properly talk to her. She just keeps apologising for inviting them to stay. She said, "I thought they might have changed."'

'People like that never change. But seriously, is there anything I can do?'

'Hmm. You know those sonic devices people put in their gardens to keep cats out? I need one of those that only works on in-laws.'

'I'll look on Amazon.'

I made us both a coffee. 'Has Colin said anything else to you about George and Edith's murders? Have the police got anywhere with their investigation?'

'I don't know, but you can ask him yourself in a minute. He's meeting me after work and we're going to the cinema. Hey, why don't you come with us?'

I was tempted. The thought of going home to Jeff and Lizzy filled me with dread. That was the worst thing about all of this. Previously, my house had been my sanctuary. I'd looked forward to going back there every evening after the stresses of work. But now I would rather stay at the office. My skin prickled with anger and frustration and I became aware that I was clenching my teeth, grinding them together.

'Elliot?'

'No, it's fine. I don't want to crash your date night. I know how little you get to see Colin with all the long hours he works.'

'Did I hear my name?' I looked up. Colin had entered the office. 'Sorry, I'm a little early. What were you talking about?'

Amira got up from her chair and kissed Colin on the cheek. 'I was asking Elliot if he wants to come to the cinema with us. He's having some . . . problems at home.'

The look on Colin's face told me he wanted his girlfriend to himself. But he said, 'What kind of problems?'

'His in-laws,' Amira said. 'Tell him what happened, Elliot.'

I gave him the abridged version and he shook his head sympathetically. As a police officer, he was used to seeing the worst of human nature – like, for example, older people getting their heads smashed in with hammers – so he didn't seem that surprised.

'Is there anything the police can do?' Amira asked him.

'Not unless they break the law.'

It struck me that if they'd thrown my bed out or got the delivery company to take it away, I could have reported them for theft. But they were too clever, too sneaky.

'It doesn't seem right,' said Amira.

Colin pulled a sympathetic face. 'If you want to evict them, you'll need to talk to a solicitor, I'm afraid.'

I explained I was waiting to hear back from one.

There was a long silence. Then I said, 'What if they *have* broken the law?'

Colin perched on the edge of Amira's desk and stroked his stubble. He really was sickeningly good-looking. Amira had told me that there were several women on a nearby estate who kept calling the police to report invented crimes, hoping Colin would turn up.

'That would be different, of course,' he said. 'Why, what do you think they might have done?'

'Well, they replaced my bed. And they drank a really expensive bottle of wine.'

I cringed as I said it, aware of how trivial this sounded.

Colin's response confirmed it. 'Hardly stealing the Crown Jewels, is it? Though I'm sure you could use it in a civil case if you had the appetite for it.'

Taking them to small claims court? That seemed pointless. I thought about telling Colin what I'd learned in Winchelsea Beach, the suspected violence towards and mistreatment of their children. But there was nothing the police would be able to do about that now, not unless Gemma, Stuart or Chloe came forward. And if they hadn't done that in the last twenty years, they were hardly going to now. I needed to concentrate on the present. Or the recent past, at least.

'I'm sure they're running from something,' I said.

'Like what?' Colin asked.

'I don't know . . .'

He shook his head.

'No, wait. Something that happened in France. I don't know what it was but I'm sure there must have been a reason why they left the country and came back here, and why Chloe was in such a state. I don't believe she really had a virus. It was more like she was having some kind of breakdown. Post-traumatic shock or something.'

I had read that stress could cause a high body temperature. It was called psychogenic fever.

'Maybe that's why they came back,' I said. 'Because Chloe wasn't well, mentally.'

Amira spoke up. 'Or they simply ran out of money.'

'That sounds likely,' Colin agreed.

'So why are they so shifty and secretive about it? They won't even tell me exactly where they were staying or what they were doing over there. But I overheard Jeff and Lizzy whispering about it one night, just after they came to stay. Something about getting away with it.'

'It could be anything,' Colin said.

I paced the office. 'If you knew them, you'd be suspicious too. I think . . . I think this is a pattern. I think they moved in with Chloe's boyfriend in France, hugely outstayed their welcome – the poor bastard – before doing the same to me. They're like cuckoos, taking over other birds' nests. Or . . .' I thought back to what George had said. 'Knotweed. They're like knotweed.'

Colin and Amira exchanged a look.

'You think I'm going crazy, don't you?' I said.

Colin made a placatory gesture. 'I think you're under a lot of strain, Elliot. Maybe you should take a break, go somewhere sunny for a week.'

'And leave those bastards alone in my house again? You must be joking. I'd get back and find *all* my furniture replaced! In fact, I'd go to France myself if I wasn't so worried about leaving my house at the mercy of Jeff and Lizzy. I could find out what they were up to. Track down Chloe's ex-boyfriend . . .' I stopped pacing. 'Hey, couldn't you do that for me, Colin? Get in touch with Interpol? Get them to look into it?'

Colin shifted off the desk. 'Elliot, mate, there's nothing for them to look into. We need a crime to investigate, not just a hunch that they might have done something dodgy.'

I glanced at Amira. She gave me a sympathetic shrug but it was clear she agreed with her boyfriend.

'Why don't you simply ask Chloe?' Colin said. 'Or Gemma, or the other one . . .'

'Stuart.'

'Yeah, him. Maybe they'll be able to put your mind at rest.'

'Or maybe they're in on it,' said Amira.

I stared at her. At the same time, Colin laughed. 'You two are as bad as each other. Come on, Amira, we're going to miss the start of the film.'

They left, Amira telling me to 'take care' and that she'd see me tomorrow. But I wasn't really listening. All I could hear were Amira's previous words ringing in my ears.

Maybe they're in on it.

Maybe I couldn't trust anyone.

Chapter 34

I fell back into my chair.

During the last few days it had crossed my mind that Jeff and Lizzy might have told Stuart about what had happened in France. It hadn't occurred to me that Gemma might know too, that she was keeping secrets from me. And as Amira's sentence, tossed off almost casually, sunk further into my head, the more anxious I felt.

Was this something Gemma and her parents had planned? Had she been out on Open Gardens day, looking for the perfect property for her and Jeff and Lizzy to move into? The perfect mug to fall in love with her?

'No,' I said aloud, but the argument raged inside my head.

Gemma had been miserable since her parents arrived – but maybe that was because she genuinely liked me and felt guilty.

She had criticised Jeff and Lizzy to my face, but she hadn't done anything to get rid of them.

She acted like she genuinely loved me – but what if it was all an act?

I took a long, deep breath and counted to ten. I needed to examine the evidence. What proof did I have that Gemma was in cahoots with her parents, that she wanted them to live with us permanently? None. In fact, everything I knew pointed to the opposite conclusion.

I knew from talking to the two anglers that Gemma had tried to run away from her parents when she was young. She had barely had contact with them over the past few years – although I was taking her word for it on that. What was certain was that she had been drinking a lot since they arrived, a sure sign that their presence made her unhappy and stressed. And then there was the way she had spoken about them in Ashdown Forest. She had sounded like she hated them. She was angry with them for borrowing money from her. She'd told me I didn't know what they were capable of.

Gemma wouldn't have said any of that if she wanted her parents to stay with us indefinitely. I relaxed a little, realising that I had allowed Amira to spook me.

Gemma was my wife. I loved her.

We were in this together.

ω

I was about to close down my computer and trudge home when an email pinged into my inbox. It was from Shirley Trent, the solicitor I'd contacted earlier, telling me she'd found the answers to my questions and that she would call me in the morning.

I couldn't wait. I figured she must still be at the office if she was emailing, so I called her.

'Have you five minutes to talk through it?' I asked.

She laughed. 'It'll take longer than that, but yes, fine.' She was in her late fifties with a warm Scottish accent, and I liked her in the same way I liked a lot of women of her age, because they made me think of my mum. 'I'll put it all in an email to you too, if you like.'

'That would be great.'

'Okay, so usually in cases like this – and I must say it's rather rare to find someone whose in-laws are refusing to move out – we would advise both parties to follow ADR, which stands for alternative dispute resolution. It's always much easier than going down the legal route.'

'I assume ADR involves talking to them and trying to reason with them?' I asked.

'Quite.'

'In that case, forget it. I've tried that already. I even offered to lend them the money they'd need to move in somewhere. They refused.'

I could feel myself about to launch into a rant and forced myself to stop.

'That's a shame,' Shirley said with a small sigh. 'If it's something you absolutely can't resolve among yourselves, the first step would be to write a letter giving them a date by which they need to move out. I'd make this fourteen days in the future.'

I wrote that number down on a pad. Two more weeks with the Robinsons. That was just about bearable. 'So what happens next? If they don't move out by the date in the letter?'

'That's when things get legal. We would serve a notice to quit. That tells them that if they don't move out within a further month – actually, I would usually advise two months when it's a family matter, to prevent further hold-ups when it gets to court . . . If they don't comply then it would go to the County Court.'

'Two months,' I said, writing that down as well. I yearned for the time, a minute before, when I'd thought they'd only be around for two weeks.

'Yes. And then it can take another two months for the court to issue proceedings, especially in London. The whole system is so clogged up.'

Again, I wrote down *Two months*. In total, we were already up to four and a half months.

'And then your in-laws would have fourteen days to file a defence, at which point they can delay things further by mounting a defence.'

'Oh, for God's sake.'

'Did you tell them they could only stay for a set period when they moved in?'

I rubbed my face. My hand felt cold, like I had no blood in my body. 'The understanding was that they'd stay for a couple of weeks. But that was informal. A figure of speech, really.'

She tutted. 'I thought that might be the case. I'm afraid that makes it easy for them to say the invitation from you or your wife was open-ended, although you can of course argue the opposite. Anyway, if they mount a defence, you would need to file a statement of truth and then the hearing would take place in court. This is where things could get really tricky.'

I almost laughed.

Shirley went on. 'If the judge finds some merit in your in-laws' defence, he or she might decide it needs to go to a one-day trial. That trial could be anything from three months to a year in the future.'

I put down the pen. 'You're kidding, right?'

'I'm afraid not. To be honest, I think it's unlikely the judge would decide it needed to go to trial, so we're probably looking at everything being decided at the hearing in . . .'

I did a quick calculation. Five months including the two weeks for the Robinsons to mount a defence. 'That would be April.'

'Sounds right. After which, your in-laws would be given up to forty-two days to vacate your house, and if they still refused to go we would have to get bailiffs involved, which can take another couple of months. But then . . .'

I stopped listening.

'Elliot? Are you still there? Hello?'

I ended the call. I couldn't bear to hear any more.

If Jeff and Lizzy refused to move out and I had to go the legal route – and knowing what I did of them, I was sure this would be what happened – it would take at least six months to get rid of them, almost certainly more. They could be here until next summer, even longer if the judge decided it needed to go to trial.

Why had I allowed them into my home? Why was the system so stacked in their favour? Like a child, I wanted to scream with the frustration and injustice of it all. Wanted to scream 'It's not fair!'

But as my mum had always said when those words escaped my lips: *Life's not fair.* I had made the mistake of letting Jeff and Lizzy into my life. And now I was stuck.

Chapter 35

Over the next few days I was haunted by an image of myself falling into a dark chute, down and down, spinning and somersaulting, reaching out in vain for something to grab on to. The sides of the chute were smooth and slippery, and although it felt like the bottom was close, I kept on falling, eternally braced for impact, for the smashing of bones, an explosion of pain, white light, blood. The end.

My days took on a familiar pattern. I went to work, where I was able to absorb myself to a degree in tasks that needed to be done, classes that had to be taught – but not fully. I never felt like I was one hundred per cent present, and part of my mind was at home, chewing over the issue of what to do about my situation, wondering how much I could trust my wife. I was asked to appear on BBC radio to talk about the government's education policy, something I would have jumped at previously, but I couldn't do it. I didn't think I'd be able to keep a lid on my anger, could picture myself ranting over the airwaves, taking out my frustration on whichever government apologist I was up against. Several times a day I would find myself consumed by blackness, an intense hatred for Lizzy and Jeff, violent fantasies involving hammers and knives and vicious dogs that thrilled me in the moment but left me sick and dizzy. Left me wondering who I was.

What I was becoming.

At the end of each day I would linger in the office until all the other lights in the building had gone out, ignoring messages from Gemma asking where I was and when I would be home. When every item of filing was put away and every email answered, I would head back, stopping off at a pub for a drink en route. Sometimes two drinks. That would take the edge off, make it possible for me to cross the threshold of my house.

Jeff and Lizzy would be there, in the kitchen, the living room, always present, their voices loud and harsh, the TV turned up. Jeff would usually be slouched on the sofa with Charlie – that furry Judas – purring on his lap. Lizzy would be in the kitchen, drinking endless cups of tea with the radio tuned to some infuriating talk station on which people would unburden themselves of their problems: the pregnant teenager, the young mother with cancer, the widower who was contemplating suicide following the death of his wife. Lizzy would sit at the table, enrapt and glowing, like a vampire growing fat on human misery.

Meanwhile, Chloe had begun to venture out of her room more often, drifting around the house, moving so quietly that it was as if she were able to float. I would come out of the bathroom and find her there, or be at my computer and sense her behind me, watching, slipping into the shadows as I turned. Some nights I was certain I could sense her presence outside my and Gemma's bedroom door, though when I got up and checked there was never anyone there.

I spent the evenings in the snug, shutting the door behind me, a stranger in my own home. Sometimes Gemma would come in and try to talk to me, looking as miserable as I felt. She tried to start conversations, to tell me about work, any topic but her parents, but her words would be sucked into the void between us and disappear. Eventually, she would give up and go to bed, and I wouldn't join her until I was certain she was asleep.

I felt like going away, leaving them all to it. But whenever this urge took hold, I would shake myself. Clench my fists and whisper, 'No.'

This was my house.

All I needed was a plan. Surely I could come up with one. All my life I'd been told I was clever. A problem-solver.

But every time I tried to solve this problem, all I could see was myself being sucked into that chute, down and down towards the bottom. A one-way journey with no end and no escape.

ω

I awoke early on Saturday morning with a brilliant plan. I made myself and Gemma breakfast – taking it to her in bed – then went back to the kitchen and emptied the entire contents of the fridge and freezer into black bin bags. The food cupboards too. I poured all the milk down the sink, chucked out the tea and coffee. I carried the black bags down the street and dumped everything in a communal bin.

I was going to starve them out. And when they left the house to look for food and tea, I would secure all the doors and get someone round to change the locks. I didn't care if I'd have to go hungry. Jeff ate constantly and Lizzy needed eight cups of tea to make it through the day. I couldn't believe I hadn't thought of it before.

I was in the kitchen when Lizzy came down. She ignored me, filling the kettle and opening the cupboard to look for the teabags. Her face creased with confusion. She opened the fridge and found it empty.

She turned to me, confusion turning to realisation on her face.

'You stupid twat,' she said before leaving the room.

Jeff's heavy footsteps came down the stairs and he appeared in the kitchen. He poked his nose in every cupboard then smirked.

He took out his phone and, thumbing it, left the room.

Half an hour later, the doorbell rang. Jeff got to the door before me and opened it to reveal a Deliveroo driver, who handed over a bag of food and two polystyrene cups of tea. Jeff tipped him and said, 'We'll probably see you again later.'

I stepped in Jeff's path as he headed back toward the stairs.

'How did you afford that? Has this mysterious person in France paid up?'

'Get out of my way, Elliot,' he said, his voice low and threatening.

'I can turn off the Wi-Fi,' I said. 'Stop you using your phone.'

'So? I've got 4G,' he said.

'How exactly can you afford your phone?'

He rolled his eyes. 'Stop obsessing over the money. Do you still not get it? It's not about the money. We like it here. We've decided to stay and you need to accept that.'

I tried to grab the bag of food out of his hands but he pulled it back, dodging my efforts.

'Careful, Elliot,' he said, stepping so close I could smell his uncleaned teeth. 'You're not a fighter, are you?'

Blood throbbed in my ears. I heard my dad's voice, telling me that I didn't have to fight, that violence would solve nothing. Except . . .

I prodded him in his chest. 'You're a parasite, Jeff. You think you're a big man, but all you can do is leech off your daughter. You're a loser.'

His nostrils flared and he pulled back a fist.

'You're a terrible dad too. Gemma hates you, Chloe's weird and Stuart's a wreck. You and Lizzy – you're the worst parents I've ever encountered. And I've met some real lowlifes.'

His fist trembled beside his face. But then he lowered it and smiled.

'I know what you're trying to do, Elliot. You want me to punch you so you can get me arrested.'

He was right.

'You might not think we're great parents, but at least, unlike yours, we're still around. The Robinsons are survivors.'

'So you're happy to be a parasite, are you?'

'You can label me however you want, mate. But tell me who you'd rather be – the sucker who slogs his guts out to build himself a nest but is too weak to protect it, or the guy who comes along and takes it from him?'

'A thief, you mean? I'd rather be the guy who works hard. Who earns the things he has.'

Jeff rolled his eyes. 'And that's what makes you a loser.'

I wanted to kill him. A rage unlike any I'd ever known had ignited inside me. I took a step towards him.

He laughed. 'You going to try to punch me, are you? Then I'd be justified in beating the crap out of you. Self-defence.'

My fists trembled. He was right. Hitting him might make me feel better for a second but it would do no good. But how could I fight someone who showed such contempt for the rules that most people – most normal, civilised people – live by?

'I'm bored of this conversation,' he said. 'There's no point trying to starve us out. We'll just send Chloe out if necessary, or get Stuart to bring us stuff. And don't bother turning off the heating and the water. We'll outlast you, mate. We've lived in worse conditions. Much worse.'

He shouldered his way past me and stamped up the stairs, leaving me behind, flushed and shaking.

It had been a terrible plan.

Chapter 36

'Talk to me.'

Sunday night, exhausted after a weekend trapped inside with the Robinsons, I trudged up to bed and found Gemma waiting for me. She was standing by the window, staring out at the rain.

'I'm too tired to talk,' I said, starting to get undressed.

She came over to me. 'No. Elliot. I'm serious. We can't go on like this.'

I laughed. 'You're telling me. Why don't you go downstairs now and tell your parents to leave? Kick them out.'

'You really think they'd listen to me?'

'I don't know. You wouldn't tell them to go anyway. You want them here.' The energy required to keep my guard up had drained away and all the doubts I'd had about her came rushing out. 'Do you want to know what I think? I think this was all part of your plan. You found some sucker with a nice house and no relatives, no one to help him, and decided to move your family in.'

The more I spoke, the more I believed it.

'You know, there's a species of ant, *Polyergus breviceps*. That's what your family are like.'

She stared at me like I was talking gibberish.

'What these ants do is, a queen goes into another colony, replaces the existing queen and takes over. She uses the colony's worker ants to look after her and then, when those worker ants die, just the parasite queen and her offspring are left.'

'Elliot, what the hell are you talking about?'

'How could you do it, Gemma? How could you have so little self-respect? Forcing yourself to screw some guy you've just met, just so you could get your hands on his house. Were you grimacing over my shoulder the whole time? Did you have to scrub yourself afterwards?'

She sat heavily on the edge of the bed. There were tears in her eyes.

'You really think I could do that? Oh my God.'

Her tears almost made me pause, but I was on a roll now, too angry to stop.

'I've worked it all out,' I said. 'The day we met, you were scoping out houses and their owners, and I was perfect, wasn't I? The perfect sucker. The whole whirlwind-romance thing, the fact that your parents suddenly needed somewhere to stay straight after we got married, it's all too convenient—'

'No!' She shouted it. 'I fell in love with you, Elliot. *Scoping out houses?* Listen to yourself. It's insane.' She swiped at her tears with the back of her hand. 'Yes, I made a terrible, terrible mistake letting my mum and dad come and stay with us. The worst mistake of my life. But the idea that I set this all up . . . How could you think that of me?'

She seemed so genuine, so shocked by the allegation. I stared at her, trying to figure out if she was lying.

'You're an arsehole,' she said, getting up from the bed. She threw herself down on her hands and knees and pulled something out from underneath. A suitcase. She dropped it on the bed and began yanking open drawers, pulling out clothes.

'What are you doing?'

'I'm going, Elliot. I'm not staying here with someone who thinks I'm part of some crazy conspiracy, someone who thinks I would only sleep with him to get my hands on his stupid house.'

She dropped an armful of underwear into the case, then moved towards the bathroom.

'Gemma—'

'Get out of my way.'

'No.' I was overcome with contrition. She was right. How could I have thought that of her? It was crazy. When I looked into her eyes I could see that she loved me. She couldn't be faking it, surely. The madness, the stress, had made me lose sight of that. She was my ally, not my enemy. And I was about to lose her.

'Gemma, I'm sorry. I was wrong. I just . . . It's your parents. The situation here. It's made me lose my mind. Can't you see that it would?'

She sat back on the bed, beside the suitcase.

'Don't go, Gemma.'

She didn't speak for a short while, then said, 'Don't ever think you can't trust me. I want them gone as much as you do. I just . . . I don't know how to do it. How to make them go. I know how stubborn they are, how awful, how . . .' She stopped short of whatever it was she was going to say.

I knelt on the bed and took her hands. 'In the forest, you said I don't know what they've done. You need to tell me.'

'It's so painful.'

'Please. Tell me.'

Again, she fell quiet. From outside came the muted swoosh of passing cars. I lifted the suitcase off the bed and put it on the floor, sitting in the space where it had been, beside Gemma. She laid her head on my shoulder.

'Do you know one of the things that attracted me to you, Elliot?' she said. 'It was when I came into your house and saw how tidy it was. How ordered.'

I laughed. 'That doesn't make me sound very cool.'

'No, but it was to me, because it was such a contrast to the chaotic home I grew up in. I can hardly begin to describe what it was like: the mess, the piles of stuff everywhere, the clutter and the filth. It was like one of those TV shows about hoarders – those people who can't look after themselves.' She grimaced. 'I've tried to talk about this to people before and they look at me like I'm a snob or a neat freak, but it wasn't just dirty and messy, it was like living inside the brain of a madman. Or madman and woman, I should say.'

I thought about the state my house had been in when we got back from Sussex. 'I've seen how messy they can be.'

Gemma shook her head. 'No, you haven't. Believe it or not, they were trying to be neat so they didn't piss you off too much when they first got here. But they can't help themselves. Their true nature leaks out.' Another shake of the head. 'This is nothing, though, so far. The more at home they feel . . .'

She trailed off, leaving it to my imagination, and I shuddered.

'Mess, though,' I said. 'That's the least of it, right?'

I put my hand on her shoulder and was shocked by how tense she was, the muscles in her upper back rigid and knotted. I remembered what the two men in Winchelsea Beach had told me. How the Robinsons' neighbour had heard yelling and screaming. Seen the children with bruises. Bite marks. Gemma trembled beneath my palm and I pulled her into a hug, felt her heart flutter against my chest.

I wasn't a therapist. I didn't think I had the tools to help her, apart from the ability to listen. To be there for her. But I had to ask. Had to know.

'When you were a child . . . did they . . . hurt you?'

'Yes,' she whispered.

She still had her head against my chest and I couldn't see her face, but I sensed that her eyes were closed and that she was seeing the past. Her younger self. I wished I could look inside her mind, wished her brain was a kind of TV transmitter that could beam her memories directly to me, so she wouldn't have to speak.

'If we were bad,' she said, 'Mum had this stick. A piece of cane. She used to make us hold out our hands. Like this.'

She pulled away from my chest and held both hands out in front of her, palms up. 'If we'd been really naughty – if I spoke back when Dad called me a waste of space, or if Stuart got a bad mark at school – they'd make us hold them the other way up.' She turned her hands over, so the knuckles were facing up. 'It hurts more like that. Does more damage.'

'Oh, Gemma.'

She clenched her fists like she could feel the sting of the cane now.

'The thing is, I could handle that. It was brief, over in seconds. Mum would usually be nice to us afterwards, as long as we didn't snivel or make a fuss. Dad might let us choose a movie to watch or give us ice cream. It was the other stuff that was harder to bear.'

'The other stuff?'

I waited, desperate to hear it, but fearful too.

'Did they . . . ?' I stopped, not wanting to say the words. 'Did they hurt you in other ways?'

She nodded, tears leaking from closed eyes, and I wanted to go downstairs, find a big stick and do to Jeff and Lizzy what they had done to their children. It coursed through me, a trembling rage, that human desire for bloody justice and revenge that is hardwired into all of us, the lust to inflict pain and suffering that we feel when we read about cases of child abuse in the paper, when we hear about paedophiles and baby killers being sent to prison and we hope they get locked up with the most violent thugs and sadists. The dark part of us that whispers, *Hanging's too good for them*. The dark heart triumphing over the cool head.

'You can still report them, you know,' I said. 'Go to the police. If they sexually abused you—'

'Elliot, no. It wasn't that. They never did that.'

'Then what? What did they do?'

And, finally, she filled in the blanks in her story.

Chapter 37

'It wasn't what they did to our bodies.' She tapped the side of her skull. 'It was the stuff they did to our heads. Do you know what it's like to be told every day that you're not good enough? That you're ugly and stupid and unwanted? It's all I can remember, from when I could first understand what my parents were saying to me. If I tried hard at school, they told me it was pointless and pathetic. They said I was trying to show I was better than them . . . When I was eleven I came home one day and found that my dad had thrown my school books, this project I'd been working on for weeks, into the fire. I had to tell the teachers I hadn't done the work.'

I was lost for words.

'I gave up after that. What was the point of trying to do well at school? I sunk to the bottom of the class. Spent my life in a daydream. And for Stuart, it was the complete opposite. He was a boy so he had to get top marks all the time, but he wasn't naturally academic. It got so bad that he ended up bullying one of the brainy kids in his class, forcing him to do his homework for him. It all came out eventually, when this kid's parents found out. That was a horrific day.'

I thought of Stuart and how, when I first met him, I'd got the impression his spirit had been crushed. Now I knew it had happened when he was very young.

'I've told you about cutting myself already,' she said. Unconsciously, she touched her belly where the scars were. 'What I haven't told you is that when I was fifteen I found God.'

I tried not to give away that I already knew this.

'My parents were total atheists. Quite contemptuous of people who went to church. There was a big sex scandal involving our local vicar and I remember how Dad found that hilarious and typical. "They're all perverts," he said. If Jehovah's Witnesses ever came round he used to chuck things at them. Mum was just as bad.' She shrugged. 'Maybe it was their contempt for religion that drew me to it. Or maybe it was simply that I wanted to feel that somebody loved me. I'd already learned that the kind of love the boys at school talked about wasn't love at all.'

What had Lizzy called her daughter? *Not-So-Precious Gem.* My flesh prickled.

'I got this Bible from school and read it in secret. And there was a girl in my class who went to a Baptist church in Hastings. I asked her if I could go along and did that in secret too. I told my parents I was going ice skating.' She laughed and wiped away a tear from her cheek. 'I loved it. They were all so nice to me, so welcoming. Suddenly it felt like there was something in the world that made sense. The love of God. The community around the church. It was like being part of a family. A proper family.'

'That sounds nice.'

'Yeah, it was. And it was incredible to feel that love, of God, of Christ, after spending my entire life feeling like nobody cared about me, that nobody was on my side. It's hard to describe how overwhelming it was for a while. How much strength it gave me.'

There were tears in her eyes.

'And then they told me that in order to be baptised, which was what I really wanted, I needed to love my parents. That I had to proclaim my love for them. I couldn't do it and I didn't understand why I needed to. It was awful. The senior pastor told me if I couldn't do it I would have to stop coming to the church. I think, looking back, that he was calling my bluff, but I didn't understand at the time. I felt like I'd been cast out. That nobody would ever understand me.'

I already knew what was coming next.

'Then I met this amazing couple called Delilah and Mickey. They lived in a caravan on the edge of the village and I'd never met anyone like them. They were so colourful and special. Mickey had this awesome Afro and played the guitar, and Delilah dressed like some kind of incredible peacock and had this lovely soft voice. They told me they travelled around the country, towing their caravan behind them, and were drawn to places where they sensed there were souls in need of help.'

This sounded like a load of nonsense to me and it must have shown on my face because Gemma said, 'I know. It sounds like hippy crap, but I was sixteen and this seemed like a better way for me to celebrate my discovery of Christ. A place where I wouldn't have to celebrate my mother and father. I told Mickey and Delilah how desperate and unhappy I was, and they said I could stay with them for a while. I was sixteen, old enough to make my own decisions. So I did. In the middle of the night, I packed a bag and moved in to their caravan on the cliff.'

'What happened?' I asked.

Her eyes were dry now. 'I'm sure you can guess. My parents found me. My dad turned up one day and threatened Mickey and Delilah. He said that if they didn't get out of the village he would kill them. Mickey tried to argue and Dad hit him. Oh, it was dreadful, Elliot. I was sobbing, begging Delilah and Mickey to help me, but they didn't. They were too scared, too weak to stand up to him. They just watched as Dad dragged me away.'

Gemma took a deep breath. 'I was insane for a while. I heard that Delilah and Mickey had moved on. They'd abandoned me. And I felt like God had abandoned me too. He hadn't protected me.' She laughed bitterly. 'I think I had a full-on existential crisis, aged sixteen.'

'Oh, Gemma.'

'For the next two years I stayed in my room at home, only going out to sit my exams. I sat in the dark in my bedroom, drank vodka that Stuart sneaked into the house, and cut myself. I did that for two years until, when I was eighteen, I ran away.'

'I don't blame you. Where did you go?'

'Not far. Hastings, a few miles down the road. That's when I moved into the squat.'

Gemma had told me about this already. This was when she had met an older guy, Henry, and went to live with him in his house near the park. When I'd asked her what happened before, all she said was that it had 'gone bad'.

I squeezed her hand. 'Do you want to talk about that too?'

'I'm so tired, Elliot. Can we talk about it tomorrow?'

'Of course.'

She lay in my arms and, pretty soon, fell asleep. I couldn't join her, though. I stayed awake for hours, boiling with hatred for the couple downstairs.

Chapter 38

I woke up from a dream about my parents in which my mum was yelling at me. *Pull yourself together, Elliot*, she shouted.

Come on, added my dad. *You're better than this.*

You're better than them.

Standing beneath the shower, I repeated their words to myself. They were right. I was better than Jeff and Lizzy. I stared at myself in the mirror and tried to give myself a pep talk. I was distracted by a twitch in my left eyelid, which I had last seen when I was a teenager. The Robinsons had brought it back.

I dragged a razor over my face, then decided I would feel better – more like my younger self – if I put on some aftershave. But my bottle of Sauvage wasn't in the cabinet. I thought about it. The last time I recalled seeing it was when I had brought it up here the night Gemma and I had gone out. The night Jeff had been in the shed. Where had I put it? Maybe I had hidden it, not wanting Jeff to borrow it again. Hidden it too well, it seemed.

I went into our bedroom wrapped in a towel. Gemma was getting dressed and the room was hot because either Jeff or Lizzy had got up before dawn and whacked the thermostat up.

Gemma glanced at me through her lashes. She had exposed herself emotionally last night and I could guess how she must be feeling now, in the aftermath. Raw. Vulnerable.

'It's going to be okay,' I said, drying myself with the towel. Despite only getting a few hours of sleep, I felt manic and charged with nervous energy. 'We're going to get our lives back.'

'Really?' She paused, eyes wide with hope. 'What are you going to do?'

'First, I'm going to talk to my solicitor . . .'

Gemma's face fell. 'You're going to go that route? Didn't she say it would take months?'

'Yes, but . . .'

'We're never going to get rid of them, Elliot. Maybe we should go. Run away, start somewhere new, where they won't find us. You could sell the house, let the new owners deal with them.'

'No! I'm not doing that.'

'Then what? What are we going to do?'

I picked up my shirt and pulled it on. 'I'm going to find proof that they did something criminal. I'm going to find out exactly what happened in France. If I have to, I'll go back further. I'm going to find something, Gemma. People like that – who treat their children like they treated you, who go around threatening arson and murder – they *must* have something criminal in their past. I'm going to find it.'

She stared at me. She seemed disappointed, but then she sighed and closed the gap between us, kissing me on the cheek.

'I'm sorry, Elliot,' she said. 'I'm so sorry I brought them into your life.'

But I wasn't really listening. I was keen to get going, to get on with my new mission.

You're better than them, I heard my dad say.

Now all I had to do was prove it.

ω

It was 8.30 a.m. and Jeff and Lizzy were still asleep. I turned the thermostat down so the heating would be off when they got up, then made myself breakfast in the kitchen. As I buttered my toast I came up with the idea of making tear gas, of filling the house with it and driving my in-laws outside, choking and blind with pain. It was a pleasant fantasy, but not something I would ever actually do. The risk of something going wrong was too great.

I needed to focus on my existing plan: searching for something incriminating in their past, starting with France. And I had an idea where I might find information to get me started.

Gemma came in to say goodbye and, a minute after she left, I heard a door open upstairs. I was pretty sure it was Chloe's door. I went to the bottom of the stairs and listened. Sure enough, I heard the bathroom door click shut and, a few seconds later, the shower came on.

I hurried up the stairs, avoiding the creaky step, and crept into Chloe's room, closing the door behind me.

There had to be something here that would tell me where in France they had been living. A receipt from a shop. An envelope bearing an address. A luggage label on one of her bags. I pulled open drawers, dropped to my knees and peered under the bed, figuring they were my drawers, my bed, so it was fine for me to be in here, doing this. It wasn't an invasion of Chloe's privacy. It wasn't like I was reading her . . .

Journal! How could I forget? Two weeks ago, when I'd come in here to see Chloe, I'd seen her slip a book beneath her pillow. It had looked like a journal, hadn't it? A notepad at the very least. I glanced at the door. I could still hear the shower running. Since getting better, Chloe had taken a lot of very long showers, using up all the hot water, so I was confident she'd be in there for another few minutes. Without hesitation, I slid my hand beneath her pillow.

There was nothing there.

So where was it? I patted the duvet, lifted the mattress, checked down the side of the bed. No sign of it. I forced myself to slow down and think. I knew this room. If I was going to hide something in here, where would I put it?

I knew the answer. When I moved in here, an electrician had come round to rewire parts of the house, which involved crawling into the cupboard where I had found Chloe hiding. He had come across an old porn VHS tape hidden in a nook inside, covered in dust.

I smiled at the memory as I got down on all fours and stuck my head into the cupboard, reaching to my left, hoping no spiders would run over my hand. And, to my delighted surprise, my fingers made contact with something. I backed out of the cupboard and sat up. I had found Chloe's journal.

The shower was still running but surely even she would be out very soon. I hesitated. I could take the journal away, but I was convinced she would notice it was missing before I had a chance to return it. Hurriedly, I began to flick through the pages, heading straight to the dates immediately before Chloe and her parents returned to England.

Chloe's handwriting was almost unreadable. Cramped and tiny, and written using a thick black pen; at first I thought she had used shorthand. But no, it was just bad handwriting and, to make it harder, the entire thing was written in French, a language I didn't speak. Like most kids, I'd studied it at school, but my abilities were limited to being able to buy bread, tell people I enjoyed watching television and asking where to find the supermarket. I would need time to make sense of this, first to decipher the handwriting, then to translate it.

I flicked back a few pages, and heard the shower shut off. That meant I only had a minute or two. Desperately, I scanned the pages and a couple of things jumped out at me. A pair of initials were used frequently: JC. And while every other page of the journal had been completed, one was blank. Friday, August 10th. The next day, the 11th, had just a few short lines, the writing thick and illegible, before things returned to normal. Quickly, I flicked back to the 9th. There was an account of a full day. I was able to make out some words I vaguely recognised. *Miel. Cassoulet. Cabécou.* Chloe was still in the bathroom but I needed to get out now. Just before I closed the journal, another pair of recognisable words swam into focus: *Victor Hugo.*

I stuck my head back into the cupboard and returned the journal to its hiding place. I was up and out of the room within seconds, and was halfway down the stairs before the bathroom door opened.

Chapter 39

On the drive to the office, I called Shirley, my solicitor.

'I want to get things rolling,' I said. 'Can you draft a letter for me, giving Jeff and Lizzy fourteen days' notice to leave? I think it would be better coming from a solicitor.'

'I agree.'

'Can you courier it over to me? I want to give it to them later.'

She agreed. I thanked her and hung up.

Amira was already there when I reached the office. I headed straight to my desk and threw myself into my chair, stabbing the button on my PC to turn it on.

'You're in a hurry to start work,' she said. 'Cup of tea?'

'Please.'

I waited for the computer to boot up and opened Google Translate as Amira came over with my drink. She looked down at the three French words I'd written on a scrap of paper.

'What are you doing?' she asked.

I explained.

'Wait. You looked through her journal?'

'Yes, I did. Don't be disapproving. This is war. All is fair.'

She raised an eyebrow. 'Okay. If you say so. But you don't need to use Google. I can tell you that *miel* is French for "honey".'

Of course. Somewhere in the depths of my brain, I'd known that.

'And a *cassoulet* is a dish, a sort of sausage-and-bean hotpot. Very popular in the south of France.'

'Oh, yes.' I'd known that too.

'I'm not sure about *Cabécou*, though.'

I typed it into the search engine. 'It's a type of goat's cheese.'

'Right. So it's a shopping list. I'm not sure how this is going to help you, Elliot.'

'I know. Although I think it's actually a list of things she bought. The day before.'

'The day before what?'

I told her about the blank page. 'Something important must have happened on August tenth. Maybe something so bad she couldn't put it on paper.'

'Or maybe that day was so boring she couldn't think of anything to write.'

I thought about it. Every other day in the diary, apart from the 11th when the entry was brief, had at least half a page of text. 'No, something must have happened that day. Something she couldn't bear to write about.'

Amira had perched on the edge of my desk. 'This is giving me goosebumps. But, Elliot, was there anything at all useful in this journal?'

I sighed. 'Not much. I need to have another look at it. The only other stuff I could make out was the name Victor Hugo—'

'Maybe Chloe had been reading *Les Misérables*.'

'And some initials kept appearing. JC.'

'Jesus Christ?'

I put my head in my hands. 'Let's not bring him into it.'

Amira laughed. 'Like you said, you're definitely going to need to get hold of that journal again. Take photos of the pages next time.'

I groaned. 'Why didn't I think of that?'

She patted me on the shoulder. 'You'd make a terrible James Bond, wouldn't you?'

ʊ

A motorbike courier dropped off the letter from Shirley at my office in the middle of the afternoon. This was the long, slow course of action; my Plan B. Although the way things had started with Plan A, I might be stuck with the less preferable alternative.

It was a bitterly cold evening and I pulled my coat around me as I got out of the car. I looked up at George and Edith's dark house and wondered how long it would be before it was on the market. Somebody, I imagined, would get a bargain; houses in which horrific murders had occurred were unlikely to go for their full value. Maybe, I thought bitterly, I should buy it and move in. At least then Jeff and Lizzy would only be the *neighbours* from hell.

They were both in the living room, watching a quiz show on TV. I watched as they mocked the young woman on the screen who had just got a question wrong.

Everything they said and did disgusted me. I had never thought myself capable of pure hatred before, but I felt it now. It was like having eels wriggling beneath my skin, a churning sensation in my stomach. I ground my teeth together and tried to push back the blood-red images that invaded my head. It was easy to see how loathing could drive someone insane. The intensity of it. The way it got your endorphins rushing, craving the release that only violence could bring.

I found Gemma in our bedroom, watching something on her iPad. I had already decided not to tell her about Chloe's journal because I had a feeling that, despite everything, she would be angry with me. She would see it as snooping.

I held up the letter and told her what it was. 'I'm about to give it to them. Wish me luck.'

'They'll just ignore it,' she said.

'I'm sure. But that's not the point.' Although there was still part of me that clung to the hope they would be reasonable. Civilised. That they would read the letter and do what was asked of them.

Back downstairs, I didn't hesitate. I went straight into the living room, walked over to the TV and switched it off.

Jeff's mouth gaped open. 'Oi, I'm going to miss the final round.'

'I couldn't care less, Jeff.' I held out the envelope containing the letter. 'This is for you.'

'What is it?' Lizzy asked.

'Just read it.'

After a few seconds, Lizzy finally took it from me, opened the envelope and scrutinised the letter.

'I hope you didn't have to pay too much for this,' she said. 'You should be saving your money, not spending it.'

'What are you talking about?'

She smirked. 'That's for me to know and you to find out.'

Before I could react, Jeff snatched the letter from Lizzy's hand and read through it.

'Move out in fourteen days?' He looked straight at me. 'Sorry, mate, no can do.'

He ripped the letter in half, then in half again, and dropped the pieces on the floor.

'Don't make a mess,' Lizzy said, wagging her finger. 'Elliot will be very cross. He might make you go to bed with no supper.'

My vision was tinged with pink. I had to leave the room. I itched to smash something, wished I could invent a machine that would shrink Jeff and Lizzy to the size of hamsters so I could pick them up and throw them out the front door. Better still, stamp on them. End them.

I went into the bathroom, took ten deep breaths and splashed cold water on my face. It was okay, I told myself. Why did I expect anything else from them? The letter had been delivered and the clock was ticking at last. I made a note on my phone of what had happened and at what time, as Shirley had advised me to start keeping a log of everything that occurred here. 'You might need it in court,' she said.

When I came out, Lizzy was on her own in the living room. I was planning to take a photo of the ripped-up letter, in case it was useful later, but it had been picked up and, I assumed, thrown in the bin. I went into the kitchen.

Jeff was making himself a sandwich while humming a familiar song, the tune clearly recognisable. *Up, up and away.*

He looked over his shoulder and winked. 'Was it a beautiful balloon your parents were in?'

The pink mist that had clouded my vision turned red. Dark crimson. How could he? How *could* he?

He turned as I marched into the kitchen towards him.

I punched him in the face.

The blow struck him on the cheekbone, just to the left of his nose. He reeled, his mouth falling open, more shocked than hurt. He touched the blooming pink spot on his face as I stood there before him, fists clenched, trembling with adrenaline and rage.

'You're a sick—'

He pulled a knife from the block on the counter and the words stopped in my throat.

'Back off,' he said. He took a step forward, holding the knife with its straight six-inch blade in front of my face.

I held my ground.

His voice was low and icy with menace. 'Do you want to die, Elliot? You know what will happen then. Gemma will inherit this house.'

'But you won't get your hands on it,' I said, surprised by how normal my voice sounded. 'You'll be in prison.'

'What, for using self-defence after you came at me with a knife? I'll have two witnesses, Lizzy and Chloe, who will back me up. You won't even be there to defend yourself. And Gemma will do whatever I tell her to.'

He held the blade closer to my face. I swallowed. My fist hurt where I'd struck him, but it was a good kind of hurt.

'Back off,' he said again, inching closer, Adam's apple bobbing in his throat.

I sensed someone behind me. Lizzy. I stole a glance and saw that she was shaking her head. Jeff caught her eye and slowly, reluctantly, lowered the knife. He placed it back in the block and went back to making his ham sandwich, as if nothing had happened.

I didn't move.

'I'm going to find out what you did,' I said, unable to stop the words coming out.

Jeff looked over his shoulder. 'I don't know what you're talking about.'

'In France. I know you had to leave France in a hurry. What did you do, Jeff? Did you stick a knife in someone else? What do you think you got away with?'

He froze for a moment, then turned around, a big smile on his face. He held up his sandwich.

'Nice bit of ham in this, Elliot,' he said, affecting a posh accent. 'Would you care for a bite?'

Chapter 40

I was woken by a vicious thunderstorm. Gemma and I had fallen asleep with the curtains open, and a flash of light filled the room, swiftly followed by another. Briefly, my sleep-addled brain thought it was a bomb falling on London, that war had broken out. The blessed end of the world, a merciful release for all of us, though Jeff and Lizzy, like rats and cockroaches, would no doubt survive.

Rain pummelled the window as thunder boomed overhead. I peered out at black clouds that prevented the sun from rising, water already an inch deep on the surface of the road, cars with their headlights on moving slowly through the gloom.

It was a dark and stormy morning, I thought as I headed downstairs and past the bedroom where my parents-in-law snoozed. I pictured them as vampires, lying in their crypt, and had a brief, happy fantasy in which I crept in and staked them both, turned them to dust that would float away on the wind. It made me smile. And God, it felt good to smile, even though I knew if I looked in a mirror I would see the grin of a lunatic, the Joker taunting Batman, the laughter that bubbled inside me as unhealthy as a gut full of poison.

ʊ

After lunch, I left the office and drove to Tulse Hill for my weekly lesson and private tuition session with Effy. My favourite couple of hours of the week. I headed straight into the classroom and waited for the kids to arrive.

Ten minutes after the class was due to start, I was still waiting. This was very strange. Had I got the day wrong? It wouldn't surprise me, the state my brain was in, but no, it was the right time and day and I was in the right place.

I waited another five minutes, then phoned Kenneth.

'Hey,' I said. 'Everything all right? Did you get held up in traffic?'

There was a long pause. 'Didn't anyone call you?'

'No. Why? What's going on?'

'I'm sorry, somebody should have let you know. We cancelled today's class.'

I was confused. 'What? Why?'

He didn't reply, just made an odd throat-clearing noise.

I paced the classroom as I spoke. 'Oh, don't tell me, the governors have decided to withdraw funding?' The board of school governors had been hard to win round, because the school had to make a small contribution towards the cost of the weekly group lesson, but I was sure they now saw the value in it. 'I can't believe it. They promised—'

'No, it's not that.'

I stopped walking. I was getting a bad feeling, a sick sensation blooming in my stomach. 'Then what is it? What's happened?'

He made that strange noise again. The sound of discomfort.

'Kenneth, what the hell has happened? And what's going on with Effy? If the school has decided they don't want me to run the main class anymore, surely it's still fine for me to do the private tuition with Effy? The school don't have to fund that. I can come and pick her up if—'

'Effy's not here today.'

'Oh. Is she sick?'

'Listen, Elliot, I've got to go. Someone will be in touch to explain.'

'This is freaking me out,' I said.

He didn't respond for a few moments. Then he said, 'I liked you, Elliot. We all did.'

Then he hung up.

ᖚ

I was perturbed for the rest of the day. I sent an email to the school's head teacher, trying to get answers, but no reply came. Amira was as puzzled as I was, but then we got swept up in the preparations for tomorrow's big meeting and I put the situation with Tulse Hill Primary from my mind. While we worked, it continued to rain relentlessly. A flood warning had been issued and there were clips online of buses breaking down in giant puddles, a river bursting its banks in a small town in Kent where residents desperately tried to save their flooded homes.

As we were preparing to leave, Amira said, 'Did you get anywhere yet, trying to find out what Jeff and Lizzy got up to in France?'

'No. I haven't had time.'

'I didn't think so. But it kept playing on my mind after we chatted. If you lived in France, what's the obvious place where you would buy the things Chloe listed in her journal?'

'A supermarket?'

She smiled. 'No. Just a market. So I searched for "Victor Hugo market" on Google and guess what? There's one in south-west France, in Toulouse. It's pretty well known, actually. Reading about it made my stomach growl and my mouth water.'

'Toulouse.'

'Yep. I've never been but it's supposed to be a nice place. The Pink City, they call it. Something to do with the colour of the stone they used to build it.'

234

I immediately looked it up, checking its position on a map – it wasn't far from the border with Spain – and skimming the Wikipedia page. It had a population of just under half a million people. That was disappointing. I'd been hoping Jeff, Lizzy and Chloe had been living in a small town or village, which would make it easier to find out what they'd been up to. I'd imagined myself flying out there, talking to the local butcher and baker, who would know all about the strange English people who had been living in their community for the last few years. A city, though. That made it harder.

Amira stood behind me as I studied the map.

'I think we can almost certainly say that Chloe was there on August tenth.'

I swivelled in my chair. 'That's amazing work.'

She shrugged. 'Hardly amazing. Also, I haven't a clue what you would do next. But I'll have a chat with Colin and see if he's got any advice.'

'Thanks, Amira.' I stood up. 'I hope you know how much I appreciate it.'

'No problem.' She patted my shoulder. 'I want you back to your old self. The sooner we sort out your personal problems, the better.'

I pulled her into a hug. It wasn't the kind of thing I would normally do with her – we didn't have a tactile relationship – but in that moment I felt the need for human warmth. I think she understood that because she hugged me back.

'Come on, you,' she said. 'Go home, get a good night's rest. Try not to have any fights with your father-in-law. We've got a big day tomorrow.'

I drove home through the rain. The streets were quiet, with everyone taking shelter indoors. I thought about Toulouse and what secrets lay among its terracotta buildings. Perhaps I should take a risk and speak to Chloe. I had little doubt her childhood had been as traumatising as Gemma's. Chloe might be desperate to get away from her parents too. But then, she might have been part of whatever it was that happened in France. Or she might be too scared to talk.

I was still mulling this over when I pulled up outside my house, sending up a spray of rainwater. I squinted through the rain. There was a man standing beneath the lamp post outside the gate, wearing a black waterproof coat, the hood pulled up to conceal his face. He was tall and broad, and standing completely still.

I got out of the car, pulling my own hood up, and the person outside my gate looked up at me. It was Effy's dad.

'Mr Mensah,' I said. 'What are you doing here?'

He took a step towards me, the rain bouncing off his coat and running down his face. I froze. Last time I saw him, he was all smiles. Now he was staring at me with anger. Worse than that. Hatred.

'What's—'

He grabbed me by the balls.

The pain was unlike anything I had ever known. He squeezed, and pure white agony roared through my body. I couldn't speak, couldn't move. All I could see was his face, close to mine, eyes wide, teeth bared.

'I trusted you,' he said.

'Please,' I managed to gasp.

He squeezed my testicles again and I thought I might faint. In that moment, I would have been happy to die if it would put an end to the pain. I was vaguely aware of the sound of a car pulling up behind me, a door slamming, footsteps hurrying towards us.

'I hope you die in jail.'

'Mr Mensah!' It was a woman's voice. 'Let him go.'

The pressure on my balls abated a little. The woman shouted at him again and, finally, he released me.

I collapsed to the pavement, retching, waves of pain crashing through my body. Effy's dad was yelling, something about perversion and castration and hell. I vomited and gasped for air. It hurt. I couldn't imagine my balls ever feeling normal again.

On all fours on the wet pavement, I looked up and saw two things.

First, Jeff and Lizzy were looking at me through the front window. They were both smiling.

Second, the female police officer who had shouted at Mr Mensah was standing over me, dressed in a black windbreaker. Behind her, a male cop was restraining my assailant, stopping him from having a second go at me.

'Elliot Parker?' said the policewoman. 'I need you to accompany me to the station.'

I threw up again, all over her shoes.

Chapter 41

The police took me to an interview room and left me on my own, sitting at a table in an airless, windowless space that stank of stale sweat and cheap cleaning products. The table almost filled the entire room, with a digital recorder sitting at one end against the wall. I'd seen rooms like this on TV, usually with some criminal slouched on one side, his lawyer beside him or her, saying 'No comment' to everything the cops asked.

I had never expected to be in this position myself. I had been arrested and cautioned but still had no idea what I was supposed to have done or why Mr Mensah had attacked me.

Of course, with that and the call to the school earlier, when Kenneth had been so frosty, I knew it must have something to do with Effy. What had her dad said? *Perversion. Castration.* My stomach clenched. Surely they couldn't . . . ? No, the notion was so abhorrent, so crazy, that I rejected it immediately.

The wait seemed designed to make me suffer. I could taste vomit on my tongue and my testicles still hurt. I hadn't been offered anything, not even a glass of water. I was about to start banging on the door and demanding to see someone, when it finally opened and two women in plain clothes came into the room. One of them was in her forties, white with short mousey-brown hair. The other was a younger Asian woman. They sat opposite me, with the older woman closer to the recorder.

'I'm DS Ackerman,' she said. 'And this is DC Syal.'

'Do I need a lawyer?' I asked.

'You have a right to legal representation, yes. Is there someone you would like us to call or would you prefer the duty solicitor?'

This didn't feel real. 'I haven't done anything. I don't even know what I'm accused of.'

'Really?' Ackerman asked, raising an eyebrow.

'Really.'

They exchanged a disbelieving look, then Ackerman said, 'You don't have to have a solicitor present if you don't want one, Mr Foster.'

'I want you to tell me what I'm supposed to have done. Whatever it is, it's going to be a misunderstanding. A total waste of your time.'

They looked bored, like they'd heard it all before. 'Let's start the interview,' Ackerman said. She switched on the recorder and told it their names along with mine. 'It's nine thirty-two on the evening of November twentieth. Mr Foster has chosen to be interviewed without a solicitor present.'

'Because I don't need one,' I said.

DC Syal was holding a manila folder. She laid it on the table between us but didn't open it.

'Do you know a child named Effia Mensah?' she asked.

So it *was* about Effy. I wasn't surprised, but that didn't stop me from going cold inside.

'Yes,' I replied, aware of how dry my mouth was. 'She's one of my students.'

'But you're not a schoolteacher?'

'If you mean, am I employed by a school, no I'm not. I am a qualified teacher, though. I have a PGCE and spent a couple of years working at a primary school.' I gave them a very brief history of my career: the website that I'd sold; setting up Inquiring Minds; what we did. I was sure they must know most of it already. 'Effia – Effy – is one of the children I teach from Tulse Hill Primary. I also give her private tuition.'

Ackerman spoke. 'Private, eh? Do you give many kids private lessons?'

'No. Effy is the only one.'

'And why's that? What makes her so special?'

I was so tense that my shoulders ached and every time I moved my head the vertebrae in my neck crunched. 'She's exceptionally bright. And her dad requested it.'

'Her dad being Samuel Mensah?'

'Yes. Well, I didn't know his first name but I assume that's him. The man who attacked me outside my home earlier this evening.' I inhaled. 'Mr Mensah asked the school, and the head of science there, Kenneth Chase, persuaded me to do it.'

'Persuaded?'

This was clearly part of Ackerman's interview technique: to take a word I'd said and repeat it back to me as a question.

'Yes. We don't usually offer private tuition because it's not the most effective use of our time. Our mission is to teach as many less-privileged children about science as possible, to inspire as many minds as we can without classes being so big they become ineffective.'

'So Effia Mensah *was* special?'

I had a horrible, horrible feeling about where this was heading. It was like being on a runaway bus, the brakes cut, speeding towards disaster. Part of me knew I should stop talking, tell them I did want that solicitor after all, refuse to answer any more of their questions until I knew exactly what I was accused of. But, whatever it was – and I kept trying to reject the worst-case scenario because it was so absurd – I knew I was innocent, and like a naive fool I was gripped by the urge to explain myself, to make them see that I hadn't done anything. Surely if they listened they'd realise this was all a misunderstanding?

'She's the brightest student I teach,' I said. 'The one with the most aptitude and enthusiasm.'

They fell silent and waited for me to speak. And even though I knew, from the shows I'd watched, that this was something the police did when interrogating suspects, I couldn't resist the need to explain myself.

'I said no initially. But Kenneth persuaded me.' More silence from the detectives. 'I thought it would be good PR, that it would help us secure more sponsorship, if I could use Effy as a case study.'

'So it was a business decision?' Ackerman folded her arms and leaned back in her chair.

'That was a big part of it, yes. Because here was this girl from a migrant family who lived in a crappy tower block, one who had none of the advantages that wealthy children get. And she was going to show people that with natural talent and good teaching, it's possible to excel at science. The plan was to get her to sit her GCSEs in biology, chemistry and physics years before her contemporaries.'

They both stared at me.

I couldn't hold back any longer. 'Listen, I need you to tell me what I've been arrested for.'

'In a moment, Mr Foster,' said Ackerman. 'Did you have a private session with Effia on the thirteenth of November?'

I did a quick calculation in my head. Today was Tuesday 20th. 'That was last Tuesday, so yes.'

'And Tuesday the sixth?'

'Yes.'

'And the two of you were alone in the classroom?'

I shifted in my chair, pain snaking its way up through my body until I thought I might be sick again.

'What am I supposed to have done?' I asked, keeping my voice as calm as I was able.

Ackerman looked straight at me. 'Effia Mensah alleges that on two occasions, during your private lessons on the two aforementioned dates, you sexually assaulted her.'

241

There it was. The runaway bus, plunging into the river. It took all my self-control not to throw up again. I was aware that I must have turned completely white, as I felt the blood drain from my face, saw my hand tremble where it rested on the table before me.

'That's insane.'

'She says that you touched her . . .'

'What?'

'. . . on the first occasion, on November sixth, she says you put your hand on her chest and touched her bottom. And on November thirteenth, you went further, putting your hand inside her underwear and touching her.'

'Oh my God.'

It felt as if my entire world was spinning out of orbit. This couldn't be real. Why were these people accusing me of such unspeakable things?

'Effia says that you told her that it was a secret, that if she told anyone you wouldn't be able to teach her anymore, that she wouldn't be able to do her GCSEs. She says you told her it was all part of her biology studies but that other people wouldn't understand.' Ackerman leaned forward. 'Do you have anything to say, Mr Foster?'

I tried to speak but there was no saliva in my mouth and my tongue felt too fat and swollen. Eventually, I managed to force the words out.

'I need a solicitor. And I'm not saying another word until I get one.'

'That's your right,' said Ackerman.

They both got up. It was clear: they were certain of my guilt.

'Wait. I'm entitled to a phone call, aren't I?' I hadn't seen Gemma at the house and, though I had no doubt Jeff and Lizzy would have taken great pleasure in telling her what they'd seen, I wanted to talk to her myself.

Ackerman smirked. 'That's an urban myth.'

'But my wife. I need to tell her where I am and what's going on.'

'Don't worry, Mr Foster. I'm sure she'll be aware. Now, do you have a lawyer or do you want representation to be provided for you?'

ω

I sat on the rock-hard bed in my cell. I had spent the night here, snatching a little sleep before waking up from nightmares in which I was trapped in a coffin, buried alive while everyone I knew walked over my head, oblivious to my screams.

Surely no one would believe I had done this?

Would they?

I didn't understand why Effy had lied. Why make up such an awful story about me? I had never touched her. I hadn't even patted her shoulder or stood particularly close to her. When we started Inquiring Minds, both Amira and I had attended child-protection training where we were told that touching a child, even a pat or hug if they were distressed, should be avoided. We had undergone rigorous CRB checks. The very notion of doing the things DS Ackerman had listed made me sick to my core. I taught children about science because I wanted to pass on my knowledge and love of science, not because I was interested in them in some vile way.

I raked my fingers through my hair, which felt thin and greasy. Why had I agreed to give Effy one-on-one lessons? Why had I broken my own rules? I had never imagined I would be accused of such terrible things, but I had allowed my heart to overrule my head. I liked Effy. It made me happy to see how much she loved science. She reminded me of myself when I was her age, though I was convinced she was naturally more gifted than me and that, with the right education and opportunities, she would go on to greater things. I'd had visions of her winning a Nobel Prize. Of making a difference.

I wanted to talk to her. To find out why. Had someone . . . ?

I sat up straight.

Someone must have put her up to this. Her dad, hoping to get a payout? No, it couldn't be him. He had looked at me with genuine disgust and anger. He believed I had done it.

Then who?

I had no professional enemies. I hadn't exchanged a single cross word with any of the parents of the children I taught. I didn't have any jealous exes or people from my past who wanted me to suffer.

I could only think of one person who would want to get rid of me, to see me languishing in prison.

No, not one person.

Two.

Chapter 42

I jumped up from the bed, ready to bang on the door of the cell, to tell the police about my revelation, when it opened.

DC Syal stood there. She eyed my raised fist and said, 'Your lawyer's here.'

I had asked the police to call Shirley, who, I knew, would be able to find a criminal lawyer to represent me. His name was Gideon Jennings and he was a few years older than me, with dark hair that, from the patches that peeped out from beneath his collar and cuffs, probably covered his entire body. I was allowed to talk to him for ten minutes before my next interview with the two detectives.

The first thing I said to him was: 'My in-laws are behind this. I'm sure of it. My father-in-law is called Jeff Robinson and his wife is Lizzy Robinson. One of them must have got to Effy, persuaded her to make up all these lies about me. Someone needs to talk to Effy now, get her to admit she's lying. Maybe they bribed her, told her—'

Gideon held up a hand. 'Whoa. Let's backtrack here. We don't want to go into this interview making wild accusations.'

'They're not wild!'

'All right. But let's come back to that. Tell me everything the police have said to you, and everything you said to them.'

I went through the whole painful conversation I'd had with the cops. He nodded, tutted and made notes.

'The whole thing is absurd,' I said at the end. 'You do believe me, don't you?' I was desperate for someone to have faith in me.

'I'm your lawyer. It doesn't matter if I believe you. We'll have to see if they have any physical evidence or witnesses, though the latter seems unlikely. Their next step will probably be to seize your computers, both home and office—'

'What?'

'It's standard procedure. I take it you haven't visited any of the websites that a paedophile might visit? You haven't been on the Dark Web?'

'No!' A horrifying thought struck me. 'But if this is Jeff and Lizzy setting me up, they might have. Jeff's always going on about how he knows nothing about computers but I've seen him using my iMac.'

Gideon got this look in his eye whenever I mentioned the Robinsons, as if I was a paranoid fantasist. 'Let's hope that's not the case. I imagine it's going to end up being your word against hers. An eight-year-old girl. Not the most reliable witness, and you're well known, have dedicated your working life to helping children, have no criminal record. If it goes to court I think we'd have an excellent chance.'

I put my head in my hands. *If it goes to court.* The thought was unbearable, and not just for me. It would be awful for Effy too. 'It can't get that far,' I said.

'Well, let's see what the police have to say about their evidence.'

He must have seen how nauseous I was feeling because he leaned across and said, 'Don't worry, Elliot. But let me do the talking, okay?'

ʊ

Gideon was great. He advised me not to answer the detectives' questions, no matter how many times they advised me to talk, to put across my side of the story. It seemed, though, that he was right: there was no physical evidence. Of course there wasn't. Less positively, he was also right about their plan to examine my computers.

As soon as they told me this, I was unable to stop myself from blurting out, 'If you find anything, I didn't put it there.'

Ackerman and Syal sat up a little straighter. 'What do you mean by that?' Ackerman asked.

Gideon shook his head at me but I needed to say it. 'My in-laws. They've been using my computer too and I'm involved in a dispute with them.'

'What kind of dispute?'

'They won't leave my house.' I put both hands flat on the desk between us. I was becoming agitated again. 'They hate me. Would love to get rid of me. I bet they put Effy up to this, persuaded her to lie about me.'

There were raised eyebrows all round.

'They're evil,' I said. 'This is exactly the kind of thing they'd do. They tried to kill me. They left the gas on in my house hoping I'd flick the light switch and ignite it.' I didn't think that was true – why would they destroy their new home? – but I needed the police to think badly of Jeff and Lizzy.

It didn't work. Ackerman and Syal exchanged a look. They thought I was a nutter. Then Ackerman changed the subject, going back to confront me with the details of what I'd supposedly done to Effy. I reverted to saying 'No comment' to everything.

Then, half an hour in, there was a knock on the door. A policeman poked his head into the room and said he needed to speak to the two detectives. They suspended the interview and left.

My heart dropped into my stomach. 'I bet they've found something on the computer,' I whispered. 'This is it, Jeff's well and truly stitched me up. My whole life is going to be ruined.'

Gideon told me to get a grip and stay calm. That was easy for him to say. He wasn't facing years in prison, his reputation destroyed, being beaten up by nonce-hating inmates, spending his life on a sex offender's register . . . The list went on and on.

Ackerman and Syal came back into the room, wearing grim expressions.

'What is it?' I asked, my voice high-pitched and panicked. 'I swear I didn't—'

'You're free to go,' Ackerman said.

I was so shocked that I thought I hadn't heard her properly. 'Free?'

She nodded, her expression thunderous.

'What's going on?' Gideon asked.

It was Syal's turn to speak. 'Effia Mensah and her father have just visited the station. She's withdrawn her statement. She says she made it all up.'

'Well. That's good news,' said Gideon. 'Looks like you owe my client an apology.'

'Leave it out,' said Ackerman.

A huge jolt of adrenaline surged through me. I could barely speak, but managed to stutter a question.

'Was I right? Did somebody put her up to it?'

Ackerman pursed her lips. 'She says that somebody spoke to her and told you were a bad person, that you'd abused other children and that you would soon do it to her if she didn't stop you. They also said that if she didn't tell this story about you, her family would be deported.' She sighed. 'It all came out after she said to her dad, "I'm so glad we can stay here now." He asked her what she meant and, apparently, she broke down and confessed.'

'I knew it! Has she given you a description of this person?'

'They talked to her on the phone. She has a mobile phone already.'

That wasn't unusual. Half the eight-year-olds I taught had iPhones.

'Whoever it was found her via social media – she's on Instagram – and got her to give them her number. We're constantly going into schools and warning kids about online security but . . .' She shook her head like she wished the internet had never been invented.

'Maybe she'd recognise the voice?' I said.

'We'll be following that up, Mr Foster. But like I said, you're free to go.'

She stood up and opened the door. The conversation was over.

ω

I don't want to exaggerate but, leaving the police station, I felt like the guy at the end of *The Shawshank Redemption*. Sweet, underappreciated freedom. But my elation at being released without charge turned to anger and bitterness as I made my way home, walking through the cold streets wishing I'd called a cab but wanting the time to think and clear my head. My phone had died overnight while the police were 'looking after' it, so I couldn't call anyone anyway, and the only taxis that passed by were already occupied.

I couldn't decide what to do. Confront Jeff and Lizzy, tell them I knew what they'd done, or keep my suspicions secret? I guessed they would be shocked when I walked through the front door and I decided it was better to keep quiet, especially if the police were planning to talk to them.

It was a long walk home and, halfway, tired and hungry, I stopped at a cafe. I ordered a late breakfast and asked if they had a phone charger I could borrow. I sat in the corner with my phone plugged into the wall, waiting for it to boot up.

As soon as it did, in rushed a flood of texts and messages and social media notifications. It was so overwhelming that I ignored them all and called Gemma.

She answered immediately. 'Elliot? Where are you?'

'I've been released without charge. I'm on my way home.'

'Oh, thank God. I've been going out of my mind. Where exactly are you now?'

'In a cafe near Denmark Hill.'

'Okay. Let me come and meet you there. We can talk.'

I was confused. 'Aren't you at work?'

'No, of course not. I couldn't go in while all this was going on. I'm at home.' I realised that she had been speaking quietly, like she didn't want to be overheard. I gave her the name of the cafe and she said she'd get an Uber.

'Listen,' she said before she hung up, 'you haven't been online since you got out, have you?'

'No. Why?'

She exhaled. 'Put your phone away, eat your breakfast and wait till I get there. I'll see you in ten minutes.'

But of course, once she said that, I had to check my notifications. And as soon as I started scrolling through them, I wished I'd stayed in my bubble of blissful ignorance.

Chapter 43

> @Elliottthescientist Disgusting pervert. I hope u die and ROT in HELL!!!

> Shocked & disgusted by the news about @Elliottthescientist. Always thought he was a nice guy.

> @Elliottthescientist I hope you get raped in prison you pedo freek.

There were hundreds more like this. I read the first couple of dozen before laying my phone face down on the table. The room spun around me like I was drunk, and I had to close my eyes for a few seconds. I shouldn't have looked. I should have waited for Gemma.

But I was unable to resist the urge to lift the rock and peer beneath.

I had been tagged in a news story in London's biggest newspaper, published this morning. The headline told me everything I needed to know.

BOFFIN TEACHER ACCUSED OF KIDDIE ABUSE

Beneath the headline was an unflattering photo of me, taken at a charity garden party a couple of years ago, standing there with a glass of wine in my hand, squinting into the sun, mouth open. There were over a thousand comments on the article but I managed to close the page without looking at them. I knew what they would say.

Somebody had leaked the story, even though I hadn't been charged. That didn't matter to the press or public, though. I remembered when the BBC had broadcast images of the police raiding the home of Cliff Richard after sexual assault allegations were made against the veteran pop star, and he had never even been arrested for anything. The newspaper report, which I had skimmed briefly, was short on substance – mainly a precis of my career so far – and nobody had asked me or my lawyer for a response.

I imagined tomorrow there would be an even shorter follow-up story saying I had been released without charge. But I knew what would happen.

People would always look at me and think, *There's no smoke without fire.*

And I had a very good idea about who had leaked the story. The same people who had persuaded Effy to lie. The same people who were trying to ruin my life.

Gemma hadn't turned up yet – I guessed her Uber must have got held up – but I couldn't sit around here waiting. I was sure people in the cafe had recognised me and were glaring at me, even though when I looked around no one was looking in my direction. It didn't matter. I could feel their thoughts stabbing me like needles. *Child molester. Paedo. Scum.* I had to get out.

I stood up too quickly, rattling the table and knocking my chair over. I put my head down and hurried out, legs wobbling like I'd been confined to bed for months.

Outside, I gulped down air and returned to my phone. There were numerous missed calls, including several from Amira. There was still no sign of Gemma so I called Amira's mobile. She answered straight away.

'Elliot! Where are you? What's going on?'

I told her I'd been released. 'Effy withdrew the allegations.'

It sounded noisy where she was. A babble of high-pitched voices. A children's playground. She must have been standing outside a school.

'It was Effy? Wait, what happened? I don't understand. I've been trying to get information out of Colin but he's gone away for the week on a training course and when I called him he said he hadn't heard anything about it.'

I started to tell her – about Effy accusing me of assaulting her, my night in the cell, how she'd confessed to lying – but halfway through she stopped me and said, 'Hang on, I can hardly hear you. Let me find somewhere quieter.' The line went silent for a short while before she said, 'Right, I'm in my car. Now, tell me again. Calmly.'

I told her everything, as succinctly as I could. I was close to tears, the aftershock of what had happened hitting me hard.

'Oh, Elliot,' Amira said. 'It must have been horrific. But thank God she came clean.'

'I can't even think about what would have happened if she hadn't,' I said. 'It would have destroyed everything we'd created.'

'It's been going crazy at the office,' she said. 'The phones have been ringing off the hook. I've just been letting everything go to voicemail.'

'Reporters?'

'Yeah. But also . . .'

'What?'

She hesitated. 'Clients. Head teachers. The local education authority. Backers. Parents. It's been rough. I didn't know what to say to anyone.'

The wind outside the coffee shop bit into me. But that wasn't why I felt so cold. 'You didn't tell them I was innocent?'

'I didn't know what was going on, Elliot.'

'But surely you should know I would never do anything like that!'

'Yes. No. I mean . . .'

'Oh my God. You thought I might be guilty? Of abusing one of our kids?'

'Elliot . . .'

'How many contracts have been cancelled?'

She sounded stricken. 'I don't know.'

'But some?' When she didn't respond I said, 'More than some?'

'Most of them, Elliot. Including Lambeth Council.'

The local education authority. Our biggest client by far. I couldn't speak.

'But we'll bring them back. I'll start calling everyone the moment I get back to the office. Are you coming in? We should both call them, together.'

I had sunk into a crouching position. Amira's voice sounded like it was coming from a very long way away. My name was tainted now, whatever happened. The mud would stick forever. And despite the good we did, the council were always trying to cut costs. Some bean-counter there would already have worked out exactly how much they'd save; they might even have reallocated the funds already. They'd be worried too, about a flood of complaints from parents.

'We're ruined,' I said.

'No! We can fight this, Elliot.'

I covered my face with my hand. 'Even you thought I might be guilty.'

'But—'

I didn't let her finish. I hung up and switched off my phone.

ϖ

I was still hunched on the pavement when a car pulled up and Gemma got out. She stood for a moment, the wind whipping her hair into her face. She was my wife, my ally. Right now, I needed her. And I needed her to believe in me.

She came over and crouched beside me, putting her arms around me.

'Come on,' she whispered. 'Let's go for a walk.'

I let her help me to my feet. 'I need to ask you something. You didn't think I did it, did you?'

'What? Of course not.'

'It never entered your head? That I might assault a child?'

'No! My God, Elliot. The moment I heard about it, I knew it was a terrible mistake.'

I hugged her. She felt like she'd lost weight, all sharp angles and bones. There was a sour odour about her too, beneath the smell of the breath mint she was sucking. Had she been drinking this morning? Most likely it was from last night, and it would be difficult to ask without it sounding like an accusation. I would talk to her about it later.

We walked hand in hand down the hill towards Camberwell. It was busy, as always, and I was sure people were looking at me. Just like in the cafe, I could hear their voices inside my head, accusing me, judging me. Wanting me to ROT in HELL.

As we walked, I told Gemma what I'd seen online. I told her everything Amira had said. She made a series of increasingly distressed noises.

'How could the police make such a stupid mistake?'

'It wasn't a mistake,' I said, as we passed the shops at the bottom of the hill and started the long walk towards home.

'What do you mean?'

'Someone put her up to it.' I explained what Effy had admitted to the police.

Gemma stopped walking. 'You think . . . ?'

'Yeah. Your parents. Who else could it be? You know what I remembered earlier? Your dad, looking over my shoulder when I was working in the snug. I'm sure I was emailing Kenneth about Effy. All her personal details and her dad's phone number are on that computer. Even someone as useless with computers as your dad would be able to find them, and I gave your parents the password so they could use it to search for properties.'

I suppose part of me wanted her to argue, to give me some solid reason why it couldn't have been Jeff or Lizzy. But she didn't. Instead, she hung her head and said, 'I'm sorry. This is all my fault.'

'No, it's not. Don't think like that. I'm not interested in blaming you. I'm only interested in working out what we're going to do.'

She started walking again.

'This legal route is going to take too long,' I said. 'The thought of having them under our roof for another day is unbearable. There's no way I can put up with them for the months it's going to take to evict them.'

A bus roared past us. I pictured Jeff and Lizzy, crushed beneath its wheels.

'The police are going to talk to them about this thing with Effy, but I know what's going to happen. They won't be able to prove it was them. If only I could find out what they were doing in Toulouse, what happened on that blank day in Chloe's journal.'

'What?'

Maybe it was the tiredness or the stress, but I had temporarily forgotten that Gemma didn't know about what I'd found. Now it was time to come clean. I told her about finding Chloe's journal and what I'd found in it.

'So you think something happened in August that made them come back to England?' She seemed shaken but not angry about me going into her sister's room and looking through her stuff.

'Yes. When did you get the email from them asking if they could come and stay?'

She took out her phone and, I assumed, looked through her emails. 'October twenty-first.'

'So they hung around in France for two months. That's weird. Unless they went somewhere else before coming here. Has Chloe said anything to you?'

'No. Nothing at all.'

'She's said nothing about having a boyfriend? Someone with the initials JC?'

'Elliot, she talks to me even less than she does to you.'

A pair of young women passed us, walking side by side and thumbing their phones at the same time.

'It seems weird,' I said, 'that none of your family had phones when they got back to England. Surely Chloe would have had one, at least. Probably full of photos of this JC guy. Full of evidence. Did you never speak to them or exchange texts when they were in France?'

'We just exchanged the occasional email. I told you, I had as little contact with them as possible.'

'Hmm. But they must have had phones, and ditched them before they came back. Maybe they contained incriminating evidence of whatever it was they did. When we get home, I want to try to have another look at Chloe's journal. I need you to distract her, get her out of her room for a while, and keep your parents away from her room at the same time. Can you do that?'

She was gripping my hand hard. 'Yes. Of course.'

'Great.' I smiled for the first time in twenty-four hours. 'Just think how great it would be if we could find evidence that would get them arrested.'

Gemma nodded, tried to smile back. But it slipped away as quickly as it had come.

I hardly noticed. I was convinced I was going to find something. I was going to turn the tables. The image of Jeff and Lizzy being led away in handcuffs while I looked on powered me all the way home.

Chapter 44

There were paint pots and bottles of white spirit in the dining room, stacked against the wall along with brushes and rollers. The tape measure I'd seen Lizzy with when they'd first come to stay was there too. Gemma had told me they'd bought the painting supplies while I was with the police, announcing their plan to redecorate, to make the place 'more to their taste'. No doubt there was more new furniture on the way too.

The kitchen stank of Lizzy's cigarettes, which she had taken to smoking indoors now, not even bothering to hide her habit anymore. I went upstairs. The smell in the upstairs hallway and bathroom was a cocktail of Brylcreem and halitosis and stale sweat. It was as if it had permeated the brickwork, clinging to the paint and floorboards. If I ever got rid of them, the whole house would need to be scrubbed and fumigated.

I could hear Jeff and Lizzy in their bedroom, talking together in low voices. Plotting, I expected. Figuring out how to get rid of me now their attempt to get me locked up for child abuse had failed. What next? An unfortunate accident? *He tripped and fell down the stairs . . . The wiring in the kettle must have been faulty . . . Poor Elliot slipped and smashed his head open on the kitchen counter . . . He must have fallen asleep in the bath.*

There are so many ways of killing someone in the home and making it look like an accident. As I headed up to my and Gemma's bedroom, I felt jittery and unsafe. What was once my haven, a place of security and comfort, now felt like a deathtrap.

Gemma had gone straight up to the bedroom when we got home. I found her there now, pacing the floor.

'How am I going to lure them out of their rooms and keep them out?' she asked, chewing her thumbnail. Her hands dropped to her belly where her scars were. I'd noticed she often touched her stomach at times like this, as if the scars throbbed when she was worried.

'I don't know. Cook them a meal? Say you want to make peace?'

She shook her head. 'That won't work. They'll be suspicious. But maybe I could say I'm cooking a special meal to celebrate you being released?'

I thought about it. 'No, then I'll need to be there. You need to make them think you're on their side.' I ran a hand through my hair. When I took it away there were several loose strands stuck to my palm. The stress was making my hair fall out. 'Okay, I've got it. In a moment, I'm going to start shouting at you. I want you to shout back. Then storm downstairs to the kitchen and start crying. Actually, you should make sobbing noises as you go past your parents' door. Chloe's too. That's bound to draw them out. They'll want to witness your pain.'

She rubbed at her belly. 'Okay.'

'Then tell them we've been arguing about them because you told me you want them to stay. Tell them you want to make up for lost time and get to know them better. Lay it on thick. Say how grateful you are that they're here, how you wish you'd never married me.'

'I might choke on the words.'

I laid my hands on both her shoulders and put my forehead against hers. 'You can do this, Gemma. Maybe you should offer to cook them dinner at that point and tell them you want to carry on talking. Who knows, maybe this will be a double whammy and you'll be able to get some info out of them that we can use. Just keep them downstairs as long as possible. And put some music on to mask the sound of me moving around.'

I kissed her and she wrapped her arms around me. The kiss lasted longer than I'd intended.

'Can't we just go to bed?' she asked, pressing herself against me. 'And do this tomorrow?'

It was tempting. So tempting. To lose myself in her, in carnal abandon, so I wouldn't have to think about anything else for a while. But no. This had to be done now.

'Later,' I whispered, extricating myself.

She visibly steeled herself. 'Okay, let's do this. Do you want to start the shouting or shall I?'

I smiled. 'Ladies first.'

We yelled at each other, back and forth, just making up nonsense, mixed in with swear words. Gemma stamped her feet and I threw a hardback book against the wall. She slammed the en-suite door and screamed at me. I shouted back, using the worst words I could think of. It felt good to get it out. Cathartic. Suddenly, I could see the appeal of those therapy sessions where people go into the woods and holler at the trees. Gemma looked slightly alarmed as I called her every name under the sun, and perhaps I got a little carried away as I imagined I was yelling at Jeff and Lizzy. After a minute, Gemma had to grab hold of me and make eye contact to pull me back into the present.

'Sorry,' I said in a soft voice, giving her a hug. 'Good luck.'

She sucked in air. 'I hope you find something. I need this to be worth it.'

'It's worth trying, Gemma. Whatever happens.'

She left the room, slamming the door behind her and stomping down the stairs. She began to make sobbing, choking noises as she descended. They sounded pretty damn realistic to me. I opened the door a crack and listened, hearing the bedroom door below open and

Mark Edwards

the bass of Jeff's voice. Gemma let out another anguished sob. Another door clicked open and I was sure they had all come out of their rooms. There was a flurry of footsteps, several pairs of feet going down to the ground floor, and then all was quiet. I waited and, a minute later, music came on, drifting up from the kitchen. An eighties radio station.

I gave it another couple of minutes, to ensure none of the Robinsons came straight back up, then trod lightly down the stairs to the middle floor.

I headed to Chloe's bedroom – my office, which I was desperate to get back – first. I immediately opened the cupboard and reached inside for the journal.

There it was, still in the same spot.

Shutting the cupboard door quietly, I sat with my back against the wall and began to leaf through the journal, looking for passages that might be important and wishing I could read French. Knowing I didn't have much time, I used my phone to take photographs of the pages immediately before the missing entry on August 10th. I flicked back further, looking for Jeff and Lizzy's names, for words like *Papa* and *Maman*. I found these a few times and took further pictures of those pages. Then, still sitting on the floor, I messaged them to Amira with a note asking if she could translate them.

This was the best I could do for now. As I was putting the journal back in its hiding place, I heard someone coming up the stairs. I froze. Was it Chloe? I considered crawling into the cupboard and hiding, but then I heard the bathroom door shut. A minute later, the toilet flushed and whoever it was went back downstairs.

I exhaled.

I went back out into the hallway, feeling deflated. I had been hoping that something in the journal would leap out at me, even if it was written in a language I didn't understand. Downstairs, the music was still playing and, above it, I could hear the babble of conversation and Lizzy's laughter. Probably chortling at the idea of me and Gemma

262

falling out, of her being on their side. The hot stone of anger pulsed in my gut. There had to be something else here that would help me.

I should look in Jeff and Lizzy's room.

I hesitated, but only for a moment. They had obliterated my privacy. If they caught me in their room, what was the worst that could happen? They would know I was looking for something to use against them. But if I didn't find anything, that wouldn't matter anyway. This might be the only chance I got.

I slipped into their room and closed the door softly behind me.

It was a scene of chaos, like the worst teenager's bedroom. Actually, chaotic wasn't the right word. It was destructive. It showed no respect for or love of the place where they were staying. By making such a mess – discarded clothes, duvet hanging off the mattress, crockery everywhere, a pile of what looked like toenail clippings scattered on the chest of drawers – it was as if they were trying to mark their territory. Stamp themselves upon it, like a cat spraying inside its owner's house.

Where should I start? Jeff and Lizzy's suitcases seemed like a good idea. One was shoved under the new bed and the other was on top of the wardrobe. The first was Jeff's. It was empty, but the luggage label was still attached. Hope flared for a second, but instead of their home in Toulouse he had written this address.

Lizzy's suitcase contained some clothes: a swimming costume and a towel that smelled damp and musty. I reached inside the inner pocket and found an envelope. I pulled it out.

Photographs.

There were only a dozen or so and I looked through them quickly. There were a couple of Jeff, standing in a garden beside a barbecue, grinning at the camera. He looked no different to how he did now, except he was in shorts and a T-shirt, indicating this was taken recently. There were a few photos of Lizzy, taken at the same event. She was in a bikini, lying on a sun lounger, cigarette smouldering between her fingers. She was saying something and seemed annoyed that someone,

Jeff presumably, was taking her picture. On the surface, Lizzy looked so much like Gemma in these photos it was terrifying. But, looking closer, Lizzy lacked something that Gemma had. It was as if her aura had been stripped away, the human warmth that made Gemma so beautiful. Lizzy should be an attractive woman. Instead, she looked like a mannequin that had learned to walk and talk.

I moved on to the final few photos. There were two of Chloe, again on the same occasion. She seemed happy, like her dad. She was wearing shorts and a vest top and wasn't as skinny as she was now. She looked young and carefree, the sun shining behind her, rendering her hair white.

In the last photo, Chloe was sitting at a small wooden table with a young man. He had dark hair and tanned skin. At first glance, the smile he gave the camera seemed genuine, but looking closer I could see something in his eyes. Fear.

Was this JC?

I slipped the picture into my back pocket and returned the suitcase to the top of the wardrobe. I turned around and my eye fell upon the chest of drawers, at the jumble of toiletries and make-up.

There, among the Brylcreem and deodorant, the Vaseline and Veet, was a bottle of Eau Sauvage. My missing aftershave.

I picked it up. Not long ago, this proof that Jeff had been helping himself to my stuff – coming up to my bathroom and taking it – would have angered me. Now it seemed trivial among everything else. But as I lifted it, the lid fell off and I caught a faint whiff of the scent.

I was thrown back in time. Back to the darkest night of my life.

Standing in George and Edith's living room. The room stank of blood and excrement. Of violence and terror. But somewhere deep in that cocktail of foul smells I could detect something else. Something sharper and cleaner. Something familiar.

At the time, I had been so overwhelmed by the sensory onslaught, by the horrors before me, my brain hadn't been able to isolate and identify the scent. And this was the first time I'd smelled it since. The first opportunity for my brain to make the connection.

I sat on the bed, still holding the bottle, breathing heavily. Was this real? Could my memory be playing tricks on me? I took another sniff of the bottle and closed my eyes, forcing myself to revisit that night again.

Instead, I was taken back to an earlier evening. Standing in my garden shed. I had detected Eau Sauvage that night too. Jeff had told me he'd been in the shed to get a break from Lizzy. And then I hurtled forward again, to when I'd found Edith, and I was sure, I was *certain*, that I could smell this aftershave. But before I could pause, to react, my memory sent me back up the stairs, back into George and Edith's bedroom, and I was crouching beside George as he said his final words. Words of warning, I was convinced.

He'd never completed his warning, if that's what it was. He had said *Not*, then began another word starting with 'w' before breathing his last.

But what if it wasn't two words he was trying to get out, but one? *Knotweed.*

I got to my feet, reeling, having to hold on to the chest of drawers for support. *The Knotweeds.* That was what he called the Robinsons.

In his final moments, the best George's broken, dying brain could manage was this word, this attempt to warn me, to tell me who had killed him.

This and the aftershave. There was no longer any doubt in my mind.

Jeff had killed my neighbours.

And at that moment, the bedroom door opened and he was standing there, his lip curled into a sneer.

Chapter 45

The mask Jeff usually wore – the no-nonsense but avuncular family man – had been well and truly ripped off. A vein throbbed beneath the taut skin of his forehead, his teeth were bared and his eyes dark. His fists were clenched by his sides.

He looked like he wanted me dead.

'Knotweed,' I said.

He blinked at me. 'You what?'

'How did you do it?' I asked, as calmly as I could. 'Get to George and Edith's and back so quickly? Why weren't you spattered with their blood?'

Jeff's eyes flicked between the bottle of aftershave and my face.

'I guess you must have worn some kind of coverall,' I said.

He stared at me.

'What did you do with the toy cars? Have you sold them? Or are they here somewhere?'

I pulled open a drawer and began rifling through, blindly, chucking socks and underwear aside before moving on to the next drawer. There was nothing here except clothes. He must have sold them already. Maybe that was how he was able to afford his phone.

Jeff moved closer to me. 'Are you going to tell me what the hell you're talking about?'

'Don't pretend you don't know,' I said, holding up the bottle of Eau Sauvage. 'You murdered George and Edith. This is the proof.'

'You've finally cracked, Elliot,' he said. But something passed over his face, so fleeting it barely registered. A look of realisation. Of surprise. Probably thinking about how he'd messed up by wearing my aftershave that night.

'No,' I said, 'I've finally seen the truth.'

'Truth? You need to be careful, mate.'

He took a step towards me and I retreated until I was almost against the wall. The window was to my left, the curtains closed against the night.

'You murdered George and Edith,' I said. 'Why? Actually, you don't need to tell me. It's because you saw Chloe whisper something to him, didn't you? You weren't really after the cars – that was just to make it look like a burglary.'

'You're insane,' he said.

But I was on a roll. 'What did Chloe say to him? It must have been something to do with what happened in France. Did you kill someone there too?' I was giddy with shock and exhilaration and fear. 'I think I know what happened. It was Chloe's boyfriend, wasn't it? JC. You murdered your daughter's boyfriend on August the tenth. That's why you had to leave the country and come back to England.'

'You have no idea what you're talking about, Elliot. And you need to be careful, throwing accusations about—'

'I'm sick of listening to you. You can tell your lies to the police.'

I pulled my phone out of my pocket and unlocked it. Jeff took another step across the room, moving down the side of the bed towards me.

'I didn't kill the old codgers next door,' he said with a shark-like grin. 'Do you really think I could have come here and gone back to the restaurant in, what was it, half an hour? And kill two people in that time without getting any blood on me? Ludicrous. You think the police will listen to your crazy theory? That bottle of aftershave is proof of nothing.'

He had a point. But he must have left DNA at the scene, surely? All I needed was for the police to take him in for questioning, take a DNA sample . . . At the very least it would get him out of my house and allow me to change all the locks. With Jeff gone, it wouldn't be that hard to get Lizzy out too.

'You can tell all that to the police,' I said, lifting the phone to my ear.

Jeff was surprisingly fast. He shot across the space between us, arm outstretched, aiming for the phone. I swept it away from him, turning towards the wall and holding the phone up high.

It was a mistake. It opened me up to the punch that struck me in the stomach. It was like being hit by a speeding car. All the breath left my body and I doubled over, gasping, feeling like I was suffocating.

I dropped the phone and it bounced on the carpet and landed beneath the dressing table.

I threw myself down and lunged for the phone, but Jeff was too fast. He stamped on my hand, snatched up the phone and retreated back across the room.

'Give it to me,' I demanded, clutching my mashed hand.

'Piss off, Elliot,' he said. He was calm, not even out of breath.

'Give me the phone!'

He laughed. 'Stop being a twat. Get this into your thick head: I didn't kill them.'

'You're lying.'

My hand throbbed. My stomach hurt from where he had punched me. There was still an ache in my balls from my encounter with Effy's dad the night before. But rage filled me, adrenaline acting as both a salve and a motor.

I launched myself at him, crossing the few metres between us in a second, aiming for Jeff's throat.

He dodged easily and I slammed into the wall behind him. The next thing I knew he had hold of my wrist, twisting it up behind my back until my shoulder screamed.

'Give up,' he said in my ear from behind me, spittle spraying my cheek. He reeked of Brylcreem and sweat and bad breath.

I tried to stamp on his foot but he was prepared, twisting my arm further until I cried out in agony.

'I said, *give up.*'

He turned me round and pushed me out of the room, a constellation of pain bursting from my shoulder joint. Gemma was in the hallway, her mouth open, eyes wide. Jeff shoved me forward, a final jolt of pain searing through my shoulder, and Gemma rushed to me and put her arms around me.

Jeff pointed a finger at her. 'You need to make a decision about whose side you're on, girl. But remember this: we're your blood.'

He slammed the door.

Chapter 46

I stamped up the stairs, with Gemma hurrying to keep up. I was incandescent with fury and self-loathing, blood close to boiling point, the bubble and rush of my speeding pulse filling my ears. The moment Jeff had entered the bedroom downstairs, my system had filled with adrenaline, ready for fight or flight. I had tried to fight, and was never going to flee, but my muscles and brain were still buzzing, my heart still pounding. I couldn't even feel the pain in my shoulder.

I stood at the centre of the bedroom and let rip a silent scream. Out of the corner of my eye, I could see Gemma, cowering in the slipstream of my rage. She looked scared – scared of me – and that realisation allowed the part of my brain that was normally in charge, the evolved, rational side, to take over. I needed to calm down. I went into the en-suite and splashed cold water on my face. It didn't work. Staring back at me from the mirror was a madman, red in the face, pupils dilated, hair standing on end.

I still needed to call the police. Jeff had achieved very little by taking my phone from me. I could use Gemma's or the house phone . . .

'What happened?' Gemma asked.

I turned from the mirror. 'It was your dad. He killed George and Edith. I smelled it, the aftershave, my aftershave, and George tried to tell me, he said "Knotweed", and . . .'

I stopped. Gemma was staring at me as if nothing I was saying made any sense, and I imagined myself telling this story to the police, trying to get them to take it seriously. Jeff was right. None of it was proof. It was nothing close to proof.

It was as if a plug had been pulled. The adrenaline began to drain out of me. I allowed Gemma to guide me out of the bathroom into the bedroom. The strength had gone from my legs and the soreness in my stomach and shoulder and hand came rushing back.

The physical pain was nothing, though. It was my pride that really hurt, and my sense of justice. For a long time I had lived under the illusion that the world was, essentially, fair. That good guys win in the end – or at least have a fighting chance of winning. Criminals are punished, tyrants are toppled. Bullies eventually go away to live their small, miserable lives.

I saw now how naive that was. There was no fairness, no natural justice. No karma.

I sat on the edge of the mattress, my head in my hands.

'What happened?' she asked. 'Tell me, slowly.'

I told her. About the aftershave and George's final words.

'What did my father say? Did he deny it?'

'Yes, of course. Maybe he thought I was recording him. I've been racking my brains . . . Do you remember if he was wearing aftershave in the restaurant that night?'

She rubbed her forehead. 'I think so. Actually, yes – yes, I do. I remember thinking it was strong as we left the house.'

'And it was my aftershave?'

'Yes. I mean, I don't recall recognising it at the time, but it definitely could have been.'

I was short of breath. 'Do you think your dad is capable of murder?'

She didn't answer immediately. She blinked and I saw tears in her eyes. Her reply, when it came, was whispered. 'Yes. Yes, I do. But I also know that if you go to the police with this, you won't get anywhere.'

We both sat in silence for a little while. 'You must think I'm so pathetic,' I said eventually.

'What? Of course I don't. You think I want you to be like my dad? You're a thousand times the man he is. You think I want someone like that? All muscle and aggression? We're not living in the Stone Age.'

I shook my head. 'I know what you're going to say. I'm more intelligent than he is. Brains should triumph over brawn. But your dad's not an idiot, Gemma, is he? And whatever you say about my qualities versus his, he's winning. He's come on to my territory and taken it over. I should be able to protect my own home. It's like this time a couple of years ago when Charlie was being terrorised by a tom that came into our garden every night. I'm like Charlie. A neutered tomcat.'

'But that other tom's not around now,' Gemma said. 'Charlie must have won in the end.'

'Only because the other cat got run over.'

'Oh.'

'Yeah.' I laughed bitterly. 'I saw him on the roadside. Unfortunately, Charlie didn't come up with some brilliant scheme to triumph over his foe. He spent a month cowering in the kitchen until his enemy stopped turning up.'

From downstairs I could hear the blare of the TV. I wondered if Jeff and Lizzy were having a similar conversation to Gemma and me, and if Jeff was feeling good about himself or if he was worried. Surely there was part of him that was afraid of the police and of going to prison? Or was he supremely confident that he'd get away with it? Just as he'd got away with everything else in his life.

Gemma looked like she wanted to say something.

'What is it?' I asked.

Unexpectedly, she burst into tears. Soon she was sobbing. I put my arm around her shoulders, pulled her close.

'Gemma, sweetheart.'

Finally, she got control of herself, grabbing a tissue and blowing her nose. But there were still tears in her eyes.

'I'm crying because you're right,' she said. 'He is winning. They both are. Trying to evict them legally is going to take forever and who knows what damage they'll have wreaked by then.' She looked at me. 'I'm scared, Elliot. Scared that we're never going to get rid of them. Scared that it's going to destroy our marriage. Unless . . .'

I waited. 'Unless what?'

Her voice had dropped to a whisper. 'I can't say it. I shouldn't even be thinking it.'

'Tell me.'

'No, I can't. I don't want you to think I'm evil.'

I stared at her. I thought I knew what she was going to say and, I must admit, I experienced a tingle of excitement, deep in my belly. I hated them. Jeff and Lizzy. They had invaded my house and humiliated me. They had inflicted untold damage on their children. They had almost certainly committed some terrible crime in France. They had tried to get me jailed for child abuse. And worst of all, Jeff had murdered the lovely couple next door, smashing in their skulls with a hammer before returning to dinner as if nothing had happened. They were evil. There was no doubt in my mind.

But that didn't make what Gemma was about to suggest any more palatable.

'Gemma, no.'

But she took both my hands in hers and looked into my eyes. She was beautiful, perhaps in that moment more beautiful than ever before, and her voice was soft but clear.

Mark Edwards

'Elliot,' she said, 'it's the only way. My mum and dad . . . The only way they're going to leave us alone, the only thing that will stop them destroying other lives.'

'Don't say it.'

But she did.

'The only way to stop them is to kill them.'

Chapter 47

'You could do it, Elliot. I know you could. For me. For us.'

'You're not serious.'

She held my gaze, unflinching, not even blinking. She was deadly serious.

'It's the only way,' she said. 'Don't you see? We'll never get them out of here alive. Not before they destroy everything we have. Everything you have, Elliot. They've already tried to destroy your career.'

'They've probably succeeded,' I said.

'No, you'll recover from that. Or rather, you will if my parents aren't still around. Because I bet you they've got a lot more planned. And it won't just be your job and your business that they target. They want to break you, Elliot. They'll try to break us so you're isolated. And then the mental torture will really begin.'

I made an incredulous noise. 'You mean it hasn't started already?'

I was astounded by how calm she was, as if she was laying out a business plan, not talking about murdering her parents. 'Not really. They want you docile, so they can carry on living here with you but without any resistance or trouble.'

'Or they want me gone. They've already tried to get me sent to prison.'

Gemma shook her head. 'I don't think they thought you'd go to prison. They probably suspected Effy would confess sooner or later. They wanted to scare you. To show you what could happen. Maybe we should leave here, start anew somewhere else.'

I pulled my hands away and stood up. 'This is insane. It's my house. Our house. This kind of thing . . . it can't happen.'

Gemma got up too, grabbing hold of me again. 'But, Elliot, it is happening. This is what my parents do. They turn the world upside down. They twist all the rules, they lie and cheat and destroy, and they get away with it. They're going to get away with killing George and Edith.'

Gemma gestured for me to sit down again. I felt drained but still wired. And all the while, as we talked, a little voice whispered questions in my ear: *Could you do it? Could you kill them?*

I opened my mouth to speak but Gemma put a finger to my lips.

'The world will be a better place without them in it. You have to agree with that.'

'It's hard to deny.'

'They've never done a good thing in their life,' she said.

'They had you. That's one good thing.'

She made a noise in her throat. 'That's debatable. But it's because they gave me life that I don't say any of this lightly. I've been trying to come up with an alternative, another way to get rid of them. But in every scenario I come up with, we fail. They either stay here or they come back. And there's part of me that thinks, *Okay, Gemma, just wait. They're almost sixty. Wait till they die of old age.*'

'But they could live for another twenty or thirty years.'

'Exactly. And I can't wait that long. I want a life, Elliot. A life with you. Maybe a family.' Her eyes shone with emotion.

'I'd like that,' I said.

'But it can never happen. Not with Mum and Dad around. Could you imagine raising a child in such a terrible atmosphere? But if they were gone, we'd be free to start our life together properly. Maybe a couple more years of being on our own, really getting to know each other.'

That was all I really wanted. Sometimes I forgot that Gemma and I had only known each other for a few months. It had been so intense. And I could imagine an outsider looking in and telling me how foolish I'd been. How none of this would have happened if Gemma and I hadn't rushed to get married and move in together. But it's easy to apply cold logic when it's not your emotions involved. Despite everything, our relationship still felt right. I loved her. There was nothing I could do about that.

This suggestion of Gemma's, though. This required rational thought. To even consider it, I had to separate it from emotion, from hatred and fear. Perhaps because I was so exhausted and numb, I was able to do this. Temporarily, at least.

'What are you thinking?' Gemma asked.

'That there's no point doing it if we would end up in prison. Have you thought about that?'

'Of course I have.'

'And what was your conclusion?'

She chewed her thumbnail and I noticed how the skin around her fingers was red and raw. 'I thought you'd be able to help with that. I mean, you're a scientist. You must know some way of doing it.'

I laughed humourlessly. 'I can think of plenty of ways to kill someone.'

'But could you make it look like, you know, a natural death?'

'Hypothetically speaking, you mean?'

She gestured for me to go on.

'Well, I can think of a few methods. Poisoning being the obvious one. There are a number of chemicals or natural toxins that you could use.'

'Right.'

'I can think of a couple that would be hard to detect in a pathology report, such as—'

Mark Edwards

The eagerness with which Gemma was looking at me made me stop. I couldn't do this. I wasn't that person.

'Gemma, this is crazy. Not just crazy. It's wrong. We can't murder your parents, no matter how awful they are. I can't kill another human being.'

'Not even Jeff and Lizzy?'

'No.'

Was that a flash of anger in her eyes? Or just disappointment?

'Then tell me how to do it,' she said, leaning closer.

I stared at her. 'You don't really want to kill them. Your own parents.'

'There's no other way.'

'No other way? There has to be. We can try the legal route. I'll go to the police . . .'

'But we have no evidence!'

'They could still—'

'No!'

She hissed it through clenched teeth, the ferocity of it killing the conversation, and then she lay back on the bed. She covered her eyes with both hands, but a tear trickled from beneath her palm and ran down the side of her face. I didn't know what to say. I wanted to reach out to her, to offer her some comfort. I wanted to make her happy. But I wasn't going to back down.

I despised Jeff and Lizzy. But I wasn't a killer.

I was about to say something about how we should go to sleep, get some rest, when Gemma spoke. She was still lying back, covering her eyes, but she wasn't crying anymore.

'Do you want to know what happened to Henry?' she asked.

My voice cracked when I replied. 'Your ex-boyfriend?'

'Uh-huh. And Mickey and Delilah. Do you want to know what happened to them?'

She sat up. Mascara streaked her face and her eyes were pink. She leaned forward and opened the bedside cabinet. To my surprise, she took out a bottle of vodka and a tumbler, pouring herself a double measure and knocking it back. She refilled the glass and offered it to me, but I shook my head.

'Let me paint you a picture,' she said.

Chapter 48

June 2005

Everything had been going so well until the afternoon Gemma came home to the place she shared with Henry and found her parents sitting around the kitchen table, drinking tea.

Gemma was only nineteen but everybody said she seemed older. *An old soul*, that was how Henry had described her when she first met him. He was twenty-five, with black hair and perma-stubble. That first time he met her in that squat in Warrior Square, when she was out of her mind on glue and strong lager, he'd said, 'You look like you've seen things.' All she could do was nod in agreement. She didn't need to tell him about her parents or her childhood. Henry could see how much she had suffered; he knew she wasn't drinking and doing drugs and sleeping on a filthy mattress in a mildew-stinking hellhole because she'd had a happy upbringing. He told her he was going to help her, and he did.

Once she'd learned to trust him, when she'd decided he wasn't abusive or violent, that he wasn't only interested in her body, she went with him to his Victorian house on the edge of Alexandra Park in Hastings and allowed herself to be looked after. To be loved. Nine months had passed now, and she was starting to believe she loved him too and that she was ready to tell him about her parents.

She should have done it sooner. Because then he would never have opened the door and let them in.

'All right, Gem,' said her dad, as if it had only been days since she'd last seen him, not over a year. She had left home on her eighteenth birthday, pausing only to say goodbye to Chloe, who was also here, sitting at the table with her eyes downcast. She would be fifteen now and was as skinny as ever but beautiful. Not for the first time, Gemma experienced a pang of guilt about leaving her younger sister alone with their mum and dad. The only thing that salved her conscience was knowing that they treated Chloe better than her and Stuart, who had also left when he was eighteen, moving to London.

'Hi, sweetheart,' said Mum, getting up and kissing her before Gemma could react. She held her cheek, shocked. She couldn't remember her mother ever kissing her before.

'How did you find me?' she said, holding on to the back of a chair.

Dad laughed and winked at Henry, who had been, so far, watching the exchange with a faltering smile. 'You make it sound like we had to track you down.'

It must have been Stuart, she figured. She should never have given him her address.

'You look well,' said Mum, appraising her. 'Looks more like me every day, doesn't she, Jeff?'

'Two beauties,' he said. He reached across and squeezed Chloe's hand. 'Three, I should say. My girls. Lucky bloke, aren't I, Henry?'

Henry, to his credit, had clearly figured out something was wrong. 'Is everything okay, Gemma?'

She managed to nod. 'Can I have a quick word?'

He followed her into the hallway, then into the bathroom. She pulled the light cord so the fan came on, knowing it would mask their conversation.

'You have to get rid of them,' she said.

'But they're your parents.'

'Exactly. The parents I ran away from.'

Henry chewed his lower lip. 'Okay. But . . .'

'But what?'

'I've kind of already asked them to stay.'

Her legs gave out and she sat down on the toilet lid. 'Oh God.'

'Listen, Gemma.' He touched her cheek. 'Clearly you have issues with your parents. But I think it would be good for you to spend some time with them on your own territory, away from your childhood home. I think it will help you see that they're not monsters.'

'But they are.'

He didn't believe her. She could see it. 'Well, in that case, it will be good for you to prove to yourself that you're stronger now. That you can cope. I think it will be really positive for you. And they said it's only going to be for a few days.'

The bathroom fan droned in her ears. Henry crouched in front of her and kissed her forehead.

'It'll be fine,' he said. 'I promise.'

August 2005

'Please. Please, Gemma. Don't go. I love you.' Henry threw himself down on his knees, clutching at her. She pulled away, shaking with disgust and fury, but he kept on begging. 'I'm sorry, so sorry. But it was them. It was their fault.'

'Get off me!' She spat out the words, retreating across the bedroom to put distance between them. She could hardly bear to stay in this room now. This room that had once been full of love and hope was now thick with the stench of betrayal.

'Gemma, please . . .'

'My sister!'

He made an anguished noise.

'She's fifteen years old! And you had sex with her. Right here in our bedroom.'

She picked up the rucksack, which was only half-full, so meagre were her possessions. She had no idea where she was going to go. All she knew was that she had to get away. From Henry. From her parents. Her sister too. At this moment, she hated Chloe as well. She loathed all of them. She burned with it.

'I was trying to comfort her,' Henry said, his voice full of snot and misery.

'*Comfort?*'

'But it's true, Gem. She told me what happened with Mickey and Delilah. She was so upset and I put my arm around her and then we were kissing.'

Gemma put her hands over her ears. 'I don't want to hear it.'

'But don't you want to know the truth? About what Jeff and Lizzy did? Why they had to leave Winchelsea Beach?'

Ever since they'd come here, Gemma had suspected they were running from something. Hiding.

And having them here had been even worse than she'd feared. The jibes, the mental cruelty, the mess and thoughtlessness. The way they constantly tried to belittle her. The names she heard them call Henry behind his back, even while they borrowed money from him and took advantage of his kindness. Gemma had pleaded with him to throw them out but Jeff was insistent they would be homeless. He told Henry the bank had repossessed their house in Winchelsea Beach. Gemma had no idea if that was true but Henry believed it. And although he had come to dislike Jeff and Lizzy, having seen what they were like, he was too much of a bleeding heart to throw a fifteen-year-old girl on to the street.

Not too much of a bleeding heart to screw her, though, was he?

'What did she tell you?' Gemma asked, not sure she wanted to know.

'She said this couple, Mickey and Delilah, came back to the village. She said you knew them.'

Gemma was shocked. She had never thought they'd be brave enough to return.

'I did. Once.'

Henry was agitated, repeating what Chloe had told him. 'She said she did what you'd done. Went to stay with them in their caravan. And then your dad found out and went mad.'

History repeating itself.

'Chloe said he dragged her out and took her home. And Gemma, listen: he went back in the middle of the night and torched the caravan. Mickey and Delilah were still inside.'

Gemma put her hand over her mouth.

'You need to go to the police,' she said. 'Tell them what Chloe told you.'

'What? And get arrested for sleeping with an underage girl?'

'Then I'll go.' This was it. The perfect opportunity to get rid of her dad, at least.

'But there's no proof,' Henry said. 'And Chloe said she would deny telling me. She doesn't want them to go to jail. She's still a kid. She's scared.'

All of Gemma's anger swung back towards her boyfriend.

'Yeah. She's a kid.'

Henry hung his head. 'I wasn't thinking straight. I'd been drinking. I was upset too.' That morning, Henry had found his beloved cat, Kenny, dead in the back garden. He'd been poisoned. 'And I know it sounds pathetic but she looks older. She looks like you.'

Gemma glared at him. 'Going to do it with my mother next, are you?'

He recoiled as if she'd slapped him. And she *ought* to slap him. He more than deserved it.

'You can have them both when I'm gone,' Gemma said. 'Chloe will be sixteen in a few months so it'll be legal. My God, I ought to call the police. Get them to throw you in prison.'

She was crying now. She had grown to love him, to finally let her guard down. That was the one good thing about her parents coming to stay. It had made her and Henry closer.

But now he had ripped their closeness to shreds.

'What are you going to do?' Henry asked.

She hoisted the rucksack on to her back. 'I'm going, Henry. You can deal with them. I never want to see any of you again.'

And she did it. She walked out. She ignored Henry's cries from upstairs. She walked straight past her sister, who was standing in her doorway, her expression inscrutable. She glanced at her mother, who was sitting in the kitchen, a cigarette smouldering between her fingers. She went out the front door and found her dad sitting on the front step, looking out at the park.

'Off, are you?'

She walked down the steps without speaking. Trying not to cry.

'Gemma!' he called.

Her body disobeyed her brain and she turned to look up at him.

'You can't escape us forever,' he said. 'We're family.'

'See you at your funeral,' she muttered, walking away.

Chapter 49

Gemma and I sat in silence for a minute after she'd finished. While she'd been talking, Charlie had come into the room after pawing at the door, and he sat on the bed, purring, oblivious to the tale of human misery.

Oblivious, too, to the danger he might be in. I lifted him and put him on my lap, stroking his back, feeling his purr vibrate through me. I had little doubt about who had killed Henry's cat.

Gemma blinked at me with wet eyes. During her tale, she had downed another two or three shots of vodka but appeared stone-cold sober.

'Those were the last words I spoke to him,' she said. 'Except I didn't have to wait for their funerals, did I? I should have known.'

'When they came here, was that the first time you'd seen them since you left Henry's?'

'Yeah.'

Why hadn't she told me that before? 'So what happened next, after you left? Do you know?'

She was sitting close enough to reach out and tickle Charlie's ear. 'I found out. Henry emailed me and told me that he had enlisted the help of some bikers from this pub he used to go to on the seafront. They turned up and literally chucked my parents out.'

'Ha! I would have loved to have seen that. If only I knew some bikers.'

Gemma smiled.

'And what did your parents do after that?'

'I'm not sure where they went immediately after. They said they'd been moving around. But a few years later they turned up at Stuart's. He'd just got married to Jane.'

I sighed. 'Let me guess. They moved in with them and made their lives a living hell.'

'Yep. They were there for ages. Nearly two years. It almost killed Stuart. He told me he actually tried to kill himself, that Jane found him with a noose around his neck and stopped him. There was another incident before that, too. Mum started a fire in their kitchen by not putting a cigarette out properly, though luckily Stuart found it and put it out in time.' Gemma absent-mindedly stroked the cat. 'So Stuart and Jane took drastic action. They handed in notice to their landlord and basically made themselves homeless. They lived in a hostel for a little while. But it was the only way they could get rid of Mum and Dad.'

That wasn't an option for us, as I owned the place.

'After that, Mum and Dad vanished again for a little while until one day Stuart got an email from France, telling him that Chloe had met someone, a French guy, and they'd moved in with him. We were relieved, even though we felt terrible for this poor Frenchman. We hoped they'd stay over there forever and we thought they might, until this August. They emailed me and then—'

'Wait.' Something had jarred. 'You mean they emailed you in October, not August, right? That's what you said earlier.' Also, I clearly remembered Gemma telling me about the email just after we got home from Vegas.

'Oh. Oh yes, of course. October.'

She averted her eyes. She was clearly lying.

'Hang on. You heard they were coming back in August? Two months before you told me about it?'

She looked sick.

'Gemma?'

She couldn't look at me. 'Yes. They emailed me.'

I shifted and Charlie jumped off my lap, landing on the floor with a mew of displeasure. 'When in August?'

'I can't remember exactly.'

'Was it before or after you met me?'

She didn't respond.

'Was it *before* or *after*?'

Her reply was whispered. 'Before.'

I sat back. The room felt smaller, the world even crueller. A cold draught crept through the window. She hadn't told me until October, when we got back from Vegas. She'd acted like she had only just received the email.

'I'm so sorry,' she said. 'I never wanted to mislead you. I'd just found out, the day before I met you, and I went round to see Stuart to talk about it. That's why I was in Herne Hill.'

I reeled, trying to make sense of this new information.

'I'd already told them they couldn't stay with me,' Gemma said. 'I lived in a tiny bedsit. But Stuart was desperate, terrified they were going to turn up on his doorstep and demand to be let in.'

'What? Couldn't he have just told them to go away?'

'I said exactly the same to him, but you don't understand how hard it is to say no to them, even after all this time. After all the things they've done to us. Stuart's weak. It comes from years and years of being controlled by my dad, by both of them. That's why he would rather have made himself homeless than live with them. And Jane's terrified of them too.'

Gemma went on. 'I was worried sick about it. I knew it would destroy Stuart and his family. I didn't know what to do. And then Stuart said, "If only we knew someone who could deal with them for us." And when I met you, I remembered that.'

'I don't understand.'

She went over to the window and peered out at the street, and I realised she was retracing her steps from that afternoon, when she had first walked along Cuckoo Lane.

'I left Stuart's and went for a walk, trying to clear my head, to think. And then I saw the signs about the Open Garden. I just wanted to see somewhere beautiful, to imagine the life I could have had.' Her eyes were distant, remembering. 'I recognised you straight away. I think I saw you on *Newsnight* once, talking about the need for better education in the sciences. I was impressed by what you said and how . . . passionate you were about it.'

I ignored the compliment. I was too busy staring at her, wondering if it could be true.

That she had decided, as soon as she met me, that I could help her do away with her parents.

'You thought . . .' I forced the words out. 'You thought that, as someone who knows about chemistry, I would know how to kill someone and get away with it?'

'I . . . No . . . Yes . . .'

'I don't believe this. I cannot believe this. That's why our relationship started? Why you told me you wanted to get married after two months?'

'Getting married was your idea!'

I hardly heard her. My mind was racing, trying to figure it all out. I guessed it didn't matter if we were married or not – not unless she wanted me dead so she could inherit my house. Despite the shock of what I'd just learned, I was willing to give her the benefit of the doubt over that one, especially as she was right. It had been my idea.

All she had needed was to move in with me, so she would have somewhere for her parents to stay. And then what? The answer seemed too awful to be true. She had known exactly how they would behave and how difficult they would be to get rid of. She had foreseen how insane they would drive me, how I would come to despise them. She couldn't have known they would try to get me charged with child abuse but she must have known they would do something to push me to the brink.

To get me to the point where she could suggest that we kill them.

That had been her plan all along. That was why she had married me. It was even why she had invited her parents to stay with us.

This wasn't a real marriage. I wasn't really her husband and she didn't really love me.

Gemma had only got together with me for one reason, and it had nothing to do with love.

PART THREE

PART THREE

Before

It was mid-September. They had been at the remote house for over a month now, waiting for Gemma to tell them they could return to England. It was testing every shred of Jeff's patience and nerve, especially with Lizzy badgering him about it every bloody hour, telling him this was a bad idea, that someone was going to turn up any day. A friend or the son and his wife. The police.

Jeff knew that with every passing day the risk increased. But he was still sure this was better than being out on the road and, besides, they had little choice. They had no money, not even enough to buy fuel, while Valérie – their unwilling host – had a larder full of supplies, a vegetable patch and chickens. She even bulk-bought cigarettes and had a large supply, which kept Lizzy from going crazy. He had also ascertained on that first day, with Chloe translating, that Valérie's son, Mathieu, was a busy man with a high-flying career and that his wife and his mother didn't get along. He hardly ever called, thinking the occasional text message was enough. He had told her if she wanted to see photos of her grandson she should join Facebook, which she refused to do. Mathieu sounded like a wanker and Jeff was pleased that he was going to teach him a lesson about the importance of family. He was going to make him wish he'd kept in touch with his mother.

But Mathieu's distance and Valérie's reclusiveness were great for the Robinsons. The only person who ever came by was the postman, leaving the mail in a box by the front gate. Fortunately, he never had any need to ring the doorbell.

So Jeff, Lizzy and Chloe were left alone. And that was fine. They were used to it, in a way. Since leaving Winchelsea Beach thirteen years ago – after that unfortunate incident with the caravan – they had been living in other birds' nests, first in England, then over here.

The major difference this time was that the house's owner was tied to her bed.

Jeff wasn't an animal, though. He had used a long rope which allowed Valérie to use the bucket he had placed in the corner. She kept crying, especially in the morning, when they would gag her to ensure she didn't wail or holler when the postman came by. She kept calling Jeff a diable. *He knew enough French to understand that meant 'devil'.*

'Why don't we just kill her?' Lizzy had asked the other morning, carrying the stinking bucket to the lavatory.

'Because we might need her alive if someone turns up.'

'That doesn't make sense. If someone comes here she'll scream the bloody house down.'

He had sighed. 'I like her, all right? I'm trying to figure out a way for her to survive this.'

Lizzy had rolled her eyes and said, 'You're going soft.'

He had pushed her up against the wall.

'Soft, huh?'

She hadn't spoken another word. She'd just glared at him till he let her go.

Now Jeff looked out the back window at the garden. Chloe was out there, collecting eggs from the hens. It had become part of her daily routine and was pretty much the only time she seemed to come alive. She spent the rest of her days lying on the sofa, staring into space. She was barely eating, didn't speak, and her skin was hot to the touch. She was like this whenever they moved on. From Winchelsea Beach, from Henry's place in Hastings, from Stuart's . . . Jeff was used to it, but she needed to pull herself together before they returned to England.

It was going to be hard enough as it was. They hadn't exactly parted on good terms with Gemma, had they? To him, it was all water under the bridge, but he hadn't been sure how Gemma would react when Chloe emailed her to say they needed somewhere to stay. He knew Gemma hated him and Lizzy. But she didn't hate her little sister, despite what had happened with Henry. And Jeff knew Gemma wouldn't want Chloe to be stuck with nowhere to stay.

Still, he hadn't been surprised when Gemma had replied to that first email, telling Chloe they couldn't come and stay because she lived in a bedsit. He thought they'd probably have to go and stay with Stuart and deal with his wife, whose name Jeff could never remember, when they got there. He'd even emailed Stuart himself, telling him to get a couple of rooms ready.

But then Gemma had surprised him. You can't stay with Stuart, *she'd written, emailing him the next day.* I'll find somewhere. It might just take a little while.

He'd written back thanking her profusely, but pointing out they didn't have forever.

Don't worry, *she'd replied.* I actually think I've found somewhere already. It's a big, beautiful house with enough room for all of us. I think you'll love it. It's on a really nice street called Cuckoo Lane.

He'd looked it up on Google Street View. She was right. It was a lovely place. It would be worth waiting for.

But what about the owner? *Jeff had written back.*

Gemma had replied straight away. Don't worry about him, *she wrote.* He won't cause you any trouble.

ω

That email exchange had been in the middle of August. Now it was mid-October and finally, finally, they were going home. Gemma had come through.

Jeff had been checking the internet ever since they'd got here, looking for news reports about what had happened in Toulouse, using Google Translate so he could understand them. To his relief, the police seemed clueless about what had happened. There was mention in a couple of the early reports that they wanted to talk to 'an English family who, according to locals, had been staying with the deceased'. There were no mentions of their names and the website said only that police were 'concerned for their safety'.

Jeff and Lizzy hadn't made any friends in Toulouse. They'd been seen around town, had frequented a few coffee shops. But nobody had ever known their real names. Jeff was confident they'd have no trouble getting on the flight that Gemma had booked for them.

There was only one thing left to do now. One loose end.

Jeff went up to Valérie's room. She was perched on the edge of the bed, picking at the rope that fastened her to it with weak fingers. She glared at him as he walked over and began to unfasten the rope at both ends.

'Come on,' he said. 'We're going outside.'

She was suspicious. She didn't want to move at first, so he had to use a knife to coax her, being careful not to touch her skin with it. He didn't want to leave any marks. He'd always been careful with the rope too. He didn't want anyone to know she'd been tied up.

Outside, he instructed her, using gestures, to stand beside the pool. Autumn was here but it was a warm morning. He let her stand there for a while, enjoying the sun on her face. He let her smoke a cigarette too. Then, with a word of apology, he pushed her into the swimming pool and, after stripping and jumping in beside her, he held her under – again, being careful not to leave any bruises – until she went limp. He left her floating face down.

An unfortunate accident. Elderly woman falls in her swimming pool. Her neglectful son, who never came to see her, would get the blame when *she was eventually found, by which point her body would be rotten, any bruises on her skin long gone.*

Jeff went back into the house. Lizzy had watched him drown Valérie but acted as if nothing had happened. She was in a chipper mood.

'Can't wait to see the back of this country,' she said, going round the room with a cloth to remove their fingerprints from every surface. She had already scrubbed everything with bleach and vacuumed like she had never vacuumed before. No doubt their DNA would be present, if anyone looked for it, but none of them were in any databases anyway. They just wanted to remove any sign they'd been there. They deleted the computer history too. Again, Jeff didn't think the police would dig any deeper.

'Is Chloe ready?' he asked, as he gathered their possessions together.

'Yeah. She keeps going on about the chickens, though. She's worried they'll starve to death.'

He tutted. 'What is it with our daughters and bloody animals?' He shouted up to Chloe, then said, 'I'd better get the car out of the garage.'

As he was about to leave the room, Lizzy said, 'I wonder what this new husband of Gemma's is like.'

'A drip, I expect.'

She sniggered.

'Just remember,' Jeff said, 'when we get there, we need to be on our best behaviour.'

'Oh, of course,' Lizzy replied with a smile. 'Aren't we always?'

Chapter 50

'So our whole relationship was a sham,' I said.

'No!' Gemma, who had been staring at the bedsheets, finally met my eye. 'I fell in love with you, Elliot. That wasn't a lie.'

'How can you expect me to believe that?'

She came back to the bed and tried to take hold of my hand again, but I shook her off and stood up, not wanting to be anywhere near her.

'Elliot, please. Let me explain. Yes, when I met you I thought you could help me, that you'd know how to kill someone and get away with it. But I didn't think I'd ever actually want to go through with it and . . . I liked you straight away. When you were stung by that bee I was genuinely terrified. I thought I was about to lose something that could be really good. Something special.' She let out a long breath. 'But then I mentioned meeting you to Stuart, and made the mistake of telling him my original thought, about you being a scientist who'd know about poisons and chemicals and so on. Joking about it, you know. And he seized on it. He said it was a brilliant idea.'

I shook my head, incredulous.

'By that point I'd already fallen for you. Do you really think I could have faked all that? The explosion of chemistry between us? It was real, Elliot. More real than anything I've ever felt. It seemed like, I don't know, a bonus that you had this amazing house. And every time I talked to Stuart, he told me it was perfect. A perfect trap; a place where we could finally free ourselves. So I let it happen. I let Stuart persuade me, thinking that we'd find some other way, that you and I could figure something out together, and then it was too late. They were here, doing what they always do, and it was like being on a runaway train.'

'And tonight you decided they'd finally pushed me far enough?' That I would agree to help you kill them?'

'Yes. But I was wrong.' She had turned so pale I could almost see the bones beneath her skin. 'All the misery we've been through since they got here has all been for nothing. My parents have won. Unless you tell me how to do it.'

'I'm not going to do that.'

'Then we're stuck. Or rather, you're stuck. Because I'm guessing you want me to leave.'

She looked bereft, as if all the colour had drained from the world. When she looked up at me there were fresh tears in her eyes.

'I didn't know they would murder George and Edith. If I'd thought anything like that would happen, I'd never have let them anywhere near this place. You have to believe that, at least.'

'I don't know what I believe anymore.'

'I love you, Elliot.'

I couldn't look at her. I should have been enraged, but I was too exhausted; punch-drunk and numb. Reeling from everything I'd learned in the past few hours. My brain couldn't process any more and my heart couldn't take it. I didn't know how much I believed her, if everything was a lie or if there was truth mixed in with the falsehoods. Maybe it didn't matter. One lie was enough. The foundations of our relationship were built on deceit. There would be no getting over this. No way forward.

'Can I stay tonight at least?' she asked. 'Please?'

'Whatever,' I said. I took a spare sheet out of the cupboard. 'I'm going to sleep on the sofa.'

ω

I was awoken in the morning by Lizzy.

'Lovers' tiff?' she asked with a smirk, poking her head into the living room. Charlie was asleep on my feet. After hours spent staring into the darkness his purring had finally lulled me to sleep.

'Go away, Lizzy,' I said.

She half-turned, then hesitated. 'It will be much easier for you if you just give in. Let us stay here. We can live together in harmony, you know. If you stop trying to cause trouble.'

I glared at her.

'Like all this nonsense about the old couple next door. Forget about it, Elliot. Let it go.' She took a step into the room. 'Why don't I make us all a nice dinner tonight? Or I could get something delivered. We've got your Deliveroo log-in so we can use that.'

She walked towards the kitchen, humming to herself.

I couldn't stay here a minute longer.

I was still wearing yesterday's clothes. Not caring that I must have bad breath and that my hair was sticking up at a dozen angles, I went out to my car and headed to the office, so desperate to get out of the house that I didn't stop to try to retrieve my phone from Jeff. I was shocked to discover it was eleven o'clock, that I'd slept longer than I thought. A floater was trapped in my vision, restarting its journey every time I blinked, and I almost collided with someone at a busy roundabout. I reached the office in desperate need of coffee and someone to talk to.

'Amira?' I said, entering the office. Going up the stairs, I had decided that I was going to sort out the mess at work, spend the day making calls. I could deal with that part of my life, at least, with Amira's help.

But she wasn't there.

As someone who had spent the past few days being struck by one bomb after another, I didn't find this as surprising as I might have done previously, even though Amira was never late, never off sick.

Maybe she had decided it wasn't worth it. That I had screwed everything up to such an extent that she might as well take a duvet day. She certainly deserved one. I thought perhaps she and Colin had decided to have a day at home together before remembering he was away on a training course until the weekend.

I would have to try to fix the mess of my professional life without Amira. I opened my computer, went straight to my contacts and, using my desk phone, began to make calls.

It was intensely frustrating. Half the people I needed to speak to were out or hiding behind their secretaries. One or two point-blank refused to talk to me. I spent forty minutes chasing the person I most needed to convince that she had made a mistake: the head of education at the local council. When I finally got through to her she was flustered.

'I'm sorry, Elliot. We just can't risk being associated with you at the moment. It's just too complicated. And what with the cutbacks . . .'

'But I'm innocent,' I said, fighting back the urge to shout it. 'Surely you heard, the girl recanted. She was put up to it. Ask the police.'

'I believe you. It's horrible for you, so terribly unfair. But it's all too unsettled, too difficult right now. Maybe in six months or a year, when people have forgotten.'

I hung up. Six months? A year? We would go broke long before that. But I refused to give up. If we could get enough small clients back on board, we could just about keep going. I started to scroll through my contacts again, but wasn't sure who Amira had already called. I went over to her desk to see if there was a list there. Amira was always making lists.

There were indeed several sheets of paper on her desktop, but when I picked up the top one I realised this wasn't anything to do with work.

Toulouse, August 10th. Next to that she had written, *Check news reports.*

Beneath that she had copied out a few headlines, surrounding them with question marks.

Amira had been trying to find out what the Robinsons had done in France. I felt a surge of gratitude. With a start, I remembered sending her photos of pages from Chloe's journal. Among all the drama of the evening, I'd forgotten about that. Amira would have been able to translate the pages. But had they contained anything useful? Had she got anywhere?

Halfway down the page, Amira had written *JC?* and drawn a box around the initials.

Just beneath that, she had written *Jean-Claude?*

I felt a tingle beneath my skin. Jean-Claude. Was that the name of Chloe's boyfriend? If I put that name into Google and looked for news reports from Toulouse from August, I might find something. I rushed back to my computer and made a start. But it was too difficult. My lack of French ability made the headlines impossible to understand without using Google Translate. And – although I could do that – putting each article through the translation tool, and trying to understand the unnatural results that came back, made the task far more arduous than it should have been.

Amira, however, spoke French pretty well. And maybe she had already found something out.

I snatched up my car keys and headed out.

Chapter 51

Amira and Colin lived in a maisonette on a quiet back street in Crystal Palace, a new-build with a neat square lawn that had once belonged to the local authority. I had only been here once before, attending their housewarming party a year ago. I pulled up outside and noticed a couple of teenagers across the road, kicking a football back and forth. They ignored me.

I rang Amira's doorbell and waited. There was no response so I rang it again.

She must have gone out. I walked back up the path and spotted Amira's red SEAT Ibiza. If she had gone out, she couldn't have gone too far. Perhaps I should wait a while and see if she came back.

It was freezing on the street, too cold to hang around, and I was about to get back into the relative warmth of my car when I paused. Maybe it was everything I'd been through over the last couple of days, but my nerves were jangling. If Amira wasn't at work or at home, and her car was right there in front of me, then where was she?

I approached the youths playing football. They were around thirteen years old and should have been at school. The taller one picked up the ball and was about to scarper when I said, 'Have you seen anyone come in or out of that house this morning?'

He looked at me suspiciously. 'You a fed?' That was what a lot of teenagers in London called the police.

I sighed. I wasn't in any mood to be messed around. 'No. I'm a friend of the woman who lives there.'

'A friend, eh?' The two boys cackled.

I put on my best teacher voice. 'Just tell me. Have you seen anyone?'

'Nah, mate,' said the taller one.

His friend said no too and they walked off.

'Thanks for the help, guys,' I said under my breath.

I went back to Amira's front door and rang the bell again. I lifted the flap of the letterbox and listened. I could hear voices. Then music came on and I realised it was the radio: the talking I'd heard had been the DJ.

It seemed out of character for Amira – who had told me off numerous times for leaving the lights on in the office – to go out and leave the radio playing.

I thought about calling the police, but without my phone it would mean a search for a working phone box, which were few and far between these days.

I went round to the back of the maisonette. A window gave a view into the kitchen. Putting my face to the glass, I could see a carton of milk on the side, next to a plate which contained a half-eaten slice of toast. The dishwasher stood open and I could hear the radio through the glass.

Something definitely wasn't right here.

Next to the kitchen window was the back door. Without expecting anything, I tried the handle.

The door opened.

I wasn't sure if it was because I was getting flashbacks to what had happened at my next-door neighbours' place, but I felt sick with dread. That time, I had disturbed the crime scene. Maybe I should do what I hadn't done then and go in search of a phone.

It would take so long, though. And, like last time, I was worried that someone – Amira in this case – might be hurt, in need of urgent medical attention. Maybe if I'd got George help sooner, he'd have survived. What if Amira was in a similar situation? I couldn't stop myself. I went inside, leaving the door open behind me.

I went through the kitchen into the hallway, terrified I was going to see blood on the walls. I had gone rigid with fear and, when I called Amira's name, my voice was hoarse and rough. I had to force myself to keep going, to walk on my unsteady legs. Common sense was screaming at me: *Go back to the car, find a public phone, call the police.* If someone had attacked Amira they might still be here, ready to do the same to me. But I had to get to her.

I forced my legs to move, going back into the kitchen, where I grabbed a sharp knife from the block on the counter.

The living room was neat and tidy, with no sign of a disturbance. There were no other rooms on this floor apart from a tiny toilet, which was empty, so I went up the stairs.

'Amira?' I said again, getting no response.

I hadn't been upstairs at Amira's before. I remembered her telling me there were two bedrooms, a bathroom, and a box room which she used as a home office. The master bedroom was directly in front of me, the door standing open. I looked inside. The bed was unmade, with a top and a pair of jeans laid out on it.

The clothes Amira had planned to wear today? Clothes that, for whatever reason, she hadn't put on. I looked around the room. Drawers had been pulled out. A jewellery box on the dresser stood open.

I was now certain that something had happened to her. Again, a voice in my head yelled at me: *Leave right now, knock on a neighbour's door and tell them to call the police.* But just like before, I couldn't stop myself. I needed to see her. I needed to know if there was any way to help her.

I opened the bathroom door and looked inside. The floor was wet and the glass of the shower cubicle was streaked with water, but the room was empty. So was the box room, which looked like it hadn't been used for months.

That left the second bedroom.

I braced myself, counting to five and trying to gather the courage to do this. Because I knew I was going to find something terrible. Something that would change the course of my life. There was still part of me that clung to a belief in a just universe; a world in which there were still a few things that made sense. A world in which I could still believe that everything would turn out okay in the end.

When I opened the door, the final shreds of optimism were ripped away and the old Elliot Foster finally died.

Amira was lying face down on the carpet. There was a deep red wound on the back of her head, blood glistening in her hair, one arm stretched out before her like she had been trying to crawl away from her attacker. The room was in disarray, with more drawers yanked open, coins and what I assumed to be costume jewellery scattered across the floor.

I approached Amira and crouched on the carpet, not wanting to touch her, to disturb another crime scene.

Her open eyes were glassy and unseeing.

I left the room backwards, eyes swimming with tears, colliding with the banister behind me and almost falling. I don't remember going downstairs. I don't remember going out to the front garden. I can't recall if the football-playing teenagers had come back, although I am sure there was someone there, staring at me.

All I remember is falling to my knees on the damp front lawn, raising my face to the sky and howling. And when the howling stopped, after the tears had dried, I felt nothing but cold and numb. Like my heart had been ripped out and replaced with a block of ice.

Cold. Numb. And knowing what I needed to do.

Chapter 52

Gemma and I sat on a bench in West Norwood Cemetery, surrounded by crooked ancient tombstones and fresh graves, a weather-beaten angel watching over us. On the way up the path, coat wrapped tight against the stinging wind, I had read a few of the gravestones. *Beloved mother and wife. Infant daughter. Dearest father.* It made me think of my own parents, who had been cremated. I had scattered their ashes on the beach in Great Yarmouth, where they had met. Were they looking down on me now? I heard my dad's voice, urging me to reconsider, telling me again that it was better to turn the other cheek, that violence should never be met with violence.

I didn't believe him anymore.

Or rather, I didn't care.

Everything that had happened after I left Amira's place and called Gemma was a blur, like a half-remembered movie or drunken night out. I think a neighbour came outside to find out what all the fuss was about. I guess they must have called the police. I remember the police coming and the shock on DS Rothermel's face when she saw me. One of the cops mentioned Colin and a terrible hush came over them. Rothermel told me that they would need to talk to me later and I nodded. I didn't tell her I was certain this wasn't the botched burglary it had been set up to look like. I didn't tell her I knew who had done it and why.

I was sure that my phone records would show that Amira had tried to call me that morning. Maybe she'd left a message to tell me that, using the extra pages I'd sent from Chloe's journal, she'd found out what Jeff and Lizzy had done in France, a message that Jeff had read or listened to and deleted. My passcode wasn't hard to guess. It was my date of birth, which would have been easy for Jeff to find. Amira's phone was missing and I was sure the police would think the burglar had taken it along with several pieces of jewellery and some cash.

I didn't tell the police any of this, because I had already made my decision.

There might be enough evidence to prosecute Jeff, but I couldn't be certain.

Not certain enough, anyway. And even if Jeff did end up in jail, which was hardly enough of a punishment for what he'd done, Lizzy would still be free; Lizzy, who was complicit in all of this, even if she hadn't murdered George and Edith and Amira with her own hands.

Jeff and Lizzy needed to be punished.

Jeff and Lizzy needed to die.

'We want a poison that's going to work quickly,' I said. 'One that's easy for me to get hold of and ideally one for which there's no antidote. I started off by thinking about ricin.'

Gemma nodded.

'Ricin comes from castor bean plants. *Ricinus communis*. It's common in ornamental gardens. In fact, George and Edith had it growing in their garden and I'm sure it's still there.' Nobody had attended to next door's garden since their death. 'I think there would be some sort of poetic justice if we used that.'

We waited for an elderly man to pass before Gemma said, 'What does it do?'

'It's a slow, painful death. Nausea, bloody diarrhoea, seizures, a burning sensation in the mouth and throat, stomach pain. And that, unfortunately, is the main problem with ricin. It's slow. It takes three to five days. It would certainly be a way of getting Jeff and Lizzy out of the house and to a hospital, but then they'd be treated and the doctors would realise they'd been poisoned. We'd have to keep them locked up and stop them communicating with the outside world until they were dead.'

Gemma winced.

'It's doable,' I said. 'And it wouldn't be too difficult to extract it from the plants. I'd probably need around forty beans to kill both of them, use a solvent to get rid of the fat, filter the residue then dry it out and concentrate it down.'

'But three to five days,' Gemma said.

'Yes. It makes it risky and it kind of negates my main reason for thinking of using ricin in the first place, which is that it's hard for a pathologist to pick up. Which leads me to the second part of the plan. For this to work, I think we need to dispose of the bodies. We don't want anyone to know Jeff and Lizzy are dead. I guess it's lucky they don't have any friends. That they never go out.'

'What do you mean?'

'Will anyone care if they disappear? Will anyone miss them?'

'No. Nobody.'

There was one problem we needed to address. Gemma's siblings. 'I'm sure we can tell Stuart that your mum and dad did a moonlight flit. That they decided to move on. From the sound of it, he'll be so relieved he won't ask any questions.'

Gemma licked her lips. This conversation was making her look pale and anxious, but she had already assured me that she had no intention of backing out. 'Yes . . .'

Something in her tone worried me. 'What is it?'

'I think we need to tell Stuart what we're going to do.'

'No.'

'Listen to me, Elliot. They've ruined Stuart's life as much as they have mine. He despises them. And he can help us. I mean, we're going to need to move the bodies, aren't we?'

'Gemma, I don't think it's a good idea. How do you know he won't go to the police? Or tell someone else?'

She took a deep breath. 'Because he'll be so happy and relieved that he'll never have to face them again. And . . . I think it would be safer to involve him. If they just disappear he'll be suspicious. He'll ask questions. He'll talk about it with Jane. I've been thinking about it ever since I first brought this up, and I really think it's the sensible thing to do.'

I started to protest again but she stopped me. 'Besides, there's an important reason why we need to let Stuart in on it. We're going to need his help to get Chloe out of the house, because we clearly don't want her around when we do this. And he's the only other person she knows in London.'

I thought about it, then sighed. I still wasn't keen on the idea, but I couldn't think of any other way to conceal what we were doing from Chloe.

'Are you sure he'll want to go along with it?' I asked.

'Of course. I told you, he wants them gone as much as I do.'

I sighed. 'Okay. I'm trusting you here, Gemma. You know him better than I do. So what's the plan?'

Another visitor to the cemetery passed by, preventing Gemma from replying straight away.

'I can ask Stuart to invite Chloe to go to his place,' she said when we were alone again. 'To babysit. He'll have to encourage Jane to go out with some friends. I'm sure she'd jump at the chance of a night out.'

'Okay. Sounds good. And he should ask her to stay over.'

I wondered how Chloe would react when she got home and found her parents missing. Would she be suspicious when we told her that they had upped and left? I would need to come up with a story. Maybe

I could persuade her that, like Henry before me, I had hired some muscle to scare them off. Perhaps I should tell her something closer to the truth: that I had found out they'd done something terrible here in London and they had fled to avoid the police.

Chloe would believe that. Because she knew what they had done to her boyfriend in France.

Earlier, while waiting for Gemma to take her lunch break, I had borrowed her phone and sat in my car, searching the internet for the words 'Jean-Claude', 'Toulouse' and 'mort'. Using Google to translate the web pages that came up, I found a news report on the website of the city's local paper, dated August 11th.

Young Man Found Dead in Guilheméry

Police were called to an address in Guilheméry, Toulouse, where the body of a man identified as Jean-Claude Giacobini was found. Mr Giacobini, 28, was found at the bottom of a flight of stairs with fatal head injuries.

I had skimmed the report. A couple of lines at the end told me this was the person I had been looking for.

Neighbours reported that Mr Giacobini, who was described as quiet and studious, had been living at the address with his English girlfriend and an older couple, although their identities remain unknown. Police are appealing for these persons to come forward to help them with their inquiries into his death.

It was obvious to me what had happened. Jeff and/or Lizzy had pushed this poor guy down the stairs, then fled. They had been living in what Google told me was a busy residential district of the city, where it would be easy to be anonymous – especially if, as seemed common with Jeff and Lizzy, you all but never went out. Again and again, the Robinsons hid themselves away in other people's houses, destroying the lives of the original residents. Unlike Henry, Jean-Claude – the poor guy who looked so young and happy in the photos I'd found – hadn't been able to get rid of them and he had ended up dead.

I was sure this was why Chloe had been in such a state when she'd first come to the UK. I had no idea where they'd been hiding out in France for two months, but during that time she must have been grieving for her boyfriend and still hadn't recovered when she arrived in London. And although she might show herself from time to time now, and no longer acted like she was about to expire, she still seemed disturbed and unhappy.

By getting rid of Jeff and Lizzy for good I would not only be avenging Amira, George, Edith and Jean-Claude – plus I couldn't forget Mickey and Delilah, who had burned to death in their caravan – I would be setting Gemma, Stuart and Chloe free.

And I would get my house back.

My house and my life.

I told Gemma the rest of the plan.

'It's going to take a few days for me to get everything we need,' I said. I couldn't believe how calm I felt now I'd made a decision. But I had to check Gemma was really on board. 'Are you absolutely certain you want to do this?'

'Yes.' She paused. 'Does that make me evil?'

I pictured Amira's body.

'We're not the evil ones, Gemma.'

It was almost time for her to go back to work. We both stood and Gemma looked around at the gravestones, taking in the reality of what we were about to do. If everything went to plan, Jeff and Lizzy would never have a final resting place. No one would bury them or scatter their ashes.

'What about you?' she asked. 'Are *you* sure?'

The image of Amira's body was seared into my vision. Layered over it, I saw Edith, dead in her living room with her skull smashed in. I remembered the life exiting George's body after he tried to whisper his last words to me. After he warned me about Jeff.

No doubt Gemma was thinking about her own scars, both those on her flesh and those in her heart. I took her hand and my breath stained the cold air as I replied.

Don't do this, whispered my father's voice in my ear.

I ignored it and said, 'I'm sure.'

Chapter 53

Jeff, Lizzy, Stuart and Gemma sat around the table in my dining room while I finished making dinner. I was serving a simple meal of pasta with a vegetable sauce and garlic bread. Low on acid and sugar.

'Wine?' I heard Gemma say to Stuart, and he nodded.

'Just a small one. It's a work night, after all.' He laughed nervously and I wished he would calm down. He looked ill, with beads of sweat popping on his forehead. His eyes kept flicking to his parents and I shot him a look over Jeff and Lizzy's heads, urging him to chill out. I was starting to regret getting him involved, even though, as Gemma had predicted, it was the only way to get Chloe out of the house.

'You not drinking?' Lizzy asked Gemma. 'That's unlike you.'

Gemma smiled. 'I think I'll have a small one too.'

She also needed to calm down. I had asked Gemma and Stuart to go easy on the booze, no matter how stressed they were, because I didn't want them to be drunk later when there was going to be a lot of work to be done.

And though it didn't matter, especially not tonight, this wine was not for guzzling. When Stuart had turned up this evening clutching a bottle, I had been shocked to see the expensive wine that had gone missing. It had turned out that Jeff and Lizzy had given it to Stuart as a birthday present and here he was now, offering it up to me with a sickly grin. I had to pretend I didn't recognise it, despite the smug expressions on Jeff and Lizzy's faces.

'Maybe I should have a glass?' Lizzy said now. I tensed. I had been banking on Jeff and Lizzy remaining teetotal as usual – because alcohol, along with sugar, can reduce the effects of potassium cyanide. I remembered a lecturer at college telling us the theory that when Prince Yusupov attempted to kill Rasputin, it didn't work because the poison was given to him in wine and cakes. The reaction could have formed amygdalin, allowing the monk to excrete the cyanide before his body absorbed it.

It was also advisable not to put cyanide into acidic food because this could create hydrogen cyanide, a gas which would disperse before it did its lethal job. Hence the pasta and vegetables, and the drink Jeff and Lizzy were sharing.

The poison was in the bottle of mineral water that sat before them now. I had chosen a water with a slightly bitter taste, which would mask the cyanide, I thought. I had spooned it into the bottle earlier, having prepared it in my little lab at work. Jeff, I estimated, weighed one hundred and eighty pounds and Lizzy weighed one hundred and thirty. It was important that the poison worked quickly and that there was no chance either of my in-laws survived. I couldn't risk them going out to seek medical help. I also thought there was a risk that Gemma or Stuart, seeing their parents keel over, might have a change of heart and try to save them. The longer Jeff and Lizzy were alive and suffering, the more chance there was of that happening. So although I probably only needed one quarter of a gram each to kill them – much less than a teaspoon's worth – I had decided to use double that. And then I'd added a little more, just to be safe.

I'd added extra salt to their food to ensure they were thirsty, but if they were going to drink wine instead, this whole plan would be screwed.

Lizzy picked up the wine bottle and inspected the label, which was written in French. I'm certain she was just trying to wind me up, but when I didn't react she wrinkled her nose and put the bottle back on the table. 'Actually, I think I'll stick to water.'

I exhaled and watched as she poured a glass of mineral water for herself and Jeff. She took a sip and Jeff did the same. I shot a glance at Stuart. I had instructed him not to stare at the bottle, not to watch his parents sipping the poisoned water. On this front, he was doing well.

I told myself to stop worrying. So far, it was all going to plan.

I finished preparing the food and carried it, steaming, to the table, then sat down beside Gemma. I squeezed her knee beneath the table. Behind me, still unopened, were the pots of paints and white spirit. I was looking forward to getting rid of them.

'I'm starving,' I said.

'Yeah, me too,' said Jeff, helping himself to a plateful of pasta and breaking off a chunk of garlic bread. Everyone else did the same. Gemma stared at hers as if it had come straight from a cat's litter tray, the prospect of eating anything making her nauseous. But it was important that she act normally.

As she lifted her fork to her mouth, her hand trembled, but Jeff and Lizzy were both too busy eating to notice.

I poured Gemma some more wine. Better that she was tipsy later than a nervous wreck now.

'This is lovely,' Lizzy said. 'Thanks, Elliot.'

'Yeah, gorgeous,' said Jeff. 'Cheers.' He raised his glass of water and took a big swig.

Lizzy reached across the table and patted my arm. 'I knew you'd come round soon enough. No point in all that unnecessary tension, was there?'

It wouldn't be convincing for me to pretend everything was wonderful between us. I wasn't going to smile and act like I was delighted for them to be in my house. I just nodded and concentrated on my food, acting beaten, like I had when I got home from my conversation with Gemma in the cemetery. I had asked Jeff if he had my phone and he had shrugged and said, 'I gave it back to you. Don't you remember?' He had stared at me, daring me to challenge his lie, because it was obvious he had destroyed it. I guessed he would have deleted any messages from Amira first, ensuring they weren't on the cloud, along with the photos I'd taken of Chloe's journal. Even a supposed tech-luddite like Jeff could manage that.

I had acted like I was too afraid of him to argue, then gone out and bought a new phone.

'I wonder what Jane's having?' Stuart said now.

Jane had, as we'd expected, jumped at the chance to go out with her friends. They were having dinner in town and Stuart had urged her to enjoy herself; let her hair down. Chloe was at their house now, babysitting.

'I don't think I've ever seen Jane eat,' Lizzy said. 'I never thought you'd end up with some anorexic bird.'

Jeff laughed and pointed his fork at Stuart. 'You used to like them cuddly, didn't you? Remember that big girl you went out with at school. What was her name?'

'Natalie,' Lizzy said, pulling a face. 'Fat Nat.'

Jeff guffawed then shovelled more food into his mouth. 'We might not be the world's greatest parents but at least none of our children ended up fat.'

'Yeah, glad to see you've lost some weight since we got here, Gem,' said Lizzy.

Gemma bristled but stayed silent. Stuart had put his knife and fork down and was clenching his fists. I willed him to keep calm.

Jeff turned to me. 'Really sorry to hear about your colleague. Killed by a burglar, was it? Tragic.'

Now it was my turn to contain my rage. How dare he bring it up? He clearly got a kick out of seeing my distress.

He couldn't resist pushing me. 'Seems to surround you, doesn't it, Elliot?' Jeff said.

'What are you talking about?' asked Gemma.

'Death.' He pointed his knife at me. 'First, your parents died in a hot-air balloon crash. I mean, what are the chances of that? Then that nice old couple next door got their heads bashed in. Another burglary gone wrong. And now your partner. I'm going to start calling you The Jinx.' He winked. 'You'd better be careful, Gem. It might be you next.'

If I'd had any lingering doubt about this being the right thing to do, it had now vanished.

'Sorry, mate,' Jeff said. 'Just having a laugh.'

'I don't think the subject is very funny.'

'Yeah. Too soon, I suppose.' He rolled his eyes.

I watched as Lizzy drained her glass of water and topped herself and Jeff up.

'Bit salty, this pasta,' she said. 'Very nice, though.'

'What's for pudding?' Jeff asked, putting down his knife and fork and sitting back, hands folded across his belly.

'I'm afraid it's just fruit,' I replied. 'Or cheese and biscuits.'

'I like cheese and biscuits,' said Stuart, who had been picking at his dinner, moving it around his plate like a fussy child. Like Gemma, he was clearly feeling too nervous and agitated to eat.

Jeff rolled his eyes. 'Yeah, me too, but only the good stuff. We got spoiled, living in France. Chloe became a dab hand at finding good stuff at the local market. All those gorgeous cheeses.'

They had both drunk over a glassful of cyanide-laced mineral water now. The poison would start to kick in very soon. I knew the science behind it, of course. When the cyanide ion became bonded to the iron atom, it stopped your body from being able to use oxygen. Heart muscle cells and nerve cells would die. With the large dose Jeff and Lizzy had ingested, it wouldn't take long.

I braced myself and thought about enzyme inhibitors and critical cells. If I pretended this was a science experiment, it helped me relax and hide how I was really feeling, that mix of terror and excitement. There had been times while I was preparing this last supper when my conscience, which had my dad's voice, tried to stop me. But then I had thought about Amira and George and Edith. I reminded myself what Jeff and Lizzy had done to Mickey and Delilah, torching their caravan. I pictured the scars on Gemma's belly.

I stole a glance at Gemma, who seemed paler than ever.

Lizzy saw the glance. 'You feeling all right, Gem?' she asked.

Gemma took another sip of wine, but the tremor in her arm was noticeable.

'You look like you're about to collapse,' Jeff said to her. 'Haven't given us food poisoning, have you, Elliot?'

And then it started to happen.

'Actually, I'm not feeling great either,' said Lizzy. She put her hand to her head and winced. 'I feel . . .'

With a terrible groan, she bent over double, her face almost touching the tabletop. Jeff jumped up from his chair and crouched beside her.

'Lizzy! What is it? What's—'

A spasm of pain must have hit him too. He clutched his chest and fell on to his knees. Stuart and Gemma were both on their feet now, staring open-mouthed at their mum and dad. Lizzy tried to get up, but her legs gave out beneath her and she collapsed on to the wooden floor.

Jeff said her name again, desperation in his voice and something else. Realisation. He was holding his belly now, and his face had turned red. He retched, put a hand to his mouth, and then vomited, all the undigested food he'd just eaten forming a pool that spread out beneath the table, filling the room with a terrible stench.

I was paralysed, unable to do anything except watch. This was actually happening. I had done this. Gemma had her hands over her eyes while Stuart stared at his parents with a kind of horrified fascination.

You did this, my dad screamed in my ear.

I wanted to vomit too.

Lizzy had gone still, eyes staring into nothingness. Still on his knees, face screwed up in agony, Jeff turned his face towards Gemma and Stuart, and then, finally, me.

'You idiot,' he said, and fell to the ground. His head struck the floor and he made a croaking noise that I will remember forever. He spasmed, arms twitching, lying beside the puddle of his own stinking vomit, and then lay still.

Chapter 54

The three of us stared at the bodies on the floor.

Stuart took a step towards them, then back, then forward again; a strange, shuffling dance. Gemma clung to the back of the chair she'd been sitting on, knuckles white.

'Are they . . . ?' Stuart asked in a hushed voice.

I crouched beside the bodies, avoiding the sick, and felt for Lizzy's pulse. Nothing. Then I did the same with Jeff.

'They're dead,' I said.

Stuart was silent for a second. Then he whooped and punched the air. He put out his hands to Gemma and said, 'High five, sis.'

To my astonishment, she high-fived him back, a smile creeping on to her face.

Stuart stepped around the table and unleashed a volley of spit on to his dad's back.

'That's for all the times you said I was a loser.' He jigged from foot to foot, unable to stop grinning. He looked manic. 'Come on, Gemma. You do it too.'

She didn't move. Shaking his head in disgust, Stuart knelt between his dead parents. He stroked Lizzy's hair. 'I told you, Mum. I told you I'd get my own back.'

He laughed again, then lifted Jeff's head up by the hair and sneered into his father's face.

He let Jeff's head drop. It thumped against the floor. Stuart got to his feet and reached over to grab my hand. I tried to pull it away but he clasped it with two hands and shook it vigorously. His hands were slick with sweat.

'Thank you, Elliot. Thank you *so* much.'

I pulled my hand from his grasp and stared at him with horror as he did a little jig of joy around the kitchen.

What had I done?

I flashed back to a year ago, when I had been putting the finishing touches to the restoration of this house. My beautiful house, in which everything was just how I wanted it, every surface, every wall, every piece of furniture. I remembered that day, when all the work was done, walking through each room, stepping back and taking it all in. All the work and money I'd put into this place. My heart and my soul. *I'm going to be happy here*, I'd thought. *This is my forever home.*

How the hell had I got to where I was now, with two corpses in my kitchen, with the son of these dead people dancing around like he'd just won the World Cup?

I knew the answer to that. Of course I did.

Gemma must have seen the way I was looking at her because she said, 'What?' The smile had vanished now and there were tears in her eyes, but not of sadness or grief. These were the tears of a victorious athlete, of an Oscar-winning actor. Tears of relief and exultation; years of wishes breaking free from their bottle.

She had got what she wanted. And it was what I had thought I'd wanted too, since I found Amira's body. I had thought I was calm, but I had acted out of rage, a man who had been pushed so far that he couldn't take any more.

Now that Jeff and Lizzy were dead and my rage had been fed and sated, I felt nothing but cold, sick regret.

And when I looked at Gemma and examined my heart, I found nothing good there either. No love. All I felt was shame and resentment and bitterness. She had done this. She had turned my perfect home into a house of horror.

While I was staring at my wife, Stuart took his phone out of his pocket and wandered out of the kitchen. I followed him.

'What the hell are you doing?' I demanded. 'Who are you calling?'

The look he gave me was shifty, and he tried to turn away from me. Needing to know who he was phoning, I lunged at him. He squirmed away, running back into the kitchen, attempting to thumb the phone as he went. I was too fast. I caught him and grabbed the phone from his slippery, sweaty hand. As Stuart backed away from me he knocked the bottle of wine he'd been drinking – my special wine – off the counter. It smashed on the ground, glass and the remains of the wine spraying our feet. I held the phone, staring at the screen. He had dialled 9-9, but hadn't got to the third digit yet.

'What the hell?' I said.

He was sweating heavily now. He tried to look confident, but he couldn't maintain eye contact.

'You were going to report me to the police? Tell them I poisoned your parents?'

He was practically dripping with sweat. He cleared his throat, glanced over at Gemma then back at me. Gemma didn't look at all surprised by what was happening and I realised, with a fresh jolt of horror, that she was in on it.

'Sorry,' he said. 'It just seemed much cleaner, you know? Better than this crazy scheme to get rid of their bodies. I mean, what if we helped you do that and got caught? We'd be accessories, at least. We can't have that. I've got . . . I've got a family to look after.'

It was exactly the kind of thing Jeff would have said.

'You're just like him,' I said.

This seemed to wound him, but he said, 'I suppose I've inherited his survival instinct. Until tonight, I'd have said Dad was one of the world's great survivors. But he finally met a better man.'

Was he really trying to flatter me now?

'Or maybe I should say he pushed a better man too far.'

I stared at him. Could he be talking about *himself*?

He wiped his brow. 'Listen, when this goes to court, Gemma and I will be witnesses. We'll tell them our parents drove you to it. You can plead temporary insanity. I mean, Jeff killed your neighbours and your friend at work. Maybe the police will even find proof to back you up. No jury will convict you.'

That was crap, and he must have known it. Even if it was proven that Jeff murdered George, Edith and Amira, I would still go down for what had happened tonight. This wasn't a movie where the vigilante is allowed to walk free at the end.

Stuart gestured at Gemma. 'Give me your phone.'

He went to move towards her and I stepped into his path. 'No!'

'Gemma, call the police,' he said.

She was still by the dining table, with her parents' bodies between us. I turned my head to look at her. She didn't appear to know what to do.

'Oh, sod this,' said Stuart, trying to dodge past me so he could get Gemma's phone.

I grabbed his shoulders and pushed him back against the counter. He bared his teeth like a rat I'd once seen cornered by Charlie, pulling back his fist to throw a punch. I am not an experienced fighter, but neither was he. I saw the punch coming and sidestepped. And as he lunged forward he lost his balance. His back foot came forward and he trod on the spot where the wine bottle had landed.

It happened in a split second. He slipped in the red wine and went down, crashing to the kitchen tiles. And as he landed he made a strange gasping sound.

I was about to dash across the room towards Gemma, to make sure she didn't call the police, but I paused. Stuart wasn't getting up. Instead, he pulled one hand up to the side of his neck which was against the floor. He took his fingers away and studied them, his face slack with shock. They were coated with blood.

I crouched in front of him. I'd thought his head was lying in a puddle of red wine.

It wasn't wine.

There was a vicious shard of glass sticking into his neck, thick and jagged and about two inches across. The pool of blood around Stuart's head was growing bigger with every second. He tried to speak and a bubble of blood popped between his lips.

A moment later, he died.

Chapter 55

'What have you done?' Gemma said.

'What have *I* done?' I marched across the kitchen, trailing bloody footprints behind me, and snatched her phone from her hand. She moved to run, to try to flee the room, but I grabbed hold of her upper arm.

'Stand over there!' I shouted, pointing at the back wall.

'You killed Stuart.'

'Shut up!'

She fell quiet. Her head fell forward so her chin almost touched her collarbone. And I tried not to panic. Because if I didn't make the right decisions now, I would be going to jail. I would make sure Gemma went with me, but even though I was guilty of murdering Jeff and Lizzy, and felt that guilt in every cell of my body, I didn't want to end up in prison.

A little voice whispered inside my head: *Things can be the way they were.*

I rubbed at my ear as if a fly were trapped there.

You can get your old life back.

But I needed Gemma's help.

I strode over to her and lifted her chin with my finger, forcing her to look into my eyes.

'We can fix this,' I said. 'We can figure it out.'

'But . . .'

I followed her gaze towards the three bodies and all the mess that surrounded them. I had no idea how easy it would be to scrub this place free of all the blood and DNA that coated the floor. At the start of the evening, I had been confident that no one would come looking for Jeff and Lizzy, that the police would never even suspect a crime had been committed. Chloe was the only person who might possibly report them missing, and Gemma had assured me she would talk to her, tell her they'd decided to leave without her, that we had discovered all the things they'd done and had told them we were going to tell the police.

Now everything was different. Stuart was dead, his blood all over the floor. Jane knew he'd come here for dinner. What would she do when he didn't come home? What would we tell her? It felt like there were bugs crawling inside my brain and I rubbed my head with my knuckles. *Think, Elliot.*

Would Jane, and the police, believe it if we managed to clean this place up and told them Stuart had gone off with his mum and dad? I couldn't believe that the police wouldn't investigate and that suspicion wouldn't fall on me. My neighbours were dead. My business partner – whose partner was a cop – was in the mortuary. I had found all of the bodies. The police knew I'd been in a dispute with Jeff and Lizzy. It could hardly look more suspicious.

Think.

Could Gemma and I convince the police that Stuart and his parents had all confessed to the murders of George, Edith and Amira, and that Gemma and I had found out? Perhaps I could say that we had confronted them over dinner and Jeff, Lizzy and Stuart had freaked out and left. I guessed that would spark a manhunt. But what would happen when they weren't found? Would they scour this place? Find traces of Stuart's blood?

I swore under my breath. 'Come on, Gemma. Help me think this through.'

I explained my train of thought so far but I wasn't sure if she was listening.

Halfway through my garbled monologue, she said, 'We should run.'

'What?'

'Leave the bodies here. Get our passports and get out of the country. We can be on a Eurostar within an hour. Then we can get another train out of France. Head east to Russia or Northern Cyprus. Somewhere without an extradition treaty with the UK. We can be thousands of miles away before anyone finds the bodies.'

'You're insane,' I said.

She looked shocked. 'No, it could work. We'll change the way we look. Change our identities.'

'No, Gemma, you don't get it. You're insane to think I'd want to go anywhere with you now, after what happened tonight.' I clenched my fists. 'You set me up, Gemma. You were going to let me go to prison.'

'No, we would have testified, told them you were driven insane and . . .' She trailed off. She must have known that would never have worked. She closed her eyes for a long moment. When she opened them, she said, 'I'm sorry for everything.'

'Yeah,' I said. 'And I'm sorry I ever met you.'

She looked like she was about to plead her case but, instead, her eyes flashed with defiance.

'We don't have time to argue right now. We need to deal with this, otherwise we're both going to jail.'

She was right. We were in this trap together. And we needed to work together to get out of it.

'What if we tell the police that Stuart did all of it? That he put cyanide in the mineral water, and that Jeff smashed the bottle and killed him before he died?'

I thought about it. 'I don't think that would work. Where would Stuart get cyanide? Even if they believed it, they would suspect me of procuring it for him.'

She was pacing the dining room, well away from all the blood and vomit, and it felt like I was seeing her properly for the first time. The way her mind operated: scheming, working through problems.

'We should go ahead and dispose of Jeff and Lizzy's bodies,' she said. I noticed how, like Stuart before, she'd stopped saying Mum and Dad. 'And then . . . maybe we can say Stuart's death was an accident. He dropped the wine bottle and slipped in the wine. Which is actually close to the truth. We'll have to make out it was just the three of us here.'

'But what about Jane? She'll tell the police that isn't true. I think we need to make out all three of them left together.'

'Oh God. We're so screwed.'

We caught each other's eye and, just for a second, it was just as it should have been. A married couple, united by a common problem. Newlyweds, trying to figure it out. Except it seemed like an impossible puzzle.

I thought, though, in my panicked state, that Gemma was right. We should go ahead with the original plan. Make it look like Jeff and Lizzy had disappeared. Then we could deal with the Stuart problem.

'We should start with Lizzy,' I said. 'She's the lightest.'

I stepped behind Lizzy and grabbed her beneath her armpits. Gemma took hold of her ankles, face turned to the side so she didn't have to look directly at her dead mother.

I heaved. Even though Lizzy weighed a few stone less than Jeff, she still wasn't light. It was like trying to move a rolled-up carpet. We couldn't lift her, so had to drag her, which meant I was doing all the work. I had only managed to get her halfway to the kitchen door and was already sweating.

'Come up this end,' I said. 'We'll have to take one arm each.'

Gemma stood beside me and we each took hold of an arm. This was easier. We pulled her through the kitchen door, gathering momentum, and found it was easier in the hallway, where there were varnished wooden floors.

Now we needed to get her up the stairs. It had just gone nine and I was aware of time ticking away. I put my arms beneath Lizzy's armpits and locked my fingers together across her sternum. Gemma took hold of her legs, beneath her knees. There were fifteen stairs but it felt like five hundred. Every two steps, we had to pause. Lizzy's head lolled to the side and her cold face made contact with my cheek, like a ghastly kiss. I cried out, but kept going, using every ounce of strength to carry her up to the landing, where I collapsed beside her.

Gemma, who hadn't taken so much of the weight, still looked like she was going to puke.

'Go and run the bath,' I said, panting. 'Just use the hot tap. Don't let the chain fall into the bath. We won't be able to reach in to pull out the plug if we can't grab the chain.'

She disappeared into the bathroom. I couldn't bear to be left alone with Lizzy so pulled my aching body to my feet and went upstairs to the bedroom where Gemma and I had been staying since her parents' arrival. I had hidden a coverall and thick rubber gloves beneath the bed and I put them on now. I grabbed the eye protectors that I'd stashed there too, and opened the wardrobe. This was where I'd hidden the pellets, storing them in carrier bags.

I hefted out one of the bags and peered inside it. Each bag was full of potassium hydroxide pellets. KOH. It was easy to get hold of, especially for someone who had an account with numerous suppliers of chemicals. If the police investigated they might wonder why I had ordered so much of it over the past few days but I had a reason ready. I was going to use it to teach my remaining students how to make soap, and I had prepared a number of lesson plans just in case I was asked about it.

I carried the bags downstairs to the landing.

'Is the bath ready?' I asked, standing there in my protective gear.

Gemma looked me up and down. 'Yes.'

'And it's as hot as you could get it?'

The hotter the water, the faster it would do its job, even though the KOH would increase the water temperature greatly, the exothermic reaction heating the water like a flame beneath a pan. Lizzy's flesh would disappear, stripped to the bone. After a few hours, we would just need to pull out the plug and most of Lizzy would disappear down the plughole, through the pipes and into the sewers. Her bones would remain but they would be reduced to a soft, squidgy substance that could be scraped out and disposed of elsewhere.

'Okay, let's get her into the water,' I said. 'Be careful not to burn yourself.'

'I didn't think you still cared,' Gemma said.

I grabbed hold of Lizzy's arm. 'I don't. I'm thinking about physical evidence.'

Once the body was in the bathroom, the next step was to heave it into the bath. In the tests I'd carried out at the lab, the KOH dissolved most materials, so it was sensible to leave Lizzy fully dressed. The zip and metal buttons on her jeans would remain, but they could be got rid of along with the remains of her bones.

'Ready?' I asked. 'We'll put the body in, and then I'll add the KOH.'

Gemma nodded, going down to the other end of her mum's body and grasping her lower legs.

Lizzy seemed to be getting heavier by the minute, although it was too soon for rigor mortis to have set in. We lifted her to the rim of the bath.

'Gently,' I said. 'We don't want to create a huge—'

A noise came from downstairs.

We dropped the body back on to the bathroom floor. In my near-hysterical state, I thought Jeff had risen from the dead. I heard footsteps, a door opening and closing. My entire body went stiff, expecting to see Jeff's corpse ascending the staircase, vowing revenge. It had been too easy. Like a monster in a horror movie, Jeff wasn't that easy to stop . . .

'Hello?' said a voice.

Gemma and I gawped at each other.

Chloe was home.

Chapter 56

I leapt up, all thoughts of walking corpses forgotten, and pelted down the stairs with Gemma following behind me. Chloe was by the front door, taking her coat off. As usual she appeared to be in her own little bubble, headphones in, head down.

Her eyes widened when she looked up and caught sight of my protective gear, which, in the rush to intercept her, I'd forgotten I was wearing.

'I thought you were going to stay over at Stuart's,' I said.

She pulled out one headphone. 'Jane got back early and said I might as well come home.'

She moved to go past me but I blocked her. I could hear Gemma behind me, breathing heavily.

'What's going on?' Chloe asked. 'Can I go to the kitchen? I'm thirsty.'

I blocked her again. 'No. It's not . . . safe.'

'There's a gas leak,' Gemma said.

'Really?' Chloe sniffed the air.

And before I could stop her, she swerved around me, dodged Gemma and went into the kitchen.

I was standing right behind her. She saw Stuart first and her hand went to her mouth. Then she saw her dad. She took a step into the room. I think I had expected her to scream; to freak out in some way.

Instead, she turned and said in a cool voice, 'What happened?'

Neither Gemma nor I replied.

'Where's Mum?' Chloe asked.

Gemma went into the kitchen and tried to put her arms around her sister, but Chloe shook her off. She went over to Stuart and crouched down at the edge of the pool of blood, peering at his wound, the shard of glass still stuck in his throat. Watching her, a wave of dizziness hit me. Chloe was going to call the police. I was going to prison. I slumped back against the wall and a voice in my head said, *You're going to have to kill Chloe too.*

I shoved the idea away, appalled with myself. Maybe Gemma's idea was the right one. I should grab my passport and run, hope I made it out of the country before the police found me or put out an APB or whatever it was called. I could lock Chloe in her room; that would slow her down, give me enough time, maybe.

'Mum's upstairs,' Gemma said. 'I mean, her body's upstairs.'

'You killed them,' Chloe said. She had gone over to Jeff's body now, looking down at it with no emotion on her face. *She must be in shock*, I thought. Any second now she's going to start screaming.

'We did it for you,' Gemma said. 'To save you from them.'

Chloe turned slowly to regard her sister. Her mouth opened then closed. I had no idea what was going through her head. She said, 'Stuart too?'

'That was an accident. He was going to call the police and there was a struggle. He slipped.'

'Oh,' Chloe said. She still didn't scream or cry. But neither did she do what her siblings had done. She didn't grin or dance to celebrate her freedom. On this night of madness, Chloe's reaction – or lack of it – was perhaps the most shocking thing of all.

'I'm sorry,' I said.

Chloe looked at me like she'd forgotten I was here.

'The world's a better place without them,' Gemma said to her sister. 'You know that. All the things they did to us. The people they've killed. Think of all the lives they ruined, including Elliot's. Including ours.'

Chloe nodded slowly. 'Yes,' she said.

'I know what happened in France,' I said, and Chloe's attention snapped to me. 'They killed your boyfriend, didn't they? Jean-Claude. That's why they had to come back here.'

Chloe held my gaze. 'You looked at my journal.'

'I did. And I figured it out from there. Though I don't understand what you were doing for the two months between Jean-Claude's death and your return to England.'

There was a long pause before Chloe said, 'Can we get out of this room? It . . . smells bad.'

We filed into the living room, which felt like an oasis, away from all the blood and death in the rest of the house. It was quiet. I could hear myself breathe. Exhausted, I slumped into an armchair, wishing I could sleep and wake up to find all my problems had been fixed. But then I became aware of Chloe watching me, still calm. Still, I assumed, in shock.

'What happened after they killed Jean-Claude?' I asked.

'We took over another house. An old lady. Dad kept her tied to her bed while he was waiting for Gemma to find somewhere for us to live.'

I swallowed. 'An old lady? What happened to her?'

'He drowned her in her swimming pool.'

Another death. Another body. I wondered how many others there had been over the years. People we didn't know about. Crimes that had never been solved. And I guessed that was why Chloe wasn't freaking out now. She was used to witnessing terrible things.

'See!' Gemma said to me. 'They're evil. We had no choice.'

Chloe didn't appear to be listening. She stared at the ceiling. 'Why is Mum's body upstairs?'

Gemma winced. 'She's in the bathroom. We're going to . . . make her disappear.'

Chloe's eyebrows shot up. 'Acid?'

'Alkaline,' I said.

Chloe nodded, then said, 'I should call the police.'

'No!' Gemma took a step towards her. 'Think about what they did to Jean-Claude. And to Mickey and Delilah. Think about how they've controlled you your whole life. Yes, Elliot and I did this for ourselves. We did it because we needed to cut this cancer out of our lives. But we did it for you too, Chloe. I wasn't lying when I said that.'

There was a long, long silence, during which the sisters gazed at each other, Gemma waiting, Chloe apparently chewing over what her sibling had said.

'So what are you going to do?' Chloe said at last.

'I don't know,' I replied. My heart was beating so fast now I thought it might explode out of my chest. 'Had Jane gone to bed?'

'Yes.'

'Then we've probably got until morning before she notices he didn't come home and comes looking for him.'

'You should text her from his phone to tell her he's decided to stay the night here.'

I nodded. Panic had stopped me from thinking straight. I went into the kitchen – Chloe was right, it stank in here, of blood and vomit – and retrieved Stuart's phone from his trouser pocket, trying not to look at his face.

'It's locked,' I said as I went back into the living room.

'Can't you use his thumb to open it?' Gemma asked.

'That won't work.' The technology relied on electrical charge, which dead people don't have.

'Try 210512,' Gemma said. 'That's Katie's birthday.'

Another person who used a date of birth to open their phone. But the mention of Katie stabbed me in the heart. We'd taken that little girl's daddy away. *Beloved husband and father.* I deserved to go to jail. The code worked, though. Stuart's phone opened, and I sent a text to Jane – *Had too much to drink and decided to crash on the sofa here xx* – before taking the phone back into the kitchen and shoving it into Stuart's pocket.

'How long does it take to dissolve each body?' Chloe asked when I returned. It seemed she'd made her decision. She was going to help us.

'A few hours,' I said, feeling sick but relieved. 'Four or five if you include the time it will take to get rid of the residue.' I explained how the KOH worked.

'We're not going to have time to do all of them,' Gemma said. 'How about this? We tell people that Jeff and Lizzy killed Stuart and then ran.'

'Except we just texted Jane pretending to be Stuart.'

'Maybe that wasn't such a good idea,' said Chloe.

'We can't put them all in the bathtub,' I said. 'I don't even know if three of us could carry Jeff's body up the stairs and into the bath. Getting Lizzy up there almost killed us.'

'And we don't know if the police will believe us and what the forensics will tell them,' said Gemma.

We were going round in circles. An ever-decreasing spiral, like water spinning towards the drain, taking my life with it. I glanced over to the mantelpiece where Lizzy's cigarettes lay and, although I'd never smoked in my life, I wondered if lighting up would make me feel better, help me think straight.

Chloe followed my gaze towards the cigarettes and something changed on her face.

'I've got an idea,' she said, going over and picking up the cigarette packet along with the lighter that lay beside it.

She flicked the lighter and held up the flame.

'Burn the bodies?' Gemma said. 'Would that work?'

But I knew that wasn't what Chloe meant.

'No,' I said. 'No way.'

'It's the only way to destroy all the evidence and get away with all of this,' Chloe said.

Gemma twigged and said, 'Oh my God.'

Chloe's idea was clever and appalling.

'You need to burn down the house,' she said.

Chapter 57

'I can't,' I said. 'I won't.'

Chloe took a cigarette out of the packet. 'Elliot, it's the only way. Most house fires start with cigarettes, don't they? And Mum and Dad have a history of leaving the gas on by mistake. I'll testify to that, if needed.'

I nodded. I had mentioned that to the police, hadn't I? When they'd questioned me about Effy.

'And Mum started a fire in Stuart and Jane's kitchen once, didn't she,' Gemma said. 'Jane will definitely remember that.'

'This is the story,' Chloe said. It was as if this crisis had brought her to life. 'One of them cooked dinner and must have forgotten to turn off the hob. Then Mum lit a cigarette and boom. The three of them were in here, chatting, we were all in bed. We managed to get out but the fire was too powerful to stop.'

'No. I can't. Not my house.'

'But you must have insurance. You'll be able to start again. A new place. Somewhere just as nice.'

I shook my head. All the work I'd put into this place. The time, the love. The hours I'd spent on my hands and knees, sanding the floors.

All the trips back and forth to choose the perfect shades of paint for every room and hallway. All my possessions: my books and vinyl, photographs of my parents and my childhood, certificates and keepsakes from all the places I'd been. To make this look realistic, I would have to let it all go up in flames.

But then, as I pictured the bodies in the kitchen and upstairs, I began to argue with myself. Apart from the mementoes of my parents, it was all just stuff. I could acquire it again. I could, as Chloe said – and if we got away with it – buy somewhere new with the insurance money. I could make another place my own, just as I had this house on Cuckoo Lane.

But my memories were here too. The happy, peaceful times I'd spent before I met Gemma. The intense, warming sensation of achievement I had felt when I finished restoring this house. And what about all the families who had lived here before me? The history of this place, stretching back over a hundred years? If we created an explosion like the one Chloe described, could any part of the building be salvaged? I guessed so, in time. The brickwork would still be here. Someone else could live here one day and be happy.

But I still couldn't bear the thought of it. Of losing my house.

'What would you rather lose?' Chloe asked, as if reading my mind. 'Your house or your freedom? What about your good name? Your reputation? Your career?'

'I don't deserve any of those things,' I said. 'Not anymore.'

'That's crap,' Chloe said, coming closer to me. 'It sounds to me like you were manipulated into this whole thing.' She glanced at Gemma. 'Driven to the brink. And Stuart's death was an accident, wasn't it?' She put her hand on my arm. 'You don't deserve to go to prison.'

'She's right,' Gemma said. Now I had the two Robinson sisters either side of me. 'You deserve the chance to start again, Elliot. I think we should do it. It's the only way.'

'You just want to save your own skin,' I said.

She frowned. She looked genuinely sad that I thought that. 'No. Despite what you might think of me, Elliot, I love you and I will never forgive myself for dragging you into all this. You need to choose. Your house. Or your life.'

I broke away from them, needing space. Needing to be able to breathe. There was a photo of my parents hanging on the wall and I approached it now, silently asking them what I should do but not wanting to hear the answer, hoping desperately that they weren't looking down on me now, that they hadn't seen what I'd done.

I had always thought they would be proud of me. But not anymore. As I'd said to Chloe, I didn't think I deserved freedom, even though I'd been manipulated, no matter how much I'd been provoked, even if Stuart's death was accidental. That didn't stop me, though, from being terrified about what would happen if I was caught.

Could I burn down my beautiful house? I pictured the paint blistering and peeling from the walls. Smoke blackening the ceiling roses. The furniture reduced to ash.

But then I thought about the blood that was congealing on the kitchen tiles. Pictured the body lying beside the bathtub above us. Remembered how it had felt when I realised Gemma was going to betray me.

This place was stained. Sullied. Burn it down and I could start afresh. Somewhere new.

On my own.

'Give me the lighter,' I said.

ᴥ

Gemma and I dragged Lizzy's body back downstairs – which was a lot easier than getting it upstairs – and into the kitchen, where, with some effort, we managed to seat her at the dining room table. Then we did the same with Jeff and Stuart, which was even harder and took all three of us. By the time we finished, we were all soaked with perspiration, but all three of the bodies were propped upright. Lizzy used a saucer as an ashtray when she smoked indoors, and I positioned it in front of her. The remains of dinner were still on the table from earlier. I scraped the plates and stacked them in the dishwasher but left the glasses, emptying a couple of bottles of wine into the sink and placing them at the centre of the table.

I took the bags of KOH out to my car – there was no one around to see me – then went back inside and emptied the bath. While I did this, Gemma mopped up the blood and vomit, as we were worried it might leave behind mysterious stains on the floor that fire scene investigators would question.

At half past one in the morning, after all this was done, we changed into our nightwear and lay in our beds for a few minutes. It felt strange and sad lying beside Gemma, knowing our brief marriage was over. There was no way back for us, although I knew we would have to act as if everything was fine between us for a while. It might look suspicious if we split up immediately after the fire.

I stared at the ceiling for the last time. Even though I was wired like I'd drunk twenty cups of coffee, there was also a part of me that longed for oblivion and I felt myself slipping towards sleep. I jerked awake immediately and turned to Gemma.

She lay on her side, facing me. Tears ran down her cheeks.

'I'm sorry,' she said. But I was sick of her apologies. I was sick of her. And when she reached out and placed her hand on my arm I felt nothing.

'I think it's time,' I said, sitting up. I had placed the lighter and Lizzy's cigarettes on the bedside table. I picked them up and headed towards the bedroom door.

Gemma didn't move.

'Come on,' I said.

She still didn't get up. She was crying properly now, tears running into her hair, sobbing with her palms over her face. I tried to conjure up some pity but it was beyond me. Our love didn't need to be consumed by the coming fire. It had already died.

'Maybe I should stay here,' she said. 'It's what I deserve.'

I tutted. 'Don't be stupid. You've got what you wanted, Gemma. You're free now. If this all goes to plan, you've got your whole life ahead of you.'

She sat up, wiping her eyes. 'You sound so bitter.'

I made an incredulous noise. 'Do you blame me?' She went to speak but I cut her off. 'Please don't apologise again. Let's just get this done.'

I left the room and, a minute later, she followed.

Chloe was already waiting downstairs. I had wondered if she would bring anything with her, like her journal, but she was empty-handed.

I took a cigarette from the packet, hoping that some last-minute flash of inspiration would come to me and I'd find an alternative to what I was about to do. But nothing came.

Back in the kitchen, I pushed the cigarette between Lizzy's index and middle fingers. Lifting her hand, I lit the cigarette. My eyes fell on the bottles of white spirit that sat in the corner with the paints and brushes Jeff and Lizzy had bought. Although not as flammable as something like kerosene, the white spirit would act as an accelerant when the fire took hold, making the fire burn even faster and hotter.

I went over to the cooker and turned on the gas.

I left the room and shut the kitchen door behind me.

Gemma, Chloe and I stood by the front door, not speaking. They were both in their pyjamas, wrapped in dressing gowns, while I wore a T-shirt and underwear beneath a long coat that I'd grabbed from beside the front door. We needed to make it look like we'd fled from our beds.

It was also a good idea for the clothes we'd been wearing to burn too, as they were no doubt covered in DNA. I stared at the floor, so tense that my chest hurt. I could almost hear the house whispering to me, cursing me for betraying it.

'How long do you think it'll take for the gas to reach the cigarette?' Gemma asked.

'A few minutes,' I said. I wasn't entirely sure. We needed the kitchen to fill up with as much gas as possible before that gas was ignited.

'Shouldn't we go outside now?' Gemma asked. 'What if it blasts down the kitchen door and kills us?'

'It won't,' I said. 'And it'll look pretty stupid if a witness sees us flee the house before the fire breaks out.'

The seconds ticked by in silence.

'Nothing's happening,' Chloe said. 'Maybe the cigarette burned out before the gas reached it.'

'No,' I said. 'It's—'

I didn't complete the sentence. A whooshing sound came from within the kitchen. Almost immediately, the smoke alarm went off.

'Let's go,' I said.

ʊ

I stood on the pavement, watching my dreams burn.

Chloe was beside me, staring up at the smoke pouring into the night air with a kind of wonder, while Gemma sat on next door's front wall, concentrating on a crack in the pavement. A few moments after we'd come outside there had been a bang and a great rush of smoke. Not long after that, flames began to flicker in the front windows. A great shudder of regret wracked my body and I fell to my knees. Glass shattered and more thick black smoke billowed outwards and upwards. I thought I could smell cooking meat, but maybe that was my imagination.

Chloe nudged me. 'You need to call the fire brigade.'

I stared at her like I had no idea who she was. 'What?'

'Elliot, get a grip. Where's your phone?'

I couldn't think straight. 'I left it inside.'

'Gemma?'

But Gemma had gone into a kind of catatonic state, sitting on the pavement and watching the flames.

Chloe swore and ran to the house two doors down, hammering on the door and yelling, 'Fire!' As she did that, someone emerged from one of the other neighbours' houses, and soon doors and windows were opening all along the street, people coming outside in their dressing gowns. But everyone thought someone else must have phoned 999 so it took five minutes before someone actually made the call. That suited me. The longer it took for the fire brigade to arrive, the better, because I wanted the three bodies inside to be burned as badly as possible. I didn't want there to be any doubt that they'd died in the fire. Didn't want a pathologist finding the poison inside Jeff and Lizzy or to spot the wound in Stuart's throat.

And we were lucky, if luck is the right word. It turned out there was a big warehouse fire a few miles away. Most of the area's firefighters were tackling that blaze. It took them over twenty minutes to reach us after the call was made. The white spirit in the kitchen had, as I'd predicted, helped the fire in the kitchen to burn like the fires of hell. By the time the firefighters managed to extinguish the blaze, Jeff, Lizzy and Stuart had been burned down to the bone.

But I'm getting ahead of myself. Because just after the neighbour called 999, a hideous thought came to me and my stomach lurched.

'Where's Charlie?' I said.

Gemma jumped to her feet.

'Was he in the house? When did you last see him?' I racked my brains. I hadn't seen him all evening. I would have remembered.

'I think I saw him,' Chloe said. 'When we went upstairs to get Mum.'

Gemma and I both whirled round to face her. 'Where?'

'In Mum and Dad's room. I'm sure he was asleep on their bed.'

I immediately broke into a run towards the house. Even standing by the gate, the heat coming from the living room was intense. But the fire didn't seem to have reached the hallway that led to the front door, which we had left open. It had burned straight through from the kitchen to the living room. I ran to the front door and peered inside, where a black cloud of smoke swirled.

'Charlie!' I yelled, as if that would do any good.

The fire hadn't reached upstairs yet. All I would need to do was to get through the smoke in the hallway, run up the stairs, grab Charlie from the bedroom and run back down again. I took one step over the threshold and stopped, the smoke stinging my eyes, the heat pushing me back. And then I felt a hand grab my shoulder and pull me back.

'Elliot, no.' It was Gemma.

'But, Charlie!' I was crying now. If my cat was alive, I might have some hope of getting through this, of recovering. Because right now, in the terrible aftermath of all that had happened, Charlie was not just a cat. He was a symbol of everything I'd lost. My final link to my life before everything went bad. 'I have to try.'

'No!' Gemma blocked the doorway.

'Get out of my way!'

'No, Elliot. I won't let you do it.'

And before I could react, she leant forward to kiss my lips. Just a quick kiss, before she stepped back into the house and slammed the front door.

'Gemma!'

I banged on the door with my fists. My keys were inside. I felt more hands on me: a guy from down the road, pulling me away from the house, dragging me towards the road, and as I tried to break free, flames appeared in the upstairs windows. I thought I saw a figure there, in the room where Jeff and Lizzy had slept, but it might have been smoke. And then it was smoke, gushing forth, flames dancing behind, and then I heard the sirens approaching from a distance. I finally broke free from the man who was holding me and as a huge explosion ripped through the house, I looked to my side and saw Chloe, flames reflected in her eyes, an enrapt expression on her face.

She turned to me and spoke in a hushed voice.

'They're all gone,' she said.

PART FOUR

PART FOUR

Chapter 58

Gemma never came out of the house. Fire scene investigators found her on the top floor, in the bedroom where we had spent most of our marriage. She had died of smoke inhalation. It was theorised that after going in to look for Charlie she had fled upstairs to escape the fire on the middle floor, where she had got trapped. But I would always wonder: had she done it deliberately? Had she known she wouldn't be able to live with what she had done?

Which was exactly what *I* was trying to do. Live with myself.

After the fire, I felt like I was living in a dream, or in a kind of existential daze, accepting everything that happened without feeling or surprise.

I didn't cry at Gemma's funeral, nor Stuart's, even at the sight of Jane and Katie sobbing as the remains of his body were lowered into the ground.

I didn't feel joy or relief when the fire scene investigators concluded that the fire was an accident, started by a cigarette. I told them Lizzy had cooked dinner that night, that she must have left the gas on, something she had done before. I had even mentioned it to the police when they interviewed me about Effy, so it was on record. Because the smoke alarm started screeching so quickly, Gemma, Chloe and I had woken up immediately and managed to get out of the house before the fire spread.

It was shock. PTSD, perhaps. I'm a scientist. I know there's a rational, medical explanation for the way I feel now. But I can't help but come up with a more poetic explanation: that I left my heart in my house on Cuckoo Lane. That it burned along with the people I killed; that it died when my wife stopped breathing. That the person who still walks and talks today is nothing but a husk, an empty shell.

I'm sure a therapist could help me figure it out, make me feel better, but I can hardly go to one, can I? I will never be able to tell anyone the truth.

The only stirring of emotion I experienced was at Jeff and Lizzy's joint funeral. Chloe and I were the only attendees, on a filthy, wet day when the sky was so dark and low I thought it was about to fall in. I'd like to say I felt regret. Guilt. But I didn't. As their already-charred bodies slid into the incinerator, I remembered everything they'd done and the kind of people they'd been, and a single word bubbled up.

Good.

Beside me, dressed head to toe in black, a veil covering her face like something from a romantic novel, Chloe cried.

She had nothing. No one left. And as we walked away from the crematorium I made a decision: it was my duty to look after her.

ɯ

'Are you ready to go?' I asked.

Chloe nodded, then smiled as Charlie came padding into the room, tail swaying. I picked him up and gave him a cuddle before wrestling him into his cat carrier. The memory of seeing him appear in the front garden, fifteen minutes after Gemma went into the house, was one I clung to during my darkest moments, when I thought about ending it. I didn't have a duty towards only Chloe. Charlie needed me too.

'We're going to our new home,' I said to him as he glared at me through the mesh wire of his carrier.

There was a beep from outside and I went to the front window.

'The taxi's here,' I said.

Because both Chloe and I had lost everything in the fire, and the house I'd been renting came furnished, we could travel to the new house by minicab. All we had were a few small suitcases containing clothes we'd bought recently, plus a couple of boxes containing a few odds and ends, mainly stuff I'd rescued from the shed; some tools and a few old cat toys.

I moved towards the door but Chloe put a hand on my arm, stopping me.

'Elliot, I just want to say . . . thank you.'

'For what?'

'For not abandoning me.' Her eyes shone with emotion.

'I should thank you,' I said.

'Me?'

Yes, I thought. *For not telling the truth. For not condemning me to prison.* Because no matter how numb I felt, it was still better to be free.

But I didn't want to say that out loud so I said, 'Come on, we should go.'

Again I moved towards the door, but she held on to my arm.

'You saved me from them,' she said. 'And I know you think you're looking after me, but I'm going to look after you too.'

I touched her hand. 'Thank you.'

There was nothing else to say.

I climbed into the taxi and put Charlie beside me on the back seat, while Chloe got in the front seat. It was a short journey from this rented place in East Dulwich, and to get there we needed to pass Cuckoo Lane. I found myself gazing out at the entrance to the street, at the bare winter trees, at the row of houses where a blackened house stood like a rotten tooth spoiling a perfect smile.

The cab moved on and soon we were entering our new street, pulling up outside our new home. It was smaller, in a less desirable area, but it could be just as beautiful as my old house. And looking at the 'SOLD' sign, at the windows of this fixer-upper, I experienced something unexpected. A flicker of hope. Of muted optimism.

Here it was. My fresh start.

Optimism's flame sprang to life. I was going to refurbish this place, using the money left over from the insurance payout, and get my business back on track. I was going to teach more children like Effy about the wonders of science so they could help change the world. I was also going to have to do some kind of PR push to deal with my tainted reputation, to remind people I had been wronged.

I was going to make amends for everything I'd been driven to do. I was going to help people.

Starting with Chloe.

ω

'I like it,' she said, wandering from room to room. 'It's got promise.' She stood at the window in what would be her room and gazed out at the back garden. It was a mess, overgrown and patchy. The weeds looked like they'd been having a wild party in the flowerbeds.

A moment of intense melancholy washed over me. Instead of Chloe, I should have been moving in here with Gemma. If our relationship had started in the normal way . . . in an alternative universe we would have found somewhere to live together, a place like this, somewhere that would be equally ours. We would have moved in, fixed it up and decorated it, had fun while we were doing it. In that universe, she wouldn't have allowed her parents to stay. She wouldn't have used me. She wouldn't be dead.

But even if the quantum physicists are right and there are many possible worlds, we can only ever know one of them. And this was mine.

I realised Chloe was staring at me and turned to her.

'It will be okay,' she said. 'I promise.'

'I hope so.'

She ran a hand through her hair. Her roots had almost entirely grown out now and her hair was the same colour as her mum's. The same colour as Gemma's.

'I'll help you with the garden,' she said. 'That can be my project. We can grow lavender and catmint, grow vegetables and herbs.'

I smiled. 'Just go easy on anything that attracts bees.'

'Oh yes. I forgot about that.' She touched my arm. 'Don't worry, Elliot. I'm not going to let anything happen to you.'

The house had come with a small amount of furniture that had been left by the previous owners, including a double bed in this room. Chloe sat down on its edge now and for a moment I thought she was going to ask me to sit beside her, which would be awkward because I really didn't want to, but then she yawned and said, 'I'm bushed. I might lie down for a little while, have a nap. Is that okay?'

'Of course. You don't need to ask permission.'

'Thanks, Elliot.'

I went downstairs and into the kitchen, my footsteps echoing in the mostly empty space. There was a cheap table and a pair of rickety chairs. Charlie had gone to hide beneath a cupboard and I tried to coax him out, then gave up. He'd adapt. It would be easy for him.

My thoughts returned to Gemma, to the way she'd insisted on entering the burning house, shutting the door so I couldn't get in. I might not have cried at her funeral – I had still been so numb – but

355

now I was fighting back tears. I struggled to hold back the fantasy in which she was here with me. The empty rooms; the dusty corners and the shadows. It would all feel so different if she were here.

I tried to shake off the melancholy, to let the anger come back. She had betrayed me. If she hadn't brought Jeff and Lizzy into my life, George, Edith and Amira would still be alive. It was her fault I would have to live with the regret and guilt that made me wake every morning in a puddle of sweat.

Except . . . except she was only a product of her upbringing, wasn't she? She had been desperate. Frightened. I had seen her scars, witnessed her pain, but how could I, with my happy childhood, ever truly understand her?

And without that understanding, how could I condemn her?

Although I had thought at first that she had entered the burning building because she wanted to die, I wondered if I was wrong. Perhaps I should take what she did at face value. She had wanted to save Charlie because she loved him like she loved all animals. And she loved me. She didn't want me to put myself in danger. Maybe, by rescuing my cat, she thought she could rescue our marriage, or at least give it a chance.

'Oh, Charlie,' I said, as he finally crept out from beneath the cupboard and began sniffing around the edges of the kitchen. 'I don't know about you, but I need a drink.'

I rummaged in one of the cardboard boxes and found his water bowl, which I filled and put on the floor. He ignored it, like always. I peered into the box to look for the kettle and mugs, needing a coffee. It wasn't in this box so I turned to the other one. Before leaving our rented accommodation, Chloe had stuffed her dressing gown – which wouldn't fit in any of the suitcases – into the top of this box. I pulled it out.

Something flew from its pocket, landed on the kitchen floor and skidded beneath the cupboard where Charlie had been hiding.

I got down on my hands and knees and reached beneath the cupboard, groping among the dust bunnies for the object, and closing my fist around something cold and metallic.

I sat on the kitchen floor and stared at the object on my palm.

Chloe appeared in the doorway, making me jump, but my heart was pounding anyway.

'I couldn't get—' she began, then saw what I was holding.

And her face told me everything.

Before

'What the hell?'

Chloe wasn't sure where she was. There was a strange but familiar coppery taste in her mouth and her limbs ached. She was burning up. The world around her appeared liquid, all muted colours and wavy lines. She was in the hallway downstairs, and there was somebody beneath her. Somebody else was standing beside her, yelling.

'You stupid, stupid—'

She tuned her dad out, but then her mum's voice cut across him, harsh and coarse, hurting Chloe's ears.

'Oh, Chloe! Not again!'

Mum's words were like a slap, bringing Chloe back into the real world, out of her fugue state, and that was when she looked down and saw that she was straddling Jean-Claude. There was something wrong with his head. Blood in his hair and the shape was all wrong, like a boiled egg that had been whacked with a spoon. There was blood on the bottom stair and more on the wall beside her. She put her hand to her lips and when she brought it away she saw red on the tips of her fingers. Blood in her mouth. How had that got there?

And then it came back to her. Upstairs in their bedroom, Jean-Claude telling her he didn't love her anymore, that he thought it was time for her to move out. Time for her to go home to England. She had accused him of *finding someone else, some local slut, maybe that girl who sold bread at the market, the one who always smiled at Jean-Claude and gave Chloe dirty looks. He denied it. There's no one else, he said. It's just . . . you. And when she had asked him what he meant by that he had averted his eyes, those beautiful brown eyes, and told her that she scared him.*

'Your parents too,' he had said in heavily accented English. 'The three of you have taken over my home. I want you gone. All of you.'

Then he had started to cry – he was always weak, and the sight of his tears made something flash inside her. He had left the bedroom then, walking towards the stairs. She had realised he was probably heading down to the cellar, to where their suitcases were stored, and she had followed him out of the bedroom. Had run out, in fact, moving at speed, and as she reached him he was at the top of the stairs. He turned towards her.

And she had pushed him, using all her strength, and he had flown down the steep staircase.

She had heard the crack when he hit the stone floor of the hallway. Had known straight away that this wasn't the kind of fall you recovered from.

She didn't remember going down the stairs. She didn't remember straddling him or kissing him, though how else could she have got his blood in her mouth?

She tuned back in to what Mum and Dad were saying.

'This is why we have to live with you!' Dad yelled. 'Because you can't be trusted.' He grabbed her by the chin, made her look at him. 'What would you do without us to protect you, huh?'

'Maybe we should leave her to it,' said Mum. 'Let her clear up her own mess, for once.'

Dad let go of Chloe and whirled around. 'No! We're family. We stick together. We always stick together.'

Mum folded her arms. 'So what are we going to do?'

Dad stood over the body, peering at the wound on Jean-Claude's head. 'We leave him, that's what. There's nothing to say he didn't fall.' He glared at Chloe. 'But we're going to have to go. We can't have the police questioning Chloe, can we? She'll probably say something to incriminate herself.'

'He was going to leave me,' Chloe said. 'I couldn't let him.'

'See?' Dad turned back to Mum. 'She'll say something like that to the police and then she'll be screwed. We need to get out of here. I'll contact Stuart, tell him we need to stay with him.'

Mum laughed without humour. 'What, after what happened last time? He'll never let us in.'

'Gemma, then.'

'But—'

'Lizzy, we don't have time to stand around arguing about this. No one around here knows our real names, do they?'

Chloe began to cry. The realisation they were going to have to leave this place, their haven, and that it was all her fault, stabbed her in the gut. By the time Mum and Dad got her into the car, she couldn't hold back. Dad kept shouting at her to shut up, but the angrier he got, the more distressed she became. Racked with self-pity, she cried for herself as they drove away into the night.

B

Since they'd come to France, Mum and Dad had hardly left the house. And Dad had made Chloe use a fake name, Clare, because – Chloe realised now – he'd always known something like this would happen. He knew that, one day, she would do it again.

Just like she had killed Delilah and Mickey, setting fire to their caravan while they slept. It was their own fault. She was fifteen and had only gone to stay with them because she wanted to see what Dad would do, and they hadn't exactly been welcoming. Not after the threats Dad had made after Gemma stayed with them.

Chloe had begged them, though. And, being good Christians, they had taken her in. She was only going to stay one night, and through the evening,

360

when they played guitar and gave her homemade stew to eat, she thought Mickey and Delilah were amusing and kind of sweet. That was until they called Dad an 'ignorant heathen' and said that he and Mum had driven Gemma away. They called her parents 'child abusers'.

Chloe had always found it hard to control her anger – the first victim was Gemma's hamster, which Chloe crushed beneath the heel of a pair of dress-up shoes after Gemma told her she was stupid – but that night the fury overwhelmed her. Made her black out. And when she came to, she was standing beside the burning caravan and she could hear Mickey and Delilah screaming, trapped inside their metal home.

After that, Dad decided they needed to leave Winchelsea Beach.

But things didn't go well in Hastings. Gemma's boyfriend, Henry . . . Well, Gemma thought the sun shone out of his behind. He had 'saved' her. What she didn't know was that he was a pervert. One day, feeling resentful towards her parents for bringing her to this boring place – even poisoning Henry's beloved cat hadn't made her feel better – she told Henry that Dad had torched the caravan. She had squeezed out some tears, and Henry had comforted her, and the comforting turned to kissing and then, well, Gemma caught them. Just as Chloe had hoped.

What a crazy day that was.

Later, they went to stay with Stuart and his wife, Jane. Chloe hated Jane from the moment she met her. She was so high and mighty, and condescending. One hot summer's day, Jane pushed Chloe too far – she told Chloe off for leaving the milk out of the fridge – and Chloe went into one of her black, hot states. When she came to, the room was filled with smoke and Dad was yelling at her, saying she could have killed them, but he had managed to persuade Jane and Stuart it was an accident, that it was Lizzy who had started the fire with one of her cigarettes.

And then later, after Stuart and Jane made them all homeless, Chloe met Jean-Claude and they came to France.

ʊ

Mum and Dad didn't have phones and they had made Chloe throw hers away in case the police used it to trace them. They drove for hours. By the time they reached the little house where the old woman lived, Chloe had calmed down enough to do what Dad told her.

She emailed Gemma. She watched impassively as Dad dragged the old woman upstairs.

Over the coming weeks Chloe spent most of the time sleeping, only getting out of bed to eat or feed the chickens in the back garden. She liked them. She called one of them JC, another Delilah, another Mickey, not caring if she mixed up their gender. And all the while, she burned inside, just as she had after she set fire to the caravan. Killing seemed to set a fire inside her, one that burned for a long time.

But never long enough.

Chapter 59

I held the toy Maserati in my palm. Chloe watched me, so calm and still, apparently waiting to see what I would do.

I got to my feet.

'You killed George and Edith,' I said.

She blinked at me. 'My dad gave it to me.'

'You're lying. I saw your face when you came into the room and saw the car. It was you. Oh my God, it was you.'

It was silent in the kitchen, just the sound of our breathing. I wanted her to deny it, to insist that Jeff had given the car to her, that I had misread her expression. But she didn't. Instead, she walked over to where Charlie was standing, watching us, and scooped him up into her arms, kissing the top of his head.

I was surprised by how calm I felt. Maybe it was a result of all I'd been through already. I didn't feel as much anymore. My heart had grown a protective layer.

'I'm sorry you had to find out,' Chloe said.

I opened my mouth, groping for words. The only one I could find was 'Why?'

'Because I needed to feel the fire again.'

What was she talking about? I had expected her to tell me my neighbours had found out some secret. That was why I'd thought Jeff had killed them, after all. I thought Chloe had told George something.

'The fire?'

'Uh-huh. The one I felt when I killed Jean-Claude. I liked it.'

She touched her belly, the same way Gemma used to touch hers when she was aware of her scars. 'I've liked it my whole life,' she said. 'That's why Mum and Dad would never let me go. They thought I'd get myself into trouble. It's why they always had to find somewhere safe for us to live.'

I took a step away from her.

She stroked the cat. 'But now I'm free, thanks to you, Elliot. Free to do what I like.'

I still couldn't make sense of it. I had been so sure it was Jeff. *Knotweeds.* George's final word could have been referring to the family as a whole. But . . .

'The aftershave,' I said. 'I smelled it in the house. Did your dad catch you there? Did he help?'

'What? Oh . . . you mean your Eau Sauvage? It was Jean-Claude's favourite too, and it reminded me of him. You didn't mind me borrowing it, did you? You took it up to your bathroom and I had to come and get it. Mum took it off me in the end, said it was morbid and that I needed to forget about Jean-Claude.'

'But Jeff used to wear it too. I smelled it in the shed after he'd been in there.'

She shook her head. 'I don't know about that. But it seems unlikely. He hated it. He said real men don't wear perfume.'

So it had been Chloe in the shed that night. And Jeff must have been lying when he told me it was him. Protecting her. Because he knew she was scoping out next door? Jeff wasn't the only liar, either. I had never been able to remember if Jeff had been wearing my aftershave the night we went to The Buzz, but Gemma had assured me he had been. Because she wanted me to think he was guilty.

'Did your mum and dad know you'd done it? That you killed them?'

She looked sad. 'Dad really told me off.'

I found myself thrown back to that night. That dreadful night when I found George and Edith. 'Wait . . . So you came back from Stuart's early?'

'Yes. I went into the garden and through the fence.' I could see she was picturing it too, her eyes bright as if there were flames dancing there. 'Their back door was wide open. I had the hammer I'd taken from your other neighbour's shed . . .' Her voice was soft and dreamy. 'I got blood all over my face.'

I remembered the police telling me they'd found traces of both George and Edith's blood in their bathroom basin.

'I had to clean and return the hammer. Then I waited for you to get home.' She looked fondly at me. 'Don't look so worried, Elliot, I was fine. The fire kept me warm.'

'And the other toy cars?' I asked.

'I buried them in the garden. But I kept that one. Touching it, holding it, brought back the feeling a little.'

She looked up at me, the corners of her mouth twitching, and I moved further away from her. There were no weapons for her here. No knife. Not even any heavy objects. But I couldn't help but be afraid of her.

I thought I had seen evil in the shape of Jeff and Lizzy. But here it was in a purer form. It all but glowed.

'Did you kill Amira too?' I asked.

'No. That was Dad. He did it to protect me because, well, you already know. She left you a message saying she'd found the news reports about Jean-Claude's death, and you'd been snooping in my journal so he was worried you had enough to go to the police with. To get them to look into it, anyway.'

She dropped Charlie and he padded away, leaving the room.

'There's no need to be frightened of me, Elliot. I'm not going to hurt you.'

'I know you're not. Because you're going to prison.' I took out my phone.

'You don't want to do that,' she said, walking over to the kitchen table and sitting down on one of the rickety chairs. She was smiling again. And in that smile I saw the truth behind her words. The reality.

Because if I reported her to the police, she would tell them what I'd done.

'Why don't you put the kettle on?' she said.

I still had the phone in my hand. I could still call the police, tell them what she'd done. I could tell them everything. Because it would be better, wouldn't it, to get this psychopath off the streets, to put her behind bars so she couldn't kill again, wouldn't have the opportunity to stoke that inner fire whenever she felt the need. It was the right thing to do.

Except I couldn't.

I couldn't go to prison. I had already lost so much, trying to stay out of jail.

And Gemma had lost her life.

I put the phone back in my pocket.

Chloe smiled. 'And you can give me the little car too.'

I hesitated.

'Come on, Elliot. I can just tell the police that I found it in my parents' bedroom. Or, you know, I could even tell them I found it among your things.'

'But—'

'Don't worry, I'm not going to. But it's mine and I want it back.'

Reluctantly, slowly, I set it on the table in front of her.

'Thank you,' she said. She patted the chair beside her. 'Now, come on, why don't you take a seat? We've got a lot of plans to make. We need to talk about how we're going to turn this into the perfect home for you and me.'

I sat down and listened to her detailing her plans for the garden and the house, all the things we could do to the living room and the kitchen and the bedrooms, how she wanted to put a claw-footed tub in the bathroom. I watched her face, and that's when it struck me. She had her dad's eyes and her mum's hair. Jeff's mouth and Lizzy's body. She sounded like them when she spoke and, in her gestures, she looked like both of them.

They were still here.

And I knew, despite her reassurances, before long she would be overcome again by the need to feel that heat she'd described. I was always going to be the easiest target. All it would take was a hidden epi pen and a bee in my bed. An accident that would not only fulfil her desires, but get rid of the only person who knew her secrets.

Which meant I had no choice.

I was going to have to get rid of the one person who knew mine.

Acknowledgments

I really hope you enjoyed *Here to Stay*. If this is your first time reading one of my books, thanks for giving me a try and if you are wondering which of my novels to read next I would recommend either *The Magpies* or *Follow You Home* first. If you're a regular reader, thank you for coming back.

Whenever I told people I was writing a book about 'in-laws from hell', the first question they asked was, inevitably, 'Is it based on real life?' I am happy to say that no, it's not. I have lovely in-laws and I would like to thank them all here: Julie and Martin Baugh, Katie and Ste Gray, Tom and Jen Baugh, and Amanda and Rob Marson. Special thanks to Julie, who was the first person to ever buy one of my books and who has remained a loyal reader (and wonderful mother-in-law) ever since.

Thanks too to my own family: Mum, Roy, Dad, Jean, Claire and Ali, as well as Auntie Jo, Martin, Louise, Elliot and Oliver.

A huge thank you to Stacey Wyke and Robert Chilcott for being so generous with their time and telling me everything there is to know about poisons and the disposal of dead bodies. I have changed some details so this book can't be used as a how-to manual!

Andrew Verlander explained just how difficult it is to legally get rid of unwanted guests; thanks to him, and to Margaret Rowe for putting us in touch.

Amber Rothermel won a competition on Facebook to have a character named after her. Hope you enjoyed meeting your namesake, Amber.

My editor, David Downing, showed tough love and helped me make this book much better than it would have been otherwise. It was great to be reunited.

Thank you to my agent, Sam Copeland, and everyone at Thomas & Mercer for making me a very happy author: Laura, Hatty, Eoin, Sana, Gracie and everyone else who helps put my books into readers' hands. Also, Sophie Ransom at Midas for helping to spread the word.

A massive 'like' to everyone on my Facebook page (facebook.com/markedwardsbooks) for all your enthusiasm and cheerleading.

And finally, the biggest thank you of all to my beautiful wife, Sara, and my kids, Poppy, Ellie, Archie and Harry. You're what it's all about.

Free *Short Sharp Shockers* Box Set

About the Author

Mark Edwards writes psychological thrillers in which scary things happen to ordinary people.

He has sold over two million books since his first novel, *The Magpies*, was published in 2013, and has topped the bestseller lists several times. His other novels include *Follow You Home*, *The Retreat*, *In Her Shadow*, *Because She Loves Me*, *The Devil's Work* and *The Lucky Ones*. He has also co-authored six books with Louise Voss.

Originally from Hastings in East Sussex, Mark now lives in Wolverhampton with his wife, their children, two cats and a golden retriever.

Mark loves hearing from readers and can be contacted through his website, www.markedwardsauthor.com, or you can find him on Facebook (@markedwardsbooks), Twitter (@mredwards) and Instagram (@markedwardsauthor).